BAD GLASS

BAD GLASS

WITHDRAWN

Richard E. Gropp

BALLANTINE BOOKS   NEW YORK

A Del Rey Trade Paperback Original

Published in the United States by Del Rey, an imprint of The Random House Publishing Group, a division of Random House, Inc., New York.

DEL REY is a registered trademark and the Del Rey colophon is a trademark of Random House, Inc.

Library of Congress Cataloging-in-Publication Data
Gropp, Richard E.
   Bad glass / Richard E. Gropp.
      p. cm.
   ISBN 978-0-345-53393-7 (pbk.) — ISBN 978-0-345-53564-1 (ebook) 1. Photographers—Fiction.
2. Quarantine—Fiction. 3. Spokane (Wash.)—Fiction. 4. Psychological fiction. I. Title.
   PS3607.R653B33 2012
   813'.6—dc23
2012019974

Printed in the United States of America

www.delreybooks.com

9 8 7 6 5 4 3 2 1

Book design by Caroline Cunningham
Frontispiece illustration: mckenna71 at stock.xchng

FOR JIM,

WHO WAS THERE WITH ME

IN THE STREETS AND TUNNELS

IN THE RED AND THE BLUE

BAD GLASS

This is the photograph you know:

The room is small and dark. The walls are industrial concrete, with no windows. It's someplace underground. A basement, maybe. A subbasement. A sewer. There's a road flare burning on the far side of the room, a spark of violet-red light barely cutting through the darkness. It illuminates the water-stained walls but doesn't touch anything else.

A half dozen flashlight beams converge on a body in the middle of the floor.

It is a man dressed in military fatigues. He is stretched out on his back. His flashlight has tumbled from his hand, resting just beyond his flexed finger-tips. The flashlight's narrow beam reveals a mop and pail set in the corner of the room.

The soldier's shirt has been torn open. There are bloodred trenches scoured across his flesh—gouge marks, the work of his own fingernails. And there, right in the middle of his chest, is an arm sprout-

ing up from his breastbone. It's a thin white arm—
sickly pale, like something that's never seen the
sun—reaching up through a puckered, jellied wound,
protruding all the way up to the bicep. It looks
like the whole arm has been punched up through the
man's body, slammed through from the floor at his
back. But the wound is small—too small for such
violence.

The arm is bent slightly at the elbow—a crooked
tree sprouting up from the dead man's chest. The
wrist does not hang limp. Instead, it is cocked
back, the gore-streaked fingers splayed with tension.
Teardrops of blood hang from sharpened fingernails.

The soldier's head is tilted back as far as it will
go, the tendons in his neck as taut as a hangman's
rope. His expression is pure agony. His eyes are
open, staring at the wall behind him.

The floor is solid concrete. The parts we can see are
smooth and unblemished. And there is nothing—save
that one horrifying limb—to suggest that there is
anything beneath the room, anything except more concrete, earth, and rock.

It is insanity, printed and framed. Pure insanity.

This image was originally posted to a website, a community
forum dedicated to Spokane. It got a lot of attention, and after
two days of intense traffic, it was picked up by the AP. They ran
a story on it. And from there the photograph spread like a virus,
appearing in newspapers and magazines, popping up on television news broadcasts. It was used in *TIME* magazine, alongside
other perplexing photos from the city. *Newsweek* ran an entire

sidebar explaining how it had been faked, how it could not possibly be real.

Unfortunately, the photograph is real.

I should know. I took the damn thing.

And I've got more. Countless inexplicable images, locked up on my hard drive—the dark heart of the city, encoded in 32-bit RGB color. Compared with some of those, this image looks downright tame.

And they're all real.

Everything you've heard about the city, all the rumors, all the stories . . . it's all true. And you're not even getting the worst of it.

I shouldn't have come here.

○1.1

Photograph. October 17, 01:53 P.M. Entering the city:

A road. There's an overgrown field at its side, littered with autumn leaves. The quality of the light
suggests midafternoon, with dark, threatening clouds
visible in the distance.

There's a standard street sign in the background,
set in the top quarter of the vertical frame. It's a
simple green-and-white sign, similar to countless
others dotting the streets of America: ENTERING SPO-
KANE. Except now the city's name has been painted
over with black enamel. Rivulets of spray paint have
dripped down, drawing lines across the reflective
green surface. The city's name is gone. Spokane—the
word, the place—no longer exists.

In the foreground—frame left—stands a soldier in
camouflage fatigues. The greens and browns of his
shirt and helmet are muted by dust and road grime.
There's a pack of cigarettes tucked away in his
breast pocket. He's holding his right hand out
toward the camera, blocking the view of his face.

Instead of eyes and nose and mouth, we see only the clean white flesh of his palm.

An assault rifle is strapped across the soldier's chest.

There's a pink bunny sticker visible on the gun's butt.

O1.2

Getting into the city was easy. Surprisingly easy.

Ostensibly, the whole perimeter is under military lockdown. There are huge, well-manned checkpoints on I-90, blocking entrance to the east and west, right at the Spokane County border. There, I-90 becomes a forty-mile stretch of dead highway, a severed artery in the heart of America, blocking traffic on the Washington State side of the Washington–Idaho border.

I first tried the direct approach, driving east from Seattle.

There was very little to catch my eye between Seattle and Spokane: Snoqualmie Pass, still dressed in autumnal browns; the Columbia River, seated in its vast, water-etched gorge. But most of eastern Washington was pure boredom. Nothing but dead grass and industrialized agriculture, stretching on for miles and miles and miles.

Traffic began to thin as I hit the middle of the state. Most of the remaining vehicles were military vehicles. I watched long convoys of Jeeps, transports, and drab-green tractor-trailers shooting west, back toward Seattle. They had I-90 pretty much to themselves and didn't seem too concerned about the posted speed limits. Once, about fifty miles shy of the city, an open-backed transport passed, heading in my direction. It swerved around my car, easily hitting 110 mph in the far left lane, and suddenly I found a dozen helmeted soldiers staring back at me over the waist-high tailgate. They all had bored, empty expressions on their faces. What did they know about their destination, I wondered, about the place looming up ahead? Were they privy to government secrets, to the things we mere civilians couldn't possibly know? Or were they, too, wandering around in the dark? I guessed the latter.

As I watched, one of the soldiers sparked a match and lit a cigarette. He protected the flame with his cupped hands and nodded the cigarette forward with his mouth, like a bird grabbing for a worm. I briefly considered trying to get some pictures of the transport—wondering how difficult it would be to dig out my camera while simultaneously flooring the accelerator—but the soldier with the cigarette lifted his head and saw me watching. A scowl spread across his face, and he flicked his match my way, bouncing it off the middle of my windshield. I let the truck go.

About a mile from the military barricade, I pulled to the side of the road and got out my telephoto lens. I sat on the hood of the car and counted soldiers through the long glass, steadying the heavy camera on my steepled knee. When the count hit thirty, I got back into the driver's seat, returned the camera to my bag, and pulled out a map. There was a whole web of smaller roads sprouting out from the city. I figured not all of them would be this well guarded.

I started the car, crossed the median, and headed back west.

I was starting to get nervous. Until now, I'd had a precise plan, a course of action I could follow step by step by step. I'd spent the last couple of days crossing items off a list: I cashed my father's final tuition check; I went shopping for supplies—photography gear, food, clothing; I packed up my tiny dorm room. For God's sake, I had a fucking *TripTik*! An honest-to-God, Triple A–endorsed map pack, showing my course highlighted in bright neon yellow. I didn't really need the damned thing—nothing

could be simpler (California to Seattle via I-5, then Seattle to Spokane via I-90)—but there it was, sitting on my passenger seat. A
course. A plan.

Now that I was off the TripTik, things had changed. Suddenly—
uncertainty. I found myself grinding my teeth, and my knuckles
had turned into tiny bone-white mountains, tensed atop the
steering wheel.

I took the first exit and started wending my way north, sticking to the largest roads I could find. There was no life here, off the
highway, nothing but shuttered strip malls and empty parking lots.
By all accounts, the phenomena afflicting the city didn't stretch
out this far, but that hadn't stopped people from fleeing, leaving
behind this . . . this empty borderland. It was eerie. Nothing but
convenience stores and gas stations. Abandoned and silent.

After a couple of minutes, the strip malls gave way to cookie-
cutter developments and middle-class suburban housing. A few
chimneys billowed smoke, but most of the houses looked empty,
and there were very few cars parked out on the streets. I passed a
woman walking a black-and-white collie. They both stopped in
their tracks and stared after me, their expressions nearly identi-
cal: wide-eyed curiosity mixed with fear.

I wondered how much looting there was out here now, how
much home invasion. Not much, I guessed. It seemed like people
just wanted to stay the fuck away from this place. And I was
guessing that that included criminals.

I passed through the last of the housing developments and
veered east, entering a small patch of well-maintained woodland.
A park. The road dipped and angled back up north, finally termi-
nating at the lip of a valley.

I stopped in the middle of the street and studied the map for a
minute. The Spokane River was somewhere down below, flowing
by at the bottom of this little gorge. I craned my neck and tried to
catch sight of the city to the east, but it was blocked from view.

I turned my car in that direction.

I ran into a barricade at the mouth of Fort Wright Road. There were just two soldiers at this one, guarding a line of orange-and-white barrels, the sand-weighted kind that you see at the side of highway off-ramps. When I first rounded the corner, the soldiers were lost in private conversation. One was standing with his arms crossed while the other gestured wildly, drawing grand figures in the air. They both had rifles slung across their backs.

They weren't exactly vigilant. It took them a moment before they saw me coming. And when they finally did, they lazily motioned me forward.

I pulled up to the orange-and-white blockade, and one of the soldiers—the one with the active hands—stepped forward and made a gesture, motioning for me to get out of the car. "Step clear of the vehicle, please," he said. He added the "please" with a smile, and that took me off guard. I'd run through the border scenario countless times during my drive up from California, trying to figure out any angle that would get me through the military gauntlet and into the city. Not once had I considered the possibility of a simple, polite conversation.

I got out of the car and shut the door behind me. I glanced up at the barricade and saw the other soldier watching us carefully. He hadn't moved from his position in the middle of the road, but he had swung his gun forward.

"Let's see some ID," my soldier said.

I got the wallet from my back pocket and slipped my driver's license free. I held it out to the soldier, noticing a slight tremor in my hand. My nerves are usually pretty good. But then again, I'm not usually trying to sneak my way into quarantined cities.

The soldier moved forward, plucked the license from my hand, and took a quick step back.

"Dean Walker," he said, reading my name off the card. He flipped the license over and glanced at its back. I don't know what he was expecting to see there. Maybe a bribe taped to the back. He glanced up at me, smiled, and nodded.

He flipped my license to the soldier at the barricade, sending it flying in a neat arc. The soldier fumbled with his gun for a moment before managing to get his hand up in time to catch the license. He studied it briefly, then picked up a two-way radio and began murmuring into its mouthpiece.

"What are you doing here, Mr. Walker?" my soldier asked. "Do you have business inside? Official business?"

"My brother . . ." I said, pausing to clear my throat. I let the anxiety into my voice, hoping it would add weight to my lie. "My family thought he got out with the evacuation. We thought he was at his mother-in-law's house in Idaho, and I guess they thought he was with us in Seattle. We . . . we don't talk too much."

The soldier held up his hand, stopping me before I could go on. "What's your brother's name?"

"Randy."

The soldier turned back toward his comrade. "Check on a Randy, too. Or a Randolph. Same last name." The other soldier let out a brief grunt and returned to the radio.

"I need to get in there," I said, nodding toward the city. "I need to find him and his wife."

The soldier shook his head. His smile was gone, and that completely transformed his face, aging him before my eyes. I'd originally placed him in his mid to late twenties, but now, with the smile gone, he looked at least ten years older. His eyes were ice blue, and perhaps a bit too wide.

"That's not going to happen," he said. "We're checking our records right now. If we ran into your brother in the quarantine zone, his name will be on the list." He tapped at the side of his nose; if this was some kind of signal, I didn't catch its meaning. "And now your name will be there, too, if it's not already. And if it is, if you're trafficking in and out . . ." The soldier shrugged, letting me fill in the consequences.

"I just want to get in," I said. "I'm not going to do anything—"

He held up his hand and shook his head, his lips set in a pained grimace. "No," he said, lowering his voice, "you don't want in. You just don't know any better. Trust me. There's nothing in there you want to see. *Nothing healthy*. And if your brother's in there . . ." Another shrug.

I studied the soldier for a long, silent moment, all of my plans, all of my lies—my nonexistent brother—stopped short by the pain in his voice. "What is it?" I asked, my voice a faint whisper. "What's in there? They aren't telling us anything."

The soldier glanced back toward the barricade; his partner was still on the radio, lost in his own conversation. "I spent some time in city center while the military was setting up infrastructure. They had us guarding the government buildings and patrolling the streets, not even doing house-to-house searches—I don't think anyone's doing house-to-house, not anymore." He paused. There was a brief tremor across his forehead, his muscles convulsing. "That place . . . it does things to you. No explanation. It just happens. There were twenty people in my National Guard unit. Three disappeared, one killed herself, and one gouged out his own eyes—he just didn't want to see anymore. The poor bastard. When I was transferred out . . ." He shook his head and managed a brief smile. "I think that's one of the best things that's ever happened to me, right up there with the birth of my baby girl. Now, out here, I get to sleep at the base, thirty miles away. And I don't . . . I don't hear things—"

"He's clean," the soldier at the barricade called. "No Dean Walker. No Randy Walker." He approached, cautiously, and handed me my license. Then he once again retreated.

"Sorry, kid," my soldier said, taking a quick step back. He cleared his throat, trying to regain his composure. "I'm sorry about your brother. If he's still in there, he's probably okay. There are quite a few civilians, and most of them . . . most of them are managing."

I stayed silent for a moment, not sure how to proceed. The city had done something to this soldier, something powerful and terrifying. But what? And did I really want to know?

Yes. *God,* yes. But more than that, more than knowing, it was something I wanted to *capture.* That phenomenon. Whatever was going on inside the city, I wanted to distill it down to its essence; I wanted to condense it into a series of perfect images—perfectly framed, perfectly amazing images.

The city had changed this soldier in a deep and profound way. And that was the type of power I wanted. I wanted people to look at my photography, and, looking, I wanted them to change. Forever.

And I needed that to happen fast.

After all, how much more time did I have? I was a college dropout, a former fifth-year senior living on the last of my father's tuition checks, his accounting job waiting for me down in California, looming over my head like the blade of a guillotine. *That is, if he hasn't already disowned me,* I thought. *And then what? Fast-food jobs? Scrambling to survive? No time for art?*

"Please," I said. "I need to get in there . . . Maybe money? If I paid . . . ?" As soon as I opened my wallet, the soldier stepped forward and pushed it back against my chest.

"Fuck, no! Are you crazy?" He lowered his voice and moved even closer, until we were just inches apart. "See the poles at the side of the road?" He gestured with an angry stab of his head. "See what's on top?"

I peered up into the gray sky, noticing for the first time the freshly driven telephone poles standing on either side of the barricade.

"Cameras," I replied, feeling my knees weaken.

"The roads are under surveillance. We can't let anyone in . . . They'd see."

The soldier stared at me for a long moment, his deep blue eyes grabbing hold of my muddy brown ones. Then something happened to his face—a crumpling inward—and the sorrow returned, replacing that momentary burst of anger. "You need to get in there, don't you? Your brother? Is that it?"

I nodded.

We stood that way for a couple of seconds, the soldier studying my face, trying to gauge my intentions. Then he looked away. "The cameras have a limited range, extending maybe twenty feet into that field over there." He nodded toward the south side of the road. "Bobby and I . . . well, we tend to get distracted."

I nodded my understanding, and he pointed me back toward the car.

I started to get in but stopped as soon as I noticed the backpack on the passenger seat. I could see my camera sheathed neatly within. I glanced up through the windshield and, for the first time, noticed the sign on Fort Wright Road: ENTERING SPOKANE. But the word *Spokane* was gone, hidden beneath midnight-black enamel.

"Wait!" I called. The soldier had already started back toward his comrade, and there was a blank, drained look on his face when he turned back my way. I reached over to the passenger seat and pulled out my camera, holding it up so he could see. "I don't suppose I could get your picture?"

For a moment, the soldier looked confused. He glanced up toward the surveillance cameras, then back down, shaking his head in amazement.

Then, slowly, that out-of-place grin reappeared.

He was a pretty good subject.

At first, he just gave me that shit-eating grin—wearing it like a protective mask—and that just wouldn't work. He was standing on the edge of something dark and unknowable, not posing with his family on a holiday weekend.

Finally, I had him grip his rifle in his left hand while holding his right out in front of his face, like he was trying to block my shot. I felt ridiculous moving the soldier around like a department store mannequin. I felt like an impostor.

Is this what photojournalists do?

Yes, I finally decided. *Anything to get the shot. Anything to tell a story.*

I didn't stage the bunny sticker, though. The bunny sticker was already there—a bright, childish icon stuck to the butt of the soldier's gun.

Before I pulled away from the barricade, the soldier told me about an overgrown lane a half mile back the way I'd come, whispering directions into my ear with a cautious glance up toward the nearest camera. It was barely there—a little woodland trail, almost invisible—and I had to jolt through a quarter mile of brush before I finally reached a small alcove sheltered beneath an umbrella of branches. A dozen vehicles were already parked back there, hidden away from the main road, some covered with a thick coat of fallen leaves, others looking car-wash clean.

I parked next to a mud-splattered Jeep and got out of my car. Judging by the carpet of leaves on its hood, the Jeep had been there for quite a while. I walked a circuit around the vehicle, peering in through its windows. The passenger-side window had been left open just a crack, and there was a puddle of rainwater standing on the carpeted floorboard. The Jeep had specialty California license plates, and there was a stacked "P.P." icon to the left of the number.

"Shit," I muttered, shaking my head. I'd seen that icon on the news. P.P. stood for "Press Photographer."

How much competition do I have? I wondered.

I knew I wasn't the first. Pictures had been leaking out of the city for weeks now—strange, beautiful pictures, unlike anything I'd ever seen. But how many photographers had beaten me here? Dozens? Were there parking spots like this at every entrance— alcoves filled with Jeeps and news vans and P.P. specialty plates?

Is my chance already gone?

Overwhelmed with frustration, I hauled off and kicked the Jeep's bumper. The vehicle rocked back and forth on its shocks, but my boot didn't leave a mark. I considered keying the car—just scratching the shit out of every visible surface—but decided to take the high road. Instead, I hauled off and spit a huge glob of phlegm onto the middle of its windshield.

Then I got my bags ready and locked my car.

My camera, camcorder, and notebook computer were all in my backpack, each tucked away in its own carefully padded compartment. The rest of my gear was crammed into an oversized duffel; my clothing and supplies were packed so tight, they threatened to burst the bag at its seams. As soon as I hoisted it onto my shoulder, the duffel's strap cut off circulation to my arm, and its weight had me walking like a drunken hunchback, tilted to one side.

I was already winded by the time I made it back to the barricade. As soon as I got near the cameras, I circled around to the far side of Fort Wright Road and made my way out into the field. The soldiers pretended not to watch, but I caught them shooting me furtive little looks. I stayed at least twenty feet from the road, and after about a dozen steps, I noticed a thin trail beneath my feet. Nothing like a well-blazed path—just a line of crushed grass and mud shooting back toward the road a hundred yards away—but I was certainly not the first one to make this detour.

As I drew even with the barricade, I glanced over and found the soldiers watching. As soon as he saw me turn, the one who had been on the radio glanced away—an embarrassed, self-conscious movement—but his comrade, my soldier, continued to watch. He flashed me a bittersweet smile, then swatted at an imaginary fly, waving his hand in front of his face. It was a completely innocuous gesture—anyone watching on video wouldn't give it a second thought—but I caught the meaning. A sort of "good luck." I returned the wave, then turned back toward the trail.

And that's how I got into the city.

02.1

Photograph. October 17, 04:43 P.M. Taylor Stray:

Most of her body is in shadow, but not her face. It
stands out like a spark of fire in a pitch-black
cave. Her skin is on the dark side of Caucasian—
vaguely Indian—but a narrow beam of sunlight makes
it glow. She's wearing a dark hooded sweatshirt; the
cowl is pulled up, tented loosely over her head.

Her eyes are dark and alert. Black pearls in milk.
Focused and strong, absolutely un-self-conscious.
The camera is the last thing on this young woman's
mind. It's barely present, the least important thing
in the room.

Beams of sunlight stab down from the ceiling—out of
frame—spotlighting dead leaves and litter on the
linoleum floor. There's a window on the left side of
the room—a square of bright, hazy light, revealing
no hint of shape or form on the other side. Nothing
but glowing white fog.

She's holding a backpack by its strap, extended out
toward the camera.

She's not smiling. The look on her face . . . it's
the same intensity that's in her eyes, mirrored in
lips, cheeks, and forehead. Reflected and amplified.

She's focused on something else. Something beyond
the camera, beyond the room.

O2.2

Weasel found me at the edge of the business district.

For the last hour, the sky had been spitting intermittent drops of rain, threatening to open wide and drown me in a torrent. There was a frigid wind blowing out of the north; it carried with it a faint taste of metal. I pulled my jacket tight across my chest and continued south, hoping I'd be able to find someplace safe and dry before the rain started in earnest.

It was a three- or four-mile hike from the barricade to downtown Spokane, and my course took me through upscale neighborhoods filled with pristine white town houses, each two or three stories tall, with abbreviated yards and narrow driveways. It was quiet here. There were no barking dogs, no growling traffic, just the rustle of leaves caught in that cold, metallic wind. As I passed down the center of the street, an old black woman appeared on one of the front porches. She watched me draw near, slowly shaking her head back and forth. I offered her a wave, and in response, the old woman raised her middle finger and thrust it out at me. Then, still shaking her head, she turned and retreated back into her house.

The buildings grew taller and more densely packed the farther south I got, until, finally, I hit the Spokane River and entered downtown proper. As soon as I crossed the bridge, I dropped my duffel bag to the sidewalk and started working at the pinched muscles in my shoulder, massaging the sore flesh and working it through a slow roll. When the numb tingle finally disappeared from my arm and hand, I pulled the camera from my backpack and started taking pictures. The view wasn't exactly exciting, but there was something here I wanted to capture. The tone. The sense of desolation. I took shots of the deserted sidewalks, up-rooted street signs, a toppled trash can lying on its side in the middle of the street. Unfortunately, the disconcerting aspect of the scene was something I couldn't capture on a memory card—the silence, the utter lack of movement.

There was nothing here. No life.

After a couple of minutes, I gave up trying to capture this absence, this *void,* and sat down next to my bag. *What now?* I wondered. *What's the plan? Find someplace to hunker down and set up camp? Look for other people?*

I once again started to massage my shoulder, trying to knead the tension from my muscles. It was much easier to work at this than wonder at my next step.

"Hey!"

The sudden noise jolted me out of my thoughts. It took me a moment to locate the source: a small man rolling out of the window of a nearby building. The man landed on his feet, with his hand still up on the windowsill; then he started toward me, slowly.

The approaching stranger made me feel nervous. I had a tripod strapped to the back of my bag—a collapsed aluminum frame that I could use as a weapon if pressed—but I didn't want to go digging for it now. I didn't want to turn my back on this man. Besides, I hadn't come here to hurt people or make enemies.

As if reading my thoughts, the man held out his hands, showing me empty palms. He was short, about five foot two, with an old-fashioned fedora pulled low over his eyes. He was dressed for the cold—several layers of flannel shirts, flashes of white long underwear peeking out through holes in a pair of ragged jeans, and all of it dirty. It looked like he'd been living rough for quite some time now.

"I mean you no harm," the man said, offering up a smile. He had a couple of decades on me, those years chiseled into deep trenches around his mouth and on his forehead. "Just curious, is all, you being a newcomer to our fair city."

"Yeah?" I grunted, trying to sound calm and hard-boiled, despite my nerves. "And you're the welcoming committee?"

"Something like that." His smile twitched with nervous energy. "There's no electricity, no cable, and radio reception's for shit here . . . I gotta make my own entertainment!" After a moment looking me up and down, he offered me his hand. "My name's Wendell."

"Dean," I said, grasping his sweaty palm.

"You a photographer?" He smiled and nodded toward my backpack. "I saw you with your camera, snapping away like crazy."

I shrugged. "I take pictures. I'm not sure that makes me a photographer, though . . . just a student, really." I gestured toward my backpack and the camera hidden inside. "For the time being, this is all just . . . play. An unrealized dream."

"Fuck, man." He laughed, shaking his head. "That's a dangerous game to play—coming *here* to take fucking snapshots."

Annoyed, I turned and grabbed my duffel bag, slinging it over my shoulder. I could feel the man—this dirty derelict—standing behind me, and I paused long enough to mutter, "Yeah, well, my father always said I didn't have a lick of sense." Then I started walking away.

"Jesus *fucking* Christ, kid. I was just kidding. We've all got our reasons." Wendell broke into a trot, trying to catch up to me. "See. See. *See.*" I turned and found him pointing, with both hands, to a wide, shit-eating smile. "All you kids, you're all so fucking sensitive. You'd think I broke your favorite toy . . . corrupted all your motherfucking MP3s."

"Just tell me where I'm going," I said.

"Sure, man. Welcome wagon and all of that shit. It'd be my pleasure." He once again pointed to that creepy theatrical smile. There were way too many teeth there. It made him look positively demented.

As we started south on Monroe, Wendell pointed to our left. There was a thin sliver of green visible between the buildings. "Riverfront Park," he said. "It's not that big—just a little slip of green—but it's nice. A nice place to watch the river. There was some type of famous carousel there once, before the evacuation. When the word came down, though, they just packed up all the wooden animals and left." An odd look passed across his face. "There are other animals there now, in the park. Not-so-friendly animals."

"Like what?" I asked.

Wendell shrugged. "Wild dogs, probably. I've heard people say wolves and bears." After a moment of silence, he added in a lower voice, "And some talk about other things, too . . . animals you won't find in any zoo."

I studied him for a moment, trying to read the blank look on his face, trying to figure out what *he* believed. "How long have you been here?" I asked. "In the city?"

"I was here when the curtain came down. Government motherfuckers came in, and I never bothered to get out. No place to go."

"You should know, then . . . you can tell me what's going on. Out there—" I nodded back over my shoulder, toward the outside world. "The stuff you hear . . . it doesn't make much sense."

Wendell pulled to a stop. I turned to face him and found a bemused smile spread across his face, not the demented smile he'd flashed earlier, but something softer, more sympathetic. "If you're looking for sense," he said, "I can't give it to you. Here, after a while, you stop looking for sense. I don't know what you heard out there, in *America*"—the word tripped over his tongue, like it was part of some foreign language—"but in here, it's just something you live with. Something in the background. There are vicious animals in the park, so you don't go there after dark. There's a warehouse on the east side—it's been on fire for three months straight. So you stay the hell away. And if you see people in the street, people who shouldn't be there, people whose feet don't move when they walk . . ." He shrugged. "You just don't see it. You don't think about it, and you try not to remember."

"And that's true? All of that stuff?"

He shrugged.

"But why?" I asked. "How? What caused it?"

He gave me an amused look, then once again started down the street. He raised his hand in a dismissive gesture, flicking his wrist like he was tossing something away. "Everyone's got their theories: chemicals in the air, contagious brain cancer, some type of terrorist attack, mutated animals, fucking *aliens* and *demons* and the dead spilling out of heaven and hell . . . Frankly, it's all just religion to me. Unknowable. Meaningless." He crossed himself and rolled his eyes in disdain. But his sarcasm fell flat; the gesture was just a bit too fluid, too practiced. "And if you came here looking for reasons, you're just wasting your time."

He picked up the pace, and I followed, staying a step behind.

After another block, he once again pointed to our left. "The government buildings are just over there, on Sprague. The military's hunkered down in the courthouse. They've got armed guards and everything, but if you leave them alone, they won't bother you too much. Same goes for the patrols and roving vehicles. The military here, they're too busy to do much actual policing."

I looked over but couldn't see anything from this side of the street. Just empty buildings and dark windows.

"What'd you bring, anyway?" Wendell asked, nodding toward my duffel bag. "What've you got stashed away?"

"What?"

"Liquor? Drugs? Anything *useful*?"

"Just clothing and supplies," I said, bouncing the backpack on my shoulder. "And photography gear."

"Shit. What a waste." He shook his head. "I'd have given you a whole shopping list to smuggle in. Some vodka. A fucking *Big Mac*. People could use some relief right about now."

"How many?" I asked. "I mean, how many people are here? In the city?"

He just shrugged and pointed me on. As we continued south on Monroe, I became aware of people watching us. At first it was just the uncomfortable sensation of eyes crawling across my flesh, then I started to see their faces—slight, pale moons peering out from the abandoned buildings on either side. Most of the windows had been broken out and covered over, replaced with haphazardly laid boards and sheets of plywood. Eyes peered from the occasional gap, and voices echoed out. A frantic peal of laughter emanated from the heart of a building on my right, and I turned to find an imposing man standing in a doorway. His arms were crossed in front of his chest, and his huge body took up the entire entrance. When my gaze lingered, the man frowned and wagged his finger back and forth, shaking his head.

I recognized the gesture: *Nothing to see here. Move along.*

"This is Homestead territory," Wendell said, his voice dropping into a whisper. "Bit of a commune, really, put together by a man named Terry." He shook his head at the name, a sad expression on his face. "People joining together. Power through numbers and all of that happy shit. They just like to fuck with people, act like they know best—bunch of self-righteous bastards, if you ask me. You probably don't want to do anything too shady around here, though, or you'll get your face beat in. For real."

I nodded, finally tearing my eyes away from the tough guy at the door.

"I would have probably joined up myself, if not for all those fucking rules," Wendell said. "Plus, they really, *really* hate me."

We turned left on Second Avenue and headed east. Slivers of glass glittered everywhere, crunching beneath our feet as we proceeded down the middle of the street. After a couple of blocks, I noticed a group of people crowded around a shattered storefront. It was on the ground floor of an old office building. Before the evacuation, it might have been a chain coffeehouse—maybe a Starbucks or a Tully's—but since then it had become something else. Changed, repurposed, mutated. Every bit of the facade had been broken down and removed—doors, windows, walls—transforming it into a dimly lit cave, open to the street. All the debris from the demolition had been pushed back from the opening, forming a semicircular drift of drywall and wood. Inside there were tables. The smell of grilled meat wafted out in a cloud of charcoal smoke.

There was a sloppy hand-painted sign above the opening. It read MAMA CASS AND THE CHAR-GRILLED MIRACLE.

"A restaurant?" I asked, surprised. I hadn't expected this level of organization.

"Yeah," Wendell replied, suddenly nervous. "Mama takes barter or money. Anything of value."

We had attracted some attention. In front of the restaurant, a half dozen people had turned our way, watching as we approached. They were dressed in the same fashion as Wendell: multiple layers of heavy clothing, ragged and dirty. I stopped and set my bag on the ground, debating whether or not to dig out my camera and get some shots of the restaurant and its patrons.

"We shouldn't stay here," Wendell said. "It's not safe for you. You're new. You're carrying all your stuff!" He grabbed my elbow and started pulling me back down the street. I took my time turning around and was surprised when he plucked the backpack off my shoulder. "Here, just, let me carry that . . . just, *here*!"

As I was turning, a figure pulled out of the crowd in front of the restaurant, and a woman's voice called after us. "WEASEL! What did I tell you? What did I *fucking* say?"

And that was when Wendell started to run, taking off with my backpack.

My backpack, I thought, suddenly terrified. *My computer. My motherfucking camera!*

○

Wendell moved fast. He ran north a block, then turned east, jumping the hood of a car parked at the corner. I followed.

I managed to stay about twenty yards back. My breath was a loud steam-engine rasp, burning its way out of my throat and lungs, but I barely noticed. Even with the duffel bag weighing me down, bouncing back and forth against my legs, the thought of losing my camera kept me moving.

I was frantic, terrified. All my plans and fantasies were in that backpack. To lose it now, right after I got into the city . . .

I tried calling out to him, but he didn't even look back. The bastard just kept on running, malnourished and scrawny but surprisingly fast.

There were kids on this street, playing baseball in the center of the downtown block. About a half dozen. I didn't pay them any heed. For me, the game was just a blur of motion in the background, a dull rumble of raucous, youthful laughter.

I gritted my teeth and managed a burst of speed, pulling within feet of Wendell's fleeing back. The sound of our chase had caught the kids' attention. They were hooting and hollering as we neared, no doubt anticipating some type of violent confrontation.

I reached out, and my fingers brushed against the fabric of the backpack—*my backpack*—now slung over Wendell's shoulder.

I threw myself forward just as he jigged to the right, his nimble form disappearing through an open doorway. Unable to stop my dive, I collided with the doorjamb, shoulder first, and the weight of my duffel bag slammed me hard into the wall, jolting all the breath from my lungs. The kids in the street let out a loud, sympathetic "Oh!" that quickly broke into disjointed laughter. I didn't even look their way, instead shaking my head and sucking in a burning lungful of air. My legs were weak from the impact, but I managed to stagger into the building. It was some type of hotel or apartment complex—a tenement, really. I could tell it had been an old, run-down wreck even before the evacuation. I entered in time to see Wendell swing around a wooden banister and up into an open stairwell. I followed, losing ground with every weak and trembling step.

I thought about ditching my duffel bag on the first-floor landing, just tossing it into a corner where I could pick it up later, but decided against it. Somebody might find it—one of the kids on the street, one of Wendell's friends—and I just couldn't take that chance. If I lost *both* of my bags within minutes of entering the city—well, maybe my father was right about me. No common sense.

The light in the stairwell was tinted a strange shade of red, as if it had been filtered through crimson cellophane. There was a boarded-over skylight at the top of the stairwell, six floors up, but the light wasn't coming from up there. It was trickling in from the landings. A low-grade hum filled the air around me: the sound of an engine grinding away in the distance, muffled by plaster and drywall and sheets of plywood. A generator? Whatever it was, I couldn't pinpoint its location; I twisted my head from side to side, but the sound didn't get any louder, didn't change in the least. *Is it in my head?* I wondered. *Is it the sound of blood draining from my brain? The tidal pull of a hard, weak-kneed faint? Did I crack my head against the door frame without realizing it?*

I heard a door slam shut on the fourth-floor landing and continued up the stairwell. I wasn't running now; I could barely manage a fast stride.

I didn't know this building. I didn't know what might be waiting for me outside the stairwell. A gang with weapons? Wild animals? Wendell, hiding in the shadows with a two-by-four?

The baseball game out on the street had started back up, and the loud *crack* of ball against bat rang out like a gunshot, jolting my heart into a stutter. The hit was followed by a loud cheer and the sound of glass breaking in the distance.

I paused on the fourth-floor landing and tried to catch my breath. My chest was sore from the collision on the ground floor, and I couldn't stop panting. There were gray spots swimming at the edges of my vision. I pushed forward, opening the door and moving through in a low crouch, just in case Wendell was waiting for me on the other side.

The fourth-floor hallway was empty. Gray light seeped in through the open doorways along its length, illuminating drifts of crumbled plaster and refuse heaped against the walls. The whole place seemed damp. The carpet—a muddy, threadbare red—squished beneath my feet, and the smell of mold and rot made the air feel heavy and foul. I paused for a second, listening for Wendell. I could hear a rhythmic squeaking—the grind of machinery, maybe? pistons?—but no footsteps, no scrambling at windows or fire escapes.

Had he gone to ground? Was he hiding in one of these rooms?

I moved slowly from door to door, easing forward to peek into each room. The first half dozen were vacant. Nothing but stripped dirty mattresses, overturned nightstands, and shattered lamps. There were wrought-iron fire escapes outside each window, but all the sashes were closed, and I could see no signs of attempted escape.

The squeaking sound was coming from a room halfway down the corridor, and as I drew near, low animal growls and panting started to drown out the more mechanical noise. Bracing myself, I peered around the doorjamb and found a man and a woman having sex on a dirty mattress. They were still dressed in their derelict tatters, and the woman—pinned to the ground—was wearing gloves, her shrouded fingers digging into the back of the man's jacket. The way they were going at it—it was something brutal and primal. All energy and friction, like dogs in heat.

Growling. Saliva flying.

They couldn't see me where I was standing in the doorway, but even if they could, I don't think they would have noticed. They were so consumed by their act, by their . . . *passion*? No, not passion. Something less human, less emotional.

Not passion. *Drive*.

I watched for nearly half a minute, lost in the spectacle, before finally noticing the kid in the closet. He must have been about eight years old. He wasn't hiding; the doors were wide open. Instead, he was just sitting there beneath the hems of abandoned clothing. His eyes were wide, his dirty face an expressionless mask. He was watching me with an intense curiosity.

And it hit me—that boy's stare—like a punch to the solar plexus.

I stumbled away from the doorway, my stomach churning, suddenly very, very dizzy, my head just about ready to fall off my neck. *I'm not right,* I told myself. *I cracked my skull. A concussion, internal bleeding, something serious and deadly.*

I continued down the corridor, away from the room with the fucking couple.

Away from the child.

The hallway made a ninety-degree turn, and I found yet more rooms stretching the width of the building. Only one of these doors was closed, and, coming from inside this room, I heard something new. To my ears, it sounded like a seldom-used window rattling open—rain-swollen wood groaning inside its frame, the sound of physical exertion vibrating through glass.

Wendell, I thought, grateful for the distraction, for the chance to refocus my energies.

By the time I got to the door, though, the sound had stopped. Now there was only silence in the building. Even the sound of fucking, back along the corridor, had disappeared. Slowly, I eased the door open.

There were two people in the otherwise empty room. One—a young woman—was lying on her back in the middle of the floor. She was wearing a thin white dress; the material looked insubstantial, far too thin for the cold October air. Her face was pale, and her bright blue eyes stared up at the ceiling. Embedded up there—in the ceiling—was a naked man, his skin a sickly shade of black. The man's body was spread facedown, reclined back against the ceiling in a relaxed pose. Where his body contacted the wood and plaster, his flesh disappeared, like a mannequin half submerged in a pool of water.

But this was no mannequin. And the ceiling was not water. This was a *human body*, and a large percentage of it was stuck—physically stuck—inside that solid surface.

The man's right arm extended down, quivering slightly in the still air. His left arm was stuck inside the ceiling, his hand and half of his forearm stretching up through its surface, outside the room—or so I imagined. Perhaps those body parts were simply gone, his form just . . . halting at the boundaries of the room, becoming nothingness on the other side. His back and buttocks, too, disappeared into that solid surface. His left knee was steepled out in a V, forming an upside-down Greek delta with the ceiling. His left ankle and foot were gone, and his right leg disappeared midthigh. His uncircumcised penis dangled down like a broken light fixture.

The man was alive. At least his body was alive; I couldn't say anything about his mind. I could see muscles twitching beneath his skin while his chest eased in and out, taking calm, shallow breaths. His eyes were wide, but they quivered wildly, rolling with the rhythm of short-circuiting nerves. There was no consciousness there, none that I could see. Just autonomous reaction: a body gone mad, without human control.

And the young woman in the white dress continued to watch, transfixed, lying on the floor beneath the body. She was just a girl, really, no older than seventeen. The man's extended right hand made it look like he was reaching down, like he was offering the girl a tender caress, or grasping for his own salvation.

My hand started to shake, and I let it fall from the doorknob. There was a smell in the room, a strong, powerfully *human* smell. Sweat. Sweat and the sharp copper scent of freshly spilled blood.

Standing in the doorway, I hunched double, trying to fight back a sudden wave of nausea and vertigo.

And when I glanced back up, I found the girl watching me. While I'd been looking down, she'd turned her head my way, and now those bright blue eyes slammed into me. Her hand fluttered up toward the body in the ceiling, and she started to speak, her lips quivering weakly. I focused on her fingers. I was afraid she was going to reach up and grasp the dead man's hand.

No . . . that was not what I was afraid of. I was afraid the man would grasp *her* hand.

I backed out of the room before she could find a louder voice. I didn't want to hear what she had to say. I desperately didn't want to hear. I retreated back the way I'd come, making it ten feet before I had to hunch over and vomit against the wall.

After that, I dropped into a kind of autopilot, letting my legs carry me out of the building.

Wendell and my backpack were long gone. They weren't even memories in my shell-shocked mind.

I'm not sure how long I sat out on the curb.

The rain started to fall not long after I made it out of the building. The baseball game in the street fell apart, and the kids scattered under the cold drizzle. They barely noticed my ashen-faced stupor. Perhaps it was common here, that look, something they saw every day.

The rain wasn't heavy, just a light, damp kiss against my face.

"You shouldn't do that."

It took me a moment to recognize the words, to parse them as human language and riddle out their meaning. A handful of seconds passed before I glanced up and saw a young woman standing before me. She had a black hoodie pulled up over her dark hair, protecting her from the rain, and there was a hard look on her face—smooth, tempered steel cast into human form. A backpack dangled from her hand.

"Do what?" I finally managed. "What shouldn't I do?"

"Trust people." She lifted the backpack by its strap and swung it back and forth in front of my eyes. It took me a moment to rec-ognize it as my backpack, and when I reached out to accept it, my hand was shaking.

The steel fell away from her face, revealing a crinkle of con-cern. When she resumed speaking, her voice was quieter. "I caught up with Weasel down the street, reclaimed your bag. That man's nothing if not predictable." She shook her head, a weary gesture of disappointment. "Don't get me wrong; he's a good per-son, but he's also an asshole. Takes advantage of the newcomers, steals their shit. I've tried to get him to stop, but he doesn't listen. He's got monkeys to feed." She tapped a gloved finger against the inside of her elbow.

I nodded.

"You should get out of the rain," she said, pointing to the hotel door behind us. Immediately, I stood up and started shaking my head.

"Not in there," I said, backing away. "No fucking way."

"Okay. Fine. We've got other options." She led the way to a small one-story building on the other side of the street. It was practically a shack, a run-down shanty, dwarfed by the buildings on either side.

As soon as we got through the door, I dropped my bags to the floor and leaned back against the wall. It was a huge effort to stay on my feet. The pull of gravity seemed absolutely immense.

"You look pale," the young woman said.

I nodded.

She pulled a bottle of Pepsi from the pocket of her sweatshirt and offered it to me. "Sugar should help. It'll keep you from pass-ing out." I took a deep swig. The liquid went down the wrong way, and I coughed up a thin drizzle of spit.

After I finished coughing, the young woman offered me a sly smile. "My name's Taylor. Taylor Stray—Gupta-Stray, actually. And you," she said, pointing a finger at me, "you're new here."

"What . . ." I began, but I couldn't finish the question. I didn't even know what I wanted to ask. I stopped talking and closed my eyes. "My name's Dean Walker," I finally said, keeping my eyes shut.

"And you're a photographer?" she asked. I opened my eyes in time to catch a shallow shrug. "I looked in your bag. After I took it from Weasel."

"Yeah. I take pictures."

"That's good. There's a lot to see here. I don't know what pictures and stories have made it out to the real world, but we've certainly got a lot to photograph." She made an idle clucking sound at the back of her throat. "Not quite sure it's smart to seek it out, but it's certainly there."

I pushed myself off the wall and peered out the shack's front window. The hotel loomed across the street—just a building, really, but suddenly malignant, hard to look at. "What is that place?" I asked. I ran my hand across the back of my skull but couldn't find any wounds. No bumps or gashes. No concussion. Nothing to explain the things I had seen.

"The hotel?" Taylor asked. She shrugged. "Just a hotel. Nothing special."

I picked up my backpack and fished out the camera. As soon as it was in my hands, I started to feel stronger. My fingers were still shaking as I took off the lens cap, but that wasn't just fear and shock, not anymore. I was starting to get excited. I had seen something inexplicable. It had been overwhelming and terrifying, yes, but that was what I'd come here to find. That was why I ditched out on my final semester and broke a government quarantine. To capture those images, to *capture* Spokane.

And now I'd become a part of it—whatever was happening here, inside this city. I'd become *experienced*.

I took some pictures of the hotel's face, moving from the windows to the doorway, trying to catch some of the foreboding I felt. But the foreboding wasn't there. It was nothing visual, just a wound inside my head.

"Feeling better?" Taylor asked. "If you're ready, I can show

34

you around, help you find a place for the night." I turned with the camera still raised to my face, viewing the room through its lens.

And that was when I noticed her eyes. They were beautiful. *She* was beautiful.

Outside, the rain was starting to let up, and the setting sun put in a final, last-minute appearance. A beam shot through a hole in the shack's ceiling, highlighting Taylor's face. And in that light, those strong, clear eyes practically shone. She was holding out my backpack, trying to get me moving. I took a couple of photographs, hoping to catch the intense look on her face.

"Just take the fucking bag," she growled, finally tossing it at my feet.

"Jesus Christ!" I said. "Watch the fucking glass!"

"Yeah." A wide smile spread across her face. "You're feeling better."

With my camera giving me strength, I took Taylor across the street to the hotel.

There was nothing there. The copulating couple, the child in the closet, the girl in the white dress with that abomination looming overhead—they were all gone.

There *was* a vaguely human-shaped stain on the ceiling of that one room, but it might have just been a trace of leaking water, a souvenir from a burst pipe sometime in the hotel's past.

And that was it. Nothing more.

And when Taylor asked me what I was expecting to find, why I insisted on scouring the hotel room by empty, abandoned room, I just shook my head. I honestly couldn't say.

But I kept my camera ready.

03.1

Photograph. October 17, 08:15 P.M. Dinner by candlelight:

The shot is off center, canted a few degrees to the
right: a group of young men and women gathered
around a long dining-room table. All of them are
dirty. Bundled in thick clothing. Ragged and disheveled. There are bowls of food set before each seat,
but nobody seems to be paying much attention to their
meal. They're lost in conversation—broad smiles all
around as a man in a backward baseball cap holds up
his hands, illustrating some grand point.

Another man is looking directly at the camera, a
dazed, contented smile on his dirty face.

There's a cluster of candles burning in the middle
of the table—all different heights, sporting
blurred fingers of flame. The picture was taken without a flash, and the whole frame is bathed in this
orange candlelight, all other colors washed away. In
this respect, it is not a full-color shot, but not
black and white, either. Instead, black and *orange*.

The photograph is blurred, the scene too dark for
any reasonable shutter speed. Filled with trails of
movement and bright, unsteady auras. But still, the
warmth of the scene comes through. The cozy happiness.

A dinner by candlelight.

03.2

It was twilight by the time we made it back out onto the street. Purple-tinted clouds were barely visible in the darkening sky, and there was thunder rumbling to the east. The thought of hunting out a place to stay, looking for a hidey-hole in the encroaching dark, was seriously daunting, and I was grateful when Taylor invited me to stay at her house. If I had to trust anyone in this place, I figured, she seemed like a safe bet. Safer than someone like Wendell, at least.

She pulled a flashlight from her pocket and led the way north, back across the river. Once on the other side, she began cutting back and forth through upscale residential neighborhoods. It was extremely dark out here on the streets. Without electricity, the street lamps stood like dead trees on the side of the road. There were a few candlelit windows, but they were rare, and the weak light seemed somehow ominous, like hooded, distrustful eyes blinking in the night.

Back in California, I'd wandered through neighborhoods like this during rolling blackouts, deep in the heart of energy-crunch summers. The feeling here was similar, only deeper, more intense. During the rolling blackouts, there had been people all around, out walking the dark streets of the neighborhoods, lounging on their front porches—or, if not visible, there had at least been the sense of people around, the knowledge that they were out there, safely holed up behind their windows. And there had been the conviction that the lights were just about to return, the belief that this silence—so eerily complete—occupied that brief moment just before the *click* and *hum* of air conditioners powering back up, just before the epileptic stutter of streetlights flickering back on. Here, there was none of that.

Just darkness and silence. An extended promise.

Taylor pointed out Gonzaga University, waving her finger into the void. She might as well have been pointing toward China in the distance. I couldn't see a thing.

With a loud *crack* of thunder, the clouds opened up and sheets of water came crashing down on our heads. My jacket was soaked through in a matter of seconds. Taylor grabbed my hand and started sprinting through the downpour, leading me the last block to her house. During the rush to get inside, I didn't get a good look at the house's exterior, but it seemed big—a multistory Victorian, painted yellow. There was a red and blue pinwheel in the flower bed at the base of the porch; it was spinning wildly, caught in a stream of water falling from the roof.

Taylor pushed through the front door, into a brightly lit entryway. "Wipe your feet," she said, nodding toward the doormat. She shrugged out of her wet hoodie and hung it on a mirror-backed coatrack. Underneath, she was wearing a bloodred turtleneck.

This was the first time I'd seen her without the hood. There was a propane lantern burning on a nearby table, but its brilliant white light couldn't touch her pitch-black hair, it was so dark, it sucked in light like a black hole, refusing to give back even the slightest glimmer. Strands hung in wet rivulets around her face, dripping water onto her shirt. She glanced into the mirror and pushed the stray hair back behind her head, smoothing it into an elegant wave.

Again, I was struck by her beauty. Her features were angular and sharp; her beauty was strong and intimidating.

And she'd invited me back to her house.

What does that mean? I wondered, setting my bags on the ground and shucking out of my jacket. *Convenience? Pity? Something more?* I tried not to get my hopes up. Already, Taylor had seen me at my worst: weak, scared, confused.

She picked up the lantern and started back into the house. I grabbed my bags and followed.

The thick scent of pot hit me as soon as we crossed into the living room. After the day I'd had, it was an enticing smell, pungent and warm, a breath of comfort and sleep in the still air. All of the room's furnishings had been pushed back against the walls, and a half dozen people sat gathered around the lit fireplace. There were four men and two women, their faces bathed in the flickering yellow light. None looked older than thirty.

"Glad to see you got the fire going without me," Taylor said, setting the lantern down just inside the door. She was greeted with smiles, nods, and a halfhearted grunt. "I was afraid I'd find you all frozen into tiny little cubes."

One of the men leaned back on his elbows and flashed Taylor a sly little grin. "You know, we got along just fine before you showed up. I myself survived twenty-four years without your help—"

"I still find that hard to believe," Taylor interrupted, cracking a smile.

"The sun rose and set without you," the man continued. There was something wrong with his voice; his words were drawn out, stretched into a dreamy singsong lilt. It was a disconcerting effect, and it made me feel uncomfortable. "Governments formed and dissolved without you. Plants sprouted, flowered, and died. The tide rolled in. The tide rolled out." Still smiling, the man lowered himself onto his back and stared up at the ceiling. I was struck by a moment of déjà vu, and I followed his eyes, making sure there was no fractured body looming up above. "And despite your help, despite all you do, things still fall apart. The world decays. The city falls into chaos."

"Yeah, Devon," Taylor said, the smile fading from her lips, her brow scrunching into confused lines. "And morons still bray nonsense."

"But we *appreciate* your help," the man, Devon, continued, ignoring Taylor's insult. "Really, we do. Working hard. Seeing the good in everybody. Out there gathering up the lost and the helpless." He gestured in my direction, a languid flick of the wrist. Then he raised a pinkie finger up toward the sky. "Plugging up the dike with your tiny little finger."

"What's his problem?" Taylor asked, turning to the other people at the fire.

A girl with short blond hair let out a giggle. "Fuck if we know. He just won't shut up. I think he found some Quaaludes or something."

When I looked back at Devon, I saw that his eyes had fallen shut. He was lying on his back with a distant smile on his lips, rocking back and forth. Taylor just shook her head and gestured me toward the fire.

Taylor made introductions.

The girl with the blond hair was Amanda. She'd been studying psychology at Gonzaga. "*Big* waste of time," she said with a giggle. "People just don't make that much sense. End of story."

The man sitting next to her was Floyd. "Pretty Boy Floyd," one of the others said with a laugh. That's what they used to call him, back when he'd been making skateboarding videos. But those days were long past. "Fucked-up knee," he explained. He rapped his knuckles against his leg and gave his head a bitter little shake. "More metal than bone." His nose was crooked, and his cheekbones didn't sit quite right. "I had the bad habit of landing on my face."

Then there was Mackenzie, a former bookstore clerk with red hair and a thick beard. I had him pegged as the oldest of the bunch, placing him at about thirty. He had a gruff voice, and his laughter was a low bass rumble, subdued and guarded. Maybe it was just the pot, but Mackenzie kept looking around the room, casting nervous glances toward the doors and windows. The smile on his lips didn't really touch his eyes.

Sabine was sitting perched between Mackenzie and the fireplace. ("Sabine Pearl-Grey," she said with a half-mouthed smile. "That's my stage name.") She was a small, delicate girl with small, delicate features—porcelain-doll cheekbones and a long, thin neck. Her hair was dyed black with stripes of bright red shooting out from her scalp like bolts of lightning. Her smile was bright and gleeful. She was an artist. "Performance artist," she said in a husky nicotine purr.

Floyd let out a laugh. "Like the take-a-shit-in-a-shot-glass type of artist."

Sabine threw a chunk of firewood at Floyd and shook her head, the wide smile still on her lips. "Fuck no! I may occasionally *yell* at strangers and roll around on the sidewalk, but that's about it. Nothing too crude. And I do charcoals, too," she added hastily. "And poetry!"

The youngest of the bunch was Charlie, and he couldn't have been older than seventeen. He was a skinny black kid with wire-frame glasses. His smile was tight-lipped, and his tired eyes looked just about ready to fall shut. "We found him wandering the streets, looking for his parents," Taylor said, whispering in my ear. "He was out of town when the quarantine hit—staying with his grandparents in Portland—but his parents were here, in the city. He's convinced they never left, but we haven't found a single trace of them." After a moment she added: "The boy's a genius. Fixed my watch when it broke." She held up her wrist, showing me a beautiful Bulova. Its crystal face was cracked, but its elegant hands still ticked off the seconds.

And then there was Devon, still lying on the floor, gently rocking back and forth. Taylor gave me an exasperated shrug. "Yeah, he's just a fuckup," she said. "Mac says he used to see him up at the Jiffy Lube on Division, working on cars."

"Shut up," Devon mumbled, the smile disappearing from his

lips. "If you don't quit talking about me like I'm not here, I'll fucking Jiffy Lube my arm and sodomize the whole damn lot of you."

"He doesn't like talking *pre-evacuation*," Sabine said, holding her hand next to her mouth, like that little barrier might keep Devon from hearing. "He's got *issues*."

"And he's got the best fucking pot!" Floyd said, suddenly dropping to the ground and planting a big theatrical kiss on Devon's forehead. Everybody laughed, Amanda nearly collapsing to the ground in hysterics.

"Speaking of, where is that shit?" Floyd asked, his voice suddenly serious. "I need another hit. I can feel the horrors starting to creep back in."

And just like that, the laughter stopped. Amanda giggled once, but there was no levity in it this time, just nerves.

Mac started to nod violently. I couldn't tell if he was agreeing with Floyd or if this was some type of nervous tic. His eyes once again made a circuit of the room before finally settling on Taylor. "And . . . and," he rumbled, his voice strained and unsteady. "Are you sure we're alone in here? Are you positive?"

After a moment, he continued, his voice dropping down into a low conspiratorial whisper: "Is there someone else in the house?"

The pipe went around the circle a couple of times, then Taylor grabbed Mac's hand and coaxed him to his feet. She took him on a circuit of the house, trying to show him that we were alone. I could hear them moving through the rooms upstairs, the sound reaching me through a pleasant, drug-induced haze. It sounded like there were a lot of rooms up there. And a lot of stairs. Three stories, maybe. Four or five bedrooms.

Moving catlike, on all fours, Sabine crept over to my side and gestured toward my bags. "Can I take a look?" she asked. She started digging through my duffel, not even waiting for my permission. Laughing, she pulled out article after article of clothing—T-shirts, sweaters, jeans, and underwear—and set them in a pile on the floor. She tossed aside my copy of the *AP Guide to Photojournalism*. Then, finally, she reached the food. She let out a delighted yelp and started stacking cans in a little pyramid.

"Amanda!" she called, startling the blond girl out of a droop-headed daze. "Shelve the fucking pasta. We've got dinner right here!" She rolled several cans across the hardwood floor.

"Thank God," Amanda sighed. Then, under her breath: "*Fucking pasta*. Every fucking day." She looked up toward Sabine's pyramid. "Got any meat . . . or bread?"

"Just canned meat," I said with a sigh, watching as my store of food moved from hand to hand. Floyd was lost in a can of pork and beans, his eyes locked on the picture on the label. Mac, just back from his tour of the house, dropped to his knees at Sabine's side and started cycling through the cans on the floor.

"And crackers!" Sabine said, lifting a box of Saltines from my bag.

"And crackers," I confirmed. I'd meant for this food to last me a while, but I couldn't—not in good conscience—greet their hospitality with selfish hoarding.

"Don't worry, Dean," Taylor said. I turned and found her standing in the doorway, surveying the room like a mother watching her children unwrap their gifts on Christmas morning. "To-night's dinner is on you, but we'll pay you back." Then, with a cryptic smile: "We look after our own."

While Amanda and Mac made dinner, Charlie asked to see my camera.

"I want to see what kind of gear you've got," he explained. It was the first time I had heard his voice, and it was stronger than I expected. I thought he'd have a weak, tentative little kid's voice, but his words were deep, self-assured, and confident.

I nodded and passed him the camera. Devon surfaced from his stupor long enough to give the camera a distrustful glare.

"Nice," Charlie said, turning it over in his hands. "Canon," he noted. "Is it a pro model? Consumer? How many megapixels?"

"Eighteen," I said. "Not quite pro, but close enough. It'll do the job for magazine work . . . maybe not glossy advertising shots, but most people wouldn't notice the difference."

Just then, Sabine crawled over to Charlie and plucked the camera from his hands. She raised the viewfinder to her eye and started snapping shots.

"Careful—" I said, but she interrupted me with a shake of her head.

"I took classes," she said with a placating smile. "I know what I'm doing." She crawled off with the camera, taking pictures of Floyd and Devon on the other side of the room. I watched her go, anxious even after she slipped the carry strap around her neck.

"Have you had anything published?" Charlie asked.

"No," I said, shaking my head. "Well, university publications. But nothing real."

Suddenly Taylor appeared at my side. I hadn't noticed her listening in the doorway. She touched my forearm tentatively and caught my eyes. It was a warm, friendly gesture. "And that's why you're here?" she asked. "To make your mark? To get *published*?" There was a note of incredulity in her voice when she said that word—*published*. She made it sound so trivial, so unworthy.

After a moment of silence, I nodded. "And I figure I don't have much time. When my father found out I was getting a fine arts degree, he absolutely flipped out. 'There's no future there,' he said, 'no money.' And he put his foot down—he actually said that: 'I'm putting my foot down!' He threatened to stop paying for my education if I didn't switch degrees. So there I was, twenty-two and short on credits, returning for a fifth year to get a degree I desperately didn't want. And once I was done with that, I could see my future laid out before me: an accounting job at my father's firm, everything arranged neatly beneath his big thumb.

"It was terrifying, seeing it like that, and I knew I couldn't escape just by taking pictures of fountains and trees, flowers and old buildings, people in contemplative poses. Everything was so tame—pictures I'd seen a hundred times before, and usually done better. There was no way I'd make a reputation doing that. No way I'd secure a job, a future." Taylor and Charlie were watching me intently, their expressions curious, genuinely interested. I felt the need to explain myself—especially to Taylor—to let them know what I was trying to accomplish here, to let them know that I wasn't just some fucking tourist. That I had goals and ambition. I struggled against the pot, trying to find the words I needed, trying to nail down the . . . *drive* buried deep down inside my chest: this powerful thing that had propelled me across three states, through a government quarantine, and into this strange wasteland. "One of my professors . . . he said, 'Great photographers don't make great photographs; great photographs make great photographers.' And the things I've heard about this place, the images that have made their way out . . ."

I shook my head, unable to find the words. Once again, Taylor touched my arm, prodding me to continue. "There's something great here," I finally said, "in the unknown, the impossible. And it's something, I think, that can make *me* great. Something I need. Desperately."

After I finished, I searched their faces for understanding. *Do they get it? Can they possibly understand such a vague, inscrutable drive . . . this thing that keeps me moving, unsatisfied?*

Taylor was nodding, a gentle, sympathetic gesture.

And a sly, knowing smile slid across Charlie's face.

God.

Sitting here, now, writing this shit down, I marvel at the depths of my stupidity.

Sneaking into the city, I *wasn't* being noble. I *wasn't* chasing down an elusive artistic ideal, shunning corporate anonymity for art and passion.

I was just being stupid.

That's it. End of explanation.

For all of my romantic notions—bullshit self-betterment,

reaching for my potential, making a name for myself—what I did, what I pursued—leaving my life and sprinting blindly into the dark—was nothing but death and confusion and insanity.

I was running in the wrong direction.

I was fleeing the wrong things.

We had makeshift jambalaya for dinner: canned sausages and rice cooked in crushed tomatoes and seasoning. Served with crackers on the side; Sabine had been adamant about that. We gathered around a sturdy dining-room table and smoked pot between bites. It was a good meal. Maybe it was just the pot, or a reaction to what I'd seen earlier in the day, but I felt genuinely comfortable here, surrounded by these people.

While we ate, Floyd and Sabine took turns telling me stories, dishing dirt about everyone in the room: how they'd found Charlie in the southern district, Amanda in the park, Floyd skating lazily through an abandoned shopping mall. And Devon, half naked, yelling at the top of his lungs. I felt a bit self-conscious being the center of attention, but they seemed happy spinning these tales, transforming their individual ordeals into humorous quips. Even Devon got into the act, surfacing from his stupor long enough to curse out everyone in the room.

Halfway through dinner, I glanced up and found Sabine taking pictures. She was holding the camera above her head, aiming it down the length of the table. Just random, blind shots, not even glancing through the viewfinder or checking the images in the LCD screen. I told myself that I'd have to clean off the memory card once I got it back.

There was a lot of laughter. The pouring rain, the quarantine, the hotel—these things seemed worlds away. It was just the eight of us, here and now, floating through this warm candlelit haze.

After dinner, we returned to the living room and once again built up the fire. It was quiet now. The food and pot had taken their toll, and it wasn't long before people started to retreat upstairs, toward beds and blankets. Amanda and Mac left together; I gathered that they were a couple. Then Devon stumbled away, followed by Charlie, then Floyd. And then, reluctantly, Sabine.

Leaving Taylor and me all alone.

We sat in silence for a couple of minutes, me on the sofa while she warmed her hands at the fire. I listened to the crackling coals. In this perfect calm, the long day finally caught up with me, and I let my head loll back against the sofa cushions.

"Why are you here, Taylor?" I asked. I rolled my head back and forth, basking in the drugged, comfortable motion. "I told you my story, but what about you? Why do you stay when everything's so . . . ?" And I thought for a moment about the body in the ceiling.

She let out a loud sigh, and I looked up to find her watching me carefully. "Family, I guess." She paused for a moment, then nodded up toward the ceiling and the people gathered in their rooms upstairs. "I can't abandon them. Not now. I . . . was dealing with some shit when the quarantine hit, and I couldn't leave. By the time things settled down, I had Sabine and Mac here with me. Then Amanda. Then Floyd and Charlie and Devon . . .

"I think they need me. And I'm not going anywhere, not if that means leaving them behind."

I grunted, and she flashed me a smile.

Family.

Her heart must be huge, I thought, *to have room for so many.* She turned back toward the fire and added more wood to the hearth.

I drowsed off for a moment, and when I opened my eyes, I found her standing over me. She was holding out a quilt. It was an old quilt—squares of faded color, its hem ripped into ribbons on every side. "You should sleep here tonight, in front of the fire. Tomorrow we can make you up a room . . . if that's what you'd like." Her voice rose, twisting the words into a gentle question.

"Yeah," I managed, still half asleep. "That would be good."

She nodded, handed me the quilt, and turned to go.

"And . . . Taylor?" I said. "Thank you. For everything. With-out you . . . if you hadn't—"

"Don't sweat it," she said, keeping her back to me. "It's what I do. In that, at least, Devon's got me pegged." Her words were soft and distant. It was as if she'd already left the room.

Later, as I drifted off to sleep, I wondered if she was seeing anyone.

And I wondered if I was her type.

I jolted awake, chased by nightmare.

Just brief images. *My hand reaching out, touching the trunk of a tree. Watching as my flesh sank in, all the way up to my forearm.*

I didn't know what time it was. The room was dark, and the fire had burned down to embers; it was nothing but a dim bed of orange crackling to itself in the hearth.

Still late, I thought, or very, very early.

I pushed the quilt aside and stood up. My entire body was trembling. I paced from one end of the room to the other, trying to shake the remnants of dream from my limbs.

I was still high. It felt like my head was filled with cotton and loosely wound balls of yarn. My mouth tasted like bread and ashes.

The house felt different somehow, and for a long moment I couldn't place the change. Then I noticed the silence. The pound-ing rain had stopped.

I moved to the window and found the street out front bathed in moonlight. The wet asphalt reflected the crescent in the sky, illuminating the upscale houses in shades of gray. All still. All deathly silent.

Then an animal appeared from the east, trotting down the mid-dle of the road. It was a large dog or a wolf—some type of canine. At least it seemed very doglike. But not quite. The way it moved was wrong. There was something wrong with its legs. An extra joint, maybe? It seemed like each time it took a step, its legs went through an extra motion—paws violently *click*ing down, toward the road, at the height of each arc. Almost curling into fists. The animal looked powerful, strong. The way it moved . . . it was attacking the ground with each whirl of limbs.

It stopped in front of the house and turned its head toward me, as if sensing my watching eyes. It presented a wolfish silhouette, outlined against the gleaming asphalt.

Its eyes caught the light, shining a faint, glimmering blue. And even from this distance, I could see its muscles quivering, a barely restrained tornado of motion, trapped in animal form, straining to break free.

And then there were more, following in the animal's wake, moving with those odd, violent steps. A whole pack of canines—fifteen, twenty, twenty-five—flowing down the street, parting around that initial animal as if it were a boulder in the bed of a stream, its head still turned my way, watching.

They moved in complete silence, a graceful play of shadows, gliding through the night.

The animal watched me until the last of its pack had disappeared down the street. Then it turned and followed, those odd, explosive legs carrying it out of view.

"You saw them, didn't you?"

It was a breathy whisper coming from the room at my back.

I turned and found Amanda standing in the doorway, a dimly lit ghost, lost in shadow. Her face was a pale crescent, only one eye visible in the moonlight. That eye was wide, hopeful.

I nodded—*yes, yes they were there*—and she returned the gesture, providing me with the same assurance. Then she faded back into the darkness.

I didn't hear her footsteps carry her back through the house. I didn't hear the stairs creak as she climbed up to the second floor.

I was high. I was high and still half asleep, and I wasn't sure what I'd seen. Maybe just some dogs.

But what did Amanda see? I wondered, remembering that breathy, hopeful whisper.

I should have had my camera, I chided myself. It was the second straight time I'd been caught empty-handed.

At this rate, I'd lose my sanity before I ever managed to get a useful shot.

04.1

Video clip. September 7, 11:35 A.M. Press conference:

There's banner text running across the bottom of the
screen, recounting headlines from around the world.
In the bottom left-hand corner, an artful blur ob-
scures the cable news channel's logo—it's a minor
edit, somebody trying to avoid litigation, but it
looks like a tiny thundercloud or a fogged and
smudged piece of glass. The date and time are
printed in the upper right-hand corner: September 7,
11:35 A.M. PDT.

The video starts in midsentence—a man at a lectern,
talking over a gaggle of shouted questions. He is
standing in front of a pale blue background, and the
Spokane city seal hangs on a flag behind his head.
The man's conservative blue suit is sharply pressed,
and his gray-white hair sweeps back from his forehead in a perfect, unmoving wave. There is a pinched
look on his face. He is starting to perspire. The
words MAYOR JEFFREY SLOCUM are printed above the
banner at the bottom of the screen.

MAYOR JEFFREY SLOCUM: . . . be assured we are investigating every violent incident. I am in constant
contact with our elected officials at all levels of
government—including the president of the United
States—and military intervention will only be considered as—

VOICE FROM OFFSCREEN: (Unintelligible) . . . reports
of hallucinations and possible terrorist attacks?

MAYOR JEFFREY SLOCUM: We are certainly investigating
all possibilities at this time, but it's important
for everybody out there—both inside the city and all
across America—to know that all of our initial tests
have turned up negative. And these tests have been
quite extensive . . . and, we've . . . uh, we've
seen no signs of chemical or biological foul play—

A VOICE BREAKS THROUGH THE GAGGLE OF QUESTIONS: (Unintelligible) . . . water?

MAYOR JEFFREY SLOCUM: As I said, we've seen no signs
of that. We're still checking the water and air, but
at this point, those don't seem to be . . . uhm,
credible vectors. (Uncertain, the mayor glances to
his right, offscreen.)

A SUDDEN, LOUD VOICE: How many dead, Mayor?

MAYOR JEFFREY SLOCUM: At this time, we don't have a
firm number to give you. We'll be releasing those
numbers when the time is right.

THE SAME LOUD VOICE: Have you finished counting?

MAYOR JEFFREY SLOCUM: Now that . . . I do not appreciate the tone of your question! This city's local

government is doing extremely well given these trying circumstances—with all you *jackals*, all the national media, watching and salivating. Let me tell
you . . . things are starting to fall into place,
and normalcy is being—

Without warning, the mayor disappears.

In one frame, he is standing at attention behind the
lectern, hammering his finger down to make a point.
In the next, he is gone. There is no break in the
tape, no sign of a splice; there is no hitch of digital editing. Just, suddenly, a vacant lectern set
in the middle of the screen, the words MAYOR JEFFREY
SLOCUM still superimposed beneath.

Now, where the man had been, there is nothing but
pale blue background. And the city seal, swaying
slightly in the air-conditioned breeze.

The mayor's disappearance is greeted with a sudden
silence. Then the entire room reacts. Some of the
handheld microphones withdraw in surprise, and
others suddenly jerk forward. Somebody bumps the
camera, and the image shakes for a moment. After a
couple of seconds, one of the mayor's staff moves
slowly across the stage, glancing back offscreen
every couple of steps. Stricken, the woman looks
back and forth, then down, beneath the lectern.
Finding nothing, she turns back and shakes her head,
her eyes wide.

The video ends.

04.2

I heard them moving about the house while I dozed. Morning sounds. Footsteps and creaking bedsprings. Quiet voices and running water. Doors opening and falling shut. The smell of cooking tickled at my nose, but my sore muscles and foggy head kept me under the quilt. Finally, a beam of sunlight found the sofa, shining orange-red through my eyelids, and I managed to pull myself awake.

By then, the house was once again quiet. The voices were gone, and there was no sign of movement. *Maybe they all packed up and left,* I thought. Or maybe, in the early-morning hours, I'd managed to dream them all away.

Still half-asleep, I got up off the sofa and went looking for signs of life.

I found Charlie in the kitchen, sitting at a table in the breakfast nook. The room looked different in the morning light: the sun poured in through the open curtains, bathing everything in a blindingly bright haze. Charlie was tapping away at a tiny notebook computer. When I stepped through the door, he cast a quick glance up, then went right back to work.

"Do you have a Gmail account?" he asked, still typing away.

"Gmail?" I grunted, wondering if I'd stumbled into the middle of someone else's conversation. I rubbed at my sticky, sleep-blurred eyes. "You can't possibly have Internet access here—no power, no landlines, no cell signal. The military's got that all wrapped up tight. Right? Communication blackout . . . all that happy shit."

"I cobbled something together," he said with a sly smile. He spun the computer around and showed me the program on its screen. It looked like a simple email program. There was a tab at the top with my name on it (next to separate tabs for Charlie, Taylor, and everyone else), and then, down below, there was space for account information, an address line, a subject line, and a large text field for the body of a message. "If you fill in your stuff, we can smuggle it out. It'll also capture your incoming mail."

I stared at the computer for a moment, then, suddenly struck by what I was seeing, spun it back around and checked its rear panel. "The battery . . . it's *charged*? Where are you getting the power?"

"We've got a source." Again he flashed that sly smile.

My shoulders slumped, and I let out a disappointed groan. I'd spent over a hundred dollars on an external grip for my camera—one that took disposable batteries in lieu of rechargeable power—and I'd stocked up on a shitload of AAs. Not to mention a second battery for my laptop.

I turned the computer back around and stared at the mail program for nearly a minute. My fingers hovered over the keyboard, tense, itching to write. But who could I contact? Who would understand? My friends in California? My father? *Not bloody likely,* I thought. At this point, there probably wasn't a soul in the world who had even noticed that I was gone.

As I was thinking, Taylor stormed into the house. She moved in a loud rush, crashing from the front door, through the hallway, into the kitchen. She saw me at Charlie's computer and let out a deep cluck. "No time for that," she said. "No time. I told Danny I'd be there at noon." Charlie pulled the computer back across the table and resumed typing, faster now, trying to get something finished.

"Next time, Dean," Taylor said. "Next batch." She pointed toward my bags in the living room. "Now, get dressed and ready to go. You've got a lot to see here, and I figure we should start at the top. Which means moving . . . *fast!*"

I'd slept in my jeans and a sweatshirt, so getting dressed just meant swapping my shirt for a fresh one and unrolling a new pair of socks. Sabine had left my camera on the floor next to my bags. I slipped it into my backpack and slung the bag over my shoulder.

"You can't take that," Taylor said, nodding toward my pack as I came back into the kitchen. "Leave it with Charlie. He'll keep it safe."

I shook my head. "No fucking way! I came here to take pictures, and I've missed enough already."

"That's not the way it works, Dean. Unless you want it confiscated, you leave your camera here."

I studied her for a moment. There was absolutely no give in her eyes. Reluctantly, I set the backpack down on the table. I dug out a PowerBar, then pushed the bag toward Charlie. "I can take some fucking food, right?" I growled, showing her the foil-wrapped energy bar. "Or do you want to tell me how to eat, too?"

"It's not like that," Taylor said, a pinched, hard look on her face. "I'm not on some power trip here. It's just the reality of the situation."

Charlie finished typing on his notebook. He pulled a thumb-size RAM drive from the USB port and handed it to Taylor. She gave him a satisfied nod, then turned back my way. "You'll see," she said. "It'll be worth it. I promise."

I was in a funk all the way across the river. The morning sun had burned away the dark October clouds, transforming the city into someplace new; it was no longer the gray, oppressive maze I'd run through just the day before. The streets seemed wider somehow, the towers overhead not quite so tall. And everything had been washed clean by the torrential rain, wisps of steam curling up wherever the sun touched the damp concrete. Unfortunately, I couldn't enjoy this new, sparkling city. I felt naked without my backpack, without my camera.

I shoved my hands deep into my pockets. Empty, my fingers felt awkward, useless.

Taylor gave me time to sulk. She stayed silent as she led me south, walking a couple of steps ahead but glancing back every now and then to check my mood. After a while, those glances started to weigh on me. I felt stupid. Here I was, pouting like some petulant child.

"Where are we going?" I finally asked, trying to regain some dignity.

"The heart of downtown," she said. "The best place to start."

After crossing the bridge, she took me west on Sprague. The street here was deserted, but I could hear voices and laughter to the south.

"Mama Cass's place," Taylor said, nodding in that direction. "It's right down there. She gets her food from the outside. Always has fresh-brewed coffee. If you ever need company, day or night, that's where you want to go."

I wasn't certain about my bearings, but I knew that the hotel from yesterday had to be around here someplace. *And the man,* I thought, *the man in the ceiling, deformed, not even human, but still reaching out.* Perhaps it was a block farther south. I stuck close to Taylor.

As we passed, an abandoned building on the north side of the street caught my eye. There were words spray painted across its face, starting way up on the fourth floor. The words stretched left to right in crooked rows, stacked one on top of the other. Each letter was about four feet tall, transcribed freehand in gentle, feminine arcs. The paint was electric blue, laid out in thick, double-wide lines. It was a poem. Or as close to poetry as graffiti could get.

It read:

inside turned out,
no longer hidden

and the weight
    of the world

and the price
    of this vision

and the height
    we will fall

and we WILL
    f
    a
    l
    l

The last word—*fall*—was inscribed in the narrow space be-tween a window and the edge of the building, plummeting all the way to the ground. The word *will* in the final line was traced over with red paint, making it stand out like an exit sign in a dark theater.

"Who did this?" I asked, halting to study the giant words.

Taylor shook her head. "I don't really know. The Artist. The Poet . . . You'll find stuff like this all over town. Poems, slogans. All in the same handwriting. There's a giant 'Fuck You' facing I-90." She took a step back, as if trying to pull the whole building into frame. "This one's new, though. It wasn't here last week."

Poetry. The word suddenly clicked inside my head. "Sabine?" I asked. "She could have done this. She said she writes poems."

Taylor shook her head. "I don't think so. All of Sabine's poems are about her vagina." She smiled at the surprised look on my face, then gestured back toward the building. "Besides, that girl's obsessed with the Poet. She wants to find whoever's doing this . . . wants to *collaborate*." She was quiet for a moment, and when she continued, there was a hint of disdain in her voice. "You know, sometimes I wonder if this is all just some big fucked-up art project for her, for Sabine. This whole fucking thing. Nothing but background color and clever commentary. A stage on which she can play. Nothing serious, no. Nothing deadly."

I turned and studied Taylor's profile, watching as her eyes scanned the poem. "And me?" I asked. "What about me and my photography?"

"You're new here," Taylor said. "You'll learn. Sabine, on the other hand . . . she should know better by now."

She glanced down at her watch and nodded westward. "Now, get your ass in gear. We've got an appointment to keep."

The courthouse was a huge, blocky building at the corner of Lincoln and Sprague. It looked like a giant four-sided cheese grater, with hundreds of small windows recessed in a tight concrete grid. The newspaper building stood across from its entrance, and a cobblestone courtyard occupied the space between the two buildings. Once a well-manicured stretch of land, the courtyard had fallen into disrepair, now cordoned off on both ends of the block and cluttered with dead, skeletal trees. A fountain stood near the courthouse's entrance, but without water, it was nothing but a twelve-foot bowl brimming with trash and leaves. There were soldiers posted at the courthouse's front door.

Taylor led me down the street at the building's side, away from the entrance. She stopped halfway down the block and abruptly turned toward the building. It was ten stories of industrial concrete, a drab, oppressive cliff face looming above us. There was a broken window three floors up, a neat black hole punched through the building's face. Taylor glanced both ways—checking for witnesses, I supposed—then, in a quick, discreet motion, grabbed something from her pocket and lobbed it up through that gaping wound. As it sailed through the air, I recognized it as Charlie's USB drive.

Why? I wanted to ask, but she started away before I could open my mouth.

I followed her back to the front of the building, tagging along like a puppy dog as she headed straight for the main entrance. The guards smiled as they saw her approach. They must not have felt threatened. They didn't even touch the rifles slung across their shoulders.

"It's good to see you, Taylor," one of the men said, greeting her with genuine warmth. "And your timing's spot-on, as usual. The captain just left."

"Awww, that's a *shame*," she said, a campy, theatrical quality entering her voice. "And here I thought to bring him a gift!" She started digging through her pockets, searching for something, then stopped with her hand buried deep in her pants. "Ah, here it is!" she said, pulling her hand out and displaying a raised middle finger.

"Think you can give him that for me, Johnny?" she asked, turning to the second soldier.

Both of the guards laughed. "I think I'll have to give that one a pass," the second soldier said. "I'm trying to *avoid* court-martials here."

"That's a good idea," Taylor said. "I still need you on the door."

"Okay, Taylor, enough of your goddamn charm." Still smiling, the first soldier gestured her over to the side of the door. "You know the drill."

Taylor nodded and held out her arms. The soldier lifted a portable metal detector from a loop of cord wrapped around his belt. He ran the wand over her entire body, up her front and back and then down the length of her arms and legs. After the scan, the soldier checked her pockets, giving them nothing but a quick, cursory pat. He waved her toward the building, then turned his attention to me.

The guards handled me with a bit more suspicion. I noticed the second soldier inching his gun forward as his partner looked me over; the soldier's hand came to rest on the gun's butt, ready to slip forward into the trigger guard. And the pat down was much more thorough, the soldier's blunt hands running all the way up into my armpits and crotch. He felt the PowerBar in my pocket and made me take it out. He studied it for several seconds— holding it gingerly, as if it might explode—then tossed it over to his partner. I was about to complain, but the soldier cut me short with a curt shake of his head.

"You guys are good to go," the soldier said, stepping up to the building and opening the door. "You know the rules, Taylor. Nothing to make me look bad."

"Don't worry. No anarchy today." Taylor smiled and patted the soldier on the arm. "I'm just catching up with Danny." Then we passed into the building.

The lobby was deserted. There was absolutely no furniture here, just one long, muddy carpet runner leading to a bank of elevators on the far side of the room. Lights were glowing overhead, but most of the fixtures had been cracked open and the fluorescent tubes removed. Taylor saw me looking and pointed up toward the roof. "They've got plenty of generators up there. The bulbs, however . . . they aren't faring too well."

The elevators were working, but Taylor walked right on by, leading me to the stairwell at the far end of the alcove. The light inside was inconsistent. I glanced up toward the roof and watched the stairwell pulse above me, the light waxing and waning with the strength of the generators. I could hear the electricity pulsing. It was a slow, slow heartbeat.

We climbed up to the third floor.

Taylor opened the door and led the way down a dimly lit corridor. The entire floor seemed deserted. I glanced through a couple of doorways and found row after row of empty cubicles. There was paper scattered across the floor. Upturned lamps on each desk. A couple of abandoned staplers.

All the furniture had been moved away from the walls. It looked as if, abandoned, these office spaces had surrendered to some previously unknown force of physics, something that pulled desks, chairs, and cubicle walls toward the center of each giant room. Maybe, in a thousand years, I'd come back and find a dense singularity in the center of each of these spaces. Nothing but compressed office furniture collapsed in on itself.

"Here we go." Taylor's voice echoed back down the length of the corridor, jolting me out of my reverie.

I found her in one of the big, empty rooms, squatting in front of a busted window. She was holding up Charlie's USB drive. "Easier than smuggling it in," she said, a sly smile on her face.

I followed her back to the stairwell, then up three more flights of stairs.

The sixth floor was bustling with activity. It had the same layout as three floors down, but the cubicles here were arranged with ruler-straight precision. And they were occupied, full of life. Each desk supported a heavy-duty notebook computer, illuminated from above by a standing desk lamp. A mix of casually dressed civilians and uniformed officers sat hunched over these machines, studying LCD screens and transcribing text from handwritten forms. A din of voices filled the air. It was standard office chatter: rat-a-tat-tat conversation, hushed laughter, muffled curses.

The difference between this floor and the one three floors down was disorienting. The architecture was the same, but the feel was radically different. Like it was the same place—the same floor—but separated by a vast period of time.

But which comes first? I wondered. Was the third floor the past or the future? Was it an abandoned, desolate space waiting for reclamation, waiting to be filled and rejuvenated? Or was it what comes next, what happens when all of these people pack up and leave, abandoning this place for good?

"This is the military command center," Taylor explained, noticing the perplexed look on my face. "You'll find the bigwigs up on the top two floors, plotting and planning, arranging the infrastructure, sending out search parties and data-gathering expeditions." She gestured into one of the rooms. "Down here, you've got the dregs, crunching numbers and cataloging information, trying to make sense of what's going on."

We continued down the main corridor, past several more densely packed rooms. Finally, Taylor turned into a smaller office. There were only four cubicles here, all of them oversized and filled with multiple monitors. At the moment, the room held only a single occupant: a soldier dressed in a natty olive-drab uniform. He glanced up from his computer as soon as he heard us enter, and a wide smile spread across his face.

"Taylor!" the soldier exclaimed. He rose to his feet and greeted her with a warm embrace. I caught the grin on Taylor's lips and felt a moment of intense jealousy; it was an irrational reaction, I knew, but it was something I couldn't control. She was practically beaming. I hadn't known her for long, but still, from all I'd seen, I wanted to be able to elicit that type of reaction in her, the sheer magnitude of that joy.

As soon as he let go, Taylor introduced us. "Danny, this is Dean. He's a photographer. He's trying to document the situation here." The soldier's arm remained draped around Taylor's shoulder, and she reached up to pat his hand as she talked. "Danny's my spy in the military-industrial complex. He helped me get in good with the soldiers."

"You make it sound like treason," Danny said. He held out his hand and I shook it. He was taller than me—about six foot two—and he had a powerful frame. His dark brown hair was sheared close to his skull, letting a glimpse of skin shine through. It made the curve of his head look like a powerful, tightly flexed muscle. He had a strong handshake. "I just help her out now and then. I figure I should do my part . . . lend a hand to the little guy."

Danny smiled. He had a perfect smile—a warm, winning smile—and that bugged me to no end. "A photographer, huh," he said, and he gave his head a tiny little shake. "You should be careful out there. The captain sees the press as public enemy number one, and he's already got a couple of newsmen locked away at Fort Lewis . . . Frankly, I think he just doesn't know what else to do."

I nodded, remembering the Jeep with the P.P. plates on the outskirts of the city. Maybe I *wasn't* falling behind. Maybe there weren't any competing photographers in the city. Not anymore, at least. But the threat of prison—not even prison, I realized, but military detainment as some type of enemy combatant—made me feel downright nauseated. *No guts, no glory,* I told myself, but the feeling refused to go away.

I took a deep breath and watched as Taylor handed Danny Charlie's USB drive. He sat back down at his computer and plugged it in, double clicking an icon as soon as it appeared on the screen. After a couple of seconds, Danny removed the drive and handed it back to Taylor.

"What was that?" I asked. "What did you just do?"

"Charlie's program," Taylor explained. "We load up all of our email, Danny plugs it into the military network, and it launches a burst of encrypted data out into the real world." She smiled at the phrase. "Charlie's got a server on the outside—decrypts all of that information and forwards it on. It also downloads all of our incoming mail, along with the latest news from a bunch of sites." She held up the tiny drive. "It's all in here, ready for us to start surfing at our leisure. We do it every couple of days. We'll get you hooked up next time around."

"And the military doesn't know? Isn't that dangerous?"

"Nah," Danny said, dismissing the concern with a wave of his hand. "Charlie's got it streamlined down to a couple of hundred packets. As long as we aren't sending out high-definition video, it's barely noticeable. Besides, I know guys who surf hard-core porn from their military terminals. Next to some of the nasty shit I've seen on their screens, this is tulips and butterflies."

"He also recharges for us." Taylor pointed to a power strip beneath the soldier's desk. "I'm sure he'd do your camera for you."

I nodded. The thought of throwing my battery charger up through a third-story window didn't exactly fill me with joy—

when I was a kid, I never played Little League, and my throwing arm was for shit—but it was nice to know I had the option.

"And now that we've got business out of the way . . ." Taylor took a step back, leaving me hanging over Danny's shoulder, transforming the two of us into unintentional conspirators. "Why don't you tell Dean about what you're doing here? Catch us up on all of that great government progress."

Danny gave Taylor a scowl, then turned back to his computer. He popped open a window and started scouring through directories, looking for something. "What do you know, Dean? About the phenomenon?"

"I've been following it on some underground message boards, and there's been some stuff that hasn't made it into the mainstream press. Some strange pictures. Some video. Vague, translucent figures, weird physics. Kids in a cell-phone video, bouncing a ball through a—" I paused, trying to think how best to describe it. "—a *sticky* space in the air, where the ball just slows down, then speeds up again, finally stopping and hovering in midair. Everybody knows *something's* going on here—there's no denying the quarantine or the government's refusal to talk—but nobody knows exactly what. Some type of terrorist attack, maybe. A chemical leak. A haunting." I smiled at this last suggestion. "Maybe something to do with an ancient Indian burial ground?"

Danny didn't smile. "Yeah, we've got a lot of scientists trying to figure it all out. Here, on this floor, we're just gathering information. We catalog incident reports—from civilians, from our soldiers on patrol—and look for patterns." He lifted a clipboard from the clutter on his desk. It held a photocopied sheet titled *REPORT OF UNEXPLAINED INCIDENT*. This particular sheet had been filled out in red ink.

Before he set it back down, I managed to read a few of the neatly typed questions:

13) What were your thoughts before, during, and after the incident? (Please be as specific as possible.)

14) What emotions did the incident evoke? (Fear? Amusement? Regret?)
15) Do you feel compelled to seek out similar experiences?

The person who had filled out this particular form had drawn a shaky red line through question 15, as if he or she were trying to strike it from existence—the question or the compulsion it described, I didn't know.

"And what have you found?" I asked.

"A lot of stuff." Danny shrugged. "And nothing." He pointed to a white dry-erase board tacked to the opposite wall. There was a list of six bullet-pointed items sketched out in bold black letters. "We've narrowed the phenomena down to six basic categories. First, you've got your *visitors*—people and things appearing where they shouldn't be, where they *can't* be. Celebrities driving through town in BMWs. Dead politicians. We've even got a cluster of random people who swear they saw the Empire State Building rising out of the west end of Riverfront Park, but I'm guessing that one's just complete bullshit. On the flip side of that, you've got our second item: *disappearances*. People and things that should be here but aren't. Things that just . . . cease to exist. There's a whole block in the industrial district out east—it used to be warehouses, with streets and trucks and loading docks. It's all gone now. Nothing but flat, bare earth. And you know the mayor, right? You've seen the video?"

"The mayor? That was *real*?" I didn't bother trying to mask my surprise. "That video made the rounds, but everyone dismissed it as a fake. I've seen page after page of analysis. There are splices! And they found the actress, the woman who goes on stage after the mayor disappears. She says she did it for her friend's video project."

"Nah," Danny said, his face lighting up with a bright smile. "All of that stuff came from us. Misinformation. Brilliant, really! We couldn't stop the video from getting out there—it was broadcast live, after all, on national television—so we flooded the In-

67

ternet with fake copies. We added splices and artifacts. We even dubbed over some of the crowd noise, to make it sound like bad acting."

Danny opened a new window on his computer screen and launched a video clip. It was the same press conference I'd seen a dozen times before, but in amazingly clean, high-definition video—better than broadcast quality, better than anything I'd ever seen. And there was no distortion, no artifacts, no obvious splicing. It showed the mayor answering questions, getting angry, then disappearing.

In front of cameras. In front of a whole crowd of reporters.

"We put an emergency injunction on everyone in the room, requiring them to stay quiet. The woman who comes on stage—" Danny pointed to the sharply dressed woman as she stepped up to the lectern; he stayed silent as she looked around and shook her head. "She was his press secretary. She's in New York now. We hired an actress to come forward and claim credit for her role."

Danny shut down the video and swiveled back around. "Truth is, the mayor's gone. He disappeared—right that day, right that *millisecond*—and he hasn't been seen since. And the video gives us nothing. Just—one frame he's there, with that pissed-off look on his face, and the next frame . . . *poof*!" He popped open his hand, showing me an empty palm.

I stood dumbstruck for a moment, trying to process this information.

"Yeah," Danny said. "Just blows your fucking mind."

I glanced over at Taylor, thinking she'd break down laughing at any moment, revealing this whole thing as a big fat joke, but her face remained perfectly still.

"Anyway, after visitors and disappearances, we've got *sounds without sources*." Danny pointed back to the whiteboard. "Voices emanating from empty rooms. Displaced screams and crying. Hell, for two *days* an invisible gun battle raged outside the convention center; a lot of people heard that one." Danny shivered, and his voice dropped. "You could call them auditory ghosts, I guess. They usually come at night. We've got people who can't sleep for all of the things they hear."

I remembered the soldier at the barricade. I remembered the wistful, nervous look on his face. He'd seemed like a haunted man, talking about his transfer out of the city, about how he no longer heard things.

"Next, we've got *creatures*. Either animals completely out of place—flamingos in the park, clouds of butterflies in the middle of the night—or things that don't exist, things that *shouldn't* exist." I nodded, remembering the dogs—the wolves—from the night before. Amanda's animals, with those strange, extrajointed limbs. "There's some scary shit out there," he said. "We've found bodies. Bodies with tooth marks or clawed nearly in half." Danny shivered again; I wasn't sure if this was a genuine reaction, or just something he did to provide emphasis.

"Our fifth category is a little more difficult." I glanced up at the board and saw the phrase "mental problems." "We're not quite sure if it's a phenomenon in its own right or a result of everything else. It's just . . . people going crazy. Acting odd, unusual. Losing memories. Going schizophrenic or catatonic. It might be a result of all this stress, or it might be something else. Another symptom of this . . . *disease*." Danny shook his head and managed a sad little smile. "In my time here I've had two commanding officers fall apart. One was struck dumb by complete amnesia. The other attacked three of his men with a knife . . . before turning it on his own genitalia."

I made an involuntary wince.

"And the final category?" I asked.

Danny gestured back toward the whiteboard. *"Miscellaneous,"* he said, offering up a pathetic shrug. "The last of our all-encompassing groups. Just . . . everything else."

I stared at the board for a long time, waiting for a pattern to emerge, waiting for some type of connective thread to surface and tie it all together. But there was no thread. There was no pattern.

The categories remained disparate, unconnected things—except for visitors and disappearances, which could have been flip sides of the same coin.

And miscellaneous? It seemed like these people, these experts, were stumbling around in the dark here. They had no idea what was going on, and their categories did nothing to illuminate the situation.

The hotel room—that frightening tableau, now burned into my memory—remained just as strange, just as alien.

I walked over and tapped the board. "In this . . . in this miscellaneous category, have you heard anything . . . like . . ." I groped for words, trying to figure out how to explain the body in the ceiling. "Has anybody seen somebody melted—a human body, just kind of *merged* with a ceiling or a wall? Limbs and body parts disappearing into solid objects?"

Danny shook his head. "No. Nothing like that. Not that I know of."

"Is that what you saw yesterday?" Taylor asked. I turned and found a concerned look on her face. Not just concerned, but startled, going pale. "You saw a body? In a floor?"

"Well, I . . ." I shook my head. Pinned beneath that intense stare, I felt flustered. I felt a blush rising up beneath my collar. "No, not really. I'm just . . ." I composed myself a bit. "I'm not sure what I saw." I shook my head, trying to dismiss her concern, trying to escape the sharp look in her eyes. "Just forget it."

They both continued to stare at me, Danny curious and Taylor . . . well, there was something strange—something hungry—about Taylor's expression.

"So what *have* you figured out?" I asked, trying to redirect the conversation. "After one, no, *two* months on the job, what have your experts deduced?"

Danny shrugged. "Nothing much. The doctors and scientists say there's some type of chemical imbalance in the population here. Neurotransmitters. In the brain. They don't know what's causing it. They've been giving antidepressants to anybody who wants them, to boost serotonin and dopamine levels. It seems to help. Some."

"Help with what?"

"With everything." He nodded toward the list on the board: visitors, disappearances, sounds, creatures, mental, and miscellaneous.

"But it isn't all mental, is it? There's genuine physical phenomenon here." I gestured toward his computer screen, where the mayor's video file—**09–07-pressconf.mpeg**— remained highlighted. "Are you saying that a liberal dose of Prozac would have stopped the mayor from disappearing? That something physical— and *impossible*—was caused by errant brain chemicals?"

"All we know is that people on the drugs are involved in fewer unexplained incidents. The correlation is there, small but statistically significant. And believe me, that's killing our scientists. It's something they just don't want to hear." Danny double clicked his mouse and restarted the press conference video. "So yeah, maybe if the mayor had been on Prozac, it would have been different. Or maybe it wasn't the mayor. Maybe if everyone *else* in the room had been on Prozac . . ."

Danny trailed off. On his screen, the mayor once again popped out of existence.

"At least it doesn't follow you out," he said, his voice hushed, suddenly sedate. "Once you're outside the perimeter, the neurotransmitter levels even back out. The weirdness stops. Things return to normal."

"It just doesn't make any sense," I said, shaking my head in disbelief.

"Yeah," Danny agreed. "Welcome to Spokane."

"We've got to go," Taylor said. She gestured toward the door with a little sideways motion of her head. "The captain should be back any time now."

Danny got up from his seat and gave Taylor a kiss on the cheek. "Day after tomorrow?" he asked.

Taylor smiled. At his touch, all the gloom and concern dropped away from her face. "It's a date."

"They're trying the hospital again tomorrow morning. They've got grappling hooks this time. Just like Batman." Danny turned and gave me another appraising look. He clasped me by the shoulder and shook my hand, once again flashing that perfect smile. "You might want to check it out, Dean. Probably some good photos in it for you."

I nodded.

Taylor led me back through the building—down the stairwell and across the lobby. She exchanged good-byes with the guards at the door and headed east on Sprague, back into the web of downtown buildings. We both stayed silent for a couple of minutes, walking at a comfortable pace.

Finally, Taylor broke the silence. "Danny's commanding officer—the captain—would shit a brick if he knew about our little arrangement. He's got an issue with civilians in the city. Wants to crack down and force us all out. He certainly wouldn't like to see us walking the halls of military headquarters. That said, he's not above breaking rules if it suits him. He's got some type of deal with Mama Cass—lets her food shipments get through in exchange for a free lunch every day." She raised her wristwatch. "Noon to one. Predictable as clockwork."

"Are you and Danny an item?" The question just bubbled out, a flash of fire from deep in my gut. A surprised look appeared on Taylor's face, and I felt an overwhelming need to fill the ensuing silence. "It's none of my business, I'm sure. It's just . . . you seemed really happy together. I was just wondering."

Suddenly, a loud gale of laughter wracked Taylor's body, the force bending her nearly double. "For a photographer, you're not very observant," she said, wiping a tear from her eye. "I'm not his type. *Really*. The way he was looking at you . . . I think you're more to his taste."

"What?" Then, after a moment: "Oh."

"Yeah. *Oh*." Taylor once again started down Sprague. After a couple of steps, she cast a glance back over her shoulder. The laughter was still there, lingering in the corners of her smile. "He's a good guy, a good friend. If you're looking for a date, you could really do a lot worse."

I blushed, feeling stupid, then hurried to catch up.

When we got back to the house, Amanda and Mac were in the kitchen making grilled cheese sandwiches. Amanda was tending to the Coleman stove while Mac leaned in over her shoulder. His arms were wrapped around her waist, and she was laughing, squirming in his grasp as he nuzzled at her neck, rasping his whiskers against her pale flesh. As soon as she saw me enter, a look crossed over her face: a momentary darkness, like a cloud across the sun.

Those animals. Those dogs. Those things. After last night, it was something we shared. A bond.

"Hungry?" she asked, momentarily breaking free from Mac's grip. She gave his hands a playful little slap.

"God, yes," I groaned. The smell of bread frying in butter and the sharp tang of cheese had already started my mouth watering. I was running on empty. I'd slept through breakfast, and Taylor's soldier friends had stolen my PowerBar.

"And Taylor?" Amanda asked. "How about you?"

Taylor shook her head. "I had a big breakfast," she said, brushing past me and sitting down next to Charlie.

As far as I could tell, Charlie hadn't moved a muscle in our absence. He was still sitting at the kitchen table, still perched in front of his computer. The only thing that had changed was the addition of a half-finished sandwich resting at his elbow. Taylor handed him the USB drive, and he grunted a distracted thanks.

"I was thinking I could show Dean the park," Amanda said. "Maybe later today." She slid a sandwich from the skillet to an empty plate, then walked it over to the table. I took a seat next to Taylor.

As she handed me the plate, Amanda gave me a slight nod, and for a brief moment, her face became pinched, her eyes suddenly imploring. It was a fleeting expression, and when she straightened back up, the look was gone, hidden beneath a smile. "You'd like the park," she continued. "People see things there . . . animals, sometimes. You might get some good photographs."

I nodded, getting her message loud and clear. When I glanced back over to the stove, I found Mac watching me with a confused look on his face. He'd seen something between the two of us, no doubt the wrong thing.

I started to say something—I don't remember what: a question for Taylor, maybe, about Danny and the military—but a loud *bang* shocked me out of my thoughts. I turned and found Charlie standing bolt upright in front of his computer, his chair overturned on the floor. He stood like that for a long moment, a stricken look on his face. Then he slammed his laptop shut and darted out of the room.

He fled the house, leaving the front door standing open behind him.

I glanced over at Taylor, but she just shook her head, her eyes wide.

After a moment of paralyzed silence, Mac started to move. He took several steps toward the front door, going after Charlie, then pulled to an abrupt stop. He took a step forward, then a step back. It was like some halting, tentative dance, a ballet of confusion and adrenaline. Amanda, meanwhile, stayed on her side of the room, fiddling with the dials on the Coleman stove.

"What . . . ?" Mac finally implored, turning toward Taylor. "What just happened?"

Taylor stood up and moved over to Charlie's computer. She opened the lid and pressed the space bar a couple of times, waking it from slumber. After a few seconds, the hard drive spun into motion and the screen flickered back on.

I recognized Charlie's email program. There was an incoming message open in the main window. Charlie's address—**cd01@gmail**

.com—was listed in the "to" field, and the subject line had been left blank. The sender was listed as **admin@spokane.wal.net.**

There was no text in the body of the message, just a single picture. File name: **sherman_today.jpg.**

The picture showed a woman standing on the corner of an abandoned city block. She was a black woman, at least forty years old, maybe forty-five. She had straight shoulder-length hair. Her body was turned away from the camera, but she was glancing back over her shoulder. It was a candid shot, and she looked distracted, worried. The street was shrouded in mist, disappearing into white oblivion a half block up. It looked like early morning, just before sunrise.

There was a street sign on the corner. The pole was bent at a severe angle—at least thirty degrees off vertical—but it was still readable, its green reflective surface practically glowing in the early-morning haze. It was the brightest color in the whole frame: SHERMAN ST.

Taylor reached out and touched the computer screen, gently tracing the length of the woman's body. She glanced up. Her eyes were wide, darting from my face over to Amanda and Mac.

"It's Charlie's mother," she said. "She's here. Downtown."

05.1

Photograph. October 18, 01:50 P.M. Between the walls:

> It is a claustrophobic space. Very little light.
>
> The photograph is framed in the vertical—walls to
> the left and right, the camera pointed straight
> down. The space between the walls is no more than a
> foot wide. There is a source of light down below—a
> dim line of electric blue, extending from the top of
> the frame all the way to the bottom. A ruler-
> straight line of color, down where the walls end.
>
> A trickle of daylight illuminates the foreground; we
> can see bare wood studs and line after line of
> joists proceeding into the darkness. There are holes
> punched through these two imposing stretches of
> wall—splintered dents, like violent, gaping wounds.
> But they are distant, and they let in only tiny fin-
> gers of gray.
>
> The wood in the foreground is damp, glistening as if
> coated with a sheen of ice.

There is a bulge in the left-hand wall, about five
feet away—a dark half-moon with a blurry fuzz
around its edge. It is off center, perched in the
lower part of the frame. Slightly out of focus.
After a moment of study, you can just make out pale
flesh in the dim light, then a wide-open, terrified
eye.

Down there, lodged in the wall, is half a face. Half
a human face—sexless—ringed in a nimbus of short,
dark hair. It is angled inward, toward the wall, and
its open mouth is bisected just to the left of the
canine tooth, sheared away where flesh meets wood.

The wide-open eye is not blurred. Not clouded. Not
insensate.

The eye is clear. And damp. And terrified.

05.2

We found the street sign on the corner of Second Avenue and Sherman Street. It was twisted like a bendy straw, just as we'd seen in Charlie's photo.

The corner was deserted. No Charlie. No mother.

"It wasn't like that before," Taylor said, nodding toward the sign. "I walk this street three times a week, and I don't remember seeing it bent like that. It must have happened in the last couple of days."

Amanda and Mac both nodded. Mac gave a single strong nod, while Amanda's head just kept bouncing up and down, like a weight on a spring.

I had my backpack slung over my shoulder—I'd grabbed it as we stormed out of the house—and on a whim, I took out my camera and tried to re-create the photo of Charlie's mother. I found the correct angle about twenty feet up Second Avenue, then turned back toward the sign and raised the viewfinder to my eye. This is where the photographer had stood. I tried to remember the particulars of the shot. The light was completely different now, with sunshine and shadows instead of early-morning mist.

My viewfinder showed Amanda, Mac, and Taylor clustered around the sign, surveying the surrounding buildings. I don't know if it was a conscious decision on their part, but they'd left a wide gap where Charlie's mother had been.

Lined up, left to right: Amanda and Mac, the sign, a large space, and then Taylor.

I could combine the photos, I thought, snapping the shot. At first it was just an idle bit of fancy, but the image that rose to mind was strangely affecting. I glanced down at the LCD screen and studied the photograph I'd just taken. I could see it now. The combined picture would have Amanda, Mac, Charlie's mother, and Taylor, all lined up in a row. Amanda, Mac, and Taylor would look confused and just a little bit bored—on the camera's screen, Taylor had her arms crossed in front of her chest and an impatient look on her face—but Charlie's mother . . . she would be wreathed in a halo of mist, glancing back over her shoulder with that scared look on her face.

It would be an interesting shot. A hole punched through the world. A hole punched through time.

"Charlie!" Taylor called. I looked up from the camera and found her turning a full circle in the middle of the street, her hands cupped around her mouth. "Charlie!"

I joined the others at the sign, and we all started craning our heads, studying the surrounding buildings. After about a minute, I noticed Charlie half a block away, standing motionless in a doorway on Second Avenue. He wasn't moving to join us. He wasn't even looking our way. His head was down, tilted against the door frame, and the way he looked—the slump to his shoulders—made me think that the frame was the only thing keeping him on his feet.

I started toward him, and the others followed as soon as they saw where I was going. When I got within a dozen feet, I slowed down and stopped, not sure how to proceed. Charlie's face was ashen-gray, and his cheeks glistened with tears. That emotion stopped me cold. I didn't know what I could do for him. *He's a kid,* I thought, *just a kid of seventeen.* I knew he was curious, painfully smart, and full of answers, but really, I didn't know him at all.

As I watched, his shoulders started to shake, trembling like branches caught in a swirling wind.

Taylor took over. She sprinted past me to Charlie's side and wrapped her arms around him, scaring up a hitching, breathless sob.

"I can't find her," Charlie groaned, expelling breathless words against Taylor's shoulder. "She was here, in the picture. She was here, but now she's gone . . . and I can't find her!"

"We'll help," Taylor said, her voice soothing and calm. "If you want, we'll help you look."

Taylor lifted her hand from Charlie's back and gestured Amanda, Mac, and me toward the surrounding buildings, using a little twirl of her finger. Trying to get rid of us, I realized. And I felt relief—then guilt at that relief—as I retreated back down the street, away from Charlie and all that raw emotion. Both Amanda and Mac kept their faces down as they moved away, disappearing into the nearest doorway on the south side of the street.

I glanced from the bent sign toward the surrounding buildings. There was nothing there, no signs of life. There were street-level stores with shuttered windows; a couple of stairways leading down to substreet levels—cafés, a shoe store, some second-rate restaurants; and, looming overhead, a cluster of old run-down office buildings.

In the picture, Charlie's mother had been facing down the length of Second Avenue, looking back over her shoulder. Her body had been turned toward the line of buildings on the north side of the street. Not much of a lead, but it was something. A place to start, at least. I headed toward that side of the road and opened the first door I came to.

On the other side of the door, I found a small alcove lined with metal mailboxes. An apartment building, then. Judging from the number of blank name tags on the mail slots, I guessed that most of these apartments had been vacant before the evacuation. There was a narrow stairway at the end of the alcove, leading up to the housing overhead.

"Hello?" I called. My voice was tentative, weak. "Anyone home?"

I waited for a response, but none came.

I started up the stairs, and a gamy, spoiled-meat smell greeted me on the second-floor landing. Not decomposing flesh or dead animal, more like deli-style roast beef left out in the sun. A thick, damp smell. Almost musty.

There were six apartments on this level, and four of the doors stood wide open. Each of these tiny two-room dwellings was completely bare—nothing but frayed carpeting stained a uniform dingy brown. The bathroom doors stood open, revealing tiny sinks and coffin-size showers.

The door to the fifth apartment was closed but unlocked. I eased it open, and the creaking hinge started my heart thudding a quick bass rhythm inside my chest. The room was dark, but I could see immediately that there was no one hiding inside. The only piece of furniture was a stripped mattress laid out in the far corner. The window here had been covered up with cardboard and uneven strips of duct tape, and someone's works lay spread out near the head of the mattress: a black-charred spoon, a lighter, a length of bungee cord, shredded cigarettes. There were empty Baggies and vials sitting on the windowsill.

The room smelled of stale sweat and fever dreams. But no trace of spoiled meat.

The final door was flanked on both sides by stacks of newspaper. One of the stacks had tipped over, clogging the width of the corridor with a jumble of yellowing newsprint, a mad collage of text and black-and-white photographs. Smiling politicians. Crowded cityscapes. I bent down and read the date off the nearest sheet: June 15, 2002.

The smell was stronger here. It was coming from inside the apartment.

I reached for the doorknob, hesitated, and decided to knock. There was a sound of movement on the other side of the door—the groaning of mattress springs, followed by the sound of a foot hitting the floor—then abrupt silence.

I knocked again and cleared my throat. "Hello? I don't mean you any harm. Really. I'm just looking for somebody—my friend's mother. Have you seen anyone? Do you think you could help?"

There was no response. I tried to turn the doorknob, but the door was locked.

I waited for nearly a minute, keeping my head cocked next to the door, but there was no sound of movement inside the room. There was nothing. *The sound of held breath, maybe,* I thought. *Held breath and paralysis.* I retreated back to the stairwell and continued up to the third floor.

There was nothing on the third floor, and again, nothing on the fourth. Just empty, abandoned rooms, the refuse of long-gone squatters.

A sound greeted me on the fifth-floor landing, a scramble of movement coming from the far end of the corridor. It was a faint, small sound, like a horsehair brush sliding back and forth over wood. But different—something foreign, alien—nothing I could place. Charlie's mother? Doing what? I quickly made my way past the other apartments on the floor, noting the empty, unremarkable rooms as they swam past the corners of my eyes. As I drew near, the sound didn't seem to get any louder. It stayed a quiet, unearthly whisper—the *shhhhhh* of a record player hitting blank grooves, maybe—and I was afraid it would peter out entirely, disappearing before I could reach that last apartment.

I rounded the open doorway and found an empty room.

My lungs were working hard now, and I stopped with my hand on the doorjamb, trying to hear over my panting breath. The sound was still there, coming from somewhere inside the room.

I stepped forward and noticed a hole in the left-hand wall. It was a ragged oval, about three feet wide and two feet tall, punched through the drywall and plaster. No, not punched, I realized. The edges of the hole jutted outward, into the room, as if scrabbling, frantic hands had pulled at the opening, trying to make it wider. Or, I thought, as if something had pushed its way through from the other side.

The hole didn't go all the way through to the neighboring room; there was no hint of light on the other side, just darkness. Darkness and sound. It was a little bit louder now. Definitely coming from the hole.

I approached the hole and paused for a handful of seconds, trying to gather the courage to peer inside. Finally, I took a deep breath and moved forward, easing my head through the opening.

The gap between the walls was about a foot wide, and I could see plumbing snaking down toward the lower floors. A tiny breeze, cool and damp, trickled up from the basement. I glanced down and saw blue light five or six floors down. At first, I wasn't sure if it was actually there; my eyes were treacherous, swimming with afterimages as they adjusted to the dark. But the light solidified, becoming a line in the distance.

Something underground, I realized. Beneath the building.

I noticed movement out of the corner of my eye and glanced to my left. There was a mass sprouting from the neighboring wall, about five feet down. At first, it wouldn't register, this thing that I was seeing. I just couldn't comprehend it. A flesh-colored mound fringed with dark fluff. Then I noticed movement on its surface, a quivering blotch of white.

An eye. A face.

I sucked breath in through my teeth—it got trapped there, in my throat and lungs. I couldn't move, not for at least half a minute.

What is it? It wasn't a body, wasn't a person. It wasn't even a head. It was *half* a head, trapped between the walls. A face, bisected. And the eye was trembling, moving in tiny, uncoordinated bursts.

A mirror! I grasped at the possibility. It explained what I was seeing: my own face—half in the hole, half out—reflected in something down below.

I reached in and ran my hand across my cheek, moving it in front of my teeth, but there was no corresponding movement on the face. The teeth and lips, sheared in two, remained clear, unobstructed.

I felt dizzy, the blood in my head rushing and pounding behind my temples. *No,* I chided myself. *None of that fainting shit!*

I scrabbled for my camera, slinging my backpack off my shoulder and digging through it one-handed. I did this blind, keeping my head in the hole. I just couldn't look away—*I couldn't*—afraid that if I took my eye off that face, it would disappear. Just some transitory phantom, caught, for a moment, in the fragile juncture between eye and world. I flicked the lens cap off my wide-angle zoom and brought the camera up to my face. The light was horrible here; almost nothing made its way in through the hole. I cranked open the aperture and tried to hold the camera steady. I took a couple of wide-angle shots in the dark, hoping to capture that line of light in the distance, then flicked on the flash. My hands were shaking as I focused on the face. It was male, I saw. Its hair was black . . . *his* hair was black.

I twisted the lens from wide-angle to telephoto, filling the viewfinder. The camera focused, and I found myself staring at a close-up of that quivering eye.

Then the eye stopped quivering—its brow steeled up.

Suddenly, there was *sense* there, in that eye. And surprise.

I heard a *click* behind my head and realized that the sound that had drawn me here—those sandpaper whispers and horsehair brushes, that crackling record player—had grown louder in the last couple of minutes, while I'd been focused on the face down below. It was behind my head now, between the walls. And there was movement in that sound. It wasn't getting *louder,* it was getting *nearer.* I braced my hand on the hole's ragged edge and turned to look.

There were dark shapes in the gap up above. A jumble of moving limbs—large and tentacled things, just inches away. Something brushed against my cheek—just the barest, lightest touch—and I immediately recoiled, my skin prickling in a wave of gooseflesh.

My hand caught on something at the hole's edge, and there was a brief burst of fire across my palm. Then I was free, stumbling back. I slipped my camera's carry strap around my neck and took a half dozen steps back. My legs were weak, and for a moment I wasn't sure I'd be able to keep them beneath my body. The sweat on my cheeks was freezing cold.

And there was movement at the edge of the hole. At first, it was just a tiny blur of black—at one spot along the top of the hole, then, a moment later, at a dozen more, all around its perimeter. Then a black, finger-thick tentacle reached out, waving, snakelike, up toward the wall, touching and repositioning itself, as if trying to find purchase. It was a dark, jointed stub bristling with whisker-thick hair.

I was holding my breath. I thought about the camera hanging against my chest, but I couldn't break my paralysis, I couldn't lift my hands and start taking pictures. Not now. I was transfixed by that hole—*consumed*—just standing there on weak, shaking legs, watching as it gave birth to . . . *whatever*.

To something dark. And bristling. And *wrong*.

Then more of those dark limbs reached out, and a form heaved itself through the hole. Considering its initial, tentative movements, it moved fast, skittering on a bouquet of long limbs. *A spider*, I thought, suddenly flush with relief. *Just a spider!* But it wasn't a normal spider. At least, it wasn't like any spider I'd ever seen. It was huge, about the size of a small cat. And its limbs were surprisingly long, out of proportion with its body. It moved in a quick, rhythmic lurch, hauling itself down the wall in drunken uneven spurts. But fast.

And by the time it reached the floor, a half dozen of its ilk had made their way through the opening.

Now that I could see what they were—or at least I could comprehend their form—I broke my paralysis and grabbed for my camera. I started taking shots, the motor in the lens whirring as I tried to keep focus on the skittering things. I got wide shots of the spiders swarming through the hole—there were dozens now, crowding the wall. I zoomed in on one, filling the frame with a single black spider against the dirty gray carpet. I even got a series of shots of one spider crawling over another; the latter was an undersized specimen, spinning in a circle. There was something strange about the smaller spider, but, caught in its tornado of motion, I couldn't see what. I lowered the camera from my eye and activated the display, scrolling back to the start of that series.

Its leg, I saw. It was damaged or stunted. Congenitally deformed. I scrolled forward, looking for a better view. And I found it. Right there, protruding from the spider's body: a limb, much smaller than its other legs. But it wasn't a leg.

It was a finger. A human finger, pale and white.

Something touched my pant cuff, and I glanced down to find a spider climbing up my leg. My skin erupted in prickles of heat—an intense, instinctual revulsion—and I shook myself violently. The spider hung on, somehow managing to continue its ascent. I swept my camera down, striking the spider from my stomach. In that brief moment of contact, I felt bristles scrabbling against my hand, and I almost fell over backward, trying to get away.

I caught my balance and looked around.

I was surrounded. While I'd been lost in the camera, the spiders had continued to swarm from the hole. And now they were everywhere: on the walls, on the floor, swarming around my feet. They were coming right at me, moving with a purpose, a goal. I took a step back and heard one crack beneath my boot. I lifted my foot and saw its legs waving wildly; a greenish ooze leaked from its fractured body. There were more—dozens, hundreds—circling around my feet, hemming me in, moving closer.

"Dean!" Taylor cried, storming into the room. Her jacket was off, and she was thrashing it against the floor, knocking spiders back against the walls. "Your leg!"

Two spiders had detached themselves from the crowd, and they were frantically climbing my right pant leg. One had just passed my knee, heading up toward my crotch, while the other scampered up over my hip. I quickly swatted aside the one on my hip, then swung my camera down, smashing the other against my thigh. I could feel it quivering through the fabric of my jeans, and I quickly swept it back down to the floor, leaving behind a wide streak of spider guts—a sticky, jellylike substance that spread across my jeans, the heel of my palm, and the underside of my camera.

Taylor continued to sweep the floor with her jacket, holding it like a matador taunting a swarm of small, ground-hugging bulls. The spiders kept scurrying, but their movement seemed unfocused now, still fast but aimless.

I noticed a spider crawl back into the hole, clambering up over the wave of traffic still fighting to get out. Then, suddenly, the whole swarm reversed. The spiders on the floor paused briefly, then retreated back to the hole, as if summoned by an inaudible command.

After the rest of the horde was gone, a single spider remained. It was the spider with the finger. The weight of that out-of-place limb kept the spider off balance, and it had to struggle to keep to a straight line, swaying drunkenly as it left the floor and climbed up the wall. The finger flexed along with the spider's legs, a feeble arthritic parody of those graceful movements. It had a long yellow nail, fractured and jagged at the tip. *It could use a manicure,* a voice cackled behind my eyes. I shook my head and pushed that voice back down into the murky corners of my skull. It was a bad voice, it was the voice of hysteria. If I listened— if I gave free rein to all the thoughts and words and images tumbling unexamined inside my head—I'd probably break down laughing. And I wouldn't be able to stop.

Finally, the spider with the human finger pulled itself into the hole and disappeared.

"Did you see that?" I asked Taylor. "Did you see the . . . *spi-*

der?" I used the word *spider* instead of *finger*. Right then, *finger* was something I just couldn't say, not without giving in to that wave of hysterical laughter.

Taylor was panting with exertion, her chest rising and falling. Her response was hushed, breathless. "Yeah. I saw the . . . spider." I heard the word *finger* there, too, left unspoken.

"And there's something in the wall. Something I can't . . ." I shook my head, unable to continue, unable to describe the face.

"I'll take your word for it," she said, shivering visibly. "I *hate* spiders. I'm not getting anywhere near that fucking hole."

I bent down and examined one of the crushed arachnids. Its legs were still moving, tracing tiny shapes in the air. It was big and its limbs seemed ridiculously long, but there was nothing terribly odd about its structure. It was just a spider.

"And what the fuck did you think you were doing?" Taylor asked. She started to put her jacket back on, then stopped, remembering what she'd been using it for. She shook it out violently, then folded it over her forearm. "You see shit like that, you leave! You don't stick around taking pictures!"

I shrugged my backpack off my shoulder and set it on the ground next to the crushed spider. I carefully wiped my camera against my leg, adding to the smear of greenish-black guts already there, then set the camera back into its padded compartment. A thin, sticky film remained on the butt of the camera, but a more thorough cleaning would have to wait until we got back to the house.

As soon as the camera had been put away, I collapsed back to the floor, slumping into a boneless sitting position. I could feel the blood rushing out of my head, a cold sweat popping out on my cheeks and forehead. I was exhausted.

That face. Was it alive? Had it seen me? At the end, right before the spiders had come, that eye had swiveled up toward me, and there had been something there, some type of intelligence, maybe. But without a corresponding facial expression, it was hard to interpret. Was it conscious of its situation, pleading for help?

Impossible.

"Dean?" Taylor crouched down at my side. "Whatever it was, it's over now. It's just the city. It's what the city does." She draped her jacket over my shoulders, trying to comfort me. I almost laughed. Almost.

I took a deep breath and forced myself to sit up straight. "What are you doing here?" I asked. "Did you follow me?"

"I didn't even know you were up here. Charlie wanted me to help look for his mom, and this is the first building I came to. I heard you cry out from the ground floor."

I didn't remember crying out, but I wasn't surprised. Maybe when that first spider had touched my cheek—my head in that hole, bristles brushing against my face as I stared up into the moving darkness. After a few more deep breaths, I shrugged out of Taylor's jacket and got back to my feet.

"Are you okay?" she asked.

"Yeah," I grunted, shaking my arms, trying to work blood back through my body. "It's just the city," I said, repeating her words. "Just the city."

I noticed the throbbing in my palm as we walked back to the house.

We moved slowly. Amanda and Taylor were trying to comfort Charlie as we walked, flanking him on both sides, bracing him with gentle hands and quiet, indistinct words. His shoulders were slumped, practically radiating a sense of defeat. Mac and I stayed off to one side, trying to give them enough space and silence.

We'd spent nearly two hours going room to room through those abandoned buildings, but there had been no sign of his mother. No hint that she'd ever been near the corner of Second Avenue and Sherman Street.

Just that photo.

I flexed my left hand and felt a burst of fire beneath my fingers. I looked and found a line of raw flesh bisecting my palm. The outer layers of skin were gone—a bloodred line stretching from beneath my pinkie all the way to the web of flesh bridging fingers and thumb.

I stared at it for several seconds before finally placing the wound. Back in the apartment. I'd had my head in the hole, and when I'd pulled back, I'd felt my hand ripping free from the wall. But how? This was no cut, no abrasion.

I flexed again, feeling the throb.

The skin is gone, I realized. *Left behind,* inside *the wall.*

Had it begun to take me? The wall? The city? If I'd stayed in that position, focused on my camera, would I have pulled back to find my hand sunk all the way through, my fingers poking out from drywall, joining the face—that horrible, conscious face— inside that claustrophobic prison?

Again I flexed, and again I felt that throb.

Is that what this is? I wondered, my stomach churning, upset with dread and revelation. *Some type of dissolution of form? Boundaries fading and merging, absorbing and consuming?*

But how? And why?

I continued to flex my hand, flexing and releasing all the way home.

Photograph. October 19, 08:35 A.M. The warren:

A cave dug into the side of a grassy hill. A slice
of darkness, partially hidden beneath a pricker
bush.

At the top of the frame, autumn-red trees reach up
from the far side of the hill, touching a clear blue
sky. The top of a clock tower is visible above the
highest branches; the clock is out of focus, the
time illegible. There are two human-shaped shadows
oast against the side of the hill, one on each side
of the dark opening. The photographer's shadow is on
the left—arms steepled up into a pyramid—and a
thin, armless apparition lurks to the right.

The grass at the mouth of the opening is trampled
into mud. Countless paw prints have warped the turf
into textured stucco.

There is nothing visible inside the cave. It is an
entrance into pure, depthless black.

06.2

I dreamed about the face and the spiders. Not the reality of the situation—I didn't find myself back inside that apartment, seeing these things for the first time—instead, I dreamed about the photographs I'd taken. My precisely cropped, color-corrected images. The same ones I'd spent hours and hours tweaking and adjusting the night before.

The pictures weren't great—the light was too dim, the focus too soft—but I managed to salvage a trio of interesting shots: one taken between the walls, capturing the line of electric blue and that eerie face (the face just barely visible after extensive masking and gamma correction); a wide-angle shot showing the horde of spiders swarming out of the hole, cluttering the surrounding wall; and finally, a close-up of the spider with the human finger. In that last shot, the bizarre subject matter had to make up for a bad angle and weak, muted colors.

After I retired for the night, these static images followed me down into sleep, changing and multiplying in my dreams.

I spent the entire night tweaking dream photos, watching as spiders took life, stepped out of my pictures, and crawled across the computer screen while I tried desperately to capture and freeze them in place with my trackpad. I was trying to create the perfect photograph, I knew, the one that would make me famous, the one that would save me from a life of accounting. But the spiders refused to hold still. And as the night wore on, I grew increasingly frustrated.

When Amanda touched my shoulder, I jolted upright, coming fully awake.

"Shhhhh!" Her pale skin and blond hair glowed in a trickle of predawn violet. "It's early," she said. "Everyone's asleep."

I nodded and stifled a cough, then scooted up into a sitting position.

I was still camped out on the living-room sofa. The photo of Charlie's mother had brought the entire house to a screeching halt, filling the rooms with a funereal stillness and putting my move on hold.

It had been a difficult evening. As soon as we got back home from Sherman and Second Avenue, Charlie had retreated to his room upstairs. The rest of us—including Devon, Floyd, and Sabine—had gathered in the living room, unsure how to respond to Charlie's pain. Should we offer him comfort? Give him time to think and heal? Ultimately, we decided to just let him be.

There was no pot that night and no laughter, and dinner proved a rather subdued affair. After we finished eating, Taylor disappeared upstairs with a plate of food. She stayed up there for the rest of the night.

I, for my part, made my own retreat, cracking open my notebook computer and immersing myself in Photoshop.

"What time is it?" I asked Amanda. My sleep had been fitful, and I was still confused, disoriented. It took me a moment to place my location. *Not California . . . Spokane. The city.*

"Seven. Seven-fifteen." Amanda sat down on the sofa and turned toward the window. In profile, I could see the skin hunched up on her forehead and the worried downward curve of her lips. "Just before sunrise."

I waited for her to continue. The look on her face was the look of someone staring out over the edge of a building, gathering up the courage to jump.

She took a deep breath. "They were out there again last night," she said. "The dogs. The wolves. They're looking for something. They're doing . . . *something*. I know it. I just *know*."

"What are they doing?"

She shrugged. "I don't have the specifics, but it's got to do with the city. It's got to do with what's happening here."

I nodded. There was a certainty to her voice—a desperate, *beleaguered* certainty. Confronted with that, there was absolutely nothing I could say.

"I have to find them," she said. "You . . . you have to help me find them." She fixed me with sad, pleading eyes; where before I had found innocent, bubbly curiosity, there was now nothing but desperation. She was exhausted. Dispirited. Emotionally drained.

"Okay," I said. "Just tell me what to do."

We left the house just as the sun touched the horizon. The day was cold, and our breath hung frozen in the air. I regretted not grabbing my gloves and an extra sweatshirt.

"Why me?" I asked as we headed west on the residential street. "Why didn't you want to take Mac?"

"He doesn't see them," she said, watching her feet. "I've dragged him to the window, pointed them out—clear as day— but he just doesn't see." She glanced up, fixing me with bright blue eyes. "Christ, I thought I was crazy! I thought I was suffering a psychotic breakdown, seeing things that just weren't there. But that's not true, is it? You saw them, too. They're real . . . Right?"

"I saw something. A pack of canines. Only different. Their paws . . ."

At my words, Amanda's face brightened noticeably, relief breaking through that mask of exhaustion. "Right! Exactly."

"How many times have you seen them?"

"I don't know. A couple dozen?" She shrugged. "The first time was at the park, right before the evacuation. I was looking for my own dog, Sasha. She escaped from the backyard—I was living in a house close to the university back then. The city was crazy—everyone confused and terrified, no idea what was going on. But the park was empty. We used to walk there a couple of times a week, Sasha and me, and I figured that that's where she'd end up."

We rounded a corner and headed south. As Amanda talked, the Riverfront Park clock tower rose into view, peeking up over the line of buildings at the river's edge. "There were three of them, and they started following me . . . just these huge canines. I was on one of the paths, moving through the center of the park, and they were about a hundred feet away. At first, I didn't notice anything wrong with them. They were just dogs, German shepherds, maybe—too fluffy to be Great Danes, although that's about the right size. They kept pace with me, following along in a stand of trees." She shrugged, dismissing her initial impressions as no big deal. "I was a bit scared, but they didn't act threatening. No barking and growling. No posturing. They seemed content to just follow . . . but they moved so *smoothly,* almost like they were floating over the ground. Not like dogs at all.

"I stopped, and they stopped. They didn't circle around and sniff, doing all of the little things that dogs do. Instead, they just froze in their tracks—three dogs, lined up single file. Staring at me. Just . . . staring—like I was the most important thing in the universe."

Amanda stopped and turned toward me, a confused look on her face. "They were so still. And even though they were pretty far away, I swear I could see the look in their eyes. So focused!" She shifted her feet, swaying awkwardly, then lowered her eyes. "I stood still for a while, watching and waiting, and finally, after about a minute, the dog at the front of the pack raised his paw and leaned up against a tree." She shook her head. "And it wasn't a canine movement at all. It was like something a human would do—resting his palm against a wall, taking the weight off of his feet.

"And that's when I noticed the odd legs." She raised her hand

and pushed her palm all the way forward, trying to illustrate. "Not normal canine joints; these dogs had an extra bend, like a knuckle. And this dog was using it like a human hand! It was eerie. Eerie and far too human. I got out of there as fast as I could.

"It's not that I was scared," she added, shaking her head. "Not really. Surprised and confused, maybe, but not scared. I was just . . . just . . . *profoundly unsettled*." She glanced back up into my eyes, and I could tell she was happy with that word— *unsettled*—happy she'd been able to provide such an accurate description of her state of mind.

"And you've seen them a couple of dozen times since?" I asked.

She nodded, then turned and resumed walking. I hurried to keep up. "I saw them a lot at my old place, a house I shared with a couple of other students, out east. And as soon as I moved in with Taylor, I started seeing them there, too, in the backyard or on the street out front. A couple of times a week, at least. I asked Taylor and some of the others if they'd seen anything doglike and strange—trying to be coy about it, trying to hide my insanity, if indeed that's what it was—but they hadn't. I was the only one." She glanced over at me and smiled, moving close to grasp my hand—the uninjured one. "And now you! Thank God! Now I've got you."

Her grip on my hand was unnerving. I could feel the intensity of her relief—all that bottled up desperation channeled into a strong clench. She was hanging on to me for dear life.

"Why didn't you leave?" I asked. "Why didn't you evacuate with everyone else?"

"Sasha," she said. "At least . . ." She trailed off, a confused look appearing on her face. "I know she's out there somewhere— I've been looking. But that can't be it, can it? *Waiting around for a missing dog?* I was studying psychology before all of this started, so I know that there's probably something more—some deep-seated reason buried in my unconscious mind. Maybe it's just that I don't have anywhere else I want to go?" She looked at me questioningly, like I might actually be able to give her an answer.

Then she released my hand and shook her head. "Everyone else in my life—my friends, my housemates—they all just went home, back to their parents, their hometowns. But I didn't want that. I *really* didn't want that. I think, given the choice, I'd prefer Sasha."

"Even if this place is driving you mad?"

"But it's not," she said, flashing me a broad smile. "I know that now. They're there, right? You've seen them, too."

I nodded, even though I wasn't quite sure. Were we seeing the same thing? I'd seen a swarm of animals in the middle of the night. What she'd seen . . . it seemed like something different, something *more*. I could tell.

In those animals, she'd found meaning. She'd found some type of promise, something that drove her, that dragged her out of bed in the middle of the night and carried her here. With me.

We rounded a corner, and Amanda raised her hand, pointing to a slash of green on the other side of the river. I recognized the empty pathways and rolling, leaf-scattered hills from my first day in the city, when Weasel had pointed them out to me.

Riverfront Park.

Riverfront Park was a small park, just a couple of blocks of greenery trapped in the middle of downtown. It would have been a crowded place back before the quarantine, or so I imagined. There would have been families here—when the weather was nice—and come noon, there would have been office workers with bagged lunches and buskers performing for change. But now there was nothing. Just Amanda and me and the sound of the wind playing through the trees.

An offshoot of the Spokane River stretched around the south end of the park, a wide, slow-moving trough that transformed the land into a thumb-shaped peninsula. The clock tower was on the tip of the thumb, looming up over the east end of the park.

It was peaceful here. Now that the city was dead, there was nothing to drown out the muted roar of the river and the desolate whisper of the wind.

As soon as we crossed the river and entered the park, Amanda pulled to a stop and looked around in amazement. "It used to be so tame," she said, a quiet awe in her voice, "so manicured." I could see what she meant. The once neatly trimmed grass now stood knee-high and half dead, with drifts of winter-brown leaves cluttering up every open space.

I grabbed my camera, reslung my backpack, and started up the nearest hill. Amanda followed, craning her neck and looking around for any sign of her mysterious dogs.

At the top of the hill, I took a series of panoramic shots, trying to capture the park in the foreground and the city on the horizon. The early-morning light made the remaining grass glow a bright, vibrant green, providing a great contrast to the gray streets and buildings. Unfortunately, the hill was too small and the surrounding buildings too high, so instead of catching city blocks stretching out into the distance, all I got were walls hemming us in. Like we were standing on the floor of an immense gray-walled box.

"Over there!" Amanda hissed. "In the trees!" I lowered the camera and found her pointing toward a patch of woods to the south. Her eyes were wide, and her voice quavered with excitement.

"Where?" I asked, but she was already running, kicking up dead leaves as she slid down the hill. "Amanda, wait! It might not be safe." I looped the camera strap around my neck and followed her down.

She entered the trees twenty yards ahead of me, immediately disappearing from sight. I plowed in behind her, then stopped, listening for movement.

"Amanda!"

There was sound everywhere: the subdued hiss of something sliding through the bushes to my left; then to my right, the brittle *snap* of a dead branch directly ahead. I couldn't see much of anything. Low bushes had grown out of control between the trees, and I watched as a sea of leaves rippled around me. *The wind,* I told myself. *Just the wind.*

And then the growling began. All around. Low and guttural.

"Amanda?" I hissed. I'm not sure why I felt the need to whisper. Anything she could hear, they could most definitely hear.

There was no response.

I started moving forward through the bushes, holding a hand out in front of me to push aside the encroaching branches. I hadn't taken more than three steps when I felt a weight against my leg—a push, nudging me forward. I stumbled over my own feet, my heart breaking rhythm inside my chest. I barely managed to catch myself. There was movement all around—the dry rustle of leaves—and the thick, dark smell of animal musk. I glanced back, but something darted in from up ahead, catching my hand in a quick, hard grip. It was an intense pressure, engulfing my palm, and a wet growl vibrated up through my flesh and bone.

I tried to pull my hand back, and a gray muzzle came into view; black lips and pink gums were wrapped around my fist. I could see yellow plaque-stained teeth. I could see blood welling up between those teeth and my hand.

I panicked and surged forward, trying to get away. My shins hit canine flesh with a dull thud, and I collapsed forward onto my knees. Onto the dog. I felt a sudden expulsion of breath puff out around my hand, and I somersaulted forward. My hand finally came free.

A loud growl swelled up from the trees behind me, radiating out of the ground cover. Then a half dozen dogs exploded from the brush, teeth bared and saliva flying. I scrambled up to my feet and started to run, bouncing off trees and stumbling over branches and roots.

They were fast, and I could feel them gaining on me. The back of my neck tingled in anticipation, bracing me for that final, brutal snap, preparing me for the razor-sharp jaws that would sink into my fragile flesh at any moment now.

There was no way I could outrun them. No way in hell.

Then, suddenly, I was free, bursting out of the trees and falling forward into a scrim of leaves and decaying mulch. I spun around on the ground and started pushing myself backward, keeping my eyes on the trees, unable to get up off my ass.

"Dean!" Amanda cried out in surprise just before I collided with her legs and knocked her to the ground.

"Move!" I panted. "Move, move, *move!*" I continued to push myself backward, using my legs to propel myself away from the trees. Then my feet began to slip, and, finally, I stopped.

The trees were still. There was no sign of the dogs.

Amanda remained where she'd landed, watching me with huge perplexed eyes. "Your hand. You're bleeding!" She crawled forward and grabbed my hand, rotating it front to back, inspecting the damage.

For a while, I couldn't take my eyes off of the trees; then a sharp pain blossomed in my palm. I sucked a breath through my teeth and turned toward her probing fingers. "The dogs, the fucking dogs," I said. "They're crazed. How'd you get past them?"

She glanced up from my palm and shook her head. "I didn't see them. I didn't see a thing."

With the tail of her shirt, she wiped the blood away from my palm, revealing a pair of deep holes. It was my left hand, and the holes were spaced on either side of my previous wound—the line of raw flesh that had been ripped away in the apartment building. Amanda turned my hand over, exposing a single puncture wound in the web between my thumb and forefinger. This was the nastiest of the holes. My stomach began to turn, and I looked away.

"Does it hurt?"

"Not yet," I hissed. The fear had begun to subside, replaced by frustration and anger. "I'm sure it will. Give it a couple minutes and I'm sure it'll be hurting like a motherfucker."

Amanda shook her head. "You must have startled them," she said. "You must have done something wrong."

I gave her an incredulous look, and she stared right back, stubborn, unwilling to hear anything bad about her precious dogs.

"You see my hand?" I asked, raising it up so the blood spilled down my wrist and dripped onto my jeans. "You see what they did?"

Amanda didn't reply. She ripped a strip of cloth from the bottom of her shirt and wrapped it around my palm. "Give it some pressure," she said. "We'll clean it up when we get home." Then she grabbed my uninjured hand and pulled me to my feet.

"This is what I was looking at when you bowled me over," she said.

I looked around, finally calm enough to take in my surroundings. We'd passed through the stand of trees and were now standing in front of an open cave mouth, an oval swatch of darkness punched into the face of a fairly steep hill. The opening was only about four feet high, and its edges were ragged, as if it had been chewed into the earth. The grass in front of the entrance was muddy, imprinted with the shape of a hundred large, hand-size paws.

I lifted my camera and took a couple of shots. At first, I tried to use my injured left hand, but a sharp jab of fire made me drop the camera back against my chest. Finally, I managed to prop it up on the palm of my right hand and gingerly stab at the shutter release with my left thumb.

"This is where they come from," Amanda whispered, a hint of awe in her voice. "This is where they live!"

Before I could stop her, Amanda took a step forward, cupped her hands around her mouth, and shouted "Hello!" I listened as that word echoed again and again—*hello, hello, hello*—getting fainter as it passed deeper underground.

Judging by that sound, those reverberations, it wasn't a cave we were facing—a shallow little grotto—but rather a tunnel, leading down into the earth.

Amanda began toward the opening, and I jolted forward, reaching out to stop her. As soon as I touched her arm, a low growl erupted from the dark tunnel— a sustained, multivoiced rumble, like rocks grinding in the heart of the earth. "We're not going in there, Amanda. No fucking way!"

She turned toward me, a blank look on her face. I raised my hand, showing her my bloodstained bandage. After a couple of seconds, she nodded, finally relenting.

"Maybe later," she said, a dreamy quality to her voice. "When you're better. When we're better prepared."

Using my good hand, I pulled her away from the dark entrance. It was hard on her, I could tell, leaving it behind. As long as the hole was in view, she kept glancing back over her shoulder, a wistful look on her face.

I remained tense as we skirted the nearby patch of trees and set off for home.

By the time we got back to the house, the shock of my injury had faded and my hand had started to throb. The bones felt sore, bruised and out of place inside my flesh.

We found Mac, Floyd, and Sabine in the kitchen.

"Amanda!" As soon as we entered, Mac swept across the room and lifted her into his arms. "I woke up and you were gone. I thought . . . I thought . . ." He paused, taking a moment to compose himself. "Tell me, *what happened*?"

"Nothing," she said, pushing out of his embrace. "We both woke up early, so I thought I'd show Dean around the neighborhood."

All eyes turned toward me, and Amanda shot me a meaningful look. I got the message loud and clear: nothing about the dogs, nothing about the tunnel.

There was silence for a moment, then Sabine shouted *"Fuck,"* finally noticing my hand. The bandage had soaked all the way through, and I was dripping blood onto the floor. "What the fuck happened to Dean?"

"Jesus," Floyd added. He stood up and backed away from his place at the kitchen table, blanching at the sight of my bloody hand. Sabine grabbed me by the shoulder and led me over to

Floyd's abandoned seat. I dropped my backpack to the ground and let her push me down into the chair.

Sabine unwrapped my blood-soaked bandage and held my hand open on the tabletop. She examined my wounds for a second, then raised her dark, kohl-rimmed eyes to my face. Her question was still there: *What the fuck happened?*

I glanced up at Amanda, and she lowered her eyes to the ground. Mac was watching her closely; he was so focused on his girlfriend, he hadn't given me or my bloody hand a second glance.

"I tried to pet a dog," I said. "A stray. He must have been hungry."

"Yeah. Fucking *brilliant*," Sabine huffed sarcastically. "Petting stray dogs? You're a fucking Rhodes scholar, now, aren'tcha?"

Sabine cleaned the puncture wounds with water and a clean cloth. The worst of the holes was as big around as a dime; Sabine moved the skin, and I could see lengths of tendon through the opening: bunches of purple-red cord quivering in the open air. It was a nauseating sight. Floyd brought a first aid kit from the bathroom, then averted his eyes as Sabine flushed the wounds with antiseptic and bound them with gauze.

Once she was done, Sabine shook her head. "Those are some pretty nasty holes you've got there," she said. "I cleaned them out as best I could, but you're going to have to watch out for infection. That could fuck you up but good." She made a clicking sound with her tongue. "And I'm not even going to mention rabies."

I nodded. That was something I didn't want to think about. Spokane was cut off from the world. Where would I go for real medical attention? The military? *Or I could always just leave,* I thought. But the thought of fleeing the city, just when I was starting to get some good photographs, filled me with dread.

"Look on the bright side," she added with a sly smile. "You're going to be rocking some pretty cool scars after this. And if you want, you're only a couple millimeters away from a real bitching hand piercing."

Floyd laughed—a loud hyena snort—and I found myself smiling despite my worry and pain.

I heard the front door swing open, and the kitchen fell silent. Everyone turned toward the entrance just as Taylor walked in. She was clutching a stocking cap in one hand, using the other to brush strands of long black hair from her sweaty forehead. She had a bright smile on her lips, but it turned a bit quizzical as she glanced around the room, trying to figure out what was going on.

"What happened?" she asked, nodding toward my bandaged hand. Now that it was wrapped in clean, white gauze, the sight was far less nauseating than it had been.

"Dean got—" Sabine began, but I cut her off.

"I just hurt my hand a bit," I said. "Not a big deal." I pointed to the bandage and shrugged dismissively. "Just a precaution."

I know it sounds stupid, but I really didn't want Taylor to know the extent of my injuries. I liked her, and I wanted her to think I was all macho and strong, not some walking disaster area.

Sabine, Floyd, and Amanda gave me perplexed looks, but they didn't argue. And Mac, for his part, remained completely impassive.

"Well, if you're up for it, I think we can still make the hospital raid." Taylor tapped at the face of her watch. "If we hurry."

"Grappling hooks this time?" Floyd said, a wicked smile spreading across his lips. "I wouldn't miss that for the world."

I nodded my consent, and Taylor smiled approvingly. She seemed to be in a good mood, and the light in her eyes made me forget all about the holes in my hand.

Our vantage point was cold. Extremely cold.

We lay perched atop a building about a block away from the hospital, completely exposed to the frigid wind blowing out of the north. Taylor had brought a couple of blankets, and the six of us lay huddled close together—elbow to elbow, with our arms braced up beneath our chins—staring across the street at the commotion a block away.

Charlie and Devon were the only ones missing. When we checked their rooms before leaving, we'd found Devon gone, and Charlie . . . well, Charlie had refused to budge, muttering a single dispirited sentence through his locked door.

I had my camera cradled in my uninjured hand, the lens cranked to its longest telephoto setting. Sabine had my camcorder, and I could hear her cooing as she played with the buttons, checking out its various features.

"They think it might be the epicenter of what's happening," Taylor said. She lay to my right, her palms cupped around her eyes in order to block out the sun. "They've tried four—" "Five!" Floyd interjected. "—*five* times before. But the people they send in keep getting lost and confused, and they stumble out hours—or days—later. And none of them can say what happens."

"And some of them don't come out at all," Floyd added.

"I don't think that's true," Taylor said, adding a dismissive cluck.

"They couldn't get through on the ground floor," Floyd said, continuing Taylor's explanation, "so they're trying farther up this time."

"Shhhh!" Sabine hissed. "They're going in!"

I panned my lens down to the base of the hospital building. There was a cluster of military vehicles parked on the sidewalk: a single open-backed transport and three Jeeps. A tent had been erected in the parking lot thirty feet away, and a massive computer console was visible through its open door. The computer was surrounded by three officers, one of them pacing nervously in and out of view.

At the sound of a loud, hollow *thump,* I panned to a group of soldiers on the sidewalk. A thin trickle of smoke spun up into the sky above their heads, following the graceful arc of a flying rope. A grappling hook hit the hospital's roof ten floors up, and I watched as a soldier pulled the rope tight, testing its strength. He strained against the rope for a couple of seconds, then handed it over to a helmeted comrade, giving him a reassuring pat on the back.

The helmeted soldier was wearing a military-green backpack; I could see a brick-shaped radio strapped to one side and a rifle strapped to the other. The cylindrical body of a camera was mounted to the top of his helmet.

After giving the rope a tug of his own, the soldier stepped up to the building and began climbing its side. He moved slowly, hunting for footholds with cautious deliberation. When he got up to the third floor, he stepped onto a window ledge, turned his shoulder against a tall pane of glass, and quickly smashed it in with his elbow.

Then, after a moment's hesitation, the soldier disappeared inside, trailing behind a length of electric-yellow rope.

For nearly ten minutes, we watched this yellow tether spool through the window frame, moving in fits and starts. It was extremely tedious. As I lay on the rooftop, I could feel my injured left hand stiffening into a useless claw—bruised muscle pulling tight beneath damaged skin—and the camera in my right seemed to get heavier with each passing second. Then the rope stopped moving, and for a handful of minutes there was nothing, nothing at all. Just boredom.

I could hear Floyd fidgeting two berths to my left. "How long—" he started to say, but motion down in the parking lot stopped him short. The three officers had stormed out of their command tent, their eyes turned up toward the building.

I panned back in time to see the soldier fly out of the window. Not fall. *Fly.*

Propelled out into empty space. Thrown, perhaps. Or maybe he dived, throwing himself out the window at full sprint.

For a split second, the soldier fell through the air, his body perfectly limp, spinning toward the sky. Then he hit the sidewalk with a loud *crack*. For a moment, his comrades on the ground stood frozen in place, unsure how to react. In fact, the whole scene stood frozen in time: that motionless body lying still on the ground, those paralyzed clumps of soldiers and officers.

Then the fallen soldier heaved himself up off the ground.

Shedding first his helmet, then his backpack, the soldier—injured and broken—stumbled away from the building, moving in a crazed, drunken gait.

07.1

Photograph. October 19, 09:23 P.M. The red guitar:

A close-up of guitar strings. Solid white lines
against deep red lacquer.

The shot is far enough back to show the curve of the
instrument's body, a pair of graceful S's just inside the top and bottom of the frame. The red lacquer is immaculate, smooth as unsmudged glass. Near
the central hole it is a dark red verging on bur-
gundy, but it lightens up as it nears the body's
edge, where it glows like a brilliant flame.

There is a hand hovering over the guitar—dirty fingers frozen in motion, caught coaxing the thin nylon
strings into indistinct blurs. The index finger has
a cracked, ragged nail, and a thin band of blood en-
circles the dirty cuticle. The pad of the finger—
turned partway toward the camera—is coated with
blood, matching the guitar's grisly color.

O7.2

I had the falling soldier on my mind all the way to Mama Cass's: his brief flight through the air, his impact, and then that odd drunken stagger. The fall should have killed him. But he got up and continued on, a spring-driven wind-up toy, too damaged to comprehend, too damaged to just lie down.

"Do you think he'll be all right?" Sabine asked as we crossed under I-90 and approached the restaurant.

"He went totally limp, like a wet noodle," Floyd said. "And noodles don't break."

"But why did he jump?" Sabine asked. "What did he find in there?"

I was watching Taylor as we walked. She stayed a couple of steps ahead, leading the way. In response to Sabine's question, she looked back over her shoulder and shrugged. Her eyes were vacant, her thoughts a million miles away.

Nobody spoke. There was no answer to Sabine's question.

Sabine grunted and looked down at the camcorder in her hand. She'd flipped open the viewscreen and was watching the video of the falling soldier. Her fingers shuttled back and forth between "play" and "rewind," as she watched the fall over and over again.

We continued in silence.

It was a little after one o'clock when we reached Mama Cass

and the Char-Grilled Miracle. We found the tables packed with hungry lunchtime customers. There were at least thirty people seated in the open dining area and another fifteen gathered on the sidewalk outside. It was a shock, seeing so many dirty faces gathered together in one place. It made me wonder just how many people were left here in the city. Two hundred? Three hundred?

Wandering the empty streets, it was easy to get caught up in the desolation of this place, easy to think that we were the only people left in the world—just our little household, along with the military, of course. But there were other civilians out there, holed up behind doors, making do without electricity and hot water, without Internet, cable, and phone service.

I grabbed my camera and started taking pictures, trying to get some candid shots. These were truly interesting people. Beneath all that dirt and exhaustion—beneath the ragged clothing, snaggled hair, chapped lips, and bloodshot eyes—there was genuine character and resolve.

These were the people who had stayed despite having every reason to leave.

"Cool it, Dean," Taylor hissed beneath her breath. "You're making everyone nervous."

She was right. I glanced up and found myself the focus of wary glances and more than a couple of threatening glares. Several people had turned their bodies away, trying to shield themselves from my camera.

"I'm sorry," I mumbled, addressing the crowded room. I unslung my backpack and tucked the camera back inside.

"Why, if it isn't my favorite band of vagabonds . . . plus one!"

I turned and found a smiling, middle-aged black woman striding our way. She was thin as a stick, and her wide smile revealed pearl-white teeth. She was dressed in stylish ski gear, impeccably clean and perfectly fitted.

"Sharon!" Sabine exclaimed with a grin, moving forward to give the older woman a hug. "When'd you get back?"

"About an hour ago. I got a lift from the infantry." She pointed to a table of soldiers on the other side of the room. In response, the uniformed men looked up from their massive plates of food and snapped off nearly synchronized salutes.

"Well, it's good to have you back," Sabine said. She cast a nervous glance toward the back of the dining area, then lowered her voice. "I didn't want to tell Bobby, but the food's suffered without you. Hell, I was thinking of taking my business somewhere else." She held a straight face for a couple of seconds, then broke down laughing, moving to hug the older woman one more time.

"Who's your friend with the camera?" Sharon asked, watching me over Sabine's shoulder. There was a hint of distaste in her voice, like the word *camera* was a bitter fruit on her tongue.

"That's Dean," Sabine said. "He's an artist. A good guy. He's staying with us while he works on a project."

Sharon shrugged. "Well, any friend of yours," she said, still sounding a bit skeptical. Then she turned and gestured toward the back of the room, once again playing the gracious hostess. "Right this way, *mes amies*. You've got the chef's table today!"

The chef's table was an immaculate hardwood oval tucked into an out-of-the-way corner. It had intricate knurled legs and was polished to a high gloss, something you'd find in a suburban mansion. Sharon seated us in mismatched folding chairs.

"Sharon was a stockbroker back before all of this shit started," Sabine said, addressing me with a sly smile as Sharon helped us with our chairs. "She moved to Spokane to retire, to live the relaxed good life. Then the world went crazy."

Sharon shrugged. "I know it sounds bad, but I was starting to get bored, anyway . . . just sitting on my ass, watching cable news. Retirement just wasn't my thing. Besides, I always wanted to open my own restaurant."

"Why 'Mama Cass'?" I asked. "Why not 'Sharon's' or 'Mama Sharon's'?"

With a smile, she said, "'Cause people say I make a *killer* ham sandwich." She waited a beat, then looked around the table, finding nothing but blank faces.

"Jesus Christ! Don't you know anything about rock 'n' roll history? *Mama Cass? The Mamas and the Papas?* Died choking on a ham sandwich? . . . Get it? I make a *killer* ham sandwich?" After a moment of expectant silence, she shook her head and tossed a stack of hand-lettered menus onto the table. "You bunch are just getting younger and younger." Muttering, she stalked away.

Sabine smiled and gestured toward the older woman's retreating back. "She's so smart, it's scary," she said with an admiring shake of her head. "And this whole situation . . . I've never seen anyone more suited to anything. She works all the angles, greasing hands and making deals. She moves in and out of the city with impunity. Somebody here will trade an old watch for a barbecue chicken; she'll take the watch to Seattle and sell it for a hundred bucks."

"And the military lets her do that?" I asked.

Floyd let out a loud snort, then pointed to the table of soldiers near the front of the restaurant. "The military fucking *helps* her."

"And you've got to admire that," Sabine said. "You've got to admire that skill."

Taylor grunted. "Yeah, in the same way you'd admire a wolf's razor-sharp teeth." Taylor was sitting directly to my left, and she kept her words low, meaning them for my ears only. I glanced over; she had her arms crossed in front of her chest, and she met my eyes with a disgusted frown.

"Uh-oh," Floyd muttered. "Here comes trouble."

I followed his eyes back across the room and found Wendell standing just inside the entrance.

Wendell. At least that was how he'd introduced himself back when we first met. Taylor had used a different name: Weasel. That name seemed much more fitting. Stringing me along, stealing my backpack, taking advantage of my naïveté. Just seeing him again . . . it made me feel so stupid.

I felt a surge of anger rising in my gut and started to stand up, but Taylor put her hand on my shoulder, keeping me in my seat. "Just read your menu, Dean. I'll handle this."

As Taylor started across the room, I followed her suggestion, reaching out and grabbing a menu. But I couldn't read it. I couldn't take my eyes off of Weasel. It looked like the last couple of days had been rough on him. He was dirtier than I remembered, and somewhere along the line, he'd lost his hat. *Good,* I thought. *Karma's a bitch.* He was standing with a pair of equally mangy men, his eyes barely open. On the nod, I guessed.

He jerked to attention as soon as Taylor entered his line of sight. At first, it looked like he was going to bolt—his body tensed up and he glanced toward the entrance. But he didn't run. He stopped and turned back toward Taylor, his shoulders slumping in defeat. They talked for several minutes, Weasel occasionally glancing over my way. I couldn't hear what they were saying, but it was pretty easy to read the emotion in Weasel's gestures—he held his hands open wide, occasionally reaching out to touch Taylor's forearm. He gave me one last glance, then turned and left, striding through the wide-open storefront. His friends didn't follow.

"He's sorry," Taylor said when she once again took her seat. "And it's genuine, I think. He's an okay guy . . . it's his monkey that's got the greedy hands. The smack. And he's working to get clean."

I nodded. I wasn't sure I believed her—it sounded like wishful thinking to me—but I wasn't the one who knew him. I was just the stranger he'd tried to rob.

"In a week, if everything's cool, I think I'm going to invite him back to the house."

I sat stunned for a moment. Weasel had taken advantage of me, had stolen from me, had made me feel like a fool. The fact that Taylor would ignore all that and invite him back into her home . . . I was surprised at how this made me feel. A little bit hurt. A little bit betrayed.

"It's your house," I finally said. "You can do whatever you want." My voice came out cold, a voice I barely recognized as my own. "Besides, do you really think I'll be here in a week? Do you think it'll take me that long to get my pictures?"

At that, I opened my menu and stared down at the neat hand-drawn text. I could feel her watching me, confused. I could feel those coal-dark eyes drilling deep into my skull, trying to probe my thoughts and emotions.

I refused to meet her gaze.

It really was a killer ham sandwich.

According to the menu, the ham had been smoked out back in a jury-rigged smoking shed, then glazed with layers of honey and Dijon mustard. It was served thick-cut with lettuce, tomato, and Swiss cheese, between slices of doughy-fresh bread slathered with mayonnaise. It was wonderful. Each bite was salty and sweet, and I tore through the whole thing in a matter of minutes.

I had cash to pay for my lunch, but I watched Floyd trade in a couple of packs of C-cell batteries for his, and Sabine offered up a handful of costume jewelry. Mac paid for his and Amanda's meal with a couple of old books; Sharon slipped on a pair of reading glasses and studied the covers and copyright pages before nodding her acceptance. Taylor produced a roll of quarters from one of the pockets of her cargo pants.

"Sharon's got everyone in the city doing her looting for her," Taylor whispered, nodding toward Sabine and her costume jewelry. "Sooner or later, everything of value ends up here." There was an anxious lilt to Taylor's voice. She was probing me, trying to gauge the depth of my hurt over Weasel.

I let out a low, noncommittal grunt. I still wasn't ready to meet her eyes.

"It was a pleasure doing business with you folks," Sharon said, flashing a wry smile as we got out of our seats. "And it was nice to meet you, Dean. If there's anything you're looking for while you're here—anything at all—just let me know. I might be able to help."

As we filed past, Sharon stopped Sabine with a gentle hand on her arm. "And if you can swing it, kid, stop by tomorrow afternoon. I might have something for you." Sabine gave the older woman a questioning look, then nodded, her eyes suddenly going wide.

The wind picked up as we walked back home. I hunched forward and pulled my jacket tight against my chest, but the wind still managed to work its way beneath my clothing, cutting straight to the skin. It started my teeth chattering, and I had to clench my jaw to get it to stop. The only warm part of my body was my injured hand, tucked deep inside my pocket; it throbbed with the beat of my heart, pulsing flush with blood.

As we crossed the Spokane River Bridge, Sabine grabbed my arm and pointed back toward the line of buildings that constituted downtown. I followed her finger and found a scrawl of graffiti etched across the third floor of an office building. It was old graffiti—faded yellow, outlined in electric blue— but I recognized the shape of the letters. It was the Poet. The Artist.

SORRY ABOUT THE TUMORS. SOMETIMES THEY AREN'T FATAL.

Sabine smiled—a broad, joyous smile —then tucked her hands into her pockets and trotted up to Floyd's side, greeting him with a playful shoulder bump. She seemed in a good mood. Practically delirious.

I lowered my head against the cold wind and followed.

As soon as we got back to the house, Taylor grabbed me by the arm and hauled me upstairs. I didn't particularly want to go, but she was insistent. Her fingers dug deep into the muscles of my forearm, and the hard, impatient look on her face said she was done fooling around.

Fine. Whatever.

She'd sided with Weasel. She wanted him around despite my feelings. And that wounded me.

What did you expect? I chided myself. *She's only known you for a couple of days. Did you expect instant love and devotion? Did you think she'd honor your wishes above all others'?* That didn't seem too likely to me. I wasn't exactly a stunning beauty, and I didn't have Taylor's smile, her charm, or her heart. There was absolutely no reason she should feel anything for me . . . anything but pity, that is.

The upstairs hallway was surprisingly long, and we went all the way to the end, passing a bathroom, three open bedroom doors, and a narrow staircase leading up to an attic-loft. Without any fanfare, Taylor threw open the final door, revealing a cramped sewing room. A sewing machine sat perched atop a card table on one side of the room, and a futon mattress lay spread across the other. A stack of plastic milk crates formed shelving along one wall, filled with bolts of brightly colored fabric. A half-finished quilt lay beneath the sewing machine needle; from what I could see, the squares of fabric formed geometric waves, all in varying shades of blue.

"Weasel stayed here off and on," Taylor said, pointing down at the futon. Several colorful blankets had been pushed down to the foot of the mattress, and dirty clothing lay scattered at its side. "It's your room now. You're welcome to stay here for as long as you like."

"And Weasel?" I asked.

She shook her head and gestured me down toward the futon. I took a seat on the thin mattress, and she sat down on the folding chair across from me. "I'm done apologizing to you, Dean. He's my friend, and he helped me through some bad shit when the city went crazy. He hooked me up with the commune—the Homestead—when that's where I needed to be. And if not for him, I doubt I'd be alive right now." She reached out and touched the sewing machine, running her hand across its domed surface. It was an idle gesture, something to occupy her hands, something to look at other than me. "I like you, Dean. Really, I do. But I'm loyal to my friends. And Weasel deserves my loyalty."

I nodded. I didn't really feel any better about the situation, but I couldn't argue with her, and I couldn't change her feelings. Her words made sense, whereas my hurt feelings did not.

Perhaps sensing this, she leaned forward, hesitated for a moment, and gave my hand a tentative caress.

"How about this," she said. She was perched right in front of me, and I couldn't avoid meeting her eyes; they were deep, dark, and filled with honest emotion. "We forget about this for a while, okay? We see if you fit in here. We see if there's something—" She halted abruptly and looked away, blushing slightly. The awkward motion caught me by surprise.

And how does that sentence end? I wondered, watching her shift uncomfortably in her chair. *We see if there's something . . . between the two of us?* Was she acknowledging—in that broken sentence, in that blush—the possibility of a relationship?

And just like that, my hurt feelings were gone, swept away with those unspoken words.

She continued: "If after a week you still don't want Weasel here, we'll figure something out. Okay? Does that work for you?"

"Okay," I said, and I smiled. It was a genuine smile.

"Good. I'm glad that's settled. Maybe now you can stop your pouting."

Taylor grabbed a milk crate from the stack against the wall and started packing up Weasel's things. There was a pile of black-and-white composition books near the head of the futon, and she took care tucking them into the bottom of the crate.

"What did he help you with?" I asked as I watched her work. "You said he helped you when the city went crazy. What did he do?"

Taylor paused for a moment, frozen over a pile of clothing. She stared into the milk crate for a couple of seconds, lost in thought, then resumed her chore, gathering up dirty flannels, wool socks, and a pair of ratty jeans. "My parents," she said. Her voice was low. When she'd been placating me earlier, her voice had been strong, cajoling. Now it was breathy and weak, like the wind had started to leak from her lungs. "Back in September, my parents . . . something happened. They were just . . . gone. Weasel helped me cope. He kept me fed. He kept me from giving in to despair."

"I'm sorry," I said, suddenly realizing just how little I knew about her and her life. "Is it like Charlie's parents? Maybe they're still here somewhere?"

"No. Not like Charlie's parents." She shook her head, a hint of frustration coming into her voice. "My mom and dad . . . they're just gone. *Gone*. And they aren't coming back."

I stood up, wanting to comfort her, wanting to put my arms around her and lend her some of my strength, but she abruptly turned and put the milk crate between us. "I've dealt with it," she said, her voice suddenly hard. "It's in the past, and it's not something I want to talk about."

I nodded.

The moment was gone. The vulnerable, caring Taylor had disappeared, chased away by my stupid questions.

I could tell I wasn't getting the whole story—about her, about her parents—but I didn't want to push her any harder.

"You should move your stuff up here. Get yourself settled in," she said. "You've cluttered up the living room long enough." And with that, she turned and left, taking Weasel's belongings with her.

After moving my stuff up to the new room, I sat down at the sewing table and started to change the dressing on my hand. The wounds on my palm had reopened a couple of times during the day, and the gauze was tacky with drying blood and pus. I hissed as I pulled it away from the skin, a sharp stab of pain radiating up my forearm.

"Shit, man. Let me help you with that."

I turned and found Floyd standing in the open doorway. He had a guitar case dangling from his hand, an old, well-used case covered in stickers and hand-drawn graffiti. The words *Pretty Boy* were drawn across the front in bright pink nail polish. He propped the case against the wall and came over to the table, taking a seat next to the sewing machine.

He lifted my hand and started studying my palm. There was a

thin trickle of blood seeping from the largest puncture. "Fuck, I can't deal with blood," he muttered, turning my hand toward the sunlit window. His face was going pale, but he didn't look away.

"You don't have to do that," I said. "I can clean the gore and blood. Just help me wrap it up when I'm done, okay?"

Floyd stood up and walked over to the window. The window was in the wall over the futon, providing a view of the street out front. "I didn't used to be such a pussy," he said, shaking his head. "Fuck, I've laughed off shit worse than that." He pointed toward my hand. "When I was living in Santa Cruz, I wiped out jumping off the side of a parking garage, fell ten feet onto a concrete divider. I broke my ulna—my fucking *forearm*," he said, seeing the question on my face. "A compound fracture. And I walked six blocks to my friend's house, laughing the whole way. Granted, I was pretty fucking delirious, but I wasn't a shrinking pussy about it."

I poured rubbing alcohol onto some paper towels and began scrubbing my open palm. "What happened?" I asked, gritting my teeth against the chemical pain. "What changed?"

"My knee," he said, reaching down and rapping his knuckles against his right kneecap. I remembered that gesture from my first night at the house; it seemed like an automatic motion, some type of unconscious reflex. "And I didn't even see the blood that time. I was in a competition, and they had a medical staff—they put me right under when my knee exploded. The kicker is, it wasn't even a spectacular wipeout! I just landed wrong, my weight coming down just a couple of degrees too far forward."

Floyd let out a disgusted grunt, a low sound, like a growl, at the back of his throat. "And that was it. No more Pretty Boy Floyd. And now I can't stand the sight of blood."

When I finished cleaning my wounds, I found bright pink rings starting to form around the punctures. I ran my finger across the puckered flesh: the damaged skin felt hot to the touch. *It's just bruised*, I told myself. *Just bruised flesh, flush with blood.*

"Help me wrap it up," I said. I hid my wounds beneath a fresh bandage, then nodded Floyd toward the roll of gauze. He wrapped my hand up tight, securing the dressing with a fresh strip of tape.

"Does it hurt?" Floyd asked.

"Yeah," I said. "It throbs. And my whole arm's sore."

Floyd went over to his guitar case and set it atop the futon. He opened it up, revealing a shiny red acoustic guitar. Unlike the case, the guitar looked like it was in pristine condition, its lacquered finish polished to an immaculate sheen. He lifted the instrument and began digging through a small compartment hidden beneath its neck. After a couple of seconds, he came up with a handful of picks and several prescription pill bottles. He studied the labels for a couple of seconds, then upended some pills onto his palm. He bounced them a couple of times in his loosely curled fist, his face screwed up like he was engaged in some inner debate, and then handed them over.

Four pills. Small green circles, light and insubstantial in my uninjured hand. "OC" etched on one side, "80" on the other.

"Oxycodone," Floyd said. "They'll help with the pain."

"No shit, they'll help with the pain." I stared at the pills for a couple of seconds. I'd had oxy once, after oral surgery, and I remembered the fuzzy-headed warmth of the stuff. I'd lost three days under its sway, camped out in front of the television, barely able to flip the channels.

But there hadn't been any pain.

"My knee still aches," Floyd explained, "especially when it's cold. And my doctor is . . . well, let's just say he's generous. He keeps me well stocked."

I hesitated for a moment, staring down at the pills. Then I flexed my left hand. The pain was immediate, enough to make me wince. The way I saw it, I didn't really have much of a choice: on the one hand, I had pain and discomfort; on the other—resting neatly on the other—I had fuzzy-headed oblivion. I grunted and tossed one of the pills to the back of my throat. It was bitter going down, a chalky floral taste.

It's just a temporary thing, I told myself, putting the other pills in my pocket. *Just until I'm healed.*

Floyd smiled. "Cheers," he said, raising the pill bottle in a toast. And: "Down the hatch." He bolted the rest of the bottle like it was a shot of whiskey.

I was pretty fucked up. After dinner, we smoked a shitload of pot, and on top of the oxycodone, it left me feeling numb, floating free from reality.

And that was a good place to be.

Here, in this place, I wasn't feeling my hand. I wasn't worrying about the shit I'd seen: the body in the ceiling, the face in the wall, the spider with the human finger. I wasn't thinking about the soldier and his fall from the hospital window, the way his limp body had spun in the air, so eerie and silent. Instead, I was just sitting there, at peace, watching Taylor from across the backyard.

And despite the evening's frigid cold, I felt warm. I felt comfortable. I felt good.

Floyd and I were sitting on a bench in the garden, surrounded by dormant rosebushes. He was playing his bright red guitar—moving from Pearl Jam, to Bowie, to the Pixies—and everyone else was on the back porch, watching by the light of a single gas-powered lantern.

Amanda, Mac, and Devon were sitting on the steps. Amanda was leaning back against Mac's chest, resting her head in the crook of his neck. She looked sedate, at ease, her dogs a million miles away. Taylor and Sabine shared an old wicker bench beneath the eaves. Sabine had her feet tucked into a lotus position on her lap. Her eyes were closed, and there was a peaceful smile on her lips.

Even Charlie was there, sitting on the floor at Taylor's feet. He'd emerged from his room right after dinner, surprising us all with his upbeat, almost cheerful attitude. Somehow, locked up in his room, he'd managed to make peace with that photo of his mother. In fact, he seemed downright ashamed of the whole melo-dramatic episode. And he didn't want to talk about it. Not at all.

And then there was Taylor. I couldn't keep my eyes off Taylor.

I looked down and noticed my camera sitting in my lap. I turned on the LCD display and scrolled through a dozen pictures: Charlie, on the ground, resting his head against Taylor's knee; Mac, kissing the side of Amanda's head; Devon, taking a huge hit off his bong; Sabine, flipping me the bird. And then there were a dozen pictures of Floyd playing his guitar, his forehead wrinkled in concentration, utterly focused on the instrument in his hands.

As I scrolled through the memory card, Floyd cleared his throat and started in on a new song. I recognized it immediately: "The *John B.* Sails."

It was an old song—a traditional folk tune—and I knew it be-cause the Beach Boys had recorded a cover of it back in the six-ties. When I was a kid, my father had played that CD a lot. Sitting in his den with a tumbler of Scotch dangling from his hand, he'd play it, and then he'd get sad. I think it reminded him of some-thing, something painful. I never thought to ask what.

> So hoist up the *John B.* sails,
> See how the mainsail set,
> Send for the captain ashore, let us go home,
> Let me go home.

Floyd played the song with a surprising amount of emotion, his voice a crooning moan, rooted deep in his chest. I put my camera down and focused on his performance. There was no care-free, surfer lilt to this version of the song, just pained longing.

He sounded so hurt. So bitter.

And I could tell it wasn't just something he was doing for us, wasn't just part of his performance. He was digging down into his very core, and after a couple of lines, I don't even think he real-ized we were still there, watching.

I noticed blood on his hand. Floyd was playing so hard that he'd cut his fingers on the strings. But that didn't stop him. He remained completely oblivious, eyes closed, heartache twisting at his lips.

> So hoist up the *John B.* sails,
> See how the mainsail set,
> Send for the doctors now, just let me go home,
> I wanna go home.

> This is the worst trip—

Then, abruptly, he stopped midsentence. His fingers halted on the bright red guitar, and his open mouth snapped shut. The sudden silence was a shock, a jarring slap at our comfortable, intimate gathering.

And for a brief moment, there wasn't a sound in the world.

"Wait, man," Floyd said, turning toward me. There was a perplexed look on his face, like he'd just suddenly come awake to find this guitar in his hands. "What the *fuck* was I singing?" There was no pain in his voice. Not anymore. Just confusion.

And that was when I noticed the snow—big, lazy flakes tumbling from the pitch-black sky.

08.1

Photograph. October 20, 01:25 P.M. A window in the snow:

A surveillance photo, set slightly askew. Peering in
through a window at a man frozen in action.

It is a second-story window, perched directly above
a protected front door. The eaves above and below
are coated in several inches of snow. On the other
side of the glass, a young man is glancing back over
his shoulder into the unseen depths of the room. He
is wearing a black knit cap and a thick winter
jacket. His mouth is open, and his arms are raised
at his side, caught in midgesture. He is talking. Or
arguing. The lines on his face convey a look of pure
frustration.

It is a moment of candid emotion, caught and frozen
in time.

There are no furnishings visible in the room behind
him, nothing but a small swatch of wall. A blue
light glows somewhere out of view, coloring the wall

a vibrant shade and tinting the man's pale complexion. It is a subtle light, but it stands out inside
that frame within a frame—a touch of color inside
an otherwise monochrome image. It makes it look like
the man is trapped under tropical water or frozen
inside a cube of polar-blue ice.

We can't see who he's talking to.

08.2

The snow was thick on the ground by the time I got out of bed. Almost five inches. Practically a blizzard by my sunny-California standards. The snow was still falling, but it was now just a tiny flurry, nothing but dust and smoke particles floating in the air.

It felt like my head had been stuffed full of foam and string sometime during the night. And my hand had resumed its loud complaints.

My jeans lay draped over the back of the folding chair, and as soon as I got out of bed, I dug through its pockets, coming up with the remaining oxycodone. There were three left and I considered taking them all, but I ended up just popping a single pill. The night before was a real blur—a slide show of motion snapping past inside my head—and I didn't want to fall back into that haze. I wanted to stay sharp. I had work to do.

Besides, I told myself, *my hand doesn't feel* that *bad.*

Unfortunately, this reassurance didn't really help, as the thought of unwinding my bandages and checking on my damaged flesh still filled me with a sense of dread. It was something I didn't want to think about, something I didn't want to deal with. Not yet.

I got dressed, adding an extra flannel shirt to my layers of clothing. Then I stood at the window for a while, staring out at the snow-shrouded street. It was a still, pristine tableau. There were no cars or pedestrians, no hint of animal life. The entire world had been hidden beneath a thick alabaster blanket. I looked for tracks in the snow, but there was nothing there. Not a single footprint.

Not a single paw print, either, I thought, remembering the surge of wolves flowing down this very street.

On the way downstairs, I paused for a moment outside Floyd's open door. He lay passed out atop his covers, fully clothed. His guitar case sat propped against the wall near his head, and his hands were smeared with dried blood. He was snoring.

The rest of the bedroom doors were all closed. The only sound in the upstairs hallway was the low, regular drone of Floyd's breath.

Downstairs, I once again found Charlie sitting at the kitchen table, typing away at his notebook computer. When I entered, he glanced up briefly, and then nodded toward a French Press sitting on the kitchen counter. "I made coffee," he said. "Help yourself." Before I could thank him—before I could say a single word—he looked back down at his computer, once again losing himself in the glowing screen. I could practically hear the gears clicking away inside his head. In those brief moments, my presence had been noted, analyzed, and filed away. His thoughts had moved on. I poured myself a cup of coffee and sat down at his side.

"When are you sending stuff out next?" I asked, idly rapping a knuckle against the back of his screen. "When does your thumb drive go back out into the world?"

"Taylor said tonight," Charlie replied, not looking up. "She's giving it to her friend tonight."

"If I wanted to post something—to a forum, a message board—could I do that? Could you program something to do that?"

Charlie's fingers fell silent on the keyboard, and he glanced up. I watched as his forehead scrunched up in lines of concentration, his unfixed stare drifting up toward the ceiling. I'd managed to capture his attention.

"Is it a public message board? What type of security are we talking about?"

I shrugged. "I don't know. You log into an account, then type stuff into a box."

Charlie laughed and shook his head, then fell silent. His stare remained fixed on an imaginary spot above my shoulder. After a handful of seconds, his eyes refocused. "You have your computer here, right? Did you browse the site recently?"

I nodded. "Probably the last thing I read."

He smiled. "Then bring it to me. I bet you ten bucks—if it's still in the cache, I can do it. I can post whatever you want."

"Thanks," I said. "That's incredible." Charlie's eyes flickered back toward his computer, and I could tell I was about to lose him again.

"Are you scared?" I asked, seizing the moment. "About what might come back? On the drive? In your email?"

He stopped, hands frozen over the keyboard. For a moment, I thought I'd pushed him too far. Then he smiled.

"No," he said. "It's them, my parents. I figured it out. They're trying to get to me, trying to tell me something. And that's what I *want* . . . to find them, to contact them.

"And when it's time, it'll all become clear. They'll reach me, or I'll reach them." Charlie once again had that distant look in his eyes, like he was grappling with some technical problem, trying to figure out how to make something work. "It's the message, you see, not the form it takes. I just have to figure out what they're trying to say."

He turned back toward his computer, dismissing me abruptly. I could see two windows open on his screen. One was filled with code, and the other showed his mother on the corner of Second Avenue and Sherman Street. Charlie had zoomed the picture in on her haunted expression.

I felt bad for him. The only message I could read there, in that close-up, was a message of fear: Charlie's mother looking back over her shoulder with that frightened look on her face, like she wasn't alone on that abandoned street, like there was something else there, chasing her. Something horrible.

Amanda and Mac were playing in the backyard when I finished up my coffee. They were having a snowball fight. Amanda was hiding behind a row of rosebushes while Mac lobbed projectiles high into the air, sending them raining down like artillery shots. After a round of sorties, Amanda popped up over the line of bushes and whipped a snowball directly at his head, sending him toppling over.

Their laughter was high and bright, a counterpoint to Charlie's insistent *tap-tap-tap*.

Amanda stuck her head in through the back door. "Me against you three," she panted. "Mac needs the help. He's getting his ass kicked out here!" A snowball hit the window at her side, and she turned, laughing, to once again join the fray.

Charlie's fingers didn't even pause on the keyboard. After Amanda disappeared, he started sucking at his teeth absently, filling the room with a wet, slurping sound. I set my empty coffee cup in the kitchen sink, then headed upstairs to start work on my forum post.

Taylor's door was right across from the stairwell, and I paused when I reached it. I listened for a moment, then knocked tentatively. There was no response. I pushed, and the door swung open. The room was empty, her bed neatly made. *Early riser,* I thought. *Already out in the world, doing whatever it is she does in the morning.*

I continued on to my room.

I spent the rest of the morning staring at my computer screen, trying to assemble a forum post. It was a stressful task. The way I looked at it, this was the most important thing in my life. It was the next step in my journey, putting my pictures out there for the whole world to see.

These were my dreams and aspirations. In pieces on my computer screen.

More than anything, I wanted to make the right first impression. I wanted to capture people's attention and establish credibility right off the bat. I wanted people to look at these pictures—really *look* at them—and take me seriously. I wanted them to recognize my passion, my skill, my *art*.

No wonder I was anxious. I had the weight of my entire future sitting right there on my shoulders.

I decided to start with some of my more mundane images. If I started with the insane stuff, I reasoned, no one would believe me. I could hear the arguments now: *Yeah, he just Photoshopped a finger onto that spider; and that face in the wall, it doesn't even look real—it's just a mask, a mannequin.*

No, I decided, it was better to start off with the stuff no one would dispute.

First up: the soldier in front of the ENTERING SPOKANE sign. Then an empty city street. Then Riverfront Park. And finally, a pair of pictures from Mama Cass's: one showing the crowd of refugees gathered around the storefront, the other showing a handful of dirty faces watching me suspiciously. I liked this final picture; I thought it ended things on the right note. It put some human faces—ragged and tired, haunted and angry—amid all the desolation.

I was laying groundwork. Setting the scene.

I'd get to the insanity later.

I spent several hours tweaking the images, trying to make them perfect. Then I composed a couple of sentences for the top of the post. I tried to keep my preface simple; I wanted to let the photographs speak for themselves.

Greetings from Spokane! Here are some pictures from my first
week in the city. I came here to document the conditions and,
perhaps, find the truth behind the stories we've all been hearing.
I'll try to post more as events and pictures happen, but my Inter-

net connection is pretty much nonexistent (I had to sneak this
post out of the city, passing it hand to hand across the border).

I added the "hand to hand" thing to take heat off of Danny, in
case this post ever caught the attention of the authorities.

After I finished the preface, I read it over a couple of times,
trying to imagine the impression it would make. I found it lack-
ing. It felt cold, clinical. There was no emotion, no hint it had
been written by a real human being, someone capable of being
moved by the things on the other side of the camera's viewfinder.
Tentatively, I typed out another line:

It's strange here. It feels like a different world.

I stared at the post for a long time, reading over that sparse
handful of sentences, studying each and every aspect of the photographs. It still felt insufficient somehow, incomplete. *It is incomplete,* I told myself. *There is no end here, no conclusion . . . not
yet.*
But it is a beginning.

Floyd stuck his head into my room just as I was finishing up
my post.

"Come here, man," he said, stifling a yawn. "There's something
I want you to see."

I saved my work and followed him into his room.

At one time, this had been a child's bedroom. There were alter-
nating rows of clowns and balloons peering out from the wallpaper, bright cartoon shapes turned bleak and gray beneath a layer
of dingy smoke residue. Across from Floyd's child-size bed, some
of the clowns had been gouged out of the wall, as if attacked with
a potato peeler. All the balloons remained intact. In the corner, a
black sweatshirt shrouded the shape of a hobbyhorse.

The room smelled of pot and stale sweat.

Floyd was still half asleep. He stopped in the middle of the room and stretched his hands up over his head, letting out a loud yawn.

"What's up?" I asked, and I smiled. "Did you have a bad dream? Do you need me to tuck you back in? Maybe sing you a lullaby?"

Floyd let out a fake laugh. "Fuck, man, you're *funny*," he said. "I didn't realize you were so fucking funny."

He grabbed my elbow and pulled me over to the window. He had his blinds drawn almost all the way to the bottom, and I had to crouch down in order to peer through the gap. "Check it out. Across the street."

The view was the same as I'd seen from my window earlier that morning. The street was covered with snow, and there was absolutely no sign of life. Then I noticed the tracks leading from our front door to the house directly across the street.

"Upstairs window," Floyd said, crouching down at my side.

I focused on the upper story, slowly scanning from one room to the next. All the windows were shuttered save the biggest one, just above the front door. There was movement there, on the other side of the glass. I couldn't be sure, but it looked like somebody pacing back and forth.

"It's Devon," Floyd whispered conspiratorially. "I've seen him over there before, but I've never been able to figure out what he's doing. Sometimes he'll go over there and we won't see him for days." Floyd let out an annoyed grunt. "And when I ask him about it, he won't tell me shit."

I went back to my room and got my camera, then returned to Floyd's side. I raised the camera to the sill and zoomed in on the window across the street.

I hadn't noticed the electric-blue light, dwarfed in that world of startling white snow. But now, magnified inside my camera lens, it became obvious. An eerie blue glow illuminating one side of Devon's face. The light moved across his features as he paced back and forth, striding quickly from one side of the room to the other. Every once in a while, he raised his hands in a gesture of apparent frustration.

I couldn't tell what he was doing. *Did he go over there to vent?* I wondered. *Is he just storming about in an empty room, blowing off steam?*

As he passed in front of the window, Devon paused suddenly and looked our way. There was a strange expression on his face— a look of both fear and annoyance—and for a moment, I thought we'd been caught in the act of spying. But I quickly realized that that was impossible. We were hidden in Floyd's dark room, staring out through a tiny crack in his blinds. There was no way he could see us here, not from that distance.

Then I noticed Devon's lips moving in the faint blue glow.

"Is he alone over there?" I asked. "Have you ever seen anyone else in that house?"

"No," Floyd said, a hint of surprise in his voice. "We're the only people on this entire block."

I started taking pictures, snapping off a long series as Devon abruptly looked back over his shoulder toward the far corner of the room. He once again raised his hands in frustration.

He was still talking. Explaining. Arguing.

"What's he doing?" Floyd asked. "I can't see shit."

I turned away from the window, putting my back against the wall and sliding down to the floor. I handed the camera to Floyd, and he raised it to his eye. After a moment of silence, he lowered the camera and took a step back from the window. There was a shocked look on his face.

"What's going on here, Dean?" he asked, his eyes wide, his voice wavering. "Who's he talking to? Who's he meeting? And why *there,* across the street from our own house?"

And what about that blue light? I recognized that color. It was the same shade I'd seen between the walls of the apartment building on Second Avenue, glowing deep down in the heart of the building. Beneath that horrible disembodied face. The memory of that face—that frantic, pleading eye—set my skin shivering.

"There's only one person who can answer those questions," I said. "And he's waiting for us right across the street."

It took us a couple of minutes to get ready, to throw on our coats and lace up our shoes. I strapped the camera across my chest and led the way, anxious to find answers, to find the link between this place and the apartment building downtown. And Devon. I needed to know what he was doing over there, what his connection was to this whole thing. To the city. To the *face*.

Floyd seemed far less eager. "There's only one set of tracks," he said, pausing in the middle of the snow-covered street. "Whoever he's meeting . . . either they came in another way or they were there before the snow started to fall."

"Only one way to find out," I said, glancing up at the house's now-empty window. "So move your ass."

The front door was unlocked. I tried to keep it quiet as I eased the door open, but the hinges let out a loud, painful groan. I paused before crossing the threshold, listening for Devon up on the second floor, but couldn't hear a thing. There were no arguing voices, no pacing footsteps.

We stepped into the foyer, and I shut the door behind us.

The house had been stripped bare. *The owners must have moved fast,* I thought. From what I'd seen, most of the houses in the area weren't this clean; most showed signs of life forced to an abrupt stop. The owners must have hired moving trucks and fled the city as soon as the weirdness started, back in July or August, before the mad rush of evacuations had forced people to flee with whatever they could fit in their cars. I started sticking my head in through open doorways. I found an empty living room, an empty dining room. The house had nice hardwood floors. It reminded me of the place my father had bought with his third wife, down in southern California.

As I surveyed the empty rooms, Floyd moved deeper into the house. "Dean," he hissed after a handful of seconds. "Come here!" I followed him into a bright yellow kitchen.

"Look," he said, pointing toward a pair of sliding glass doors. He kept his voice low. "There's nothing in the backyard. Not a single footprint."

Floyd was right. There was nothing but pristine white snow out there, stretching across the entire yard. Whoever was here had been here for a while. And they hadn't had time to flee.

Floyd met my eyes, his bottom lip trembling slightly. He pointed up toward the second floor. His expression was easy to read: *They're up there. Waiting.*

And, no doubt, they'd already heard us coming.

We returned to the foyer, and I nodded up toward the second-floor landing. "You and Devon are friends, right?" I whispered. "Call up to him. Let him know we aren't a threat."

Floyd nodded, his eyes still wide. "Devon?" he called. "You up there, man? What are you doing?"

We both held our breath, waiting for a reply. After a half minute of silence, I gestured toward the stairs. Floyd shook his head and backed away, making me take the lead.

The upstairs hallway was dark. Most of the connecting doors stood wide open, but the windows in each of the rooms had been boarded shut, blocking out the snow-white light. After my eyes adjusted to the darkness, I poked my head into a couple of rooms, finding them just as empty as the rooms downstairs.

Floyd put his hand on my shoulder and pointed to a door up ahead. It was the only closed door on the entire floor, and its position put it even with the downstairs entrance. It was the room we'd been watching from across the street. Devon's room.

Floyd stepped up to the door and knocked. "Devon?" he called. "Seriously, man, what *is* this shit? What's going on?" There was no reply. As the silence started to stretch, I watched the expression on Floyd's face morph from tentative discomfort all the way to annoyance. "Fuck, man, we know you're—" Floyd's voice was cut short as he threw the door open, revealing yet another empty room.

The unshuttered window gave entry to a blinding white light, and I was left momentarily dazzled, trying to blink away the starbursts in my eyes. Floyd stepped into the room, looked left, then right, and immediately stormed out again. I could hear him rushing from room to room along the upstairs hallway, looking for Devon.

For my part, I turned slowly just inside the door, studying the walls, trying to figure out where that eerie blue light had come from. There weren't any visible problems with the room—no ragged holes punched into the walls, no disembodied limbs—but that didn't stop my heart from thumping hard inside my chest. I turned to my right and ran trembling fingers along the nearest wall. I didn't know what I was feeling for. Something horrible. Something I couldn't see.

"He's not up here," Floyd said, rushing back into the room. "There's nobody up here."

I stepped over to the window and stared out at the bright afternoon. "Is there an attic or a cellar?" I asked. My hands were still shaking with adrenaline, but I could feel my heartbeat starting to slow. "Is there someplace they could hide? I mean, they have to be here, right? We saw Devon just a couple of minutes ago. And that blue glow . . ."

"Hey, hey, *hey*!" Floyd exclaimed, a hint of surprise in his voice. "Did you see this?"

I turned away from the window and found him moving toward the far side of the room. There was something tucked away in the corner, something I hadn't noticed earlier: a small metal console, about the size of a shoe box.

"It's a radio," Floyd said, settling down in front of the box. He hit a switch, and it hummed to life. A bright digital display illuminated the front panel, and static crackled from its speaker. "Some type of CB radio. Battery-powered. And that's not all." Floyd reached behind the radio and picked up a pair of binoculars. There was a worried look on his face as he handed them over; his eyes kept darting back and forth between my face and the sleek black piece of equipment. He understood exactly what the binoculars and radio meant.

I took the binoculars back over to the window and raised them

136

to my eyes. I scanned across the front of the house, spending brief seconds on each of the upstairs windows before finally panning down to the open living-room blinds. I adjusted the focus, zooming in on the sofa. It was a good pair of binoculars. Staring through those high-quality lenses, I could make out the stains in the sofa's upholstery. Hell, I could count the number of crumbs trapped between its cushions.

I spent two nights on that couch! I thought, letting out a frustrated grunt. Somebody could have been watching me the entire time.

I lowered the glasses and returned to Floyd's side, giving him a faint head shake as I crouched down on my heels. He took the binoculars from my hand and set them back where he'd found them.

"I thought radios didn't work here," I said, nodding toward the console. "I thought the military was jamming all of the channels."

"Yeah, but I wouldn't be surprised if they were keeping some frequencies open so they could communicate with each other." He frowned. "But they'd be monitoring those lines, keeping it all military all the time."

"Do you think this is military business, then?" I asked, pointing to the radio.

"Devon? *Military*?" Floyd grunted in disbelief. "No way! I just can't believe that."

"Then who?" I asked. "Who was he talking to?"

Floyd shrugged and leaned forward, studying the radio more closely. There was a large "transmit" button on the front of the console, and the frequency was set to double zero. Floyd leaned over the top of the box and began running his hands along its back side. "Wait a second," he muttered beneath his breath. "What do we have here?" He got up into a crouch and started moving his hands across the wall behind the console. "There's a wire here, coming out of the radio."

"An antenna?"

Floyd shook his head, more interested in following the line than answering my question.

I got up off my heels. I could see the wire now, a thin white line pressed into the angle between floor and wall. Once he got to the door, Floyd stood up straight, following the wire as it continued up along the outside of the door frame. The thin white line touched the ceiling, then continued down the length of the hallway, back the way we'd come.

"It's held in place with staples," he said. "We've got to follow it, find out where it goes."

"Hold on a second," I said, turning back toward the room. "We left the radio—"

I halted, shocked motionless before I could take a single step back into the room. The console was still lit, illuminated by the sharp digits glowing bright on its face. Double zeros, drawn out in glowing blue lines.

The light was bright enough to bathe the entire room in eerie electric blue.

I groaned, suddenly feeling very, very stupid.

It's nothing but coincidence, I chastised myself. *The glow in the apartment building, this room . . . it's just a fucking color.*

I shut off the radio and followed Floyd out of the room.

Floyd had a tiny flashlight on his key ring. He focused its narrow beam on the wire, tucked up against the ceiling, and started following it down the length of the hallway.

"Tell me about Devon," I said as we followed the tiny white line. "I've barely seen him. It seems like he's gone all the time."

"Yeah, he hasn't been around much. Not since you got here." We reached the stairway, and Floyd traced the wire back down the wall, where it disappeared over the edge of the landing. "He's always been a bit of a flake, but . . ." He stopped in his tracks and turned back toward me, a perplexed look appearing on his face. "Actually, he asked about you last night, asked about your photography. He wanted to know what you were planning to do with all of your pictures."

Uneasy gooseflesh prickled up along my back. *My pictures.* Was that it? Was this all about me?

"What did you tell him?"

"Nothing. I told him the truth: I have no idea what you're doing." Floyd paused for a moment, his face contorting as he tried to piece it all together. "What's going on, Dean? Why's he spying on us? And who's he talking to on that radio?" He held out his hands, then looked left and right, a gesture that encompassed the entire house. Then his voice dropped down to a whisper: "And where'd he go?"

"I don't know. I'm new here, remember?"

Floyd stared at me for a couple of seconds. His eyes were cold and accusing, like he didn't quite believe me.

"Really, Floyd," I assured him. "I'm as lost as you are."

Finally, after a couple more seconds, he nodded, relenting. Then he turned and started down to the foyer.

The wire crossed over the side of the landing and proceeded down the wall, continuing to a doorway recessed beneath the stairs. The wire disappeared inside, squeezing between door and door frame.

Floyd nodded me forward, once again making me take the lead. His eyes were wide, and they kept darting back and forth between me and the door. His nerves were contagious. I paused with my hand on the doorknob, suddenly paralyzed by fear and doubt.

Is Devon waiting for us? I wondered. *Does he have a weapon?*

Or is there something worse in there? The thought made my blood pump cold inside my chest. *Something* not *Devon. Or just part of Devon. An arm or a face, jutting out from a broom closet wall.*

I cast the image aside and pulled the door open, releasing a gust of cold air that buffeted my face, making my eyes water. On the other side of the door there was a stairway leading down to a cellar. Only a couple of rough-hewn steps were visible in the dark, and the smell of damp earth gusted up from below.

"*Fuck,*" Floyd grunted. "Are we really going down there?"

"That depends. Do you want answers?"

Floyd let out another grunt. "I don't know. I'm getting pretty good at living with mystery."

"C'mon," I prodded. "Shine your light on the steps."

Floyd's flashlight was tiny, and it barely scratched the thick veil of darkness. I took the stairs one step at a time, pausing to feel ahead with the tips of my toes. Our footsteps did not echo in the dark; every sound was absorbed and consumed inside a heavy, damp silence. I paused when we hit the concrete floor and fumbled my camera from around my neck. I worked the buttons from memory, turning on the LCD display and scrolling back to one of the pictures of Devon inside the house's snow-shrouded window. It was a bright picture, and it lit the display like a fluorescent panel. I turned the camera around and used it to illuminate our surroundings.

The cellar was only partially finished. The walls and floor on the near side of the room were smooth stretches of dingy gray concrete, and the ceiling overhead was an exposed grid of joists. Three-quarters of the way across the room, the concrete gave way to damp earth, breaking off in a ragged arc that surrounded a hole in the far wall. The hole was a gaping dark void—about five feet around—and it absorbed the light from my camera, swallowing every trace like a giant hungry mouth.

"A tunnel," Floyd whispered in surprised wonder. "A motherfucking tunnel!" I heard his jacket rustle as he sat down at the base of the stairs.

The dirt floor slanted down into the tunnel's mouth. I panned the light across its width, finally noticing the thin white wire. It entered the tunnel halfway up its wall.

"Where's the dirt?" Floyd asked. His voice remained a thin, breathless whisper. "The cellar's empty. Where'd they put the dirt?"

I panned the camera around the room. Floyd was right: there were no mounds of displaced dirt, no equipment, nothing at all to support the logistics of such a massive project. "I guess it's on the other side," I said, taking a step toward the tunnel's mouth.

Floyd was at my side in a matter of seconds, grabbing my elbow before I could even reach the damp earth. "You're not serious," he hissed, still keeping his voice low. "We can't go in there. We have no idea what might be waiting."

"Devon went this way," I said. "He had to. There was nowhere else he could go! How dangerous could it be?"

"He could be working with anyone, Dean. And if he saw us, if he knows we're following . . ." I heard him choke down a nervous swallow. "And that's just the human threat. You've heard all of the stories. You *know* what could be waiting for us in there."

He was right. I clenched my hand around the camera and felt the dull pain of my wounds ratchet into a white-hot bolt of fire. After I loosened my grip, the pain of my wounds continued, radiating all the way up the length of my forearm. *The dogs had a tunnel just like this,* I reminded myself. *What if they're in there, waiting?*

"Just a little ways," I said. "Just to see where the wire goes."

Floyd's hand remained on my elbow, an unyielding vise, holding me in place.

"Don't you want to know what Devon's doing?" I pleaded. "Don't you want to know who he's working with and why they're watching us?" After a moment of silence, I let my voice drop down into a whisper: "C'mon, Floyd. He was asking about me!"

Finally, Floyd's grip loosened on my arm. "Just a little ways," he whispered. "Just in and out."

I nodded and started forward.

I tried to take pictures inside the tunnel, but the camera refused to focus in the dark and its flashes illuminated nothing but dirt—just dirt and more dirt, proceeding into the distance. I tried to take a candid shot of Floyd in the tunnel behind me, but he wouldn't cooperate; he just pushed me forward with a frustrated growl.

The tunnel slanted down. Its walls were marked with long regular grooves that looked too precise to be the work of unaided hands. *Some type of earthmoving machine,* I thought. *Or a finishing tool, something to even out the dirt.* The thin white wire was embedded in one of these grooves, about shoulder-high in the right-hand wall.

"Do you know what Devon used to do?" I asked, trying to push aside the claustrophobic silence. "Before the city went to hell?"

"I . . . I don't know," Floyd said. His voice was hesitant, shaky, torn between anger and fear. "Mac says he saw him working at a Jiffy Lube once, before all of this started, but Devon never says . . ." Floyd trailed off, suddenly lost in thought. "Wait a minute! Do you think he could be involved in this somehow? I mean, *really* involved? Do you think he helped get it started, working for the military, or terrorists, or something like that?" He paused abruptly, and when he continued, that brief spark of excitement was gone from his voice. Now there was nothing but breathless terror. "Or maybe he didn't even exist back before all of this started. Maybe——"

"Get a grip, Floyd," I said. "You're starting to sound crazy." I swung the light forward, indicating the wire. "Let's just follow the line and find out where it goes."

Floyd grunted at my abrupt dismissal, but he didn't complain, following me wordlessly into the continuing dark.

After a couple of hundred yards, the walls of the tunnel fell away, opening into a circular room about ten feet wide. A chill broke over my flesh as soon as we entered; it felt at least ten degrees colder inside this small space. The ceiling remained low, and we had to stay hunched over to keep from hitting our heads.

I slowly panned the camera from left to right, spilling light across the dirt floor. There were tunnels reaching out in every direction, like spokes sprouting from a circular hub.

"What the hell is going on?" Floyd whispered, moving up to my side. "Who could have done this?"

"I don't know," I said. "I wouldn't even think it was possible." I moved to the mouth of the nearest tunnel. Its dimensions seemed to match the earlier passage: about five feet around, with a flattened floor. A trickle of wind blew in from the darkness. It smelled of autumn leaves and fresh clean snow. "There are no supports on the walls or ceiling, nothing to prevent a collapse." I drew my finger through the damp earth at my side, watching as it spilled to the floor. "Nobody would do it this way. It's too dangerous. Damn near suicide."

I turned and found Floyd perched on his knees in the middle of the room, his eyes pointed down at the floor. It was a strange position, and for a moment I thought I'd caught him in midprayer. *Or maybe he's fainting,* I thought. *Maybe this is all just too much for him and he's ready to topple face-first into the dirt.* Then he raised his hand and beckoned me over. He had his little flashlight out, and he was shining it down at a box embedded in the middle of the floor.

The box was constructed from matte-black industrial-grade plastic. It had eight thin white wires sprouting from its squat body—two on each side—and a corresponding row of pinpoint LEDs glowed on its top. I turned and raised my camera, following a wire across the floor and into one of the gaping maws.

"It's a junction box," Floyd said. "It links wires from all of these tunnels."

"A network?"

"A secret underground network," Floyd said, glancing up at the dirt above our heads. "And I mean that in both a literal and figurative sense."

After a moment of silence—both of us lost in thought—I stood up and started taking pictures of the box. "For Charlie," I muttered when Floyd glanced up. "He knows about this type of shit, right? He might be able to tell us something." The light from Floyd's flashlight helped me focus on the box. I got a couple of midrange shots, then cranked the lens down into macro mode to catch the finer details.

When I was done, I settled back into a crouch and started to flip through the pictures on the LCD screen. The pictures looked good. The focus was sharp, especially on the macro shots, and I could make out a product number on the box's bottom edge: PDL-0001A.

As the seconds stretched into minutes, Floyd started to fidget at my side. He stood up and paced the length of the room a couple of times, then moved over to the mouth of one of the tunnels. He pointed his flashlight down the tunnel's length, but its meager light did nothing to illuminate that inky-black space.

When I finished checking out my shots, I glanced up and saw his outline in the dark. Its edges were barely visible, gradients of gray in a sea of black. It was a beautiful scene: Floyd standing at the mouth of the tunnel, staring into its deepest, darkest heart. I raised the camera and took a couple of pictures. The strobe flash shattered the darkness, replacing black with omnipresent earthy brown. And in those brief instances, Floyd's bright clothing stood out like a neon sign, a flare of color in an otherwise drab world.

Suddenly, Floyd let out a startled gasp and stumbled back from the opening. The gasp was a panicked, frantic sound, a loud *hisssssssss*, like the sound of gas leaking from a pressurized tank.

He dropped his flashlight, plunging the chamber into complete and total darkness.

I fumbled with the camera, turning it back around and frantically working the buttons with my uninjured hand. By the time I had it lit, Floyd was at my side, his hand gripping my arm. "Did you see him?" he whispered, his face pressed up against my ear. "Down the tunnel? In the flash?"

"I didn't see a thing," I said. "What is it? What did you see?"

"It can't be," he whispered. "Those eyes, those eyes . . . like they were underwater, like they've been underwater for a year. Since . . . since . . ." Then a deep shiver ratcheted through his bones, stealing his voice.

And I could see his fear. All of it. It was in his eyes, the scathing, terrified depths of the thing, that primal, bestial terror. He watched the tunnel for a couple more seconds, then abruptly turned my way, fixing me with that same unbreakable stare.

"Let's go. Let's go *right now*!"

He pulled me to my feet, not waiting for an answer, and plunged us into the nearest tunnel.

09.1

Photograph. October 20, 10:50 P.M. Naked flesh:

Abstract blur of Caucasian skin. Gold candlelight on open denim. The barest shape of an erection, jutting out of indigo blue. And stretched lips.

It is a simple image. All blurred colors, with no sharp lines. Too abstract to be pornography. Too explicit to be art.

09.2

At first, I thought we were lost. I thought Floyd had pulled us into the wrong tunnel.

There was just dirt around us—damp, featureless dirt. Nothing to distinguish one tunnel from another, nothing to recognize, to cling to in the dark. *We've come too far,* I told myself. *We should be in the cellar by now!*

I imagined us wandering, lost, through these tunnels.

The camera battery would die soon. Without its light, the darkness and dirt would swallow us whole. And then we'd be really and truly lost. We'd be buried alive.

Using our hands. Stumbling blind. Moving deeper and deeper underground.

And what would that do to Floyd? I wondered, peering into the darkness ahead. He was already freaking out. Much more of this and he'd be a complete nutjob, panicked and hyperventilating.

Finally, without warning, we reached the cellar. Floyd let out a loud sigh of relief, breath hitching in his throat. Then he pulled me from the mouth of the tunnel, out onto the concrete floor. When I paused, lifting the camera to view the empty room once again, Floyd continued on without me, dropping my arm and darting ahead into the gloom. His feet made a terrible racket as he stumbled his way up the dimly lit steps.

The door banged open above me, letting light into the cellar. After the darkness, that dim gray rectangle burned like a super-nova at the top of the stairs.

When I reached the foyer, I found Floyd sitting with his back against the front door. He was digging through his pockets. After a couple of seconds, he pulled out a pill bottle and spilled a cou-ple of oxycodones onto his shaking palm. He bolted them down and closed his eyes, his entire body falling slack with relief.

"What did you see?" I asked. When he didn't respond, I tried again: "How about we talk about it?"

"How 'bout we shut the fuck up?" Floyd replied, his anxiety rushing out in an exhausted gasp. "How 'bout we just . . . *shut the fuck up?*"

He remained still for a couple of seconds. Then he hugged him-self, rubbing at his arms like he was trying to get warm. "I was seeing things," he said. "I just let my imagination get the best of me."

"Then tell me what it was," I prodded.

"Jesus fucking Christ, Dean," he growled. His eyes popped open, and he fixed me with an angry glare. "This isn't something I talk about, okay? So shut the fuck up! There ain't going to be a tender moment here . . . and no fucking group hug!"

He pushed himself up off the floor and threw the door open, storming out in an angry huff. After a couple of seconds, I fol-lowed, tracing his path back through the snow.

As soon as I entered the house, I heard Floyd's bedroom door slam shut up on the second floor. I thought about following him up but decided not to press my luck. He'd taken his pills. He'd be calmer soon. If he wanted to talk, he'd talk.

"What was that?" Charlie asked, emerging from the kitchen. "It sounded like a freight train running through the house."

"It's nothing," I said. "Just Floyd. I think I pissed him off."

Charlie nodded dismissively, then turned back toward the kitchen. He paused at the threshold and looked back over his shoulder. "If you want to do your forum post," he said, "you should get me your computer soon. I don't know when Taylor's friend's going to show up."

I grunted my assent, then went upstairs to grab my notebook computer. I paused briefly in the hallway outside Floyd's door. I could hear him pacing back and forth inside his room. Whatever he'd seen down there in the tunnels, he hadn't escaped it yet. It was still with him, chasing him back and forth, back and forth.

When I got back to the kitchen, Charlie popped open my computer and set it on the table next to his own. He immediately began shuttling through my file system, popping from window to window with uncanny agility. It was too fast for me to follow; his hands were a blur, careening back and forth atop the keyboard. After a couple of minutes, he made an encouraging sound and started typing code into his own machine.

I let him work, turning my attention to the camera.

The camera was getting dirty. Before coming to the city, I'd treated my Canon with great care. It was my prized possession, and I kept it clean, in pristine shape. In the last couple of days, however, I'd let all of that slide. Now I was dismayed to find dings and scratches all along its matte-black body. Not to mention the mud and the layer of grime where I'd been touching it with my dirty hands. I used the hem of my shirt to wipe away most of the mud, then removed the lens cap and turned the camera up toward the light. I could see specks of dirt all across the green-tinted lens, countless dots of black, marring my precision optics. I let out a deep sigh and replaced the lens cap. There was no way I was going to try to clean my good glass with a dirty shirt. I had a cleaning kit upstairs. I'd give it a good working over tonight, before I went to bed.

After I finished inspecting the camera, I turned on the viewscreen and flipped back through the pictures I'd taken in the tunnel. Most of them were worthless. They were blurred, out of focus, or showed nothing but deep brown dirt. The pictures of the junction box, while technically fine, were incredibly boring;

they were nothing but industrial detail with absolutely no hint of mystery or art. And the pictures of Floyd in the hub were too dark, his pale face floating in a sea of black, staring off into even more black. He could have been standing in any dark room, cave, or midnight forest.

I zoomed in on the last couple of shots, trying to figure out what he'd seen in those brief camera flashes, but the pictures showed nothing new—just his face, contorted in sudden horror.

I shook my head and scrolled back to a picture of the junction box. "Do you know what this is?" I asked Charlie, holding up the camera for him to see.

Charlie glanced up from his notebook. His eyes swam for a couple of seconds—out of focus, as if he'd just surfaced from a dream—before he finally managed to lock in on the camera. He took it from my hand and studied the image. "It's a networking hub." He found the navigation buttons and began zooming in on different parts of the picture. "I don't recognize the product number. PDL-0001A—I'm not sure what company that would be. It certainly doesn't look like a consumer model."

"What does it do?" I asked. "What would somebody use it for?"

Charlie shrugged. "Standard stuff. Connecting computers in a network." He held up the camera and pointed at the image. "Those wires are heavy-duty coax, so this setup could potentially cover quite a bit of ground. And the LEDs on top? Each indicates a live connection—a computer, another hub, a printer—so there are at least eight nodes on this network. Possibly more if they've chained together additional hubs."

"Would it work for audio? Voice traffic?"

"Sure. You could send pretty much anything down this type of line. As long as it's digitized."

I nodded. I'd already guessed at most of these answers; it was all pretty standard stuff. It was this next bit I really wanted to know: "Let's say you were able to get your hands on one of these lines, in the middle of a network. Would you be able to listen in? Would you be able to hear what's going down the wire?"

Charlie paused, a concerned look on his face. "Yeah. At least theoretically, you'd be able to sniff out all of the information flowing over the network. You might not be able to understand it if it's encrypted, but you'd be able to get it."

I nodded and smiled.

"What is this, Dean?" Charlie asked, moving uncomfortably in his seat. "Is this part of the military's setup here in the city? Did you take this picture at the courthouse?"

For a moment, I was tempted to tell him the truth. I was tempted to tell him all about Devon's radio, and the tunnels, and the network hidden beneath the city. But finally I decided against it. He had enough to worry about. Besides, I wanted Taylor to hear it first. When it came to this house, and the people in it, she was in charge. She would know what to do.

"It's nothing to worry about," I lied, forcing a smile onto my lips. "There's abandoned computer shit all over the city. I was just wondering what it might be worth back home."

Charlie managed a surprised flurry of blinks. Then he offered up a sly smile. "Hell, if that's your scam, don't waste your time with *this* junk." He held up the camera, indicating the junction box on its screen. "After I finish up with your forum post, I'll point you toward the real moneymakers . . . for a small cut of the profit, of course." He let out a loud laugh, then turned back toward his computer.

There was a wide, boyish grin on his face as he got back to work. It was good to see him smile. For a time, at least, he actually looked his age.

Taylor and Danny showed up a little after sunset, carrying a cardboard box filled with booze. Bottles of Wild Turkey and Bombay Sapphire.

"Some guys in my unit went AWOL for a couple of days,"

Danny explained, flashing a lopsided grin. "I covered for them, and they were so grateful, they brought me back some gifts. I thought I'd share the spoils."

We built a fire in the living room and sat around drinking bourbon and gin out of mismatched glasses. Amanda and Mac joined us, but Charlie stayed in the kitchen, finishing up work on the thumb drive.

"Where's everyone else?" Taylor asked.

"Sabine's with Mama Cass," Amanda said. "I think they're working on something. Some type of project."

"And Floyd's upstairs, brooding," I added. "As for Devon . . ." I just shrugged. For all I knew, the tunnel had swallowed Devon whole.

Or maybe he's standing right across the street, I thought, *watching us from his second-story window. Watching us drink. Taking notes. Planning diabolical plans.*

I stared down at the bourbon in my glass. It glowed gold in the firelight, shining like liquid honey. Those first few sips had hit me hard, heightening the effects of the oxycodone in my blood. I flexed my hand and felt the skin tighten around my wounds. The pain was still there, but distant, a tickle up and down the length of my forearm. Distant, as if I were experiencing a wound on someone else's body.

I glanced up and caught Amanda midsentence: "—so hard. I thought he was dead for sure!"

"Yeah," Danny said. "Fucker's lucky to be alive. He fell three stories and walked away with nothing but a bad bruise and a sprained foot." Danny paused, and a thoughtful look came across his face. "Of course, he hasn't said anything yet, and we can't figure out what happened. He's in some type of . . . waking coma. The medics have to keep him sedated all the time; otherwise he tries to get up and walk away. It's like that's the only thing he knows how to do anymore. Walk. Like that's the only thing left in his head."

I shivered, remembering how it had looked: the soldier plummeting from the hospital window, hitting the ground hard, then getting up and lurching away.

"They aren't planning any more expeditions into the hospital," Danny said, shaking his head. "Everyone's frustrated. We aren't getting anywhere, running into walls and cliff faces everywhere we turn. And we have no idea what to do next." After a moment of thoughtful silence, he raised his glass and smiled. "Let's drink to the military—science and religion, but with guns!"

Amanda laughed. "Hear, hear!" she said, raising her glass.

I took a small sip from my drink. I was already feeling tipsy, and if I wanted to stay conscious, I knew I'd have to take it easy.

Taylor scooted over to my side and clinked her glass against mine. She smiled at me. It was a warm smile, but there was a hint of a question in her steepled brow. "So tell me," she said, keeping her voice low. "What happened with Floyd? Why's he brooding?"

Before answering her question, I cast a quick glance around the room. Amanda, Mac, and Danny had moved closer to the fireplace; they were warming their hands and laughing, their voices rich and loud in the first flush of intoxication. Charlie was still in the kitchen. For the moment, Taylor and I had a certain amount of privacy. We'd found our own little world here, seated at the foot of the sofa.

"We followed Devon across the street," I said, glancing over toward the living-room window. Right now, the window was nothing but a dark square blacked out by the night, but I remembered the view from across the street. Standing at his perch, Devon would have a clear view of our conversation. "He's been spying on us, spying on the house. With binoculars." I didn't mention the radio. "But that's not what bothered Floyd . . . We found something over there, under the house. Tunnels."

Taylor nodded. There was concern on her face but no surprise. She skated right over the part about Devon's spying, making me think she already knew, or at least suspected. "What did Floyd see?" she asked instead. "What did he see down there?"

The question caught me off guard. I'd been expecting questions, but nothing that direct. "I don't know," I said when I once again found my voice. "He wouldn't tell me."

She read the confusion on my face and patted me on the forearm. "That's just what happens," she said. "That's what the city does. To each of us."

She nodded toward my drink and smiled coyly. "Now drink up. Tomorrow we can worry. Tomorrow we can plan. Tonight . . ." Her smile grew, and she once again clinked her glass against mine. "Tonight we have booze."

"Come on, Dean. Let's go upstairs." Her voice was a hushed whisper against my ear. An audible smile. "We should be together. The three of us."

Taylor smiled and ran the back of her fingers across my cheek. I pulled away, laughing. I could feel hot blood rushing through my flesh. I was drunk, fucked up, and the whole situation seemed unreal.

Danny and Taylor each grabbed an arm and helped me to my feet. The room swayed for a moment, and then we headed for the stairs.

"You up for this?" Taylor whispered in my ear.

"Yeah," I said with a surprised laugh. "I guess I am."

We staggered into Taylor's room, and my head spun in the darkness. Then Taylor struck a match and started lighting candles. There were a half dozen total, and she laughed as she stumbled about the room, from candle to candle, trying to keep the match lit.

Danny put his hand on my shoulder, and I turned to meet his grinning face. "You've never done anything like this before, have you?" he asked.

I shook my head. "No. No. Never fooled around with any guys. I never had the inclination. No offense," I added lamely.

"Well, it's just like with girls," he assured me.

"Only manlier," Taylor said.

"Only *better*!" Danny corrected.

This struck me as extremely funny, and I started to giggle. I should have been nervous, I guess, given the situation and my white-bread upbringing, but I wasn't feeling it. I wasn't feeling much of anything. I was trapped inside an envelope of perfect, comfortable warmth, and nothing bad could reach me here. The feeling only seemed to grow as Taylor took my hand and pulled me down onto the bed.

Taylor propped herself up on one elbow and leaned out over my body. She used her free hand to stroke my face, tracing my unshaven jawline before moving up to my ear. Her touch was soft and tentative, but the act itself—her body over mine, the feel of her breath against my cheek—seemed incredibly intimate. My body responded to her touch, desire and need erupting like a bloom of heat inside my muscles. There was a dreamy look on Taylor's face, and I reached out to pull her close, but she caught my hands and pushed them back down, moving to lift the sweatshirt off my chest.

The air was cold. Her hand was colder still as she moved it up and down my naked flesh.

There was a sudden pressure against my crotch, and I tensed in surprise. I looked up and found Danny sitting at the foot of the bed, his hand kneading the flesh beneath my jeans.

"Relax," he said.

I leaned back and watched Taylor's face as Danny unbuttoned my pants. I was surprised at the intensity of her gaze; she looked absolutely spellbound—transfixed—as she watched Danny tease my cock free. *Lust.* It was lust in her eyes. *She wants me.* Immediately, my cock pulsed rock hard, even before Danny wrapped his hand around its shaft.

"Nice," he muttered. Then my entire cock was engulfed in his hot mouth.

I groaned loudly, shutting my eyes at the intensity of the sensation.

Danny's blowjob was like nothing I'd ever had before. The

girls I'd been with had all been tentative and gentle, like they were afraid they'd break my cock if they worked it too hard. Danny knew better. I put my hands on the back of his head and started to thrust in and out. He took it without complaint.

I heard a loud, mechanical *click* and opened my eyes. Taylor was kneeling beside me with my camera pressed up against her face. She was shooting pictures down the length of my body. I let out a surprised, breathless laugh, then reached up and grabbed her breast. I could feel an erect nipple through her shirt; I could feel her heart beating wildly inside her chest.

At my touch, she let out a surprised gasp and dropped the camera to the bed. Her hands darted up and immediately covered her face.

Before I could pull my hand back, she was pushing me away. She kept one hand on her face, hiding her eyes and nose and mouth, and grabbed my wrist with the other. Her grip was strong as she pushed my hand back down to the bed.

Right then, Danny's mouth went into overdrive, tightening and speeding up. My legs tensed involuntarily, and I let out a low groan. After a couple more seconds, the friction of his tongue pushed me into climax, and my rigid body fell limp.

When I recovered enough to open my eyes, I found Taylor watching me carefully. Her hands were back down in her lap, gripping the hem of her shirt. Her complexion looked ashen in the candlelight; the smile she gave me looked forced and a little bit grave.

"You really needed that, didn't you?" Danny said, wiping his hand across his mouth. "I could feel it."

Taylor smiled down at me and nodded, as if in agreement. Then she reached out and grabbed my hand. I could feel her body quivering as her fingers gripped me tight.

I ended up giving Danny a handjob while Taylor watched. After what he'd done for me, I figured it was the least I could do.

His cock felt odd in my hand. He was thicker than me and un-circumcised. And his scrotum was smooth and hairless.

He let out a loud growl as he came. Then he collapsed back against the bed and muttered a single breathless laugh. It was an absurd sound, without meaning or reason. He reached over the side of the bed and lifted a bottle of Wild Turkey into view.

The three of us lay in silence for a while, passing the bottle back and forth. I took deep swallows. Whatever clarity I'd had during the adrenaline-sharp sex, it quickly began to fade.

I was warm. I shut my eyes every time the room began to swim.

I opened my eyes and found Danny and Taylor huddled together at the door. Danny had his boots in one hand and the bottle of Wild Turkey in the other. When he saw my eyes flicker open, he flashed me a smile and a quick nod. Then he gave Taylor a peck on the cheek and disappeared into the dark hallway.

I closed my eyes again.

Later.

The room was dark, and I could feel Taylor moving beside me. Tentative fingers brushed against my arm.

"I'm sorry," she said, her mouth a couple of inches behind my ear. She was nothing but a voice in the darkness, floating, disem-bodied. "I should have told you. I just . . . sometimes—most times, really—I can't be touched. I just . . . can't abide it." Her voice was breathy, tripping over the emotion in her throat. "But I didn't want that to come between us. I didn't want to scare you away."

I should have said something. Right then. Right there. I should have reassured her. *It doesn't matter.* Or: *Together we'll figure it out.* Or maybe: *I really don't give a shit if we're touching or not. I'd be happy just standing ten feet away from you.* But I couldn't man-age it. I couldn't say a thing.

I grunted incoherently and fell back asleep.

10.1

Video clip. October 21, 08:15 A.M. Dead end:

The video starts midsprint, the entire screen jittering as the camera operator runs forward. Judging
by the quality of the clip, the camera is a fairly
cheap consumer model—strictly low-def. The color is
muted and washed out. The audio is inconsistent,
distorting in the upper registers.

The first couple of seconds take place outdoors, at
the edge of a field. The ground is covered in snow,
and the trees—swinging into view as the camera
sways back and forth—are wreathed in a thin layer
of frost.

The camera steadies long enough to show a hunched
figure disappearing through an opening in the side
of a hill. The opening is a rough mouth dug into the
dirt, and the figure has to bend down to make it
through. The camera follows in pursuit, heading
toward the hole.

The volume is cranked up loud, and the operator's breath rasps like a steam engine. Footfalls crunch through the thin layer of snow.

The camera swings to the side, revealing a disheveled young man, also in pursuit. This man pulls to a stop at the dark opening, directly in front of the camera. He lights a flashlight, then darts inside.

THE MAN'S VOICE—A DEAFENING, FRANTIC HISS: Mac!

The video is swallowed in darkness. There is an occasional blinding burst of light as the flashlight beam swings into view, but it does little to illuminate the scene. The squelch of muddy footsteps and the loud rasp of breath drown out all other sound.

THE MAN'S VOICE AGAIN: Mac!

The video jolts suddenly, and the tape hitches, sending up a single line of static. There is an inaudible curse from behind the camera, and this is greeted with a loud *shhhhh!* For a brief handful of seconds, the camera is relatively still, showing the dark earthen walls as the flashlight pans back and forth.

There are three open tunnels here, leading into the darkness ahead.

THE CAMERA OPERATOR'S VOICE, DEAFENINGLY LOUD: What the fuck is this? . . . (Followed by an unintelligible, breathless rush of words.)

The man with the flashlight sprints into the middle tunnel, and the camera follows. Fifteen seconds

pass, filled with panting breath, loud footsteps,
and momentary bursts of light. Then the man with the
flashlight slows to a stop. The camera pans around
him, revealing another man kneeling at a dead-end
wall. His ear is pressed into the dirt, and his
hands are splayed at his side. Tears streak his
muddy face. His mouth is moving even before he
starts to speak.

THE KNEELING MAN, IN A DISTORTED WHISPER: (Unintelligible) . . . her singing?

All three people freeze like statues, holding their
breath. The camera catches the kneeling man as he
closes his eyes and pushes his face deeper into the
mud.

After a couple of seconds, a bare hint of noise
swells up above the background hiss of videotape and
speaker distortion. It is a melodic, wordless whisper, muffled and muddy, without place or direction.

It is sweet and warbling. And it is a long, long way
away.

10.2

"Dean."

It was a breathy, feminine whisper, hanging in the darkness above me.

"Please, Dean. *Please* wake up."

There was a hand on my shoulder, shaking me gently, trying to pull me up from the depths of sleep. I resisted. I kept my eyes shut and rolled away from the voice, burying my face in the pillow. It was warm there, inside the pillow.

Inside the pillow, there was nothing but heat and sleep and dreams.

"Where is she, asshole? What have you done?"

Mac grabbed the back of my sweatshirt and pulled me off the bed. The sweatshirt ripped at the seams, and I fell to the carpeted floor. My right elbow hit the ground hard, numbing my entire arm.

"What the fuck?" I gasped, pushing the question out through gritted teeth.

He grabbed me by the hair and pulled me across the room, my feet scrambling beneath me as I tried to relieve the pressure on my scalp. He pushed me up against the wall and wrapped his fist around my neck. His thumb dug into my windpipe, making my eyes water; I saw his bearded, frenzied face through a blur of pain. There were tears in his eyes. The muscles in his jaw trembled with seething emotion.

We were alone in the room. Taylor was gone.

"Where is she?" Mac yelled, spraying saliva across my face. *"Where the fuck did she go?"*

"I . . . I don't know," I managed, my voice a thin croak, barely making it past his clenched fist. I thought he meant Taylor. *Did she flee?* I wondered. *Why?* Was it because of our night with Danny? The sex had been dizzying, overwhelming, and I didn't know what to think of it myself. *Or is it because I touched her?*

"Mac! Mac! What the fuck are you doing?" It was Sabine's voice, coming from the hallway.

Without taking his eyes off me, he raised his free hand, waving a crumpled piece of paper toward the door. "She's gone," he growled. "And this little piece of shit's responsible."

"Calm down," Sabine said. "Let him go." Her voice was placating but firm. She moved into my line of sight, pushing her hands up against Mac's chest, trying to get him to relax his grip.

I was quickly losing my vision; the edges of the world contracted inward, like an aperture sliding shut over my eyes.

"I said *let . . . him . . . go!*" Sabine yelled. She threw her body forward, slamming hard into Mac's chest and knocking him backward. My head snapped forward as he lost his grip on my throat.

As soon as he let go, I sucked in a great big gulp of air. The rush of oxygen set my sight spinning. My head felt like an over-inflated balloon, ready to float up toward the ceiling. Then my knees buckled, and I slid down to the floor. As I gasped for breath, Sabine stepped out in front of me, holding her hands out toward Mac.

He kept coming after me, but each time he took a step forward, Sabine pushed him back. His frenzied eyes darted back and forth between us, but he seemed reluctant to turn his anger against Sabine.

"Calm down," she said. Mac took another step forward, and she once again pushed him back. "Calm the fuck down!"

"What's going on?" Floyd asked. I turned and saw him standing in the doorway. He was rubbing his eyes and yawning. "What time is it?"

Sabine gave Mac one last push, and the strength left his legs. He collapsed to a sitting position on the edge of the bed. His shoulders slumped forward into a defeated slouch. "Look after him, Floyd," Sabine said. "Keep him away from Dean. Sit on him if you have to."

Sabine crouched down at my side. She stared into my eyes for a bit, a concerned look on her face. "You still there, Dean? Everything okay?"

I tried to speak, but my voice got caught in my throat. I swallowed, pushing saliva over my freshly damaged larynx, and tried again. "Yeah," I croaked. "But I won't be singing . . . in no choir . . . anytime soon."

I glanced over her shoulder and noticed Charlie standing in the open doorway. His eyes were wide, and he wasn't moving. He looked like a statue, a marble effigy carved into the threshold.

"What the hell was that, Mac?" Sabine growled, turning on her heels. "What the fuck did you think you were doing?"

Mac was sitting like a forlorn lump on the edge of the bed, his eyes pointed down at his stocking feet. Floyd was sitting next to him. There was a piece of paper in Floyd's hand: the crumpled sheet Mac had been waving around. Floyd started to read aloud: "There's something I need to do, someplace I need to be. I know you don't understand. I'm sorry, Amanda."

After he heard Amanda's words, Mac's head shot up, the anger suddenly back in his eyes. "It's all his fault," he said, nodding toward me. "They've been sneaking around. He's been feeding her delusions. Fucking wolves, my ass! He's been telling her all of the things she wants to hear!"

"Amanda's gone?" Sabine asked, in surprise. "When? When did she leave?"

"She was gone when I woke up. At first, I thought she was just getting food or making coffee, but then I saw the note. Her boots and jacket are gone, but the rest of her stuff is still here."

"Maybe it's nothing," Sabine said. "Maybe she just went out for a walk."

A cold, bitter smile appeared on Mac's lips. His eyes remained fixed on my face. "Tell us where she went, Dean. Tell us where you made her go."

His voice was scary calm. If his earlier assault had been an act of thoughtless passion, this new voice . . . this new voice promised cold-blooded, premeditated murder.

"I might know," I croaked, looking away from Mac's angry eyes. "There's a place she wanted to go."

We found her clothing in the park, near the mouth of the tunnel. Each garment was folded and stacked in a neat pile: jacket, sweatshirt, jeans, long underwear, panties, and socks. Her boots stood on either side of the stack like perfectly matched bookends.

As soon as it came into view, Mac darted ahead and knelt down by the pile of clothing. He quickly sorted through the entire stack, carefully lifting and turning each neatly squared garment, as if he were expecting to find Amanda hidden inside some random fold. When he reached the bottom of the pile, he glanced up and stared fixedly at the mouth of the tunnel. There was a line of perfect footprints leading into the darkness.

"No way," Floyd said, taking a startled step back as soon as he saw the dark hole in the side of the hill. "There's no way I'm going into that fucking hole!"

"You don't have to," I said, my voice low, a damaged rumble. "You can stay out here if you like."

Sabine reached out and put a comforting hand on Floyd's shoulder, at the same time flashing me a confused look, surprised at the vehemence of his reaction. Charlie stayed back near the copse of trees, a good dozen feet away.

It was just the five of us.

I'd searched the entire house before we left, but it looked like Taylor had performed another one of her early-morning vanishing acts; she must have left sometime before dawn, as I lay asleep in her bed. *And what was that about?* I wondered. Why was she constantly disappearing without word or explanation? Frankly, it was starting to piss me off. Maybe it was my fault; maybe I'd scared her away. But after our night with Danny—and I blushed briefly at that thought—it felt like she was toying with me, using me to slake her own inscrutable desires, then disappearing as soon as I needed her leadership and support.

She would have been able to keep Mac in check, I told myself. *She would have gotten to the bottom of this.*

Sabine lifted my video camera to her eye and started filming, focusing on Mac as he hovered over the pile of abandoned clothing. She'd grabbed the camera as we were heading out the front door; I wasn't sure why. Did she consider this part of some elaborate art project? Or had she become infected with my compulsion, my need to document and probe the fraying edges of reality?

"She must be freezing," Sabine said, noting the obvious. "She's naked. In the snow."

Mac let out a strangled sob. It was the sound of sudden dawning horror, as if the thought hadn't yet occurred to him. He let Amanda's jeans tumble from his fingers, then abruptly bolted toward the mouth of the tunnel.

"Fuck," I muttered, and started after him. I gestured for Sabine to follow. "C'mon. Before he gets away."

Mac didn't even hesitate when he reached the dark hole, plunging headlong across its threshold. We followed twenty feet back.

This time, I came prepared. I paused at the mouth of the tunnel and pulled my flashlight from my pocket. The beam illuminated a wide swath of muddy earth. Here at the entrance, the floor had been worked into a narrow trough, and I could see the imprint of fist-size paws all along its perimeter. The enclosed space reeked of wet, musty fur, a savage primal musk.

Before the thought of those giant sharp-toothed wolves could root me to the spot, I ducked and started forward. Sabine followed at my heels. I could hear her boots squelching in the mud behind me.

"Mac!" I called. My voice was shaky. I wanted to reach Mac as fast as possible, but that desire couldn't override my fears. There were horrible things living in these tunnels—I knew that—and I could imagine countless eyes popping open at the sound of my voice. Amanda's oddly jointed wolves. Floyd's apparition. Other things—much, much worse.

"Mac!" I called again. My voice didn't echo in the dark.

After a couple of seconds, the walls disappeared on both sides, and I pulled to an abrupt stop. Sabine collided with my back and let out a loud curse as the camcorder made hard contact with her face: *"Motherfucker!"*

"Shhhhhh," I whispered, then swung the flashlight left and right.

The tunnel opened up into three different passageways here, and all three looked exactly the same; they were the same size, had the same rough walls, and displayed the same level of use on their muddy floors. *Which one leads to Devon's house?* I wondered idly. I glanced around, but couldn't see a single wire embedded in the walls.

"What the fuck is this?" Sabine asked, a note of awe in her voice. "Out there, I thought it was just a cave, but . . . *fuck*!"

"Shhhhhh," I prompted again, cocking my ear toward each of the tunnels in turn. I thought I heard a scraping sound—a distant sandpaper scratch—down the middle passageway. I shone my light forward and moved ahead.

Mac was running, I thought. *He was frantic. There's no way we'll catch him.*

I was just about to slow down, to reassess the situation, when Mac's bright clothing resolved in the darkness ahead.

Here the tunnel ended in a wall of dirt, a frozen cascade blocking the entire passageway. Mac was on his knees, digging like a dog; his hands were scrabbling at the cave-in, pulling fistfuls of dirt into the tunnel behind him. He had his ear pressed into the mud, and his eyes were closed.

"Do you hear her?" he asked, his voice a tiny whisper. "Do you hear her singing?"

Sabine and I both fell silent. I held my breath and listened for Amanda's voice.

There was nothing. The only sound I heard was the sound of Mac's hands moving in the dirt.

After a tense handful of seconds, Mac jumped to his feet and headed back into the darkness, pushing us out of the way. "There were branches," he said, his voice filled with terrified urgency, "farther up the tunnel. I've got to get around. *She needs me!*" Then he sprinted back the way we had come.

Sabine and I exchanged a worried look, then followed him into the darkness. He quickly escaped the reach of my flashlight beam. By the time we made it back to the junction, there was no way to figure out which direction he'd gone. On a whim, I chose the right-hand passageway, pulling Sabine along behind me.

This tunnel ended about fifteen feet in. The first time my flashlight beam swept across the cave-in, I thought I saw Mac standing there, his hands pressed up against the dirt. But it was just a momentary illusion. I blinked, and there was nothing there, nothing but dirt and empty space. Sabine and I turned and retraced our steps back to the other tunnel. The left-hand tunnel went about thirty feet in before it, too, ended in a cave-in. Mac wasn't there, either.

"He must have gone out," Sabine said, scanning the dirt with the camcorder. She sounded confused, uncertain. "Maybe he missed the junction in the dark and just kept on running."

I nodded and said "yeah, yeah, yeah," but I already knew that wasn't the case. I knew we wouldn't find him.

I'm not sure where this certainty came from. Maybe it was the flash I saw in the other tunnel, that momentary vision—seeing him standing there at the dead end, his hands up, trying to push his way through the cave-in—but I *knew* that he hadn't missed the turn. I *knew* he hadn't run outside.

No. Mac had found a way *in*.

Sabine and I walked the tunnels several times, but we found absolutely no sign of Mac. He was gone. Charlie and Floyd had been standing at the entrance the entire time, and they assured us that he hadn't made it out.

He was just gone. As far as I could tell, he'd followed Amanda down into the dark.

I failed them. I let them go.

In fact, I don't think I could have handled the situation any worse. Amanda had come to me in the middle of the night—I remembered that now, putting her face to that faceless voice—shaking me, looking for my help, and I'd ignored her. I'd just rolled over and buried my head in the pillow. And now Mac had slipped right through my fingertips.

I could have stopped them, I was sure. I could have saved them. But I didn't.

It was a horrible feeling, this impotence. It seemed like everything I touched turned to shit.

I wanted to bury my hands deep in my pockets and never take them out. I wanted to run away. I wanted to do something to protect the world from my horrible, infectious failure.

We abandoned the search without saying a word. I was so frustrated, I just turned around and walked away.

Sabine, Charlie, and Floyd followed.

11.1

Photograph. October 21, 07:25 P.M. Spray-paint spiders:

Two flashlight beams illuminate a weathered brick
wall. The shutter speed is set a bit too slow, and
there is blurring around the staggered bricks; sharp
lines of mortar have been rendered dull. The bottom
half of a window is visible at the top part of the
frame, and there's a glimpse of sidewalk down at the
bottom. Otherwise, the picture is all faded red
brick punctuated by lines of glossy black paint. And
there is a hole in the center of the frame—a ragged
crater, punched through the wall in some gesture of
extreme violence.

And crawling out of the hole: a swarm of spray-paint
spiders.

It is a vast army of simple shapes, sketched out in
black lines—multijointed legs sprouting out from
squat bodies. They are densest near the hole—where
individual limbs reach out from the shattered
crevice—and become sparser as they near the edges
of the frame.

Only one spray-paint spider has made it all the way
up to the window frame. Its bottom half is sprayed
across brick and wood, and its top half is gone,
vanished through a crack in the dirty glass.

11.2

The sun was blindingly bright after the dark tunnel. It struck diamond flares off the melting snow, dazzling my eyes. There was a smell of electricity in the air, and I could once again taste copper on my tongue; it was the same sensation that had greeted me on my way into the city.

It felt like a different world out here, in the sun, and none of it seemed real. All around me this bright, still city: nothing but plastic and cellophane, a dime-store mask hiding the true face of the world. And it was a dark face, underneath it all, distorted with disease and rot, with eyes closed and mouth wide open, leaking pure midnight ichor.

We walked back to the house in silence. Floyd spent the first couple of minutes shaking an empty pill bottle; then, as we crossed the bridge to North Spokane, he pulled his arm back and launched it out into the river. He moved with a slow, exaggerated grace. His eyes were unfocused, hidden beneath drooping lids.

"What do we do, Dean?" Charlie asked as we rounded the corner to our block. "Amanda and Mac just disappeared . . . into thin air. So what do we do now?" His voice was a quavering whisper. He seemed far less confident—less substantial—without his computer in front of him.

"I don't know," I said. "If you've got any bright ideas, feel free to chime in." I couldn't keep the annoyance out of my voice. This was just about the last thing I wanted to hear: people turning to me for answers.

"Where's Taylor?" Sabine asked. "She'll know. She always knows." And somehow, this seemed a million times worse than Charlie's question.

I shot Sabine a dirty look and headed straight for our front door.

There was water dripping from the eaves when I mounted the porch. The day was getting warmer, and the snow was transforming into slush. Before long, the streets would once again be bare. *No more snowball fights,* I thought, remembering Amanda and Mac playing in the backyard. The memory drove a cold spike through the middle of my stomach.

I continued up to the privacy of my room, shutting the door behind me.

I sat down on the futon mattress and dropped my head into my hands. I felt awful. I'd woken up in a rush of adrenaline—Mac pulling me out of Taylor's bed—and I'd spent the whole morning so far jumping from one long adrenaline spike to another. Now that that ride was over, however, and the chemical rush was gone, a massive wave of sickness came flooding in, and suddenly I felt nauseated, hungover. My head was throbbing. My injured hand was on fire.

And Taylor wasn't there for me, I remembered. The thought popped into my head unbidden, washed ashore on that wave of misery. *She ran away in the middle of the night. She ran away . . . from me.*

I gritted my teeth and lashed out, kicking the back of the folding chair. It skidded into the sewing table on the other side of the room and collapsed in a loud clatter, falling flat like a deflated lung.

I seethed for a full minute, gritting my teeth and clenching my hands. Then I got up and righted the chair.

After I calmed down, I settled into the futon and got a couple of hours of sleep. It was a restless sleep, tainted by pain and nausea. I don't remember my dreams, but I'm sure they were bad. Dark tunnels and singing voices. Expressive eyes peering out from plaster and wood. And Taylor, always Taylor, retreating from my touch.

The light was still bright when I woke up, shining a midafternoon orange against my closed blinds. My head still ached, and my wounded hand felt hot and wet.

I slowly unwrapped my bandages, wincing at the change in pressure against my flesh. The smell hit me even before I was done: a gamy vinegar tang that turned my stomach. I opened the blinds and raised my hand into the light. The whole hand was swollen. There were red tendrils snaking up my forearm, fleeing the gray withered holes—crucifixion holes—one in my palm and two in the back of my hand.

My hand was infected. Badly infected—*mutant wolf*-infected. And I couldn't ignore it any longer.

I needed antibiotics.

There were only two places I could think to go for help: the military, which would almost certainly get me kicked out of the city, if not arrested, or Mama Cass. And really, that wasn't much of a choice. Still, I found myself conflicted. Taylor had made her dislike for Mama Cass perfectly clear.

But she can't be worse than the alternative, I told myself: military scrutiny, expulsion, imprisonment. *Besides, if Weasel's any indication, Taylor's not exactly the best judge of character.*

I left my hand unwrapped, careful with the sensitive flesh as I shrugged into my jacket and tucked it away in my pocket. Then I slung my backpack over my shoulder and fled the room, quickly making my way down the stairs and out the front door.

Sabine called after me from the kitchen: "Dean! Where are you going?" There was surprise and concern in her voice, but it was cut short as I slammed the door shut behind me.

It was about four o'clock when I reached the restaurant, and the sun was almost gone. There were a half dozen people crowded around the entrance and another twenty inside, seated at the mismatched tables. I didn't recognize any of the customers, but some of them must have recognized me . . . and remembered my camera. As soon as I entered, a ripple of whispers spread throughout the crowd, and a large number turned my way, fixing me with wary, suspicious eyes. One woman got up from her seat and started edging back toward a side entrance. Her movements—nervous, with shifty-short glances back and forth—made her look like a tiny bird ready to take flight. I nodded in her direction, and that set her off. She flashed me a startled grimace and ducked out through the door.

I stopped a waiter carrying a pair of ham sandwiches. He was bearded and burly, and his hair was tied back in a greasy ponytail. There was dirt smeared across his forehead, and a splatter of mustard dotted his flannel shirt. The impression as a whole was rather unsanitary. As soon as I got his attention, I asked after Mama Cass.

"What do you want her for?" he asked, gruff and impatient. His eyes roamed about the room as we talked, checking on each table in turn.

"Just tell her there's something I need."

The waiter let out a sly, knowing smile. Apparently, this was a familiar conversation. "Yeah, yeah. I got it, I know . . . there's *always* stuff we need." He delivered his sandwiches, then disappeared into the back room.

Mama Cass stepped through the door a couple of minutes later. She glanced around the room, spotted me, and summoned me back with a wave of her hand.

A burst of steam hit me in the face as soon as I opened the kitchen door, greeting me with the spicy scent of pepper and simmering tomato sauce. It was a good-size kitchen, but it was mostly deserted. The central work space was lit up bright with gas lanterns, but the periphery of the room remained dark and empty. A breeze flowed in through open windows along the back wall, cutting through the steam and spice with a damp, earthy chill.

There were bins of fresh vegetables stacked three deep in front of an unplugged industrial-size refrigerator, and a coffin-size footlocker blocked the rear entrance. The locker stood open, and I could see snow and ice packed around containers of store-bought meat. Mixed in with the ground beef and cuts of chicken and steak, I could see at least a dozen prepackaged Hormel hams. *Hand-smoked, my ass,* I thought. There were three people working back here: the burly waiter, assembling sandwiches at a side table; a heavily tattooed girl, stirring pasta sauce on a camp stove; and a rail-thin old man, sweating over a generator-powered griddle.

Mama Cass—*Sharon,* I corrected myself, remembering her real name—flashed me a bright smile and ushered me into her office. In stark contrast to her employees, she looked clean and sophisticated. *The consummate professional,* I thought. *A perfectly composed, unflappable businesswoman, ready to step from the pits of hell straight into the nearest Fortune 500 boardroom.*

Her office was a small room branching off the kitchen. I imagined it had once been a pantry before she'd taken over, now stripped of shelving and filled with office furniture.

"Well, this is a pleasant surprise," she said, gesturing toward a chair. She sat on the edge of her desk, a couple of feet away. "It's Dean, right? Sabine's friend, the photographer? I was wondering if I'd see you again."

"Yeah, well, things happen, I guess," I said lamely. "I was hoping I could get your help with something. I've got money. I can pay you." I reached for my backpack to show her the color of my money, but she dismissed the gesture with a flip of her hand.

"Don't worry about that now, Dean. Just tell me what you need. We can work out payment later. Okay?" She smiled. It was a warm smile, and if it was part of a mask—a calculated gesture meant to instill confidence and trust—it was a good mask, one she wore well.

"I need some drugs," I said. "I've got an infected wound, and I need something to keep my arm from falling off."

"Show me," she said, pushing herself up off her desk. She made a lifting gesture with her finger, like she was flipping over a rock to study the ground underneath.

I nodded and pulled up my sleeve, revealing the swollen red flesh.

Sharon bent down over my hand and gently turned it toward the light. After a couple of seconds, she produced a pair of reading glasses from her blouse pocket and bent even closer, staring deeply into my palm. Her face crinkled up in concentration. She looked like a fortune-teller trying to make a difficult read.

"How long would it take you to find me some antibiotics?" I asked.

She dropped my hand and leaned back on her heel. There was a slightly amused look on her face. "Are you kidding me? This whole place is just one big rusty nail, crawling with disease. I've got a room full of the stuff over there." She pointed out the door, toward the other side of the kitchen.

I let out a loud sigh, and my stomach suddenly unclenched. Hearing those words . . . it was a huge relief. One less thing to worry about.

"It's a really nasty wound," she said, nodding toward my hand. She kept her eyes on my face even as her head bobbed up and down. "How did it happen?" There was something odd about her voice—too much curiosity, maybe, or just a bit too quiet, too careful. It made it seem like she was trying to pull a fast one on me, trying to trick me into revealing sensitive information.

"I stepped on a rusty nail," I said.

She chuckled and shook her head. Then her hand darted up to my forehead. She moved fast, and I didn't have time to pull away. "You've got a nasty fever, too," she said, resting the back of her hand against my flesh. "If you'd waited any longer, I'd be calling in a chopper. Or digging you a hole."

She stood up and left the room. I could hear her exchanging pleasantries with the kitchen staff as she crossed to the other side of the restaurant.

When she came back, she was holding a canvas bag full of medical supplies. "Amoxicillin," she said, pulling out a pill bottle. "Twice a day for ten days. And if it doesn't start getting better in the next twenty-four hours, come back and I can give you a shot. I'd be surprised, though. The pills should do the trick. I've seen them work on worse."

I nodded and accepted the pill bottle.

"Take one now," she said, fixing me with steady, forceful eyes. She pulled a can of Coke from her bag.

I swallowed one of the pills, chasing it down with a swig of warm soda. She nodded in approval and dug back into her bag.

"When was the last time you had a tetanus shot?" she asked. Her voice was clipped and fast, without a trace of emotion. It sounded like she was giving a perfunctory reading from a very familiar script.

"A couple years ago," I said. Then I smiled. I actually *had* stepped on a rusty nail for that one.

"Then you're fine." She pulled a syringe from her bag and lobbed it into the outgoing mail bin on her desk.

After a moment of thought, she pulled another bottle of pills from her bag and tossed it my way. I grabbed it from the air reflexively and let out a pained *hiss* as my injured hand clenched shut around the hard plastic. I muttered a curse, then turned the bottle in my steepled fingers. The pharmacy label read "Hydrocodone," but the word *Vicodin* was printed underneath in shaky letters. The name of the patient and prescribing doctor had been gouged out of the paper label. "For the pain," Sharon said with a smile. "It must be screaming like a bitch right about now."

My eyes darted from the pill bottle back up to her face. She was still smiling, a sly understanding smile. *This is how it happens,* I told myself. *This is where I become indebted to her. It's one thing to accept antibiotics. Narcotics, on the other hand . . . that's a completely different beast.*

If I accept these pills, I become complicit.

I moved to return the bottle but stopped with my hand only partly extended. Sharon raised her palm and shook her head, warding me back like a traffic cop. "Don't worry about it, Dean. Really, it's nothing. Your hand is injured. It's messed up pretty bad. I'd feel awful if I didn't help."

"What do you want?" I asked, letting out an exhausted sigh. I was too tired to argue. I just didn't have the strength. "What's the price?"

"Nothing. This is a community service, an act of fellowship. Hershel out there would call it a mitzvah." She nodded toward the kitchen, and I guessed she was referring to the rail-thin man working at the griddle. "We're in a dangerous situation here, and we all have to look out for each other. Am I right?"

I nodded in wary agreement. Then I waited for the other shoe to drop, for her mercenary intentions to become clear. I didn't have to wait long.

"Although," she said, that sly smile returning to her lips, "if it's not too much of a problem, there is an errand you could run for me. A simple errand. Actually, it's something you might enjoy, something you might find . . . illuminating."

And with that, her smile widened.

Sharon put new bandages on my hand. She dug antiseptic and clean gauze from the depths of her bag, then cleaned and dressed my wounds, going about the task with the care and competence of a trained nurse. Every now and then, she glanced up and gave me a reassuring smile. It was the smile of a confident mother. A saint. A perfect, loving angel.

And it bothered me.

The way this was going, I couldn't tell if she was trying to fuck me or trying to tuck me in for the night.

When I couldn't take it anymore, I pulled my hand out of her grip. "Don't you think this whole thing is incredibly crass? What you're doing here, to these people?" I nodded out toward the crowded restaurant. "You're taking advantage of the situation. You're gaining profit and power from these people's misery."

Sharon sighed and rolled her eyes. "Yeah, well, I'm not exactly alone in that boat, now, am I, Dean?" She seemed exasperated by the accusation but not surprised, as if she'd been waiting for this, as if she'd seen it coming. "Think about it. Think about what *you're* doing here. You're not coming into this situation as a scientist or a policeman; you're here as a photographer, a journalist." She nodded toward my camera bag, and I fought the urge to push it back behind my chair, out of sight. "You're not looking for a fix or a cure. You're not invested in the situation; you don't have family to protect, or even property. And you're certainly not trying to save lives. No, what you're doing . . . you're looking for the next cool shot. You're looking for fame. Your own special kind of fame."

She leaned forward and patted my knee. The annoyance was gone from her eyes, and now there was nothing but sympathy and understanding. "I'm not operating under any illusions here, Dean. I'm no saint. But you might as well face that truth yourself. You're invested in the status quo, just like me. You're invested in the city *staying* strange. So you can take your pictures. So you can explore and report. And the reason you're here, the reason you came here, of your own free will, is because you'd rather be here, inside this weirdness, than anywhere else in the world."

I leaned back in my chair and looked away. I opened my mouth, then closed it again. "I'm still getting my feet wet," I said lamely. "I'm still waiting for the big picture."

Sharon let out a laugh. It was a loud, barking laugh, and it surprised me. "Big picture? You're waiting for the big picture?

Well, let me tell you, Dean, from where you're standing, you won't see a thing." She smiled and gave me a wink. "From where you're standing, you won't be able to see the forest for the forest fire."

She waited for me to respond. When I didn't, she gave me a nod and went back to work on my wounds.

Her words struck hard. They were a sucker punch to the gut, a big, strong jolt of truth.

And it is the truth, I realized. *That's why all of those people out there in the restaurant gave me those withering looks. I came to the city to take pictures, while they scratch and scrape just to survive. I'm exploiting their hardship. I'm turning it into a product, some-thing to study—dispassionately—and consume.*

I could have lied to myself right then and convinced myself that I did have noble intentions, that I was looking for the truth, trying to show the world what was going on inside the military's oppressive media blackout. But that wasn't the truth. Carrying my camera, street to street, day to day, I'd never even thought about those things.

I just wanted people to see my pictures. I wanted them to be amazed. By me. By my skill. I wanted to save myself from a mun-dane future.

Not exactly a noble endeavor.

I was lost in thought when Sharon finished with the bandage. After a vague, shapeless length of time, I looked up and found her leaning back on the edge of her desk, studying me with cool, sympathetic eyes.

"Don't worry about it, Dean," she said. "Whatever's happen-ing here, it's not the real world. We all just have to do what we do and hope there's no judgment in the end."

"If it's not the real world, then what is it?" I asked, my voice high, almost pleading. "What the fuck's going on?"

She shook her head. "If you're suggesting I might have some real knowledge, I don't. If, on the other hand, you're asking me what I think . . . well, I think we're all going insane. I think there's some previously unknown agent at work on our minds—something synthetic, maybe, or some naturally occurring ergot. And what we're seeing, what we're experiencing, it's all just the ravings of a city gone mad."

"But my pictures . . . all the shared experiences . . ."

"Yeah, well, I don't have all the answers," she said with a dismissive shrug. "It's just what I think, what I feel."

I nodded, preoccupied. I was considering her suggestion.

Could an insane mind grasp its own insanity? And if not, what would a city full of insane minds look like? Would they share delusions? Would they create their own scattershot mythology?

"Well, one thing's for certain," Sharon said, offering me a gentle smile, "you're not going to find any answers sitting there with that confused look on your face. It's time to get moving, Dean. My errand's not going to run itself."

I took Sabine with me on the delivery. That was Mama Cass's final request before she pushed me out the door. *It's important,* she said, *for Sabine.*

Taylor was there when I swung by the house—I could hear her voice up on the second floor—but I managed to grab Sabine and get out without attracting her attention. Certainly, I wanted to see her, to set things straight, but I figured that this was not the right time. Not while I was out running errands for Mama Cass. And besides, my own feelings remained ambivalent. I wanted to be close to her, but she kept pushing me away—both literally and figuratively—and that was driving me nuts.

I needed more time. I needed time to figure out what she wanted from me . . . and what I wanted from her.

It was nearly six o'clock when Sabine and I hit the streets, and the last traces of sunlight had already fled the sky. The moon and the stars were hidden behind a thick layer of clouds, and again I was struck by how unnatural the darkness seemed.

Cities were never supposed to get this dark. That was their purpose, right? To keep the darkness at bay.

Both Sabine and I had flashlights, and as we walked back toward the river, we sent twin beams racing across the pavement ahead. Objects emerged from the darkness like strange alien fish swimming up from the depths of a deep, dark sea: ordinary items, cutting sharp shapes across our wavering circles of light—cars, mailboxes, trash cans—made alien in their stark isolation. I played my light across a snow-shrouded yard and found a ten-speed bike lodged up in the branches of an apple tree.

"What did Sharon say?" Sabine asked. "What does she want me to do?"

"I don't know. She gave me a package and asked me to deliver it to St. James Tower on Maple Street."

"That's near Homestead territory."

She was quiet for a moment. I think she was waiting for me to respond, to react, but I didn't know the Homestead, and I didn't know how I was supposed to react. Was she expecting fear, maybe, or amusement, or annoyance? The Homestead was some sort of commune, I gathered—Weasel had mentioned it during his quick prelarceny tour—but that was about all I knew.

"Maybe Taylor should have come," Sabine continued. "She's the Homestead expert. She worked with them for quite a while."

I nodded but didn't say a word. Sabine was probing, pushing buttons, trying to figure out what was going on between Taylor and me. But that was my personal business, and I didn't feel much in the mood to share.

After crossing the bridge, I let Sabine take the lead. She knew the city well and didn't hesitate as we moved from one street to the next, first heading south, then west.

The buildings grew in height the farther we got from the river. Here, on this side of the water, there were actual signs of life scattered across the cityscape. Laughter came from a tower to our east, followed by dueling jovial voices. I could see dim flickering lights in a couple of the windows above our heads, and the tinny sound of a portable stereo echoed down, losing its coherence and becoming a monotonous whisper inside the vast canyonlike street. A loud, jangling crash sounded in the distance, followed by a muted yell—angry and confrontational.

Suddenly, Sabine broke into a trot. She ran halfway up the block, her flashlight bobbing up and down in the darkness. Then she pulled to a stop on a vacant stretch of sidewalk.

"Here, check this out," she said when I finally caught up. I couldn't see her face behind the flashlight's glare, but I could hear the smile in her voice. She raised the flashlight beam from the sidewalk, revealing words spray-painted across a concrete wall.

It was a simple phrase, painted in crimson red: THEY'RE BEHIND YOU NOW.

I turned around.

"This is one of my favorites."

Sabine panned her light to a brick wall on the far side of the street. There were black shapes covering its surface, and at first, I couldn't tell what they were. Burn marks? Mud? But they were far too intricate, too regular . . . too planned. And, as my flashlight beam joined Sabine's, the marks seemed to move.

A cold chill rocketed up my spine. *Spiders.* There were spiders all over the wall, climbing out of a hole in its center.

I took an involuntary step back, remembering the feel of spider legs crawling up my thigh. Feeling it again, this time on my back, on my shoulders, on my neck. I dropped my flashlight and started to brush at my clothing. For a moment, I lost myself, transported back to that empty apartment building, to the feel of those spindly legs, to the fear of being trapped and vastly outnumbered.

"Relax, Dean," Sabine said, a note of perplexed amusement in her voice. "It's just spray paint. Just fucking art!"

I forced myself to stop, clenching my hands down at my sides. My fingers ached, shaking as I fought the urge to brush at my neck and face. I closed my eyes for a brief moment and took a deep breath. *There are no spiders. Not here, not now.*

But the painting was so close to my memory. Spiders swarming out of a hole in the wall. It was like the mural had been plucked straight from my head, a moment from my past, sketched out line for line.

I moved forward, crossing to the middle of the street. Then I stopped. I wanted to study the image up close, to look for a single stubby-jointed spider leg amid all of those crudely drawn figures—something that might represent a human finger—but I didn't want to get too close.

I took the camera out of my bag. It was a comfort, moving through these well-choreographed motions—setting my backpack down, unzipping the topmost compartment, lifting my camera out, popping off the lens cap, raising it to my eye—and it settled me into a calmer state of mind. I had a task to perform, and it was a task I enjoyed, a task I wanted to do well.

"Fix the flashlight beams, one on either side of the hole."

Sabine complied. She grabbed my flashlight from where I'd dropped it to the street and moved the two beams into place.

I took a couple of shots with the flash on, but I was afraid all the subtle colors would be lost in that artificial glare, and I had no idea how the glossy paint would react to the light. I played with the camera's settings—switching the flash off, increasing the ISO, cranking the aperture as wide as it would go—then took a couple more shots. Even with the adjustments, I had to use a fairly slow shutter speed, and I fought to hold the camera steady.

They don't have to be perfect, I reassured myself. Mostly, I wanted to compare these images with the ones I'd taken back in the abandoned apartment building. I wanted to compare the two sets of spiders.

What would I see, I wondered, when I held these fake spiders up against the real ones? Would they match up? Would the number and placement be the same?

Impossible.

"How long has this been here?" I asked, lowering the camera.

"At least two weeks," Sabine said. "Probably longer."

I grunted and continued to stare.

Sabine moved the flashlight beams back and forth across the

wall, finally focusing on the deep, dark gash in the middle of the mural. It was the focal point of the entire piece: the nexus, the birth canal, from which all those spray-paint spiders emerged. The flashlight beams failed to illuminate anything inside. Nothing but inky black.

If I stuck my head in there, what would I see? A dim blue light? A face, staring back at me, fixing me with accusing eyes? Maybe a *spray-painted* face—a bright yellow smiley face, mocking me.

"Let's get out of here," I said, once again storing my camera. "This place gives me the creeps."

"And go where?" Sabine replied. The smile was back in her voice; I could hear it playing at her lips. "We're already here."

She raised her twin flashlight beams, casting the spider-infested wall back into darkness. Three floors up, I could see a square of light trickling out around the edges of a boarded-up window.

"Welcome to St. James Tower," she said. She laughed and started toward the front door.

12.1

Photograph, 1990. Joyous Iraqi soldier:

A brilliant sun, beating down on hardscrabble desert. Sand-colored grass sprouting out of sand-
colored earth. And a soldier, walking toward the
camera.

The soldier's dark Middle Eastern features are contorted in a joyous smile—radiant, beaming—and
there are tears spilling from his eyes, etching dark
rivulets all the way down to his jaw. He is dressed
in military brown, but his shirt hangs open, and
there's a sweaty red cloth wrapped around the top of
his head, protecting him from the brilliant sun.
There is an automatic rifle lying on the ground behind him, abandoned in the sandy dirt.

The soldier's arms are raised. A white cloth dangles
from his left fist.

He is surrendering. Joyfully.

12.2

After entering St. James Tower, we plunged from a dark foyer into an even darker stairwell. We found both doors—the door to the stairwell and the door to the street—propped open with stacks of books, volumes from a timeworn set of the *Oxford English Dictionary*. Despite a cold breeze from the street, the air inside was thick with the smell of rot; I made an effort to breathe in through my mouth, trying to keep that horrible stench out of my nose. Sabine swung her flashlight across the width of the stairwell, revealing a mound of trash bags stuffed into the space beneath the lowest flight of stairs. Some of them had split open, spilling a litter of apple cores, coffee grounds, animal bones, and soiled paper to the concrete floor.

"Fuck," Sabine said. "I think it's time to call the health inspector."

She started toward the base of the stairs, then stopped abruptly.

There were twin glowing lights up on the second-floor landing, small metallic orbs floating about a foot off the ground. They winked off for a moment, then started moving forward, sliding noiselessly through the air. Sabine jerked the flashlight up and let out a relieved laugh.

The light revealed an orange-striped tabby perched on the edge of the landing. Its bright eyes narrowed under the flashlight's sudden glare, and it stared down at us for a moment, its tail swishing angrily. Then it resumed its descent. It stayed close to the wall, watching us with suspicious eyes, and when it was about five feet from the ground, it suddenly leaped forward. It bounded down the remaining steps and out the sliver of open door.

Sabine let out another shaky laugh. "There aren't too many animals left," she said. "They fled even before the evacuation. I haven't seen a dog or a cat in months."

"Yeah?" I grunted. I clenched my bandaged hand as if trying to refute her claim, if only to myself. Already, my wounds felt better. The antibiotics were doing their job.

"Hell, they're smarter than we are," she said with a laugh. "They took the hint. They left when it was time to leave." Then she started up the stairs.

There was light creeping from beneath the door on the third-floor landing. A hand-lettered sign had been duct taped over the doorknob. It read, in giant block letters: FUCK OFF!!!

Sabine gave me a quizzical look and cocked an eyebrow. I shrugged, then stepped forward and knocked.

A man pulled the door open before I could even drop my hand. At first, he seemed nothing but wild hair and wilder eyes. "Did you see a cat?" he asked. "A fucking cat, clawing at the fucking door?" His eyes darted back and forth between Sabine and me. He was shorter than both of us and at least three decades older. His shoulder-length hair was reddish-brown, and it jutted from his scalp like strings from an unused mop head. Despite the cold weather, his shirt hung open, revealing pale pockmarked flesh.

"It's always here, that fucking cat. I try to lock it out, but somehow it manages to get back in. And then it's trapped, and that's a million times worse. It howls like an injured baby. *A fucking baby!* The bloody thing's driving me insane!"

"It left," Sabine said, taking a cautious step back. "When we came in. It ran out the door."

"Good," the man said. "It's a motherfucking miracle." He leaned forward and cast a skeptical look down the dark stairwell.

When no cat came screaming out of the shadows, he let out a satisfied "harrumph" and pulled back into the doorway.

He stood there motionless for a time. The look on his face morphed from one of frantic mania into a sudden guarded skepticism, as if he had just now noticed us standing on his doorstep and, seeing us there, remembered an intense fear and distrust of strangers. He crossed his arms in front of his chest and started scratching at his forearms; the flesh there was red and dry, flaking away beneath his yellowing nails.

"Do I know you?" he finally asked, sounding genuinely perplexed. "What do I want—?" He closed his eyes and shook his head violently. "I got that wrong. I mean, I mean . . . what do *you* want?"

"Mama Cass sent us," I said. "I've got a package for you."

At this, the man's tensions abruptly eased. The lines on his forehead and beneath his eyes disappeared, and his shoulders dropped, muscles falling slack.

"Well, why didn't you say so?" he said. He took a step back and ushered us inside.

The man's apartment was absolute chaos. It was a studio apartment, and the ceiling, fifteen feet above our heads, was a maze of naked ductwork. Rows of bookcases crisscrossed the room from one end to the other, laid out in disjointed, meandering lines; it was like something designed and jotted down by a drunken architect, without the aid of a ruler or steady hands. The shelving was packed full of notebooks and sheets of loose paper. The clutter was so dense, it filled every open space, spilling from bookcases, across the surface of card tables and down to the floor below.

There was a truly extravagant amount of light in the room; at least a dozen battery-powered lanterns—perched on tabletops, bookcases, and hanging from the walls—kept it lit as bright as day. *And that can't be cheap,* I thought. *There can't be that many batteries left in the city anymore.*

"Do you want anything?" the man asked, nervously fidgeting

from one foot to the other. "I think I've got some beers in back if you're thirsty."

I shook my head no, and Sabine didn't respond. I don't even think she heard the offer; her eyes were too busy roaming about the room, lost in the chaos.

"Okay, then," the man prompted. "You have something for me?"

I opened my backpack and retrieved Mama Cass's package. It was about the size of a football, wrapped in canvas and taped shut. The bundle was heavy for its size, and it rattled like a maraca. When I handed it over, I noticed that the man's eyes had become fixed on my open backpack; the lens of my camera was visible, protruding out of the opening like a headless neck. When I zipped it shut, the man's eyes jolted back up, exploring my face for a couple of seconds before darting abruptly away.

"I, I—" he said. Then his mouth snapped shut, and he retreated to the far side of the room, disappearing behind a wall of bookcases.

"Look at this place," Sabine said in a hushed whisper. "This is more than two months' worth of junk . . . he was a shut-in long before this weirdness started."

I made my way over to the nearest table and ran my hand across the mess of paper on its surface. The feel of the paper surprised me; it was a thick, glossy stock, a very familiar weight. I flipped a sheet over, revealing the front of a photograph. It was a picture of the Spokane River at sunset, seen from Riverfront Park. The sun was so bright, the world over the river was nothing but a radiant shade of yellow. And the ripples on its surface formed stretched-out geometric shapes, etched across the water like art carved into a slab of black marble.

I grabbed a handful of paper and flipped it all over, setting off an avalanche of brightly colored photographs. Dozens of glossy images slid across the surface of the table, some reaching its edge and tumbling down to the floor. The cascading motion unearthed a three-ring binder buried near the center of the mess.

Moving slowly, as if in a trance, I flipped open the notebook and found page after page of celluloid negatives. Each line of film had been slotted into a translucent sleeve: dozens and dozens of perfectly preserved images, each its own captured moment, crammed into a tiny, unreadable rectangle. I lifted a page and squinted through the colored plastic. I could see buildings hidden inside the plastic. I could see people.

"From before I went digital." I turned and found the man standing on an overturned bucket in the middle of the room. He kept his back to me as he grabbed a dark lantern from the top of the nearest bookcase. "I still use film on occasion, but it's hard to get. At least, it's hard to get here." He cracked open the lantern and replaced the battery inside. The lantern lit up in his hands, but the effect on the room was negligible. The room was already so bright.

"Who are you?" I asked, suddenly apprehensive. The number of photographs—if in fact all these bookcases and tables were filled with photographs—left me positively awestruck. In fact, it scared the crap out of me . . . the sheer magnitude of this place—thousands and thousands of images, each a potential gem, hidden away inside this chaos. It made me feel claustrophobic.

The man smiled. It was a relaxed smile, and it made him look completely different. He was no longer the erratic, crazy man who'd answered the door. "My name is Cob Gilles. I was a photographer . . . once."

The name was familiar. I'd seen it in my photography books back in school. Unfortunately, I couldn't remember the images it had been attached to. "You're famous," I said with a note of awe. "You've got a reputation."

He nodded and stepped down from the bucket. He continued to avoid meeting my eyes. "Yeah," he said. His voice was quiet, not much more than a whisper. "I had a reputation." Then, with a bitter smile, he picked up the bucket and started toward the back of the room. He turned a corner and disappeared into the stacks, his voice trailing behind him like a limp, lifeless tail: "But that was outside, back when it mattered."

I glanced over at Sabine, and she just shrugged. Then I hitched my backpack against my shoulder and followed Cob Gilles into the maze of bookcases.

Sabine stayed behind. The last I saw, she was walking the perimeter of the room, running her hand along the wall as she slowly surveyed the photographer's loft.

There was no order to the shelving, at least none that I could see. Just books and folders, filling up every inch of space on the shelves and piled into tall stacks on the floor. There were photography books mixed in with the unlabeled notebook spines, and I recognized a couple from my collection back home.

I pulled a folder from a shelf at random. Inside, I found a six-by-eight-inch print pasted to the first page. It was a black-and-white portrait, framed so that the subject's face was missing; there was an ear and the nape of a neck in the center of the frame, but the picture ended midcheekbone. A square of flower-print wallpaper was visible behind the subject, taking up the entire left half of the photograph. Somebody had taken a red pen and drawn a circle around the wallpaper. An arrow extended beyond the frame to the empty space beneath the image. The word *DISTRACTING* was written in large block letters. Then: *dodge/blur*. I flipped through the rest of the folder and found a dozen more shots from the same photo session, all annotated in the same way—hastily drawn words questioning composition and technique.

The last page had a head-on view of the anonymous model positioned in front of that same swatch of flower-print wallpaper. The subject's entire face had been scribbled out, lost beneath the tip of a permanent marker. And the pen had been thorough; there was absolutely nothing visible beneath the thick wash of red ink. I couldn't even tell if the subject was male or female.

I slid the book back into place and started looking for the photographer.

After the first line of bookcases, I turned right and found myself confronted with three more pathways. The way out wasn't obvious—down each path I could see nothing but row after row of cluttered shelving—and the photographer was nowhere to be seen.

"Mr. Gilles?" I called out hesitantly.

"This way." His words drifted back into the maze, a distant grunt muffled by wood and paper. I followed his voice down the left-hand path and, after one more turn, emerged from the far side of the makeshift library.

I found the photographer seated at a mahogany desk with his back against a line of boarded-up windows. What once must have been a spectacular view of the city had been fitted with precisely cut pieces of plywood, blocking out every hint of the outside world. Day or night, I'm sure the apartment would have looked exactly the same: lit from inside, completely divorced from the weather and the sun, from the city and the world.

There was an array of camera equipment spread across the desk before him. And between his hands, Mama Cass's football had been ripped open to reveal batteries and a cracked-open bottle of pills.

"I saw your camera," Cob Gilles said. "You're a photographer, right? You're here on assignment?"

"I'm here on my own," I said. "I want to report on what's happening."

The photographer smiled and nodded, and his eyes explored my face. I got the impression that he was judging me as I stood there in front of his desk, that he was looking for something in my expression. Something important. A sign, maybe. A twitch. A subtle hint of understanding.

He was trying to figure out if I was worthy. He was trying to figure out if he should take me seriously.

Finally, he leaned back in his chair and shook his head, passing judgment. "You're just a kid. You don't know what you're doing."

I took a step closer. "Fuck that," I said. I could feel my face growing flush with blood, and this time it wasn't just a fever making me hot. "I'm doing just fine. I'm getting my shots. I'm holding it together." I cast an accusing look around his apartment; the place was a sty, an absolute pit. Then I looked pointedly at the constellation of pills spread out across his desk.

Who was he to judge?

He nodded and sighed. "Yeah," he agreed. "Fuck it. Whatever. No lectures."

He reached beneath his desk and produced a can of Budweiser. He popped the top, then spent a couple of seconds staring blankly at his desk, like he was waiting for something to happen, like he was waiting for his eyes to come into focus or for one of his photographic subjects to settle into a pose. Then he swept some pills into his hand and downed them quickly with half the can of beer.

"I guess Sharon wanted us to meet," the photographer said. "Mama Cass, playing the motherfucking matchmaker. I wonder what she was expecting. Did she think I'd choose you as an apprentice? Or . . . or . . . *fuck* . . . is this some type of cautionary visit? 'Watch out, photography boy, or you'll end up like crazy old Cob Gilles'?" He closed his eyes and downed the rest of his beer. When he continued, his voice was much quieter. He sounded thoughtful now and a bit confused. I got the impression that, at this point, he was talking primarily to himself. "Or maybe that's not it. Maybe that's not it at all. Maybe *you're* the message. To me. Some type of reminder?"

"No," I said, and I offered him a sympathetic smile. "I'm Dean. I'm not a message. I'm not 'photography boy.' Just Dean." Despite his abrupt dismissal—of me, of my talent—I couldn't stay mad at him. The man was quite obviously damaged. He was somebody to be pitied, not hated.

The photographer laughed and shook his head. "Well, it's nice to meet you, Dean. It's a real motherfucking pleasure."

Cob Gilles again offered me a beer, and this time I accepted. I sat down in front of his desk and raised my can in a wordless salute.

Then we settled into a thick silence.

The photographer's eyes roamed about the room for nearly a minute before finally settling on an unremarkable spot halfway up the nearest wall. I studied him closely as he fixated on that spot. I watched as he slumped bonelessly into his chair. I watched as his eyes lost focus, going dull like clouded glass. He didn't seem to mind my scrutiny. *Too drugged out,* I guessed.

"Which of your photos would I know?" I asked, breaking the silence. "What made you famous?"

His eyes snapped into focus. "I was—" He cleared his throat. "I was embedded with the army during the first Iraq war. Desert Storm. I was there for the start of the ground assault, and I got photographs of Iraqis surrendering. People liked those pictures. They liked them a lot." He stood up unsteadily and made his way over to a stack of framed pictures propped up against the boarded-over windows. After shuffling through a half dozen, he came up with a three-foot-by-three-foot frame. "Here. It's the fucking pinnacle of my career."

The left half of the frame was taken up with a single photo: an Iraqi soldier walking toward the camera. The soldier's arms were raised, and a white scarf fluttered from his left hand. There was an automatic rifle lying in the sand at his feet. The soldier was smiling, and there were tears running down his face. He looked positively jubilant. The entire scene was bathed in warm, golden sunlight, a slice of the world dipped in amber.

Next to the picture, mounted on the right side of the frame, was an oversized gold medallion.

"This . . . this is a Pulitzer Prize," I said. I wasn't asking a question or voicing surprise. The words just fell out of my mouth, without emotion or real understanding.

Cob Gilles grunted. "Yeah, well, the photo's a fucking joke. The guy pretty much collapsed right after I took that shot. He had a fever of 103 and a wound on his leg that was going gangrenous. He was mewling in pain as he walked—just, just fucking mewling, like a pistol-whipped kitten. And that expression in the picture? I swear to God, it was never there. It must have been a freak twist of the mouth in between sobs of pain."

He grabbed the photo from my hands and tossed it to the floor, spinning it back toward the other framed photographs. There was a loud *crash* as it hit the wall.

"I was so proud of that shot. So fucking proud! And it wasn't even real." He gestured toward the shattered frame. "That's not what was going on over there, in the desert. It was a fluke. Nothing more."

"Does it matter?" I asked. "You got the shot. You were in the right place at the right time. The soldier's expression was there, and you caught it. And the emotion . . . it resonates. So what if it was a fluke?"

"You *are* a reminder," Cob Gilles said with a smile. "You're a fucking blast from my past. I thought the exact same thing back then." He stuck out his thumb, once again gesturing toward the broken frame. "I thought: if you click the shutter enough, if you burn through enough film, you'll eventually get a shot. Not *the* shot, mind you, just *a* shot. And that's photography: a fluke occurrence, something absolutely unforeseen. The collision between chance, preparation, and time. And it doesn't even matter what it is as long as it looks good.

"But it's not true. It's just not true. There are lies to every image. And the things you choose to show, the things you keep . . . they do much more than just illustrate. They change things. They alter opinion and mood. They change *minds*. And not in an objective, reasoned way, but deep down, on a powerful, instinctive level." He let out a tired little chuckle, very cold, very bitter. "And you lie with pictures just like you lie with words. You can't help it, you can't control it.

"And I'm not just talking about news photography, about subjects steeped in politics and scandal. I'm talking about a sly smile on your lover's lips. I'm talking about the expression on your child's face." He closed his eyes, and his Adam's apple bobbed up and down, making it look like he was trying to swallow something, like he was choking down a rough ball of emotion. "All of that stuff turns dark. Through bad glass, it all gets tainted."

Cob Gilles finished his beer and crushed the can against the edge of his desk, letting the crumpled shape fall to the floor. "You'll see," he said. "You're young. You'll learn."

I nodded, not quite sure how to take this exceedingly bleak view of photography. If there were lies to photography, I figured, there was truth, too, truths we'd never see if not through the dispassionate glass eye of a camera. *How'd he lose sight of that*? I wondered. *How'd he get so bitter?*

"And what are you working on now?" I asked. "Who sent you here? *Newsweek? TIME? Rolling Stone?*"

He shook his head. "No. That's not me. Not anymore. No fucking way." His face contorted into tight pale lines, as if even the thought of work gave him pain. "I mean, I still take pictures—I guess, I guess it's a compulsion with me, something I have to do— but I delete them now. Immediately. Especially if they're . . . weird. If it's the city." He forced a tense laugh. "*Fuck!* Most of the time now, if you see me taking pictures, I'm working without a memory card. It's just, just—fucking *click* and consigning it all to the ether."

"Why?" I asked. "What happened?"

He shrugged. "I just stopped trusting. I stopped trusting all of this." He gestured vaguely at the photography gear laid out before him. "It's no good. The images it shows . . . it's all lies now, Dean. It's all bad glass. And I just don't want to spread it anymore."

He once again reached beneath his desk, this time coming up with a half-empty bottle of Scotch and a pair of glasses. I wondered briefly what else he had squirreled away down there, around his feet.

I watched him fill the glasses. His hands were steady but slow.

"What do you think's happening here?" I asked.

He stared at me for a second, then turned the question back around. "What do *you* think, Dean?" He handed me my drink.

"You're new here, right? You haven't been tainted yet . . . at least not much. What do you think's happening here?"

I paused for a moment, thinking. I didn't have an answer, and I didn't really want to venture a guess. "Mama Cass thinks it's some type of hallucinogen, something in the environment that's making us all crazy."

Cob Gilles nodded. "Yeah. That sounds like her. We're all broken, hallucinating, and she's the only one taking it in stride. At least that's what she'd like to believe . . . the only one strong enough to ride it all out—this strange and dangerous trip—and walk out the other side with money busting her every seam."

"You don't agree?"

"No." He smiled. "No, we're not insane. It's deeper than that. It's the *world* that's gone insane, not us. It's the world." He bolted a swallow of Scotch and leaned forward in his chair, swaying slightly before his hands found the edge of the desk. "It's a tumor," he continued in a confidential whisper. "It's a cancer—*brain cancer*—somewhere deep in the core of the city. Growing, distorting the shape of reality. Spreading. Metastasized. Terminal. It's eating us hollow. We're eating *ourselves* hollow."

I glanced down at my glass, focusing on the beautiful glowing liquid. It was easier to look at, easier to comprehend. When I glanced back up, I found him watching me, his eyes suddenly bright and jovial. Those eyes told me his entire story. He knew how crazy this all sounded, but he no longer cared.

He had his booze. He had his pills. He'd made himself ready for the end of the world.

"I saw it, Dean. I actually saw the tumor."

For a moment, I thought he was kidding, or at last speaking in glib abstractions. But those eyes were not the eyes of a jokester; they were the eyes of a man who really didn't give a fuck what I believed or how I reacted. He was speaking in order to speak, in order to hear his own words. Nothing else mattered.

"It was in the hospital, I think, though I'm not quite sure. We started way out east, in the industrial district, but where we ended up . . ." He smiled widely and shrugged. "Jesus Christ, it was fucked! We were underground for . . . I don't know. A long time? And I don't remember most of it—moving in a drunken trance, like snatches of memory from a weeklong bender. I remember it was cold at times. And sometimes we were in earthen tunnels, sometimes in basements and corridors.

"There were six of us at the start, but only two of us made it to the room. I really don't know what happened to the others. I remember glancing around and seeing fewer and fewer people, but it didn't really register. It was like my higher brain functions had been shut off. I was dizzy, and I think I threw up a couple of times."

He raised his glass back to his lips. His hand was shaking now, and I heard the glass *clink* against his teeth as he finished off his drink. He lowered the glass and refilled it quickly, spilling another tumbler's worth across the surface of the desk.

"We must have climbed back out of the underground at some point, but I don't remember any stairs. Just the room. It was halfway down a carpeted corridor—the entire expanse gray with predawn light, all the color stripped out of the world. And then there was this . . . room—" As he said these words, Cob Gilles's voice swelled with awe. "There was this room," he continued, "with *golden* light spilling out, onto the floor of the hallway. And we were there, at the threshold, looking inside. We *must* have been aboveground, because there was an entire wall of picture windows on the far side of the room, blinding us with the most beautiful golden light. We were at least ten floors up, and the city outside was gorgeous and new—I don't even think it was Spokane. And there was a big table stretching down the middle of the room, with people sitting all around. It was some type of boardroom, and everyone was dressed in business attire, sitting motionless, staring at us. Staring at us with unblinking eyes. At least twenty of them, both men and women.

"I don't know what they wanted, but their eyes were absolutely huge, expectant. Like they knew something was going to happen—and that something, whatever it might be, was going to be absolutely terrible. And then—" The photographer's eyes scrunched up as if he were trying to riddle out some complex problem or trying to remember something that desperately did not want to be remembered. "—and then they stood up, all at once, in freakish unison. And then . . ." Cob Gilles shrugged and once again raised his glass to his lips. Before drinking, he mumbled around the glass: "And then . . . I just don't remember."

I joined him as he drank deeply. My head was swimming, and the sharp bite of Scotch did little to straighten things out.

What the photographer was saying was absolute insanity— boardrooms and businessmen! If anything, it supported Mama Cass's theory. What he was describing was a drug trip, a hallucinogenic break from reality.

The photographer let out a bracing hiss and set his glass back down. "When we came to, we were sitting on a bench downtown, and it was just the two of us. The others were gone. And they stayed gone. We never saw them again."

"And that's the tumor?" I asked. "A boardroom filled with stuffed suits?"

The photographer shook his head. He didn't seem put off by my abrupt summation. He just seemed very, very tired. "There was a sickness there, Dean; I could feel it. There's something horribly wrong with the very nature of the universe, and it was centered right there, in that room, at that meeting. Like suddenly physics had gone awry. Stars had collapsed, and atoms had split. And it was tearing everything apart. And this—" He gestured about the room, but it was clear he meant the city and not the chaos of his apartment. "—this is a symptom. This place. This feeling."

I shrugged and lifted my palms into the air, a gesture of pure frustration. "It could have been a delusion, a chemical state that imbued your visions with a sense of importance, with spiritual clarity." As I talked, memories of Psych 101 came flooding back in. "That's what religion is: epiphanies and euphoria. Just neurons misfiring."

Cob Gilles smiled and shook his head. "I saw through the veil, Dean. During that trip, the scales—as they say—they fell from my eyes."

He once again reached for the bottle of Scotch, this time almost knocking it over. Instead of refilling his glass—a task I don't think he could have managed—he drank straight from the bottle. "And what I saw . . . that was the reality. And this world—this whole fucking world—is the delusion, nothing but a fever dream spinning away inside a dying mind."

He paused for a moment, then continued: "And what happens, Dean? What happens when that mind dies? What happens when there's no one left to hold it all together?"

"Dean!"

Sabine's voice was shrill and frantic, and it sounded a long way away.

At the sound of her cry, Cob Gilles started in his chair. He'd been so focused on me—and his booze and his story—I think he'd forgotten all about Sabine, left to wander through his apartment as we talked, as he let the drugs and alcohol work their magic on his body and nerves.

I spun around and started toward the confusion of bookcases, then decided to bypass that maze altogether. Instead, I stayed near the wall, passing a small, garbage-strewn kitchenette before finally reaching the front door and picking up Sabine's trail.

"Dean!" She was closer now, and her voice sounded more frantic, more desperate.

"Sabine!" I called back, but she didn't respond.

What will I find? I wondered. *Her body, sunk into the floor? Her eyes, pleading for help?*

I collided with a bookcase and sent a shelf of notebooks cascading to the floor. A binder popped open, and the air filled with photographs.

I turned a corner and found Sabine standing in the narrow space between the wall and a row of bookcases. Her face was contorted with confusion and anxiety, but she looked healthy, un-harmed.

After a moment of tense silence, she turned and faced me. "It's the Poet," she said, her voice congested, breaking into a breath-less sob. "It's the Poet . . . and she won't speak to me!"

I followed her gaze back down the narrow space. There was a woman sitting on a stool about a dozen feet away. She sat per-fectly still, facing away from us. Her back was ramrod stiff, and her whole body looked tense, ready to spring.

She was wearing a hood. It was a black leather fetish hood, and it covered almost her entire head, leaving just her eyes, mouth, and jaw visible. A spill of dark brown hair cascaded out from beneath the back of the hood, falling over the collar of a gray, paint-spattered peacoat. I could see her face in profile. Her pale lips trembled with suppressed energy, and her bright blue eyes—framed in cut-out ovals—quivered as she looked pointedly away.

"Sharon said she wore a mask," Sabine gasped, her voice harsh and breathy. "That's why she sent me here—so I could find her! But she won't say a word!"

Unleashing a sudden burst of anger, Sabine turned back toward the masked woman. *"Fucking say something! Fucking talk to me!"*

The Poet remained still. I thought I could see her eyes widen at Sabine's outburst.

A hand grabbed my arm and jerked me back. My foot slipped on a loose photograph, and I almost fell to the floor. "It's time for you to go," Cob Gilles growled. He was drunk and unsteady, but that didn't diminish the force of his hand, or his words, as he pulled me toward the front door. He launched me in that direc-tion with an abrupt shove, then went after Sabine.

"You better fucking leave her alone!" he yelled. "She's my angel—*my* angel!—and she's been through enough shit without some crazy bitch yelling at her!"

He grabbed Sabine's coat and pulled her back, but unlike me, Sabine *did* fall. The photographer didn't wait for her to regain her feet. He just kept pulling, dragging her across the hardwood floor. Sabine kicked out, knocking stacks of books across the floor and setting one bookcase tottering precariously. Finally, one of her flailing arms struck Cob Gilles's shin, and he lost his grip on her coat.

"*Get out!*" he roared, falling back against the wall, overwhelmed with emotion. There were tears streaming down his cheeks. "Get the fuck out of our home! You aren't welcome here. You aren't welcome!"

He collapsed to the ground and buried his face in his hands. "You aren't welcome," he continued to sob, losing energy and volume. "*You aren't welcome.*"

Sabine jumped to her feet and started toward him. Her jaw was clenched, and there was dark venom in her eyes. I stopped her. I grabbed her in a tight bear hug and rotated her away from the photographer, putting my body in between the two of them. "*Shhhhh,*" I said, trying to make a comforting noise in her ear. "Shhhhh. He's done. It's all over."

After a handful of seconds Sabine stopped struggling, and I let her go. She took a step back, then adjusted her jacket across her shoulders. "Fuck this shit," she muttered, and fled the apartment, violently ripping the front door open and letting it bounce off the wall.

I turned back toward the photographer and gave him one last look before following her out. He was still sobbing in his hands.

And as I watched, he toppled over.

That's how I left him, the great Cob Gilles, Pulitzer Prize—winning photographer: sobbing, curled into a fetal ball on his apartment floor.

13.1

The picture is lit with a flash. *Washed-out gray concrete. Sharp shadows pointing to the left.* The toe
of a single out-of-place boot is visible on the
right side of the frame—a stray object intruding on
an otherwise stark scene.

And set in the middle of the photograph: fingers,
protruding from the concrete floor. They sprout out
of the ground like thick-stemmed plants, only
different—not pushing out displaced dirt, instead
reaching up from a perfectly smooth unblemished surface. The surface cuts below the knuckle on all the
fingers save the pinkie; the pinkie's knuckle is bisected neatly in two. And only the tip of the thumb
is visible, little more than a thumbnail, sending up
a glimmer of reflected light.

The angle is low; the camera is perched about a foot
off the ground. And even though it is not a macro
shot, the image is close and clear—razor-sharp de-

tails, blown up larger than life. The flesh on the
fingers looks ghostly pale in the glare of the flash,
and the ragged, dirty edges of the fingernails are
all visible. The knuckles have been scraped raw,
dotted with tiny tags of gray-white skin, ripped up
to reveal a glimpse of rosy pink beneath. It is not
a bad scrape, just the result of unintended friction, the kind of wound you'd get wrestling an un-
wieldy box through a narrow doorway.

It is a desolate shot. Gray and lonely.

13.2

"What the fuck was that?" Sabine barked as soon as I caught up to her out in front of the photographer's apartment. She let out a feral growl and kicked at a bloated paper bag lying on the sidewalk; it burst against her boot, sending fast-food wrappers and a crumpled-up cup skittering across the concrete. "I had plans. I wanted to help her, for God's sake! I wanted to help her with her art! But she wouldn't even listen."

"Yeah, well, I don't think she wants your help," I said. "And whatever your plans are, I don't think she's in any condition to lend a hand."

"Yeah," she said. "I gathered that."

Sabine let out a loud sigh; it was an exhausted rush of air, and in it I could hear her anger deflating. When she continued, her voice was imploring, and it sounded like she was asking me to do her some abstract favor, maybe change the very nature of the world around us. "I just . . . I was expecting something different, you know? Magic, not silence."

I nodded and tried to give her a reassuring smile. It felt weird on my lips, and I thought I might be doing it wrong. "I know," I said. "It's disappointing. But maybe we shouldn't be putting so much faith in other people."

Sabine gave me a questioning look, and we passed a couple of moments in silence.

"He was a photographer?" she asked in a gentle voice. "Just like you?"

"Yeah," I said, flashing a wry smile. "Just like me." I shook my head and walked away, moving out into the middle of the street.

Sabine caught up to me as I started to retrace our path back through the dark city.

Even more than before, the streets of downtown Spokane seemed deserted. It was late, approaching midnight, and there were no lights in the surrounding buildings. There was no laughter, no screams echoing in the distance. Just silence. Silence and the sound of our feet on wet pavement.

We were a long way from the world I knew.

I glanced up into the sky, expecting to see the face of the earth floating overhead—like maybe we'd been transported to the moon or to some alien asteroid hurtling through space—but there were only clouds up there, and the muffled outline of a moon packed in cotton.

I wanted to get home. I wanted to get home to Taylor.

When we reached the house, we found Taylor seated alone in the kitchen. There was a single candle burning on the table, and its steady flame etched shadows beneath her eyes. She looked tired. She looked like a haunted woman, drawn in heavy charcoal lines.

Sabine grunted a halfhearted good night and retreated up the stairs to her bedroom. I don't think she was trying to avoid Taylor and me or our upcoming encounter. I think she was just tired and disillusioned. I think she wanted to crawl into bed, where she could think about the Poet . . . and dwell and curse and seethe in peace.

"I heard about Amanda and Mac," Taylor said.

"Yeah."

"That . . . that situation . . ." She paused and finally, at a loss for words, finished her statement with a cryptic shrug.

"Yeah," I agreed with a smile. "We're on the same page there."

I sat down opposite her, and she gave me a blank, emotionless stare. "I'm sorry I left this morning. I had things I had to do . . . personal things, and I didn't want to wake you." She leaned back from the table and tilted her head, as if she were trying to see me from a different angle. "And I guess there were things I didn't want to deal with, too . . . things between us. I just wanted to let them lie. I wanted to give myself time to think."

I nodded, feeling surprisingly calm, surprisingly focused. My visit with Cob Gilles and the Poet had changed things for me. Before, I'd been so angry at Taylor. And for what? For some perceived slight, some juvenile feeling of abandonment? Now, none of that seemed to matter. It just . . . didn't matter.

If Cob Gilles was right—if the world was crazy, if photography was shit—then what did that leave? What was *he* still clinging to? What was keeping him alive?

The Poet.

"Don't worry about it," I said. "It's fine, I—"

"No, Dean, it's *not* fine. It's stupid. Us—" She raised her hand, flicking a finger back and forth between the two of us. "This, whatever it is . . . it's stupid, monumentally stupid. I'm not going to be able to give you what you want. You're not going to be happy. And I'm going to feel like shit just yanking you around."

"I'd be perfectly happy with a little yanking."

She was silent for a moment, and then her cold facade cracked and she let out an abrupt laugh. It was an odd, strangled laugh, having to fight its way past reluctant muscles. But it was a laugh. And she shook her head in surprised puzzlement, like she didn't quite know what to make of me. "I suppose we could leave the yanking to Danny."

"See! There you go," I said, raising my hands. "Problem solved. It's not my natural inclination, mind you, but that's a sacrifice I'm willing to make. For you."

She continued to stare at me, those perplexed eyes jittering back and forth. And the smile faded from her lips. "What are you doing, Dean?" she asked. "I'm trying to give you an out here."

"Yeah, well, maybe I don't want out," I said. "Maybe it's not the sex that's got me all smitten. Maybe it's you. And everything else—every fucked-up feeling and unexplained horror—can take a giant fucking leap."

She smiled and reached across the table to grab my hand. Her touch was light, a trembling paintbrush drawing indistinct shapes across my palm. "I didn't realize you were such a saint."

"Oh, yeah, that's me," I said. "I'm all about the piety and the motherfucking goodness."

She continued to smile, and it was such a warm and genuine smile. Sitting right there, in its path, it felt like I'd found the most beautiful place in the world.

"Then come along, Saint Dean," she said. "It's been a long day. We deserve some rest."

I took my antibiotics and a couple of Vicodin, and then we settled in for some sleep. Taylor wanted me in her bed. We lay side by side, perfectly chaste, holding hands in the dark.

"Are you still concerned about Devon?" she asked as the Vicodin began to hit, lifting me about an inch above her queen-size mattress. "I think I know what it is. I think I know who he's spying for."

I grunted. Devon and the radio. The underground tunnels. It seemed so long ago, separated from me by a gulf of time and weirdness—by Amanda and Mac, by Mama Cass, by the photographer and the Poet. I found it amazing, how all of that horror and confusion—so intense in the moment, so overwhelming— could just fade away. *It's some type of psychological defense*, I figured, *some type of coping mechanism*. Somewhere along the line, I'd started living in the moment, letting everything just wash over me without fully taking it in, without dwelling.

"I didn't want to tell you until I was sure," she said. "But maybe you should be there with me." She squeezed my hand. There was caring and vulnerability in her voice, and I got the sense that she was offering me another gift here, that she was opening herself up, including me in her secrets. For someone with her issues, I imagined that this was a great act of intimacy.

"Yeah, okay," I said. And then, a moment later: "Wait . . . go where?"

"Shhhh . . . tomorrow. I'll show you tomorrow."

I grunted again. And then the Vicodin caught me. It grabbed hold like a warm wave, lifting me up high, then washing me back down, into a comfortable, dreamless sleep.

Danny showed up in the morning. He was seated at the kitchen table with Charlie when I finally made it downstairs. Taylor was standing at the camp stove.

"Good morning," Taylor said, greeting me with a warm smile and a cup of coffee. She looked relaxed and happy. "You looked tired, so I let you sleep."

"Yeah, it's—what?—ten-thirty?" Danny said, giving me a nod. "I've been up since five. And I swear, I'd kill everyone in the city just to keep your type of hours." I blushed as soon as I saw him, suddenly struck by the memory of his stubbled head bobbing up and down in my lap. He, for his part, didn't seem at all embarrassed, giving me that perfunctory nod as if there was nothing at all strange between us. Perhaps there wasn't. Perhaps I was the queer one here, unsure of the protocol, unable to look him in the eye.

I've never been accused of being a prude, but Danny's utter nonchalance made me feel old-fashioned and out of step.

"I got a fresh load of data," he said, nodding toward Charlie, who was once again seated at his notebook computer. I could see the thumb drive jutting from the computer's side.

Charlie looked up and smiled, beaming with pride. "It worked. Your post . . . it posted. And you've already got comments." He spun the computer around, gesturing me toward an empty seat.

A flutter of nerves erupted in my chest.

I immediately recognized the website: Chasing the S. As far as message boards go, this one was fairly standard; there were countless more just like it out there on the Net, all assembled from the same free software packages. The view on Charlie's screen was a simplified version of the site. All the standard images were missing: there was no black-and-white banner at the top of the page, featuring the name of the site flanked by satellite imagery of Spokane itself, and there were no tiny avatars to the left of each posting. Charlie had streamlined his application. He had programmed it to pick up text and formatting information while leaving all the bulky pictures and ads behind. The resulting design was stark and no-nonsense, and more than a little disconcerting.

I quickly scrolled through the topics on the front page. The title of my post—"Photos of Spokane: Views from Inside (week 1)"—was at the top of the list. According to the stats next to my entry, there were already seventy-six comments and over five thousand page views.

"It was up for twelve hours before Danny scraped the forum," Charlie said, following my eyes on the page. "Right now it's the only post getting any attention."

I hesitated before clicking through to my thread. I was more than a little nervous. What if they hated my pictures? What if those seventy-six replies were all negative, nothing but dismissive mockery?

I braced myself and clicked through. Beneath my dismembered post—Charlie's program had stripped away all the photos, leaving just a couple of sentences and a line of broken links—there was an avalanche of comments, a mad rush of words.

—Is this for real??? Is this bullshit???
—Please, can someone confirm?
—It's Spokane. That's Riverfront Park, and I recognize that storefront with all the people. It was a Tully's before they evacuated us.

—It's Photoshopped, you morons! They aren't letting
   anyone in. You've seen the barricades and checkpoints!
—But that's not true! There are civies inside! They
   catch people going in and out all the time!
—They're real. According to the tags, someone used
   Photoshop (a student CS edition), but probably
   just to resize . . . It's not so hard to believe,
   is it? We know there are people in there, and
   they can't be in too good shape by now. Hell,
   even the weather matches. That's Eastern Washington at the start of winter.
—Where's the ghosts?
—Why aren't we seeing this shit on the news? It's a
   disaster area in the middle of America! It's Katrina all over again!
—It is _not_ Katrina. These morons can leave anytime they like. Hell, they'd get _paid_ to leave!
   Big fat government checks!
—Where's the ghosts???

After a half hour of short, gut-level reactions, the postings
started to get longer, and they started to address me directly.

—Nice pictures, intheimage [this was the name I
   used on the forum, dating back to the summer
   months, when the first vague news stories had
   begun to escape Spokane]. Tell us more about the
   city, if you've got time. What are the conditions
   like? The people look destitute, how do they get
   along? And what is the military doing?
—If you are, indeed, in there (and I have my
   doubts), how'd you do it? You've got a picture of
   soldiers there, did you have to bribe your way

in? I've heard people talk about that, here, but
I want some firsthand info. Are they willing? How
much would it cost?
—Your pictures are pretty mundane, considering the
reports we've been reading. Are the stories over-
blown? Have you seen anything strange?
—Cool! Post more!
—Please, intheimage, I don't know if you'll get
this, but I was wondering if you've met someone
named Travis Paulson in the city? He's thirty-two
years old, brown eyes, brown hair (though he usually wears it shaved bald). He lived in a house
on W. Garland, up north. Here's a picture of him,
from about a year ago. [Where the picture should
have been, there was nothing but a small red x.
Charlie's program had left the picture behind.]
We haven't heard from him since they closed the
city, and his family is terrified. *Please, please,
please* email me with anything.

There was more, but after that last message, I didn't go on. I got
the gist of the thread. There was healthy skepticism, doubt, and
a lot of questions. But nothing damning. There was no derision or
outright dismissal. And perhaps the most heartening thing here
was the sheer number of replies and the number of eyeballs that
had found my work. Over five thousand page views in the first
twelve hours! That was good exposure. The thought of all of
those people looking at my photographs got my heart racing.

Now I needed to figure out my next move.

Obviously, I had to post again, but what should I include? The
spider with the human finger? The face in the wall? The underground tunnels? Should I continue to take it slow, or should I
jump right into the strange heart of the city?

"I don't have anything ready to go out today," I said, "but I might have something tomorrow or the next day. A new post. More pictures. Will that work?" I looked up at Charlie, then across the table at Danny. Danny was smiling.

"Yeah," Danny said. "I think we can make that work."

"But not now," Taylor said. She was standing at the camp stove, scraping eggs out of a sizzling pan. She cast me a significant look as she carried over a plate of eggs and toasted bread. "You're having breakfast, Dean, and then we're going out. We've got errands to run and people to see."

My stomach growled at the sight and smell of food. I hadn't had much appetite in the last couple of days. My stomach had been tied in knots of anxiety, confusion, and fear, not to mention the nausea caused by my wounds and infection. But after reading those replies, I felt suddenly ravenous.

I was headed in the right direction, it seemed, and that did a lot to allay my fears.

I downed my antibiotics with my last swallow of coffee. I didn't bother with the Vicodin or oxycodone. My hand was feeling pretty good. Hell, *I* was feeling pretty good. Then Taylor and I hit the streets.

It was surprisingly warm out, and almost all the snow had melted from the ground. The only remaining patches of white were hidden away in the shadows: circles around the trunks of trees, small drifts piled against houses. I watched Taylor as she walked beside me. She wasn't watching the pavement in front of her feet. Instead, she was looking far into the distance. It made her look strong. She wasn't squinting despite the bright sun overhead. Her skin was perfectly smooth, a beautiful tea-soaked ceramic. I wanted to touch her, to run my thumb across her smooth cheek. But I could imagine her pulling away in horror, recoiling from my touch, and the thought of that reaction was enough to hold me back. I didn't want to cause her any type of distress.

She glanced at me from the corner of her eye. "Why are you

looking at me like that?" she asked, a perplexed smile appearing on her lips. "You're kinda freaking me out here, Dean."

"I'm just thinking about taking your picture," I said. "I'm thinking about capturing the way the sun illuminates your skin and sets your eyes on fire. I'm thinking about the lens I'd use, the framing I'd try to get, the stuff I'd keep in the background."

We continued to walk, and I continued to study her face.

When I didn't move to unholster my camera, Taylor let out a warm laugh and shook her head. "Okay, Dean. Just keep thinking about that photograph."

"Always."

As we continued downtown, she kept glancing my way, a self-conscious smile on her lips. I watched as her cheeks blushed a gentle shade of red—a rosy, pinkish red—and my chest filled with warmth. There was a smile on my lips. It felt goofy—big and unrestrained—but I couldn't dial it down. It had taken over my entire face and wouldn't let go.

Looking back now, this was by far my happiest time in Spokane. I was with Taylor, and I'd managed to make her happy; maybe I made her feel beautiful and loved.

And maybe, for a time, she made me feel the same.

"Let me do the talking," Taylor said as we turned south on Monroe. "These guys are all right, but they can be pretty intense. They're territorial and very touchy."

"Homestead?" I asked, guessing at our destination. I recognized the street from my first day in the city. Weasel had escorted me past these very buildings, bitching about the Homestead and all of its rules. I remembered people staring out at us distastefully, peering from doors and windows. But looking back, I realized that those disgusted looks might have had more to do with Weasel than with the stranger entering the city for the first time.

"Yeah," Taylor said. "They know me. I lived here for a while, before I found the house. They'll let us in."

Taylor led me to a street-level door halfway between First and

Second Avenue. The building itself was squat and unremarkable: a two-story structure sandwiched between a pair of taller neighbors. As soon as we got within a dozen feet, a man stepped from the shadows inside the building. He was big and thickly muscled, and he had a kinked black beard that masked most of his face. There was a baseball bat clenched in his hands, and he was holding it like he was getting ready to drop down a bunt: his right hand down on the knob, his left wrapped around its thick barrel. I could see an eagle tattooed on the back of his hand. I stopped dead on the sidewalk, but Taylor continued forward. As she approached, the man shifted the bat up against his shoulder and pulled himself to his full height.

"What are you doing here?" the man growled. "I thought you'd left for greener pastures."

"I can't pay the old man a visit?" Taylor said, her voice cold, confrontational. "Do you really think Terry's going to turn me away?"

The man grunted. "Maybe not, but that's *his* weakness. In my opinion, the gone should stay gone. If they have nothing to offer, they have nothing to offer."

Taylor made a clucking sound at the back of her throat, and then she flashed the man a mocking grin. The grin looked out of place on her delicate lips. "Since when did you get so deep, Mickey? And since when do you guard doors?"

The big man let out a frustrated sound—something between a grunt and a deep-throated growl—then he lifted his chin toward me. "If you go in, you leave your *boy* behind."

"No," she said, shaking her head. "We go in together. That's what Terry would want."

The big man glowered, stone-faced, for a couple of seconds, then he flexed his fingers against the bat. It was a gesture of pure frustration, his fingers pulsing with pent-up energy. "Fine," he said. "I don't care! This place is going to hell. No rules. No fucking order!" With that, he turned and disappeared into the building. Taylor followed. I had to break into a trot in order to catch up.

There was a second man standing just inside the doorway, and he stayed behind as Mickey led us back into the building. All the exterior windows had been boarded over with sheets of reinforced plywood. It looked like the Homestead had battened itself down for a hurricane. Or a military assault. Mickey produced a flashlight and waved us forward impatiently.

Before the evacuation, the building had housed a number of small businesses. Every door sported a different name and slogan. We passed MATTHEW FRANK DISCOUNT AUTO INSURANCE, TEMPLE SMITH OFFICE SUPPLIES, and, toward the back of the building, perhaps the sketchiest acupuncture clinic I'd ever seen, labeled simply ACUPUNCTURE. Then Mickey led us up a narrow flight of stairs, and we started back toward the front of the building. Halfway there, Mickey stopped at one of the boarded-up windows. He hit the plywood with a sharp, practiced rap, and the large sheet of wood swung aside. Outside, a five-foot plank spanned the distance to the neighboring building.

Taylor didn't hesitate. She climbed over the sill and crossed the gap, disappearing into the building on the other side.

Mickey gestured impatiently for me to follow. It wasn't a long way down—maybe fifteen feet—but I still took my time. I held my hands out for balance and placed my feet with care. When I reached the middle, the board suddenly started to bounce, and I looked back to see Mickey crawling out of the window behind me. The thought of that behemoth bouncing along at my heels— the thought of the wood cracking beneath all that extra weight— was enough to speed me up.

I stumbled over the windowsill on the far side, but thankfully Taylor was there to stop me from falling. Mickey jumped down a couple of seconds later.

"What the fuck is this?" I asked. "What the hell are we doing?"

"Precautions," Taylor said. She gave me a brief, placating smile but didn't offer any further explanation.

We were in a short hallway. There was a small bathroom to our right and an even smaller office to our left. The floor was a beautiful polished wood, and Taylor's footsteps thumped solidly as she took over Mickey's lead. I followed a couple of steps behind, and I could feel Mickey looming at my shoulder.

The hallway opened up onto a large, mostly empty room, and we stopped at the threshold.

It was a ballet studio.

I was surprised at our destination. I'm not sure what I was expecting—a small, smoky room, maybe, or some type of fortified bunker—but this was not even close. The room was light and airy. The far wall was nothing but glass, providing a view of Monroe Street directly outside. And the wall opposite was glass, too, panels of flawless mirror, reflecting the sun-dappled room. There was a bar bolted to the mirror, and I could imagine ballerinas stretching up and down its length, their pointed toes raised to the sky as they limbered up lithe, supple bodies.

A hint of rose lingered in the air. It was the last remnant of a fleeing ghost. A sense memory: powdered perfume over stale sweat.

"Taylor!"

There was an old, ratty sofa sitting in the corner of the room, facing out toward the massive window. Surrounded by stacks of books and a jumble of discarded clothing, it looked completely out of place on the barren expanse of hardwood floor. Like a pile of trash dropped into the middle of a perfectly manicured garden.

There was an old man struggling up from the low sofa. "Taylor!" he repeated, a wide smile on his face. "My darling girl!" The man was at least sixty-five years old. His hair was salt-and-pepper black, but his temples had faded to pure white. His wide smile was caught in a web of wrinkles, and there were thin lines radiating out from his joy-narrowed eyes.

"I saw you pass by outside," he said, nodding toward the window. "But I thought you were going to just keep on walking. I thought you were going to give this old man a wide berth."

Taylor shook her head. A bright smile spread across her face, and she broke into a trot, running up to the old man and sliding smoothly into his arms. I was surprised at the intimacy of the gesture.

In the hallway behind me, Mickey let out a disgusted grunt. Then he turned and left. I heard him scramble back off the windowsill and across the plank to the neighboring building.

"I see Mickey hasn't changed," Taylor said, backing out of the old man's embrace. "Still pissed off . . . at everyone and everything."

"Mostly at me, I think," the man said. "I'm sure he thinks he could do a better job. Thankfully, no one in their right mind would follow where he wants to lead."

The man noticed me standing on the far side of the room. He flashed a smile and nodded in my direction. "Why don't you tell your friend to come over here, Taylor. This isn't a peep show. He's more than welcome."

I approached slowly, and Taylor turned her wide smile my way. "Dean, this is Terry. He started up the Homestead. He's done a lot for me. He . . . well, I guess he saved my life."

"I don't know about that," the old man said with a smile. It was a relaxed, weary smile. He offered me his hand, and we shook. "It's not like I did her any favors. She's strong. I offered her a place to stay, but she more than paid her dues."

"Modest as ever," Taylor said. She turned away from the two of us, then crouched down and started to shuffle through the books on the floor. "Agricultural texts? Gardening? You're still trying to start that farm?"

"That's the dream," Terry said. He let the words hang in the air for a second. Then an exhausted sigh escaped his lips. He gave me a nod—an apologetic dismissal—and retreated back to the sofa. Despite his slight frame, the sofa cushions sagged under his weight. It looked like the ratty old thing had reached its last couple of springs. "It's not going to happen. Nobody's interested. They'd rather scavenge than farm. Or get what they want from Mama Cass."

"What happened?" Taylor asked. There was genuine concern

in her voice. She sat down on the sofa's armrest and focused all of her attention on Terry's exhausted face.

"Nothing. Nothing happened. I figure this is just the way it works. There's no movement, no change in our situation. The government isn't opposing us anymore; they aren't making progress with the city, and they aren't trying to kick us out. And nothing we do seems to make a difference. The buildings still fall apart. People get tired and lonely. And on occasion they disappear. It's only natural the Homestead should fall apart. What good is an organization—what good is *society*—if it can't keep entropy at bay, if it can't protect and unite its people?" Terry shook his head. Despite his dire words, the exhausted smile remained on his lips. "There were—what?—fifty people here when you left? There can't be more than thirty now. Mickey wants to do more to keep them. He suggested a . . . a recruitment drive. He wants some type of paramilitary force. He wants to raid Mama Cass's supplies!" He let out a short laugh. "*Ha*, he even wants to levy taxes!"

"But . . . the work you do. The support you give . . ."

"It's not a bad thing," Terry replied. "I'm still here. And I'll help anyone who wants my help. I'll give them structure, help them get their heads on straight. It's just . . . no one seems to want that anymore."

Taylor seemed at a loss. She extended her hand, to put it on Terry's shoulder, but the old man shook his head and pulled away. A broad smile spread across his face, and I could tell that it was a massive effort on his part, casting aside all that gloom, trying to appear jovial. "Hell, maybe it's all a sign of my success. Under my umbrella, people get strong enough to leave. I'll think of it like that, okay? I help them, and they get strong enough to make a go of it on their own. Hell, just look at you!" He held his hand out toward Taylor, palm up, like he was presenting a beautiful piece of art to a gallery of viewers. "You're looking great. Are you happy?"

Taylor smiled and cast me a sly glance. There was a touch of blush in her cheeks. "Yeah, I'm doing well. But you're the one who set me on that path."

Terry smiled. And this smile seemed effortless.

"I guess you're here to see Weasel?"

"*What?*" Confusion warped Taylor's face, and she jolted back in surprise.

"I assumed that's why you came. He's been here for three days now."

"I thought you were done with him. I thought you refused to let him back."

Terry shrugged. "I've mellowed in my old age, I guess. The rules just don't seem as important . . ." He shook his head. "Anyway, he's your friend, and Johnny pleaded for him."

"Jesus Christ, Weasel," Taylor hissed to herself. Then she turned back to Terry. "And why the fuck are you listening to *Johnny*?"

Terry didn't reply.

"Fine," Taylor said. She closed her eyes for a moment, and as I watched, the anger faded from her face; once again, there was nothing but caring, warm emotion, though perhaps not as warm as before. "No, Terry, why we're here, what I want to know . . . do you have Devon spying on my house? Are you keeping tabs on me?"

Terry let out a laugh. "Yeah, yeah, that's me," he said. "I didn't think you'd catch on. I've had him stopping by once or twice a week to tell me how you're doing. It's all innocent, though. Nothing nefarious. I'm just trying to keep track of my favorite girl."

"And you're paying him for this?" Taylor asked. "You're paying him to spy on me?"

"Not much—just some food, some pot—and if you're worried about his character, I'm not making him report anything too personal or bad. I just want to know how you're doing, if you're in trouble, if you need help." He flicked a finger in my direction. "He told me about Dean last time he was here. He said you seemed happy."

"When?" I asked, jumping into the conversation. "When did you see him?" I was excited. This seemed like a miracle to me. Finally, here was the answer to a mystery, an explanation that actually made sense, that didn't get lost in a jumble of magic and religion.

"A couple of days ago," Terry said. "Just after Weasel moved in."

"And where'd you get the radio?" I asked. "How'd you wire up the tunnels?"

Terry met these questions with a look of confusion. It seemed genuine. "Radio? Radios don't work here. And tunnels?" Terry shook his head. "No. No, I don't go near any tunnels."

I looked over at Taylor, and she returned my gaze, confused. I hadn't told her about the radio and the wires. After a moment, she offered me a halfhearted shrug. "Maybe it's something Devon did on his own. Maybe it's not important."

I shook my head. No, that wasn't it, but I didn't bother trying to argue. Taylor hadn't been there. She hadn't followed the wire down into the dark; she hadn't seen the vast network of tunnels. There was no way that that didn't *mean* something. And there was no way Devon could have done it all on his own.

"Where's Weasel?" Taylor asked Terry. "I want to see him. I want to make sure he's okay." She cast me a nervous glance, looking for my reaction. But I didn't react. There was just no energy there, no anger. Not anymore. Weasel wasn't a threat; he'd never been a threat. Taylor could like me and still want to help her friend, even if that friend had tried to fuck me over. I could see that now. I guess I was getting more secure in our relationship.

"He's in the tower, down in the basement," Terry said. "I don't know if he's there right now. Frankly, I haven't seen him since he moved in."

Taylor stood up and made to leave.

"Don't be angry with me," Terry said. "I didn't mean anything bad. I just want to see you safe. I want to see you happy."

Taylor nodded. "I know, Terry," she said. "I'm happy. I'm safe. But it's *you* I'm worried about." She bent down and gave him a kiss on the forehead. And then, in a quieter voice: "But don't spy on me. Don't you dare! I don't want to end up hating you. Okay?"

"Okay," Terry said, once again flashing that exhausted smile.

Then Taylor turned and walked away.

Taylor left through the front door. I followed her to the threshold, then paused, turning to look back into the room. Taylor continued on without me.

Terry was still seated on the sofa, facing the wide window. His hand was up on his forehead in a pose of absolute fatigue. Struck by the tableau, I fished the camera out of my backpack and started taking pictures. I framed it so that the bottom part of the vertical photograph showed barren hardwood floor, struck slightly out of focus. And then, up in the top third, there was Terry, seated on that ratty old sofa, surrounded by stacks of books. He was front-lit, as sunshine broke through the clouds on the far side of the glass. His shadow—nothing but a slumped head perched atop the sofa's elongated width—stretched back into the room, darkening the polished floor.

The Weight of the World, I thought, considering titles. *No . . . The Weight of Civilization.*

When I thought I had the shot, I holstered the camera and re-slung my backpack.

"Take care of her, Dean," Terry said, still holding that pose, head down, hand up on his forehead. He must have heard the shutter from across the room. "Don't let anything happen."

I nodded, even though I knew he couldn't see me. Then I followed Taylor out the door.

We climbed stairs up to the third floor, then crossed to the next building over, once again making our way across a makeshift bridge. The buildings on this block were all close together, but still, crossing these spans, feeling the wood wobble beneath my feet, was a nerve-racking experience, and each time I found myself holding my breath and keeping my eyes fixed on the far side.

Three floors up, the fall might not prove fatal, but it certainly wouldn't be pleasant.

When we reached the third building, we continued to climb. The building ended up on the fourth floor. We stepped out of the stairwell onto a tar-papered roof.

"Terry likes heights," Taylor said. There was a small tent set up on the corner of the roof. Arrayed around its entrance were several potted plants and a small charcoal grill. A thin ribbon of smoke curled up from the grill, guttering up toward the sky. "He linked up all of these buildings to give us territory, but he himself prefers to sleep out in the open." She was smiling widely, her affection for the old man beaming through. "The first floors of these buildings are all boarded up. There are only two entrances, one on each end of the block, and Terry keeps them guarded. It's his own medieval castle, you see. Only here, no one's trying to storm the gates."

The next building on this side of the block was much taller than the one we were standing on. In fact, it was the tallest building in sight, stretching at least ten stories tall, an imposing brick edifice, each side a dark red face stubbled with tiny windows. Taylor stepped to the edge of the roof and gestured up toward the building's top floors. A lot of the windows up there had been covered over, and I could see the glint of aluminum foil in those recessed squares, glimmering like silver teeth between narrowed lips. "The tower," she said. "I used to live up there . . . for a while."

The buildings here were not quite even, and the bridge over to the tower was skewed, slanted down at a fifteen-degree angle. Thankfully, somebody had set up a handrail, though it didn't feel much sturdier than the planks bouncing beneath my feet. Once again, I held my breath, not letting it out until Taylor grabbed my arm and helped me down on the far side.

We ended up in a stairwell. Taylor pulled a flashlight from her pocket and led the way down, casting shadows back and forth across each riser as I struggled to keep up. She didn't pause when we reached the bottom. She shouldered her way through a heavy fire door into a cold and musty basement.

It was like stepping into a long-abandoned crypt: the penetrating cold, the touch of moisture, a slight hint of rot floating in the thick, stale air. There was a dim light at one end of the main corridor. Taylor touched my arm—a brief, tentative touch—and started toward the light.

The corridor ended in a large industrial kitchen. There were stainless steel tables running along all four walls, and a cooking station stretched down its middle, complete with stove tops and a wide ventilating hood. The floor was dark red tile, and it dipped down toward a drain in each of the room's four corners. The smell of rot was stronger here.

The light was coming from a pantry on the far side of the room. Taylor gestured with her flashlight, then led the way over to its entrance.

There were three people in the pantry, and all three lay stretched out on the floor. At first, I thought they were dead, then one of them—a large black man wearing a bright red knit cap—groaned and turned over, burying his sweaty face in a blanket on the floor. The other two—a girl sporting wild black dreadlocks and a stick-thin man with a scraggly, unkempt beard—remained still. The girl had her face pressed up against the man's chest. She was shivering, despite the sheen of sweat glistening on her cheeks.

There were lit candles scattered around the room and a single battery-powered lantern burned in the corner. The batteries must have been dying, as the lantern gave off only the dimmest orange glow. There was a candle and a charred spoon at the girl's feet, and she had a pair of panty hose cinched tight around her bicep. The smell of ozone, sweat, and cooking heroin lay thick in the air.

"Shit," Taylor muttered. "Motherfucker!" She crouched down next to the bearded man and began slapping his cheeks, first softly, then with increasing strength. After the sixth slap, the man's head snapped up off the floor.

"Fuck, man," he said, wearing a distant, shit-eating grin. "What the fuck . . . ? *Taylor?*"

"Yeah, Johnny," Taylor said. "You're a motherfucking piece of work, aren't you?"

"I try," Johnny said, still wearing that lunatic smile. He let his head drop back down to the floor. "I'm a work of art . . . always in progress."

"Just tell me where Weasel is," Taylor said, shaking her head. "Tell me where he's staying."

Johnny was silent for a handful of seconds. His eyelids began to droop, and then, abruptly, they fell shut.

"Motherfucker!" Taylor growled. She clamped her hands over both of Johnny's ears and started to shake his head back and forth. His eyes snapped open, and there was a look of fear there as he tried to get a fix on Taylor's angry eyes. "Where's Weasel, Johnny?" Taylor continued to growl. "Just fucking tell me!"

The violence jolted the dreadlocked girl out of her stupor. She pushed away from Johnny and frantically rolled across the room, finally coming to rest against her other roommate. She pressed herself tight against his sleeping body and curled into a fetal ball. Her eyes remained open. She watched Taylor and Johnny from beneath drooping, heavy lids.

"Fuck," Johnny groaned as Taylor continued to shake him. "Just stop! Stop! I'm going to be sick."

Taylor grabbed the collar of Johnny's shirt and pulled him up into a sitting position. A ribbon of spit poured from his lips, and I thought he really was going to be sick. "The other . . . the other end of the hall," he said, trying to prop himself up with a shaking arm. "He emptied out a broom closet. Won't fucking come out."

Taylor put her hand against Johnny's face and pushed, hard, sending him tumbling back to the floor. Johnny let out a loud groan and grasped his head between his palms. He closed his eyes and started rocking back and forth.

"Leave Weasel alone, Johnny," Taylor said. "Terry might be letting your shit slide, but I won't let it go. I'll fuck you up—

absolutely *fuck you up*—if I ever, *ever* see you near him again. Okay? *Okay?*"

Johnny let out another groan. I took that as a sign of agreement.

"We've got to get him out of here, Dean," Taylor said as we crossed back through the kitchen. She paused and looked back at me over her shoulder. There was a hint of fear in her eyes, a glimmer of trepidation fighting its way past all of that seething anger. "He's going to die here if we don't do something. We've got to get him home."

"Yeah," I said. "It's fine. I understand."

After seeing Johnny, I really couldn't argue with her logic. I wouldn't wish that kind of punishment on anyone.

A grateful smile flickered across her lips. And then she was gone. She barreled out of the kitchen and back down the main corridor, quickly making her way to the other end of the floor.

There were a half dozen storage rooms at this end of the basement, but Taylor barely paused as she darted past, sending a brief flicker of light across each open door. I struggled to keep up. Finally, at the end of the corridor, she pulled to a stop. There was a jumble of debris strewn across the floor, here—a mop, several brooms, rags, a bucket filled with dirty gray water—and it barely left enough space to let open the broom closet door.

Taylor stepped up to the closet and knocked. "Weasel?" she said. Her voice was tentative, weak, a stark contrast to all the energy she'd unleashed against Johnny. She knocked again, this time a little bit harder. "Let me in. I want to help."

There was no response.

"Please, Wendell," she said, her voice cracking. She continued in a low whisper: "I'm sorry. I forgive you."

Then she opened the door.

There was no one inside. The closet was a tiny space, barely large enough to house a sleeping man. There were blankets layered in a stack on the floor, the top blanket turned down in a neat triangle. It looked like a child's bed, prepped and ready for a good night's sleep.

"Fuck," Taylor said, letting out a nervous laugh. In the backwash of her flashlight, I could see tears glistening on her cheeks. "All of this work . . . I thought we'd find him dead, and the fucker's not even here."

She played her flashlight across the floor of the closet. The blankets took up most of the space, but there was more of Weasel's stuff inside. There was a stack of flannel shirts folded into a pillow at the head of the bed and, lying next to it, Weasel's fedora. I remembered it from my first day in the city. He'd doffed it like a gentleman as he greeted me.

Taylor once again panned the flashlight across the small room, finally settling on a stack of notebooks tucked into the corner. They were cheap notebooks. I recognized the style: black-and-white marbled covers, the words *Composition Book* and *College Ruled* stamped across the front. There had been stacks and stacks of these things at my university bookstore—nearly a full pallet, dumped right inside the front door—on sale for fifty cents each. A worn-down nub of pencil lay on top of the stack, and there were wood shavings scattered across the floor.

Taylor let out a curious grunt. "His journals," she said. "He's always writing. Every fucking day." She got down on the blanket and pulled the topmost notebook into her lap. She held up her flashlight and flipped through the thin pages. I could see densely packed words scrawled in pencil and ink.

She leaned forward to put the notebook back, then paused in midmotion. Her eyes widened, and her left hand started to move slowly at her side, gently caressing the blanket down by her leg, feeling . . . something. I couldn't see what she was doing. After a couple of moments of tentative exploration, she scooted off the edge of the blanket and pushed it back violently, bunching it up against the far wall and exposing the concrete beneath.

And then she let out a sudden, strangled sob.

"No, no, no," she hissed. She clamped her eyes shut and fell

back against the wall. Her legs went dead, and gravity pulled her back down to the floor.

There were fingers in the concrete. Four fingers and the tip of a thumb, sticking up from the broom closet floor.

Fingers, reaching up from the world below.

Taylor dropped her flashlight, and it rolled slowly across the floor. The fingers were at the edges of its light, but they still cast sharp shadows: tapered pyramids stretching across the concrete, pointing up toward the left-hand wall. The flashlight stopped rolling, but the shadows didn't remain still. The fingers were quivering. Not strong, conscious movements, but rather an electric tremor, tendons adjusting beneath skin, pulling tight against bone.

Taylor let out a weak groan. "It's Weasel," she said. Her voice was a raw, guttural whisper. She kept her eyes clenched shut. "It's Weasel," she repeated.

I didn't say anything. My heart was beating fast, but I was not afraid.

I was numb. I was astounded.

I got down on my knees and pulled the flashlight over to my side, fixing the fingers in the center of its beam. The fingernails were ragged and packed with dirt, and there was a bruise beneath the middle cuticle. The knuckles had been scraped raw, but otherwise there seemed to be little damage. And the concrete itself was absolutely perfect—no cracks, no crumbling, no hint of violence of any type.

I glanced back at Taylor. She had her hands up over her eyes, as if she were trying to hide, as if she were trying to retreat from the world into the comfort of her pressed palms. I left her alone. Instead, I grabbed my camera and started taking pictures.

14.1

Journal. Undated. Weasel's words:

(A composition book, battered and creased. The first twenty pages are filled with cramped, handwritten letters—messy and uneven, often deviating from the light blue college-ruled lines. The first couple of pages are written in ballpoint ink; then pencil takes over midsentence.

Entries are generally short—brief bursts of words separated by thick horizontal lines. The horizontal lines are bold; they've been traced and retraced, scribbled back and forth with a heavy hand. The entries are undated.

As the pages pass, the words become larger and sloppier, and the last couple of handwritten pages are barely legible. Left-leaning letters spill off the rule. Lines and curves refuse to meet, as if the words are losing cohesion, breaking apart and scattering across the page.

The second half of the notebook is completely blank.
It is untouched by pen or pencil. It is an empty
canvas, waiting for paint.)

I've made mistakes. I've done a lot of things I shouldn't have done. And each hole I dig buries me deeper.

There's something wrong with me, I know. Something very, very wrong!!!

And that's why I belong here. That's why I'm never getting out.

- - - - - - - - - - - - - - - -

Yesterday, about three, I met Johnny and Trent in front of Mama Cass's. They were tweaking on something, bouncing up and down like ADD children on cotton candy and crack. They had these wide shit-eating grins, and they kept glancing at each other and exchanging looks, like they had some motherfucking secret and I didn't measure up to share. I almost turned around and left right then. It was all just bullshit, bullshit I didn't need. But I didn't have anywhere else to go.

They took my arms and started guiding me east, Trent braying that ridiculous laugh of his, like it was all so fucking funny, and they wouldn't tell me where we were going. Just Johnny saying, "It's a surprise. It's your motherfucking birthday party."

I was already feeling like shit. Last night's Jack Daniels was a rotten lump in my stomach and I wanted nothing more than another pull. On something, on anything, to keep it all down, to keep it all settled. When I asked, they both shook their heads and Trent repeated that giggling, hysterical laugh. He told me "Just wait, buddy. Fucking wait. We've got something better." Then they pulled me into the building.

The place had been a high-end fashion store before the evacuation. I would have hated it, I'm sure—all gloss and empty space.

Somebody had done a half-assed job boarding up the windows before they fled, and a lot of light still flooded in through the front, between crisscrossed planks of plywood. The glass in the door had been shattered, and the place had been looted. Or maybe not. Maybe that's how it was <u>supposed</u> to look. Sexy destruction, postapocalypse glamour. That type of shit.

Trent laughed and pointed back toward the rear of the store, where there was a short alcove lined with dressing rooms. His laugh faded into a manic giggle, and he started to clench and un-clench his hands compulsively. He was fucked up—quite obviously fucked up on something hard—and there was a very bad energy coming from him.

I should have left right then. I should have run away. And there <u>was</u> a dim voice in my head telling me to do just that. But there was <u>another</u> voice in there, too, this one more insistent, telling me to continue on. (And maybe that was my <u>true</u> voice, trying to give me what I deserved. Doom. Destruction.)

There was a sound in the back of the room. A mewling. At first I thought there was a kitten back there, cowering in one of the dressing rooms. That's what it sounded like, a sick, tiny kitten. Mewling, chewing on the air.

Fuck. A kitten. If only that had been it.

- - - - - - - - - - - - - - - -

In the dressing room there was a kid. No, that's not right. It was a thing, not a kid. Really, I don't know what it was. The light was dim, but I could see that it was wearing ragged pants and nothing else. It was smaller than me, and it was cowering in the corner, shivering. Its skin was pasty white, almost glowing in the gloom. And that skin, it looked thin and brittle, like paper stretched over a Halloween skeleton.

Johnny pulled a syringe from his pocket, and Trent, still laughing like a fucking hyena, rushed ~~the kid~~ the thing and pushed it down to the ground holding his shoulders. Johnny's syringe was nasty. The needle was fucking <u>bent</u>. I didn't move, I couldn't fucking move. And Johnny squatted down and grabbed <u>the thing's</u> arm. And its mewling got worse. It was a keening, a squeal, like a pig in a slaughterhouse. It started to struggle and a stench filled the dressing room as it shit its pants.

"Help him," Johnny said. "Hold it down."

I moved, on autopilot, and grabbed its legs. They felt like tree branches wrapped in canvas. I held it down as it tried to kick. And Johnny

- - - - - - - - - - - - - - - - -

Fuck, I can't write this. Tomorrow. I'll try again tomorrow.

- - - - - - - - - - - - - - - - -

I tried to visit Taylor last night, but I didn't make it past the sidewalk in front of the house. The front window was bright with light from a fire, and I could hear laughter from the living room. Mac's drone. Amanda's titter. Taylor's voice, clear and sharp as ever.

It was cold outside and I was, mostly, sober. The whole fucking world was riding shotgun on my nerves, and I could feel my eyeballs straining to pop from my skull.

I'm really not doing well. It's that stuff. It's like a toxin in my blood, and it's pooling, growing in my brain. It's not right, <u>nothing's right</u>, and the voices in the house, the laughter, after a while it started to claw at my brain.

I wasn't welcome. I didn't want to be there.

- - - - - - - - - - - - - - - - -

Back to the dressing room. That thing.

It was like a dream. You're doing things and you can't explain why. You just know that that's the right thing to do. No, not right. There's no right or wrong about it. You just know that that's the way things happen, and you do them without thinking.

Johnny stuck the thing's arm and pulled back the plunger. The blood, or whatever it was, didn't draw smoothly. It was red, but not blood red, closer to red house paint, with a splash of white mixed in. And it was clumpy. The plunger would stick, and then a lump would shoot through into the barrel.

The thing was squealing. I looked into its eyes and it was terrified. Its mouth was trembling but it couldn't speak. I don't think it knew how. Like it was a baby, and all it could do was squeal. Its eyes were wide and terrified as Johnny drew out its blood.

When he pulled out the needle the thing stopped struggling and collapsed, limp, to the floor. Its squeal petered out. Trent and I let ~~him~~ go and ~~he~~ closed ~~his~~ eyes and pressed ~~himself~~ tight against the wall (it, fucking it, I mean). Its fingers clawed weakly against the floor.

Then I turned toward Johnny and found him smiling down at the filled syringe. Trent skittered across the tiny room on his hands and knees and held his arm out toward Johnny. He was laughing, fucking laughing, and there were tears in his eyes as he pulled back his sleeve and clamped his big hand around his bicep, right beneath his armpit, making the vein in the crook of his elbow stand out.

Johnny nodded and put the needle in. He didn't sterilize, didn't do anything. It went straight from that thing's vein, directly into Trent. And Trent groaned. It was a truly pornographic sound. Then he lowered himself against the wall and leaned his head back. There was a smile of pure rapture on his face and he let out a contented sigh. Looking at him, he could have been lying in a summer field, just relaxing, basking in a bright ray of sunlight. It was like he was on a fucking picnic.

The syringe was still three-quarters full, and Johnny came toward me after Trent collapsed back out of the way.

"You'll like this, Wendell," he said. Johnny never calls me Wendell. He calls me Weasel, like everyone else.

I started to inch back, but stopped. It was that voice again, or maybe just my body freezing up.

But I didn't stop him. He pricked my skin and tilted the needle up, and I watched as the clumpy red liquid swirled inside the syringe. Then Johnny hit the plunger and I was gone.

- - - - - - - - - - - - - - - -

It was incredible. It was perfect. There was warmth inside my veins and I could feel it, I could fell it _moving_ inside me. It was like I was mainlining comfort, like stuffing a down blanket into my arm. When it hit my brain . . . I don't know, it was indescribable. Not an explosive energy and confidence, like meth, or a mellow, numbing euphoria, like H. It was something else. It was like nothing I'd ever done before.

I fell back on my ass and braced myself up with my hands. In my palms, pressed against the ground, I could feel the city beneath me. It was like this . . . again, it was like comfort. Really, words fail me, and that's all I can say. It was _comfort_. Comfort and happiness, the warmth of the womb, radiating up through my body. It sounds stupid to say I felt _at one_ with the world, but I _did_ feel part of something larger. The city, maybe. I was not alone.

And Taylor didn't matter, the way she looked at me—hope or disappointment—the understanding and sympathy I never saw anywhere else. At that moment, I didn't miss her, I didn't feel ashamed that I'd forced her away. I was part of something bigger, and I couldn't see those _small_ things anymore. No matter how large they might look back in the real world, back down in that place where I was nothing but a tiny, weak failure, a loser sporting big thoughts and small resolve. Here, all of that was <u>nothing</u>.

Trent giggled again, somewhere in the dressing room. I couldn't see where he was and I didn't want to move my head to look around. I felt my own laughter bubbling up inside my chest and I understood him, I totally understood his braying, moronic glee. A hand grabbed my arm and pushed me down to the floor. It might have been Johnny. Or it could have been that kid, that skeletal, shivering kid with gold in his veins. I couldn't see and I didn't really care.

- - - - - - - - - - - - - - -

The dressing room was empty when I regained my senses. Johnny and Trent and the thing with the golden veins were all gone, and the room was dark. The sun had almost fully set.

I still felt high, and I staggered out of the store. I made my way back to the Homestead. I've been living here for several days now, but I'm always surprised when they let me back in. They shouldn't. They have no reason. And, really, I don't think anybody wants me here, just Johnny. I'm a fucking disaster. I don't know why Terry agreed.

- - - - - - - - - - - - - - -

Johnny seemed confused when I asked him about the stuff we took. I wanted more, but he just shook his head and stared at me like I'd lost my mind. He offered me some H, but the thought of heroin made me feel queasy, like I was going to throw up right there.

"Yesterday," I said. "You and Trent met me at Mama C's and we went to that place, that store, right? In the dressing room?"

He shook his head. "No fucking way. Wasn't us. We were here. We had Bailey go out and get us food. Trent couldn't fucking move!" Trent was sitting on an overturned milk crate on the other side of the room and he started to laugh. Johnny shook his head and shot me a look, a private look, mocking Trent.

"But you pulled blood from his veins," I said. I was getting agitated and confused. This happened, right? I didn't hallucinate all of that shit, did I? "We shot it. It was, it was . . ."

Johnny gave me a really strange look, like I'd just unzipped my pants and started peeing on the floor. He actually inched away from me.

"Take this, man," Johnny said, holding out a baggie of H. "You need it."

I looked at the bag and suddenly I found myself vomiting, splattering acid bile across the floor, across my shoes. Just looking at that stuff and I felt queasy and off-balance, like the whole room had just tipped over the edge of a cliff.

"Fuck man," Johnny said. "You're cleaning that up. If you can't hold your shit together, I'm certainly not holding your hand . . ."

- - - - - - - - - - - - - - - - -

I tried to see Taylor again last night. I made it through the front door this time, but there was no one inside. Then I heard music coming from the backyard. They were all back there, gathered around Floyd and his guitar.

I stood in the kitchen for a while, watching them through the sliding glass door. They looked so happy. They looked so far away.

I could only see the back of Taylor's head, but she looked comfortable out there. And that new guy was sitting across from her, wearing an idiot grin. Just like Trent. I'd be surprised if there were even an ounce of brain behind that smile.

But I would have apologized to him in a second. I would have begged his forgiveness, begged Taylor's forgiveness, if it got me out there, into that semicircle. But it wouldn't. There was simply no way out there, no path I could take. They were just too far away.

- - - - - - - - - - - - - - - - -

My veins have collapsed. They're flat as a pancake now. Just a minute ago, I was flexing and trying to work blood into my arm, but there was nothing there. I'm empty. The pinhole from my shot in the dressing room is turning dark, and I started working it with my finger and . . . _fuck!_ I don't know. It opened up. That tiny hole opened up and my finger slipped inside. There was no blood in the wound and it all felt very, very strange.

My stomach flipped as I watched my finger moving beneath my skin. All the way up to the second knuckle. I could feel suction in there, like my heart was trying to suck my finger into my circulatory system. And as I sat there, with my finger inside my arm, my vision started to dim, and my heart grew loud inside my ears, beating, beating, beating. It was a heavy, distant sound, and the beats started to fall farther and farther apart. Gray spots gathered in the corners of my closet.

I pulled my finger out and immediately I started feeling better.

There was no blood on my finger. None. Instead, it was sticky with some type of mucous or bile. Slimy. Chunky and gelatinous. Is that what's in my veins now? Is that what my heart is pumping?

Fuck. None of this could have happened, right? It's not possible. There's just _no way._ I'm just hallucinating, right? Fuck, next the walls will start to pulse and my balls will disappear. The sun will rise in my closet and I'll go blind.

But. But the wound is bigger and darker now, and the vein leading away from that spot is turning black. It's like someone drew on me with a fucking Sharpie. No, it's like someone drew _inside_ of me with a fucking Sharpie.

238

I want some more of that shit. I need it! The boy with the million dollar veins. Is he still out there? Is he looking for me?

I need to feel that again. I need to push back against this stupid fucking body.

- - - - - - - - - - - - - - - -

This is it, isn't it? <u>Game over.</u> This is how it happens. This is how it gets you.

Fuck. I. Just

(The next page is missing. The rest of the book is blank.)

14.2

Taylor didn't say a word. She kept her hand pressed against her face as she picked herself up off the broom closet floor and retreated back into the hallway. I packed up my camera and followed.

I still had Taylor's flashlight, and I watched with growing concern as she staggered back and forth in its light, swaying from side to side in the dark hallway. Maybe it was just her obscured vision that was throwing her off balance—she refused to move her hand, keeping it steepled across her face—but probably not. *It's all emotion,* I thought. The sight of Weasel's fingers had hit her hard; it had knocked her punch-drunk.

I wanted to comfort her, but I didn't know how. My fingers itched to pull her close, but I held them back, remembering her fear of contact. I ended up making some bland, soothing sounds at the back of my throat, and then I muttered something, just some stupid comforting words—I'm not sure what—hoping I might stumble across some magical combination that would set her mind at ease. But Taylor didn't respond. She let out a deep-throated sob and shouldered her way through the stairwell door.

I felt absolutely useless. I felt like a ghost, following along in her wake, unable to make any real impact on the world. Unable to touch her, unable to do anything but watch as she tore herself apart.

She led me up the dark stairwell, across a new bridge on the other side of the building, and then back down to the street. There were no guards at this entrance. It was all the way up at the north end of the block, and the street here was silent and empty.

Taylor collapsed against the nearest wall, just outside the Homestead's entrance. She pressed her hands flat against its surface and lowered her head, resting her cheek against the dirty brick.

"Taylor—" I said.

"No, Dean," she whispered, shaking her head slightly. "Don't say a fucking word. I can't hear it."

She put her back against the wall and slid down to the sidewalk. After a couple of moments just sitting there, frozen, she lifted her butt off the ground and reached back, struggling to pull something from the waistband of her pants. With a trembling hand, she produced one of Weasel's notebooks. The ratty black-and-white notebook had been folded down the middle. The cover was creased and stained, painted brown with dirt and dried liquid. The upper right-hand corner had been torn back like a scraped tag of skin, still attached to the book by a precarious tongue of cardboard.

Taylor flipped back the cover and started to read.

She kept her head down. Her face was buried in the book for nearly ten minutes. Then her shoulders started to shake, and the notebook fell out of her suddenly limp hands.

There were tears trickling down her cheeks, but I only got to see them for a couple of seconds before she once again buried her face in her palms.

I opened my mouth to say something, then closed it once again, remembering her request: *Don't say a fucking word. I can't hear it.* Looking at her, I knew that that instruction still stood.

So I left her alone. I picked up Weasel's notebook, flipped to the first page, and started to read his story.

The last page was gone. It had been torn from the book, the final entry cut short, severed midsentence. All that remained was a ragged strip of lined paper that still clung to the binding.

But I knew how the story ended. With fingers sticking out of smooth concrete.

As soon as I reached the end, Taylor pulled the book from my hands and got to her feet. "I did this," she mumbled, her frantic eyes darting back and forth. "I did this to him." And before I could stop her, she ran away, heading toward Riverfront Park.

15.1

Object. A skateboard:

It is an oblong piece of wood, about three feet long
and caked in mud. One sloped end has been shattered.
The layers of pressed maple have come apart, splin-
tering into jagged, weather-darkened fragments.
There's a crack in the middle of its length; it
looks like a jagged rictus, reaching from one edge
of the skateboard halfway to the other.

The mud is thick, but there's an image visible on
the board's bottom side, peeking out through the
dried and flaking dirt. Just parts and portions: a
beatific face, wings in flight. White lines on a blue
and black background, with starbursts of yellow—the
Milky Way—glowing in the distance.

The skateboard is turned up on its back. Its wheels
are still spinning.

15.2

I didn't find Taylor in the park.

The park had changed in the last couple of days. Maybe it was just the snow and the ensuing melt, but it seemed much more desolate now, quiet and still. Like an animal holding its breath, or, maybe, like an animal that's no longer got any breath left to hold. The trees had lost their last leaves. Lush branches had transformed into skeletal limbs, with sharp fingers reaching up to scratch a painfully blue sky, and the ground beneath was carpeted in a thick layer of decaying brown mulch. And where there weren't any trees, there was dead grass, vast stretches of wild straw pressed flat against the ground. There was no longer even a hint of green, just sickly, jaundiced yellow.

I couldn't tell if this was just the normal transition between fall and winter here, or something different. Something permanent.

In my search, I found an old man sitting cross-legged at the top of a hill near the base of the clock tower. If I hadn't been looking for Taylor, my eyes would have skipped right over him, just a lonely old man growing like a lump out of the crest of a hill. *A goddamned Methuselah,* I thought as I drew near. He was stick-thin and had a scraggly white beard. His eyes looked haunted, sunk deep into the bony angles of his face.

He didn't respond when I tried to talk to him, when I asked

after Taylor. He didn't even look up. I'm not even sure he knew I was there. He just kept staring off into the distance—down the hill, across the river, out toward the heart of the city. I didn't try very hard to get his attention. I just left him sitting there.

As I made my way through the park, I didn't see any dogs. In fact, except for the old man, I didn't see anything alive. No animals. No people.

I stayed away from Amanda and Mac's tunnel.

After about an hour, I gave up the search and started home, hoping Taylor had beaten me there.

Charlie was in the kitchen, and Sabine was upstairs, locked in her room. The rest of the house was empty. There was no Floyd, no Devon, no Amanda, no Mac.

And no Taylor.

I stood in Taylor's doorway for a while, staring at her empty bed. Her smell was thick in the air. It wasn't a particularly clean scent—we were living rough here, after all—but there was a hint of sweet amber and rose beneath the smell of sweat and dirt. It smelled like flowers, I thought, sprouting from rich soil; this was a horribly romantic notion, and it left me feeling a bit disgusted at myself.

I was losing my focus, my drive—*I should be hunting down photographs, looking for images that will rock the world!*—but it seemed like there was absolutely nothing I could do about it. I couldn't put Taylor out of my mind. No matter how many times she ran away, no matter how distant she remained.

I gave the room one last look, then shut the door.

Before heading back downstairs, I gulped down a Vicodin. Then, after a moment's hesitation, I chased it with my last oxycodone.

I found Charlie sitting at the kitchen table. "It's getting lonely here," he said when I entered. He sounded wistful. "Sabine's hiding upstairs. Floyd and Taylor are off doing their own things. Amanda and Mac . . . well, they're just gone." He shook his head at the word *gone*. "And Devon—I haven't seen Devon in days and days."

"Yeah, Devon," I repeated, remembering the conversation Taylor and I had had with Terry, right before we found Weasel's disembodied fingers.

Devon. His tunnels. His radio. The subject was a welcome distraction. It was something I could grasp hold of, something relatively solid.

"Remember that networking hub I showed you? You said you could access it, get information. Can you still do that? Can you figure out what it is?"

"Now?"

"Yeah, now."

"I can try. If it's standard hardware, standard networking, I should be able to just plug right in." Then he shrugged. "What that'll tell us, however, I have no idea. Maybe nothing."

"Then get your stuff," I said. "It's time to go."

The house across the street was filled with a still and unnatural silence. There were muddy footprints leading back and forth from the front door to the basement stairs. *Did Floyd and I leave those behind the last time we were here?* No, I realized. Our tracks would have only been going one way, from the muddy tunnel out to the street. Someone else must have been here.

Charlie crossed the threshold behind me and then pulled to a stop. He looked around the empty house, perplexed. "There's a networking hub in *here*? Right across the street? But why? And *who*?"

I shrugged. "I don't know, Charlie. Those are the million-dollar questions."

I led Charlie to the room upstairs. The radio was still there, but the binoculars were gone. So somebody *had* been here. Devon, maybe? Come back to collect his property? They were nice binoculars; I probably would have come back for them myself if they were mine.

"Do you need the hub, or can you work with this?" I asked.

Charlie shrugged and headed straight for the radio. He sat down at its side and bent low over the matte-black console. "This should work," he said, unhooking the cable with a soft *click*. There was a small box at the end of the line and a couple of different wires sprouting from its end. "I don't even need to dig out a connector. This thing goes straight from coax to cat-5."

He set his shoulder bag down at his side and started setting up his computer. "Did you listen to it?" he asked as he went to work. "It's some type of networked radio, right?"

"There's nothing but static."

"Static?" he said, glancing up. There was a perplexed look on his face. "Like white noise? Hiss?" I nodded. "That doesn't really make any sense. There'd be nothing like static on a network like this. Unless . . ." The lines on his face softened as a new thought erased his confusion. "Unless this network connects up with a broadcast node somewhere else, somewhere outside the range of interference."

"So this could actually contact the outside world?"

"Maybe. If the cable . . ." He lifted it toward me briefly before plugging it into the side of his notebook. "If the network and the hubs lead all the way outside of Spokane—miles and miles away—If it's hooked up to some type of broadcast antenna or a satellite somewhere. If that's the case, this thing could be linked almost anywhere. Anywhere on the planet." Charlie paused for a moment, and we both let that sink in. Then he continued. "The military's using something like that for their data traffic, but according to Danny, it's all aboveground, stretching straight down the middle of I-90. And they've got a fleet of engineers maintaining the lines."

"So what is this shit?" I asked, but I didn't really expect an answer. I was just giving voice to my confusion.

"It's a darknet," Charlie said.

"A what?"

"A *darknet*. A private, secret network—something not hooked up to the world, isolated and secure, running on its own wires, using its own protocols."

"Who would do that?"

"I have no idea," he said, once again bending low over his computer. "But there's a . . . fanciful notion out there—nothing real, you understand, nothing concrete, just whisperings—about a shadow Internet. A network running parallel to the Internet we know, but somehow different, and very, very secret. Controlled by financial giants, the people who'd have the resources and the power to do something like that. It's all real illuminati stuff, you know, just paranoid speculation. But if it existed, I imagine it would be something like this—all hidden wires and clandestine hardware." Charlie looked up from his notebook and smiled slyly. The computer had finished booting up, and a multiwindowed program now filled the screen. "But we're getting ahead of ourselves here. Perhaps it's just a couple of lines connected to an antenna outside of the city. Hell, maybe it's just feeding someone's addiction to NPR."

I knew better. I'd been down in the tunnels. I'd seen the wires sprouting out in eight different directions.

Charlie was silent for several minutes as he scrolled past screen after screen of numbers and acronyms, arcane listings that looked like nothing but gibberish to me. "It looks big," he finally said. "I don't know how big. Depending on what type of router they're using and how many they've got, I might only be seeing a small corner of the network here. But there's traffic . . . a fair amount of traffic." He opened a command window and typed in a string of letters, and a media player appeared in the center of his screen. After a couple of seconds, an error message popped up, accompanied by a soft *bing*. "It's encrypted. I can't get at it."

Abruptly, he unplugged the network cable and slotted it back into the radio. "The radio's just a very specialized computer, set up to isolate and decrypt an audio feed that's been meshed inside the network traffic, and maybe broadcast back out. There's got to be hardware decryption somewhere inside this thing."

He turned the radio on and immediately jumped back, startled by an insistent voice that leaped from the speaker. Beneath the voice there was a whisper of static, a low ebb and flow, like water and gravel echoing down an empty pipe.

"—three things we need to look out for: an expanding border, changes at a cellular level, and communication. If it breaks through to the populace, we need to know immediately. It's getting worse—that much is certain—but we're not quite sure *how* it's getting worse, we're not quite sure in what manner, and we have no idea what that might bode for the future."

Charlie shot me a startled glance. "That's Devon," he hissed. "That voice, I'm sure of it . . . but what he's saying, that doesn't sound like him, not at all." I nodded in agreement. I'd only spent a matter of hours with Devon, but I recognized his voice. And this clear, quick delivery couldn't have been further from the stoned, incoherent ramblings he'd subjected us to at the house.

After a pause, Devon continued, his disembodied voice filling the room. "Containment is another matter. One we can actually do something about."

"Don't worry about Charles." This was a new voice—a man's voice—barely rising above the hiss of static. It sounded faint and distant, a trickle of words beamed from the other side of the world. At the sound of the new voice, Charlie blanched, literally blanched, his face turning a sickly shade of gray. The voice continued, "If it comes down to it, we'll deal with Charles."

"I'm sure you will, but just in case, I've got my own contingencies moving into place," Devon said. "No offense intended. I'm sure you can do your job, but I did not get to the place I'm at by taking other people at their word. We've got to plug these leaks, no matter what your familial concerns may be."

"I understand," the man replied, his voice still a muted whisper. Static and distance had stripped away all hint of emotion.

Devon's first words had knocked Charlie back on his heels, but this second voice hit him even harder, leaving him perched motionless on his folded knees, his mouth hanging open in a lower-case "o." Now he broke his paralysis and scrambled forward, his hands darting across the front of the radio. Finally, he managed to find the big red "transmit" button.

"*Dad*," he called, his voice catching on the final note, the raised lilt that would have transformed the word into a question. "Dad, it's Charlie. Is that you?"

The static continued for a couple of seconds—tense seconds—as we both waited for the voice to respond. Then the static stopped, and there was only silence. Devon and the mysterious voice—*Charlie's father*, I thought. *Is that even possible?*—were gone, leaving behind the sound of mute wires.

Charlie sat still for a couple of seconds, and then he turned his ashen face toward me. His eyes were wide, and he looked stricken, shocked absolutely senseless.

"How could you be sure?" I asked. "It was a whisper. I could barely hear him. It could have been anyone."

Charlie shook his head. "No, I know that voice. It was him."

And then, more quietly, "It was him," he repeated. He dropped his eyes back to the radio and stared at it expectantly, as if he were still waiting for it to resume speaking, waiting for it to morph into the face of his father. There was a lot there in that look: confusion, expectance, fear. Hope.

"Why would your father be talking to Devon?" I asked. "You said your parents were here, in the city. You've been looking for them. Why? What are they doing? What does this mean?"

He glanced back up at me, but his eyes remained distant. There was little there but shock and, just maybe—deep down inside—a dawning horror, a seed of understanding that was just now starting to take root. I could see it: a widening of the eye, a quiver in the lip.

And I wondered again, *What does this mean?* If anything, that look of horror on Charlie's face said that his father's voice coming from that radio meant *something*, something important.

"What's his job, Charlie?" I asked. "What does your father do?"

He didn't respond to my question. His eyes just slipped back down to the radio. And he continued to wait.

I tried to wait him out. I tried to wait for the shock to subside, for the answers to start coming, but Charlie remained mute. He just sat there in the middle of the room, fixated on that matte-black radio.

After a couple of minutes, a sound erupted in the quiet house, and it made me jump. It was a loud, prolonged creak, like a tight hinge slowly swinging open, and it came from downstairs.

I jumped to my feet and started toward the door. Charlie remained seated. He didn't even raise his eyes. I didn't even think he'd heard the sound. I left him sitting in front of the radio and quietly moved out into the hallway.

My nerves were frayed by the time I reached the top of the stairs, and my heart was beating hard. I had no idea what I might find downstairs. *Maybe Devon,* I thought. *Maybe he heard us and he's sneaking up from the tunnels, setting up an ambush, getting ready to deal with us. Maybe this is what he meant by "containment." Or maybe it's not Devon. Maybe it's something else, something much, much worse. Amanda's dogs or Weasel's disembodied fingers. Ghosts. Monsters. Swarms of mutant spiders.*

"Hi, Dean." The voice was quiet and subdued, drained of all energy. It was the type of voice a sponge would have, if the sponge had been taking sedatives for a month straight. "I didn't know you were here."

It was Floyd. He was in the downstairs hallway, sitting with his back against the front door, the exact same spot I'd found him in the last time we were here, after he'd fled the tunnels in absolute horror. The cellar door stood open across from him, and a fresh trail of mud stretched from the gaping dark maw to his muddy boots.

I made my way down the rest of the stairs and stood over him for a moment. When he didn't look up, I sat down at his side.

"I found a flashlight," he said, lifting a large metal Maglite from his lap. After a moment, it dropped back down to his thighs, his arm collapsing under its weight. "Much better than your camera screen."

"I thought it scared you," I said, trying to keep my voice calm and soothing. "I thought we couldn't drag you back underground."

He shrugged. "I had to. It was . . . calling to me." He laughed, a cold and lifeless chuckle. "Isn't that stupid? It called, and I came, again and again. And here I am, the king of running away. But I just had to see. I had to see him."

"Who?"

He looked up from the flashlight in his lap. His eyes were out of focus.

"They aren't working anymore," he said, ignoring my question. He dug into his jacket pocket and pulled out a pill bottle, shaking it upside down to show me it was empty. "I've taken, like, six now, and I'm perfectly sober."

I nodded, humoring him.

His shoulders slumped even lower. "It was my brother," he said. "When we were underground before, I swear I saw my younger brother down there, in those tunnels. He was sitting there, cross-legged in the middle of one of those offshoots—you know, the one I was looking down when you were taking your pictures? When you hit your flash, I saw him sitting there, in the dirt. And then the next flash, he was starting to stand up, heading toward me." Floyd tilted his head back against the wall and sighed. I could hear energy seeping out in that exhausted breath. Pretty soon he'd be an empty husk, puddled on the floor like a deflated balloon. "So I ran. That's me. I always run. But now . . . now I can't stop thinking about it, about him. No matter what I fucking do, what I fucking take."

"What happened to your brother?" I asked. "Why was he down there?"

Floyd tilted his head toward me and smiled. "I killed him, Dean—that's what happened. I fucking killed him."

There was a surprising warmth in his voice and a tiny little smile on his lips as he talked, as he tried to explain. And those two things remained even as his words turned to horrible things. Warm voice and tiny smile. They were a jarring contrast to the tears clinging to his cheeks and the pain and helplessness in his roving eyes.

"Byron. His name was Byron. And he idolized me. He wanted to hang out with me and talk like me and skate like me. And I tried to make time for him, really I did. I tried to look out for him. My father left when we were both pretty young, and my mom, she had her own problems—trying to support us and raise us right—and I wanted to take some of the weight off her shoulders. You know how it is, right?" He looked up at me, pleading, and I nodded. I could understand, even if I'd never had a brother, or a sister, or a parent who'd had to scrape and sacrifice just to make my life a little better. "I let him tag along when I went skating. Me and my friends . . . he was like a fucking mascot or something, and it kept us both out of my mom's hair, so she didn't complain. He was a pretty good skater. Not great, but good. I don't know if he could have really gone pro, but being my brother and all, that certainly helped. The company reps took him seriously, and when we hung out, they always wanted to give him free stuff. I worked some consulting shit for a company called F*ckstick—kind of a poseur company, with a little fucking star instead of the 'u' in their name—but they had me testing boards, giving input on design and image and stuff. Hell, they were even going to release a signature deck under my name, put my face in the ads and the whole celebrity endorsement shtick. Bullshit like 'Ride Pretty Boy Floyd's pretty-boy stick.' And God, man, isn't that just about the most awful thing you've ever heard?" Floyd let out a little laugh. It ended in an abrupt, wheezing gasp, as if he'd just been punched in the stomach. "Byron would tag along whenever I went to their offices in San Diego. This was right after I dropped out of high school, so he couldn't have been more than thirteen. He was there so much, they ended up making him his own board. Probably just trying to kiss up to me, really—buttering up my brother and all that—but he was so fucking proud of that board. Their graphic designer even did a caricature of him, in midflight, with wings sprouting out of his back, like a motherfucking angel—it was right there, blazed across the hardwood. It's corny, I know, but really, I've seen worse. They probably could have sold it in stores. Anyway, they never did release my deck—I think they were just stringing me along, really, trying to get my expertise on the cheap—but Byron still loved that board. He kept it pristine, never wanting to ride it. He just kept it propped up on top of his dresser, standing there like an icon, like some type of religious shrine." Floyd shook his head. "I don't know, maybe it was his future he saw up there: flying through the air on a skateboard, fucking angel wings on his back. Just like his motherfucking brother."

He paused and reached up to touch the side of his face, brushing his fingers against his cheek. His grin remained, but it had turned hard, an expression of perplexed bittersweet nostalgia. He ran his fingers from his temple down to the curve of his lips. His touch was light, as if he were exploring a brittle ceramic mask, something ready to crack and crumble and fall away.

After a moment, his eyes looked up and found me, locking on my face for a second before swiveling back to the cellar door.

"We lived in Santa Cruz at the time, and my friends and I had this little place in the woods, just off 17, near the base of the foothills. It was just a little clearing where we hung out, drank and smoked. Where we talked about boarding and tried to hook up with the skater chicks that were always hanging around. There was a fire pit out there, and most nights we had it burning. It wasn't far off the road; it was just a little country lane type of thing, branching off of the highway. And the clearing was so close, if you stood on the shoulder, you could see the fire sparking down in the mess of trees and brush, just down an incline and a hundred yards away. Fuck, I'm surprised we didn't burn down all of California with those fires." He paused and was lost in thought for a moment. "But anyway, I took him there a couple times. Not a lot. Not often. And I didn't let him drink or anything. Just . . . we'd just be hanging out there with all of my friends, and that was something he really loved.

"He was just trying to be close to me. I know that. The kid fucking idolized me. And I humored him. I looked out for him. I tried to include him. That was my job. I figured it was my duty. But it was more than that, I guess. I guess it was something I loved. I was his big brother, man, and I loved being his big brother. I loved that look in his eyes, that simple adoration." Floyd's smile widened, and for a brief moment it didn't seem quite so creepy.

"And then . . . one night—this was in late September—he got in a fight with my mom. It was all your typical teenage bullshit. He was concentrating too much on skating, and his grades were starting to slip, yadda yadda yadda —spending too much time out on his board or daydreaming about his board and not enough time studying. My mom was smart. She'd seen it all before—it was the exact same thing that happened to me—and she didn't want that for him. She didn't want him dropping out of school and wasting every last cell inside that thick teenage skull of his. So she grounded him. He bitched and moaned and kicked and screamed, and really, like I said, it was all your typical whiny teenage bullshit. But he knew I was going out with my friends, so he snuck out and tried to join us. But . . . he never made it there."

Floyd paused. The mask cracked a bit, and there was a flicker of movement in the corner of that horrible grin. His eyes were glassy and brimming with tears.

"Have you ever heard a mountain lion scream?" he asked. I had a hard time parsing the question. It seemed like such a non sequitur, just random words strung together. "It's a type of mating call that the females make—a shrill, yowling sound. And in the dark, it can sound like a human scream or a baby crying.

Well, I heard some that night, out by the fire, and it was like an omen. It set my teeth on edge and had my arm hair standing up straight. I turned and mentioned it to one of the girls we were with—how creepy it was, how scary—and she just laughed and called me a pussy. But there was another scream right then, shrill and labored, and that shut her up real fast. It was a very, very creepy sound, just this loud yodeling howl out there in the woods, all pain and horror. After a while, though, we managed to laugh it off, and we went back to our drinking and bullshitting. Mountain lions are pretty common in Santa Cruz, after all, and we knew that as long as we stayed by the fire, we'd be fine . . . no matter how scary they might sound, screaming out there in the dark.

"Byron didn't show up that night, and I had no reason to think there was anything wrong. The world felt the same to me, even though it had changed, even though it had become something fundamentally different. There was no thunder in the sky, no proclamations, no buildings crashing down around my head. But things *had* changed. I just didn't know it yet; I *couldn't* know it. Not then. I just went back home and crashed. I didn't even know he was gone until the next morning, when my mom woke me up. She was pissed off, and she started calling around to all of his friends. She grilled me—like I might have something to do with it—she tried to pump me for information. She thought—we both thought—that he'd just run away, that he was hiding somewhere with his friends, that he'd make his way back home any minute now.

"We didn't report him missing for three days. Jesus! Three fucking days! What kind of monsters are we?" he asked. Then, without skipping a beat, he went on with his story. "It was raining pretty hard by then, and we were both getting nervous. His friends hadn't seen him. Nobody had seen him."

Floyd paused. His mouth opened and closed, and it looked like he was having trouble picking out the right words.

"I . . . I . . ." He paused again and then changed tack. "The police released information, and there were blurbs on the local news. Someone reported seeing a kid hiking along the shoulder of 17, and the police organized a search of the woods. We found him almost immediately. I was in the dragnet. I heard the yells and came running. He was right near the clearing, right near the fire pit—this place that I'd fucking shown him, this place where he knew I would be!" The edge of Floyd's mouth was quivering now, and emotion was starting to leak through. "He was maybe a dozen feet off the path, at the bottom of the hill. He'd fallen in the dark, and he must have hit the ground just horribly wrong, just the worst possible way. His arm was shattered, and when I got there, I could see the bone sticking out—the fucking thing had torn through his long-sleeved shirt. His leg was bent backward, and there was a massive hole in his chest. The cloth around it had dried into a rain-washed red . . . He was dead, of course. He'd been dead for days. A fucking stick had punctured his abdomen. After the fall, he managed to pull it out—it was still there, clenched in his hand—but he'd bled to death in less than an hour."

"The medical examiner . . . he timed it, he placed the time at . . ." Floyd's mouth once again began to quiver, and then, finally, it collapsed into convulsions and he was sobbing. I moved to put my hand on his shoulder, but he batted me away. His hand stung against my chin, and I dropped back onto my heels.

"I was there, at the fire, while he was out in the woods," he finally managed, rubbing his palms against his wet cheeks. "And the mountain lions . . . there was absolutely no sign on his body, nothing, nothing trying to . . . trying to eat his body. There was no fucking . . . no fucking mountain lion out there in the night." He paused once again, and after a final heave, the sobbing stopped. His face settled back into an emotionless mask. Thankfully, there was no hint of a smile this time, no eerie grin. "He was there as I was walking out. He was less than a dozen feet from the path. Bleeding. Unconscious. Dying. And I was stupid and oblivious, a little bit drunk, a little bit high. And he was there. Fucking dying. Alone. Alone in the woods. Alone in the dark."

He shook his head, a slow arthritic shake.

"*Jesus fucking Christ,* I was probably laughing at the time, as I walked by. I was probably fucking laughing. And those mountain lion screams? Out there in the night?" He closed his eyes and let his head drop forward. "How . . . how could I be so stupid?"

He was silent for a time, and then he looked up. There was anger on his face as he turned toward me.

"What the fuck, Dean? Things were fine before, in the city. Things were cool. And then we had to go down there. Jesus Christ! Why the fuck did we have to go down there?" He picked the flashlight up off his lap and threw it across the entryway, through the cellar door. I heard it cascade down the flight of wooden stairs, and there was the sound of cracking concrete when it finally hit the bottom. "I was free, right? I was away from it all. Away from that house, away from my mom's bland words and her distant eyes—it was like they wouldn't focus anymore, at least not on me. I think she thought she had forgiven me, I think she genuinely believed that, but there was that look in her eyes. And she didn't know about the screams. I never told her about the screams." He shook his head angrily. "So I move on to San Diego, New York, motherfucking Brisbane. And then . . . I'm falling through the air, toward that wooden ramp, and fuck it if that plummet doesn't feel right. And maybe I don't turn when I should. Maybe I don't go limp. And then I come here . . . and I'm away. Finally. I'm free! And I'm barely thinking about him. This place here—I don't know—the weight of the air, the quality of the light . . . it's not all that easy to think, you know? And I'm free."

He nodded toward the cellar door. "And then we had to go down there," he repeated. He closed his eyes and heaved a brief sob. "Why'd you take me, Dean? Why'd I have to follow? And should I curse you for that, or should I thank you?" After a moment, he looked up and managed a tortured little smile. "Right now, I'm thinking I should just shank you in the fucking face."

His eyes held mine for several seconds, and then his shoulders collapsed. I could see all of that animation, all of that emotion, draining away, leaving behind an empty vessel. I moved closer and put my hand on his shoulder. This time he didn't push me away.

"Maybe you shouldn't be here," I said, keeping my voice low, trying to radiate calm. "Maybe you should leave, get out of the city. It's not good for you here." And after a prolonged beat, I added, "It's not good for any of us."

"But he's down there."

"He's dead."

He shook his head. "But he's down there. And I'll find him this time. I won't run away."

He turned away from me and reached through the living room door on his far side. "Look," he said, pulling something back into the entryway. "I found this. He wasn't there this time, but I found this, down in the tunnels." He handed me a skateboard. It was cracked in the middle and covered with mud. "It's his, the one he loved. See—" He brushed aside some of the drying dirt, revealing a picture on the bottom of the board. "—it's him. See? He's flying."

The board felt surprisingly heavy in my hands.

"We didn't find it in the woods. We didn't even know it was gone, not until later, not until after his funeral. I went to look for it, but it wasn't in his room, it wasn't on his dresser." I looked up from the board and saw Floyd smiling. It was a different smile now. It was reflected in his eyes, in the subtle lift of his shoulders. It no longer looked out of place on his face. "It means he's here, Dean, he's real. Just like the board. It's here. It's real."

I looked back down at the board and remained silent. No matter how much I wanted to tell him otherwise—tell him that he was wrong, that the city was just messing with his head, that his brother was gone, and that he should flee as far and as fast as possible—I couldn't.

The board was here. The board was real.

And I had no idea what that might mean.

16.1

News clipping. "A Hole in the Map: Spokane, and What They Aren't Telling Us," the *Seattle Times,* November 7, pages 7A and 12A:

The article has been clipped from a daily newspaper—aged, yellowing newsprint with sharp, scissor-cut edges. It is in two pieces: a narrow lead column stapled to a wider three-column continuation. It has been well handled. The ink is smeared, and words have been lost beneath smudged fingerprints. The paper is a webwork of creases; it looks like it has been crumpled into a ball and then smoothed back out.

The article describes the quarantine, several months in, and revisits official press releases. It quotes government officials, and there are several "No comments" scattered throughout the text.

There are two pictures incorporated into the final column of type, stacked one on top of the other—large blocks of ink reduced to abstract blurs by ex-

cessive handling. The topmost picture is nothing but
a dark morass of ink, with the barest hint of a face
lurking in the bottom corner. The bottom picture is
easier to parse but still difficult to understand.
Underneath the maze of creases and beneath the
smudged ink, where a sweaty fingertip has traced
body and limb, it looks like a spider. A giant spider, perched atop seven spindly legs and one outstretched human finger.

16.2

I put Floyd to bed. Then I watched him sleep.

I don't know how much oxycodone he actually took, but his breathing was shallow and he lay perfectly still. He didn't toss and turn or fidget and mumble. In fact, there was very little motion in his body, very little life. I'm not sure what I would have done if his breathing had actually stopped—CPR, I guess, even though I didn't have any training or knowledge on the subject— but I didn't want to leave him alone. I wanted to be there in case he needed me. In case he needed me to—I don't know—to do something, anything to keep him safe.

I just . . . I had the feeling that if I turned my back, if I shut my eyes, he would disappear. He would just . . . be gone. As if it were my attention, my concern that was keeping him rooted to the world, and without that he'd just fade into the ether.

And that would be that. One fewer person in Taylor's house.

And I didn't want that. I really didn't want that. I liked Floyd. I liked his relaxed skater charm, his playful smile, the way he laughed so easily and with such an inviting warmth. I didn't want to see the house without that. I wanted the chance to once again sit out in the backyard, listening happily as he played his guitar.

At least Charlie isn't here, I told myself. That—the two of them together—would have been too much for me to handle.

As far as I knew, Charlie was still in the house across the street. When I'd tried to tell him what was going on, when I'd tried to get his help with Floyd, he'd just grunted distractedly, barely even acknowledging my presence. I ended up leaving him behind. Now, sitting on the edge of Floyd's bed, I could see the blue glow of the radio in the second-story window across the street, and I could imagine Charlie sitting there in the growing dark, frozen like a statue, his mind stuck inside some faulty programming loop. Waiting—just waiting—for something to break him free.

And it was my fault.

Taking Floyd down into the tunnels, showing Charlie the radio—I was certainly doing some powerful work here. I was destroying people left and right.

Shit, I'm a fucking tsunami, I thought, *a wave of destruction rolling through the house!* First Amanda and Mac, then Sabine, and Weasel, and Taylor, and Floyd, and Charlie. I wondered how I was fucking up Danny's life. *I probably gave him some mutant STD or something. He probably has spiders burrowing deep into his brain.*

Jesus! I was like a motherfucking plague.

On this house. On the people in it.

When Floyd's breathing started to sound a little bit stronger, I darted into my room and grabbed my camera and notebook computer. I set up my gear on the floor next to his bed and started to work on my second post, pausing every couple of minutes to check on his breathing.

First I transferred pictures from my camera, then I spent a couple of minutes checking up on my hardware. The camera batteries were still half full; the computer was down to 45 percent. I tilted the surface of the zoom lens back and forth in the wash from my computer screen, and then I tried to clean the dirty glass, carefully brushing aside dirt and dust, using an alcohol spray to wash away a pair of errant fingerprints. When it was suitably clean, I capped the lens and put the camera back into its bag.

Then I stared at the computer for a while.

I didn't want to go on. I felt an incredible sense of dread at the thought of those pictures lurking on my hard drive.

My enthusiasm was waning . . . and fast. Whatever I'd come to the city to find, to see and to document, I was starting to think it just wasn't worth it. No matter how great the images were.

This was not a good way to get a reputation, I realized. This was a good way to die, to disappear.

Then leave, an urgent voice cried inside my head. It was a distant voice, and I got the sense that it had been screaming for a long time now. That one word, over and over again: *leaveleaveleaveleaveleave.* I just hadn't heard it.

But I couldn't leave. I couldn't leave Floyd. I couldn't leave Charlie. I couldn't leave Taylor.

And frankly, I couldn't leave the dream. My dream.

No matter how disillusioned I got—how stupid and myopic the urge became—I still wanted to take those beautiful photographs. I wanted to create something amazing. Art that would change the world! Even if it wasn't smart. Even if—my life on the line—it wasn't objectively worth it.

So I sat there, listening to Floyd's breath—it was stronger now, I was sure of that—and I popped another couple of Mama Cass's Vicodins, trying to gather up the strength to go on. And when I felt the warm roll of the drug start to surge inside my head, I leaned forward and launched my image viewer.

I tried not to think about what I was doing, tried to get lost in the simple step-by-step process: select several days' worth of photographs, right click, "open all," and then page through each individual frame. It was easier if I didn't think about it too much.

Just images without context. Just blocks of color on my screen.

There were over two hundred photographs, and my computer slowed to a crawl as it opened window after window after window. I started closing them one by one, picking out the best of each set and tossing away the ones that were out of focus and boring. A street scene, poorly framed; the tunnel in the park—without context, these didn't look like anything special. It was a pretty random process. Very intuitive. If I had stopped to think about what I was doing, if I'd been perfectly sober and unemotional, I would have spent a much longer time on each picture. I would have considered framing, the quality of the light on the subject, the oh too clever game of analogy and meaning, and the way the viewer's eye traveled across the image—whether the lines pulled you in, toward the subject, or pushed you away. Instead, I went with my gut reaction.

Did the image move me? Did it provoke emotion?

In the end, the ones I discarded were the ones I *could* discard. And the remaining seven were the ones I just couldn't close, the ones I had to keep looking at.

The first one was a technical mess. It was off center and poorly lit. And I hadn't even taken it. Sabine had, at my first dinner in the city, playing with my camera, holding it up above her head. I remembered sitting at the dining-room table—stoned out of my mind, relaxed and very, very warm—the whole room bathed in candlelight. I was actually in the photograph, sitting at the table, smiling vaguely at Sabine and the camera. And I was surrounded by the entire household.

When I looked at it, I was once again flooded with that feeling, that warmth, the belief that I had actually found something here, inside the city. *The good old days,* I thought. *They sure didn't last long*.

The next picture was something completely different. It was the face between the walls, and it was cold and terrifying and alien. I'd already worked on the photo some, making the face easier to see inside that narrow space, and I didn't spend long looking at it now. Seeing the pale flesh—remembering the way it had trembled, the way its eye had rolled blindly—made me feel sick to my stomach. I considered closing it—just trashing the image and hoping my memory of that horrible specter could somehow disappear with it—but ultimately I couldn't do it, I couldn't let it go. So I paged on to the next image.

It was the spiders, crawling from the hole in the wall. Gooseflesh erupted across my back. I didn't spend long staring at the image; instead, I shrunk it down into a small window and brought up the picture the Poet had sprayed on the front of Cob Gilles's building. It was the same scene. Or close enough. The two holes were a similar shape, and the spiders were about the right size. And while the placement of each animal wasn't quite the same, the similarity was uncanny. My photograph and the Poet's painting . . . these were two different representations of the same event. But how? According to Sabine, the painting predated my photo by at least a week.

Maybe it's a common occurrence, I thought. *Massive spiders. Complete with human fingers. Swarming like a tide, pushing out of gaps in the city, trying to engulf and consume everything they can reach. Maybe it happens once a month. Or once a week. Or every other day.*

I grunted and paged on to the next image. It was a close-up of the spider with the human finger. It was a truly awful image—just bad photography—grainy and poorly framed. But I couldn't ignore it, couldn't discard it. *I've got to post this,* I told myself. *If nothing else, I've got to give my public the finger.*

It was a bad joke, I know, but it made me smile—a goofy, half-drugged smile. But the smile died as soon as the next photograph popped into view. And suddenly the joke didn't seem funny anymore. It seemed cruel and sinister.

Weasel's fingers, embedded in concrete.

It was actually the best photograph of the bunch. It was a

close-up shot, not at all cryptic or confusing, and the focus was tight. Despite the horrific nature of the subject, there was absolutely no missing what it was. It was a set of fingers trapped in solid concrete. Period. End of paragraph. And I liked the lighting. I liked the look of Weasel's flesh against the gray concrete. The background was bright, lit by the camera's flash, but shadows sprouted from the base of each finger, traveling across the floor and landing on the wall. The foreground was dark and desolate; the toe of Taylor's boot was visible frame right. Looking at it now, I was surprised I was able to get such perfect focus in such a dark environment. *It's a fast lens,* I thought. *Good glass*.

I closed my eyes and paged forward to the last image.

It was the picture Taylor had taken, the two of us in bed with Danny. *How did it get here, at the end?* I wondered. I must have been rearranging during my first pass through the photographs. I must have put it here. But was it random chance, or was I trying to tell myself something? Was I trying to end on a high note, trying to remind myself of the good that still remained here inside the city?

The picture was out of focus and pretty much incomprehensible. Danny's head in my lap, but you really couldn't make that out. It was just a blur of blue denim, dark hair, and warm skin.

I didn't know how to feel about the picture. Conflicted, I guess. Certainly, there was a warmth and comfort in it. This was the closest I'd ever come to Taylor, but reaching up and feeling her breast, it was also the moment that the line between us had been drawn. I could come *this* close, maybe, but not an inch closer. And looking back, it was proof that she had feelings for me, genuine feelings, just like the ones I had for her. No matter how damaged those feelings were, how damaged she was.

I saved the seven images to an empty folder, then created a new text document and put together my post. It was a very simple post, just html tags for each picture, one after another: dinner table, face between the walls, real spiders, spray-paint spiders, close-up of spider, and then, in closing, Weasel's fingers. I considered including the picture of Danny and me but decided against it; even blurred and almost incomprehensible, it was too revealing.

My hands hovered over the keyboard for a couple of minutes as I considered captions. But what could I say, really? *This is true, this is real, this is what the city is?* It wouldn't do any good. They would believe me or they wouldn't. And I don't think I really cared anymore.

I'd been in the city for just under a week now, but I was already having a hard time imagining the world outside its borders. Were there people out there, still going about their daily lives? Were they sitting in front of their computer screens, looking at my pictures and daydreaming about Spokane, about the strange and the forbidden and the horribly, horribly romantic? Were there college classes going on right now? Was there nightly television and pizza delivery? Was there bus service and traffic jams and drive-through windows? Was there a government out there, looking out for the public good?

And was there a physics? Was there a reality? Was there comfort and warmth and happiness?

I didn't know. I couldn't tell. It just didn't seem real anymore.

I saved my work and shut down the computer. Then I curled up on the floor, rested my head on my backpack, and let the steady in and out of Floyd's breath lull me to sleep.

My second post on the Spokane message board was the one that started attracting media attention. I'm not sure I would have launched it out into the world if I could have foreseen the response, or, more accurately, if I could have foreseen my reaction to the response.

When I first got into the city, of course, I wouldn't have hesitated. Not for a moment. That was the whole point, after all: getting attention. Attention for me and my photography. But by the time I heard—by late November, when Danny brought me that first article from the *Seattle Times*—I doubt I would have bothered.

The person who had taken those photographs, who had composed that post, had in the intervening weeks become someone completely different. He'd packed up his cameras and gone to ground. And he just didn't give a shit anymore.

The article was mostly speculation. It recounted the standard government lines—about environmental contamination and tainted topsoil, carcinogenic buildings and ongoing threats to the public's health and well-being, and, as always, the need for further study—but it did ask some important questions.

What exactly is the threat, and why is cleanup taking so long?

Is the river tainted, and do the towns downstream need to worry?

Is it in the air?

And where exactly did this threat come from, and why is there such a need for secrecy and security?

In response, the article quoted an unnamed army general:

"First and foremost, we need to assure the people that there is absolutely no need for panic or distress. We have the Spokane situation well in hand. And while we can't go into the specifics of the threat for fear of jeopardizing ongoing investigations and research, we can tell you that we know exactly what's going on. We are still testing—under the purview of the EPA and with the assistance of some of the nation's greatest environmental scientists—in order to ensure that every last molecule of contamination has been removed from this great city. The safety of the good people of Spokane is our primary concern, and we are not going to rush our efforts, not when we have the health and happiness of our citizens on the line. Only when every last one of our concerns has been addressed—only then, and not one second sooner—will we consider reopening the city to residents. In the meantime, the good people of Spokane have been well compensated for their inconvenience."

When asked about a class-action lawsuit filed by cancer victims and surviving family members, the commander general replied, "No comment."

Up until this point, the article seemed like a standard-issue snow job—the government shoveling out the shit and the media repeating it ad nauseam. But in the last paragraphs, the writer gave voice to several of the conspiracy theories that had been floating around since day one. Was Spokane the site of a bioweapon experiment gone awry? Was it ground zero for a terror attack, something the government felt compelled to hide?

Or was it something stranger?

Perhaps hoping to stoke controversy or, more likely, trying to end on a note of humor, the newspaper went on to print two of my photographs: the face between the wall and the spider with the human finger. The low-res black-and-white reproductions were almost incomprehensible, but the writer went on to describe them: ". . . what appears to be a disembodied human face and a spider with a human finger in place of one of its legs. Purported to have been smuggled out of Spokane, these pictures recently appeared on **the-missing-city.com**, an Internet message board devoted to Spokane-related speculation. The photographer is currently unknown."

There wasn't any commentary on the photos, but the writer's message, in including them, seemed clear to me. It was a threat, a warning.

Without official word from the government—without comprehensive explanation and media oversight—the public would go about creating its own crazy theories, filling the giant vacuum left by the government's bloodless and insincere "no comment"s. Including my pictures in the article . . . this was just a taste of things to come. Without the truth, the media would be stuck publishing more and more ridiculous speculation—and there was some truly strange speculation floating around out there, some downright sinister and paranoid stuff. With my pictures, it seemed like the writer was trying to force the government's hand, trying to force it—in the face of panic and confusion—to respond with information and truth.

But, I wondered when I first read that article, *what happens when the truth rivals even the craziest Internet rambling?* In that case, what could the government actually share?

And what does it take to drive a country insane?

17.1

Photograph. October 23, 08:45 A.M. Entryway:

The house has been abandoned. The front door stands
open. There are signs of forced entry here—cracked
wood around a canted doorknob. The photo frames the
gaping maw, a large rectangle around a smaller
nested frame. The welcome mat is cut in two by the
image's edge. "WELCOME."

A wedge of sunlight illuminates a Persian rug on the
other side of the doorway—an indistinguishable
black and red scene spread across the white tile
floor. Windblown leaves and pieces of junk mail form
patterns on the tile and on the rug, describing eddies and gusts, describing neglect and desolation.
It is a language punctuated by streaks and blobs of
mud.

In the background, the house disappears into depthless gloom, hidden away from the sun's feeble reach.
There's a portico back there, leading toward the
rear of the house, and the dim outline of a stair-

case—graduated shades of gray reaching up toward
the top of the frame.

There's a landing at the top of the stairs. And in
the corner, away from the ledge: two pinpricks of
light, hidden in the dark shadows. Lidded slits,
reflecting a glimmer of electric red. A shiny metallic pink.

Eyes. Animal eyes. Peering down at the camera.
Peering down at the photographer.

17.2

There was light coming through the window when Danny woke me up.

"Rise and shine," he said. "The world can't turn without you." He had a box of doughnuts in one hand and a thermos of coffee in the other.

"What the hell happened?" he asked, smiling, bemused. He crouched down next to me and handed me the thermos. "Charlie's downstairs on the sofa, you and Floyd are up here having a sleepover, and no one else is home. Taylor's gone."

I ignored the question for a moment, instead focusing on the thermos. As soon as I got the cap off, my stomach started to growl, the smell of the coffee hitting me hard. *When was the last time I ate?* I wondered. *Yesterday morning?* I poured steaming coffee into the thermos lid, bolted it down, and then turned my attention to the doughnuts.

"What happened?" I finally said, echoing Danny's question as I fumbled with the box. I had a hard time forming the words. I was tired, and the muscles in my jaw were tense and cramped. "Fuck if I know. The city happened. Weasel happened . . . I happened."

Danny nodded and didn't press me for details. He'd been in the city long enough to understand; there was no point in explaining

274

the unexplainable. He watched as I bolted down a couple of doughnuts.

"How's your hand?" he asked as soon as I started to slow down.

I paused, my eyes darting down to my bandaged palm. My hand! It had completely slipped my mind.

When was the last time I'd taken the antibiotics? I felt a rush of panic and immediately grabbed for my backpack. I found Mama Cass's pills and swallowed a double dose. Then I started to unwrap the dirty gauze. I took it slow, my fingers shaking. I was afraid of what I might find.

What I found, however, was a pleasant surprise. The infection was gone. Completely gone. Underneath the bandage, which was stained a disgusting phlegmy yellow, there was nothing but a hardened scab. The surrounding skin was pale white, without even a hint of red. And even the gamy, rotten smell was gone.

I held up the hand, and Danny nodded his approval.

"And how's he doing?" Danny asked, turning his attention to Floyd. I turned toward the bed, and, as if feeling the weight of our eyes, Floyd let out a pathetic groan and rolled toward the window. His hand crept up and covered his eyes. "Did our boy have a rough night?"

"Yeah. He overdid it on the oxycodone."

"Fucking lightweight," Danny said with a smile. The smile didn't last long. He turned back toward me, and his expression collapsed into serious lines. "And what about Taylor?" he asked, his voice hushed, concerned. "She's usually here this early. I brought her some breakfast."

I shrugged, dejected. "I don't know. Yesterday . . . she just ran away from me. We found Weasel—" I didn't want to describe it. I didn't want to tell Danny about the fingers in the floor. "It's just . . . Weasel's gone, and she freaked out. She ran away. And I don't know where she went."

"Did you try her parents' house?"

"*What?*"

"Did you try her parents' house?" he repeated, more slowly this time, as if my incomprehension were the result of poor enunciation. "She goes there a lot. She visits them almost every morning."

"Her parents are here? In Spokane?" I was shocked. This information . . . it seemed ridiculous to me, utterly strange and unlikely.

Danny nodded, his eyes suddenly going wide. "I guess she doesn't talk about them too much, but I assumed . . ." He paused. "I'm just surprised she didn't tell you. She likes you, man. She likes you a lot."

What *had* she told me about her parents? I tried to remember.

She'd said that they had disappeared. She'd said that they were gone.

"Where do they live?" I asked. "How do I get there?"

Danny watched me for a second. He was wearing an expression of concern, and for a moment I didn't think he was going to talk. *Why? Is it something he sees?* I wondered. *Something written across my face? Something that scares him?*

Then Danny pulled out a small pad of paper and started drawing me a map.

It was gray out on the streets—still early morning, but you really couldn't tell. Under that low, gray ceiling, it could have been morning, noon, or almost night. The clouds could have been ready to spit out rain or snow or just break apart and let the sun shine in.

It was waiting-room weather. Purgatory weather.

I left Danny behind with Floyd and my computer. Charlie had shown him how to transfer outgoing information onto his thumb drive, and he agreed to upload my latest post. He wasn't too happy about it, though. He had a couple of hours away from the courthouse and didn't want to spend them baby-sitting Floyd and mucking around with my computer. He wanted to go with me to find Taylor. He wanted to make sure she was okay.

276

But I didn't want that. I didn't want him coming along.

And I couldn't even give him a valid reason why. I just told him no. Sorry—really, I'm sorry—but no.

Danny's map took me east on Mission, then south toward I-90. I stayed off the main road as I rounded the university, instead crossing to the residential street one block to the east. I probably didn't need to bother. There wasn't a soul around. The only sound in the still air was the rasp of my breath and the sharp echoes of my footsteps.

I took pictures of the abandoned houses as I walked. Most still looked pretty good—it hadn't been that long, after all—but they all showed signs of neglect and abuse. In the first month after the evacuation, the yards had sprouted out of control, crowding sidewalks and invading lawns, and then they'd died. The streets and sidewalks were plastered with wet leaves, and there were broken windows up and down the street. A couple of the front doors hung wide open.

I approached one of the houses and took a picture of its shattered door; there was a splintered dent to the left of the knob where a boot had staved it in. Looters, scavenging for food or money, or maybe just looking for a warm place to stay. Since that act of violence—maybe a month ago, maybe more—the world had slowly started to make its way into the house. I crouched just outside the door and took pictures of the entryway. Dead leaves and dirt littered a nice Persian rug. Lumps of wet, shapeless paper—once-glossy magazines, a stamped handwritten letter—adhered to the tiled floor. There was a whiff of mold in the air and hard-water stains on the dingy beige walls.

I took a half dozen photos before I noticed the line of muddy paw prints stretching from the front door to the rear of the house. The prints were large, and as soon as I noticed them, I thought I caught a hint of animal musk in the air. It was the barest tickle at the back of my nose—probably just my imagination, really, nothing more—but it was enough to transport me back to the tunnel in the park. And once again I was there, following Mac down into the dark, searching for him as he faded away, as he found entry into Amanda's world. A world of dogs and wolves. A world of savage eyes and teeth and blood and flesh.

I recoiled from the entryway and retreated back to the middle of the road.

After that, I didn't linger. I stopped taking pictures and instead just concentrated on covering ground.

There was graffiti on a building near the 290 bridge, clearly visible from the middle of its span: overlapping green and black lines scrawled across white stucco.

It was the Poet's work. I recognized the writing.

Just one sentence, but it left me feeling perplexed and just a little dizzy:

I THOUGHT WE WERE FALLING, NOT FLYING.

I took a couple of pictures and moved on.

Danny's map was surprisingly precise. It ended in a neat series of squares sketched out along Second Avenue, filling the space between Pittsburg and Magnolia Streets. There was a circle around the middle square and an arrow pointing to a phrase at the edge of the piece of paper: "blue tarp on roof."

I rounded the corner and immediately spotted the house with the tarp. It wasn't a very nice neighborhood, sitting right there at the edge of I-90, but the blue-topped house looked well cared for. It was boxy and small: two stories tall, but the second floor couldn't have been much more than a single slant-ceilinged room. None of the windows were broken, and the hedges at the yard's perimeter looked as if they'd been trimmed recently. The tarp on the roof looked fairly new as well, bright blue and still perfectly placed, despite the weeks of wind and rain and snow. There was absolutely no way it predated the evacuation.

I paused and turned a full circle before approaching the house. The street was still and silent. There were no people, no animals.

The nearby stretch of I-90 was deserted as well, the western road-block miles away, the military occupied elsewhere.

I was alone here, near the center of the city, and it was all very . . . calming.

This was a feeling I'd been having for a while now, something I'd been circling around, narrowing in on, as I walked the empty streets and thought about the empty city. Away from the eyes of people, I could do anything and it really wouldn't matter. It wouldn't change the world. It wouldn't change a single mind.

And that was very liberating. For so long, I'd been trying to impress others. I'd been trying to impress my father, my peers, the girls in my life, the professors at school. And then there was the whole photography thing, nothing but a desperate attempt to impress the whole world.

But here I'd found something different, something new. I'd found comfort in not making an impression, jumping into the ocean and not making a splash, not leaving a single ripple.

I can't imagine that this was a very healthy thought—it was the height of solipsism, after all—but it *was* calming. And there was still Taylor. I still wanted to make an impression with her. With her, I wanted to make a big-ass splash.

I stayed to the side of the house as I approached, rounding a chest-high hedge and ducking beneath the nearest window. I raised my head and looked in through the slats of a venetian blind. The front living room was empty. There was a sofa and an armchair arrayed around an unlit fireplace, and an end table sup-ported a stack of magazines at its side. I continued toward the back of the house, stopping in front of a kitchen window. Some-one left the room just as I raised my head to look in. I only caught a brief moment of dark-clad back as he or she turned the corner into a hallway on its far side. The person was nothing more than a blur of motion in the doorway; I couldn't tell if it was Taylor or one of her parents.

I continued on. There was a screen door at the rear of the

house, hidden inside a tiny garden. The garden was well maintained but not very lush. Slumbering for the winter. I carefully picked my way through the garden and glanced in through the back door window.

There was a narrow hallway on the other side of the door, leading all the way to the front of the house. Taylor was standing in its center, facing away from me. There was a blanket strung across the corridor at about breast height—a makeshift clothesline barrier, partitioning the hallway into a number of smaller spaces—and she was peering over its edge, down toward the floor on the far side. She was talking to somebody, somebody hidden out of sight, and gesturing with both hands. I couldn't make out most of what she was saying. Only a couple of her words, raised loud, made it through the doorway: "not staying," "not safe," and a single, pleading *"please."*

There was an answering voice from the person on the other side of the blanket, but it was low and calm, and I couldn't make out a single word.

It was strange, this scene, and I couldn't tell what was going on. Who was she talking to? One of her parents? And why here, in the middle of the hallway? And what was up with the partition?

I held my breath and tried to concentrate on the muffled sound of Taylor's voice, trying to pick meaning out of that muted cadence. But there was nothing there, just the dull rumble of argumentative voices, or, rather, the rumble of one argumentative voice set against the reassuring calm of a patient and soothing one. This didn't go on for too long. After a couple of minutes, the conversation ceased, and Taylor was left standing there, vibrating with mute energy. Then, in a gesture of complete frustration, she pulled the blanket aside and stormed toward the front of the house.

As she made her way to the front door, pushing aside a second barrier, the blanket closest to me slipped from its clothesline and fell to the floor, spilling with a quick, fluid motion. And what it revealed . . . well, I actually jumped at the sight, and my hands, pressed flat against the screen door, bounced wildly off the metal barrier.

It was a man, merged with the hardwood floor. The top half of his body looked perfectly normal: a Middle Eastern man dressed in a white button-down shirt. But the shirt stopped midbelly, at the floor, and the bottom half of his body was gone. His hands moved against the floor and walls, slow, languid, and completely insensate. His head lolled, and a line of spittle spilled from his lower lip. I couldn't see his eyes—his head was moving, and he was over a dozen feet away—but I could imagine them rolled back inside his skull.

There was a woman seated next to the man's stunted body, a white woman in her fifties, propped up in a comfortable nest of pillows. *Taylor's mother?* She jumped at the sound of my hands bouncing off the screen door, and a startled cry escaped her throat. Her eyes widened when she saw me standing at the window, looking in. With one hand, she reached out and grabbed the man's shoulder comfortingly; the other started scrambling toward the blanket on the floor, trying to reassemble her makeshift blind.

"Taylor!" she cried. "Taylor!" Now the woman's voice was loud enough for me to hear, frantic and shrill and filled with a primal, instinctual fear. "What is this? *What's going on?*"

I looked up and saw Taylor towering over her parents. Her eyes were locked on me, narrowed and filled with a cold, biting anger. She wasn't moving. My presence here had frozen her solid.

Her mother continued to struggle with the blanket, trying desperately to throw it up and over the clothesline. She worked one-handed, refusing to release her grip on her husband. "Help," she said, turning to look back at Taylor. "Please, Taylor, for the love of God, help!" Her words came out frantic and disjointed. There were tears running down her cheeks.

Finally, Taylor stepped forward and put the blanket back in place, carefully draping it over the clothesline. Once it was back up—and her parents hidden from view—Taylor pointed at me and gestured me away from the window. It was an angry, dismissive shooing gesture. And at that moment, I swear, there was genuine hate in her eyes. At that moment, I think she couldn't fucking stand me.

I backed away, horrified.

What had I done?

I sat down in the dirt and waited for Taylor to appear. There was a frigid wind blowing down from the north, and the clouds were getting darker overhead, a dense slate-gray weight perched above the city. It felt like snow.

I didn't know what was going to happen with Taylor. I'd looked in on something private here, a secret, and didn't know how she was going to react.

Her parents. Her father, melted into the floor, consumed by the city.

I thought it was unheard of—this phenomenon—I thought it was something that I alone had been carrying around. I thought it was mine. But Taylor had seen Weasel; she'd seen his fingers. She was a part of it now. I'd infected her.

Maybe it would be for the best if she pushed me away. Maybe I was a cancer that needed to be excised from her life.

"What the fuck are you doing here?" she asked, rounding the corner of the house. She stopped on the other side of the yard, crossing her arms and leaning back against the wall. "Did you follow me? Did you fucking follow me?"

"Danny told me about the house, your parents' house. I was worried about you. You ran away . . . after Weasel. I wanted to make sure you were okay."

"And how the fuck did Danny know? I didn't tell him. Has *he* been following me?" These words brought a sour look to her face, a look of wounded betrayal. "Are there no fucking secrets around here? No privacy?"

I shrugged. "I don't know, but I didn't mean—" I struggled for a moment, trying to figure out what I did mean, what I'd been hoping—or expecting—to find on the other side of her parents' window. Finally, I managed: "I didn't mean to scare your mom. I didn't mean to hurt you. I'm sorry." Taylor's face remained impassive, set in stone. "And I'm sorry about your father."

There was a hint of emotion then, a slight twisting at the corner of her lips. Taylor remained still for a while. Then she pushed herself away from the wall and let out a loud sigh, her anger transitioning into a desolate sadness.

"She won't leave him," she said. "My mother. She thinks he's still in there. The sounds he makes; she thinks he's communicating, thinks he's saying her name. Miriam, fucking Miriam. But he's not. It's just stupid, senseless noise." She clenched her arms tighter across her chest, like maybe she was just now starting to feel the cold October air. "She's set up camp right there, next to him, and she won't leave . . . Yet she won't let me stay in the house! She wants me out of the city. She wants me gone."

"She loves you. She wants you to be safe."

Taylor clenched her body even tighter. I could see her shivering now. "I don't see why," she said quietly, a bitter hint of self-loathing in her voice. "She should hate me. I ruin everything I touch."

"That's not true," I said, shaking my head. "That's just not true. I don't know . . . maybe it's me. You remember what Danny said? There were no reports of anything like this before I showed up. Nothing. Nowhere. It's just around me—people falling through walls, losing cohesion. It's something I brought into the city, something the city brought out of me. You just got too close . . . And I'm sorry for that. I'm just so, so sorry."

"No, Dean," she said, her voice calm, suddenly devoid of energy. She was stating fact now; there was no room for emotion. "It's not you; it's not even the city. It's me. I'm doing this. Everything around me." Then, more quietly: "It's what I do. People get close to me and they fall apart."

"That's just not true."

"This happened a month ago, Dean," she said, gesturing frantically toward the house, toward her father trapped inside. "Before you got here. We were fighting. I was yelling at him—fucking yelling—and he stepped through the fucking floor. He put his foot down, and it just didn't stop going. And it's not just him, Dean. I see this a lot. It's happening all around me . . . You saw Weasel!"

I stood up and started toward her, wanting to give her some type of comfort, but she held up her hands and took a step back, shaking her head violently. "Jesus Christ, Dean. No! Just stay back." Her voice hitched, and tears started to pool in her eyes.

"What must she think?"she whispered forlornly, staring back toward the house, toward her mother. "She knows, right? She's got to know. But what must she think . . . of me?"

I tried to give her a warm, reassuring smile. "You've got it wrong, Taylor. It isn't you. I'm not sure what it is, but it isn't you. Your mother understands that. It's the city . . . it's just the city."

"But how can you know that? You can't know that. No one knows that!"

"I do," I said. "I just do." I paused, remembering the man dangling from the ceiling back on my first day in the city. "I saw something like that—" I gestured toward her father. "—when you weren't around, when Weasel stole my backpack. So it can't be you . . . Hell, I thought it was me."

Taylor stayed silent for a handful of seconds, staring at me like she was trying to figure me out. "You're lying," she finally said. "You're a lying bag of shit, and you're just telling me what I want to hear."

"I may be a bag of shit," I said. "But I'm not lying." I took a single step forward, and this time she didn't retreat. "I'm close to you, right? We've slept in the same bed. You've been happy with me, you've been mad at me. Well, I'm still here, aren't I? I'm fine. And Danny's fine. And Floyd and Charlie and Sabine—they're fucked up, but they're still fine. They're not falling apart." I shook my head once again. "It's something else, Taylor, some other process. It's got to be. And whatever you think you know, you don't. You really don't."

Taylor watched me for a moment, her face impassive, absorbing my words. Then she shook her head, refusing to believe.

"You aren't saying anything here, Dean. Your mouth is open, but there's nothing coming out."

She turned abruptly and started back around the side of the house, heading toward Second Avenue. "Now get the fuck out of my mom's yard, before she finds her shotgun shells."

I followed Taylor through the city streets. She stayed about ten feet ahead of me. Each time I tried to catch up, she put on a burst of speed, leaving me behind. She was pissed off. I couldn't reach her.

Her father had fallen through the floor over a month ago. She'd been living with that, bearing that responsibility. How could I prove that it wasn't her fault?

I can't, I realized. Unless I somehow managed to figure out this whole thing, there was absolutely nothing I could do to convince her otherwise.

And then—

There was a great tearing sound in the sky just as we reached the middle of the 290 bridge. It was loud and violent, and it shook me so deeply that I nearly fell over. At first, I thought it was an earthquake, but the ground wasn't moving. It was just a sound, so loud that it confused my senses, a physical pounding in my eardrums.

I covered my ears with my hands and turned toward Taylor. She was doing the same thing; her hands were pressed against the sides of her head, and there was a pained, confused grimace on her face. She was looking up at the sky.

The clouds above our heads were coming apart, like eddies of water spilling downhill. It couldn't have been a wind in the upper atmosphere; it was moving too fast, fleeing a point in the sky somewhere over the middle of the city. Massive dark gray thunderclouds gathering, clumping, and spilling away, all in a matter of seconds. And the sky they left behind—

I felt my breath hitching in my throat. For a dozen seconds, I couldn't remember how to breathe. I couldn't remember anything but that sky. My God, that sky!

The sky was red. Varying shades of red—a vast field of shifting density—from neon pink all the way to dark oxblood crimson. It was an unnatural paint box of color.

The clouds were gone in a matter of seconds, leaving behind nothing but that depthless red plane. The earth-shattering sound disappeared with the clouds. *It was the sound of a massive vacuum cleaner,* I thought absurdly as I stared up into the crimson void. *The sound of the clouds being sucked away, like a bucket of spilled sand.*

"What's going on?" Taylor yelled, partially deafened.

I shook my head.

A corner of the sky lit with an electric spark of light, followed by a loud momentary *crack*. The sound of artillery fire or a dead tree snapping in two. It was nowhere near as loud as the original rending noise that had shaken me to my very core. This was followed by another burst of light and another *crack,* lighting up a different portion of the sky.

"Is that lightning?" Taylor asked.

"I don't know."

She grabbed my hand and started pulling me down the street, west, toward the center of town. It seemed like her anger was gone. For the moment at least, it had been preempted.

People were emerging from the buildings up and down the street. Dirty, ragged refugees, some rubbing their eyes as if just awakened from a solid sleep. They were all staring up at the sky. Mute. In shock. *If they weren't in shock,* I thought, *if they were capable of reacting in an appropriate, rational way, there'd be screaming and panic. Chaos and prayers and violence.* The sky was bleeding, after all. Up above our heads, the sky had fallen. And this . . .

This was its bloody corpse.

"Dean!" Taylor called into my ear, startling my eyes back down to the street. She was pulling at my arm violently. I'd stopped without realizing it. "We've got to find out what happened. We've got to find somebody who knows!" I got my legs moving once again, and we continued west. Toward the courthouse, I realized, toward Danny and the military.

We found Mama Cass at Post Street. She was sitting in a lawn chair in the middle of the road, directly in front of her restaurant. Her customers stayed back on the sidewalk, but her old Jewish cook—*Hershel,* I thought, remembering his name—stood at her side, his hands tucked beneath a tomato-stained apron. She had a bottle of beer dangling from one hand as she stared up at the sky. There was a bemused look on her face.

Taylor was going to run straight past, but Mama Cass stopped us. "Where do you think you're going?" she asked in an amused voice. "Running to the military, maybe?" Taylor pulled to a stop and turned back toward Mama Cass, pure hatred burning in her eyes. Mama Cass was watching us with a sly grin. "That won't get you very far, darling." She sounded drunk. Or high. Or out of her fucking mind.

Taylor dropped my hand and looked down the length of the street, in the direction of the courthouse. For a moment, I thought she was going to sprint off without me.

"Your friends in the military have been driving, pell-mell, up and down the street." She pointed along the cross street, first toward the hospital, then toward the courthouse. "Their fucking Hummers—they almost ran me over. They don't know what's going on. They have no fucking clue. They think we're under attack. They think that *that*—" She waited for a handful of heartbeats until a fresh *crack* rang out in the sky. "—is artillery fire. They think somebody's lobbing shells at us."

"It's got to be atmospheric," Hershel said. For someone so old, his voice was surprisingly strong. "Vapor in the air. Colliding fronts. The red—it's got to be refracted light bouncing off of something in the atmosphere."

"Red sky at night," Mama Cass recited, nodding, but the smile on her lips suggested that she thought Hershel's explanation was complete bullshit. "Sailor's delight." She raised her beer bottle to the sky, toasting the chaos, and took a long swallow.

Taylor looked back down the street.

"They're not going to help you," Mama Cass said, not even looking in Taylor's direction. "They don't know what's going on. They don't have any fucking idea. You might as well just sit back and enjoy the fireworks."

She gestured toward my backpack. "And you . . . you might want to take some pictures," she said. "I'm sure your Internet fans would love to see what's going on."

I spent a moment staring up at the bloodred sky, that violent, roiling sea above our heads. Then I shrugged off my backpack and followed her suggestion.

18.1

A piece of paper torn from a lined notebook. Undated. Hand-printed words:

> *(The piece of paper has been crumpled repeatedly. The left-hand side is a ragged tear, torn from a notebook binding. Large, shaky words cover the top part of the page—smeared pencil, inscribed by a palsied hand.*
>
> *The paper is aged and well handled. It is no longer crisp; instead, it has been transformed into a fragile cloth, by folding and refolding, by damp and greasy fingertips.*
>
> *Dingy and gray; smeared graphite. Sprinkled, dipped in water, then dried once again.*
>
> *The words are barely legible. But they are legible.)*
>
> —there's nothing left in me, Taylor. Not anymore.
>
> I'm sorry.
>
> I failed you. I couldn't stop failing you.

18.2

The sky stayed red for about twenty minutes.

I had a hard time taking pictures of that sky. Without anything in the foreground, it looked like nothing but a red, fluid pattern, an abstract collage of crimson and pink and electric blood. Finally, I went wide-angle and focused on the eastern skyline, down the length of the street. It was a view of the city from the floor of a concrete valley, with the walls on either side reaching up (and bending out) before opening onto the wide red sky. I set the camera to burst mode and shot five frames a second until I caught a couple of frames with the lightning—or the artillery fire or whatever it was—above the left-hand line of buildings.

After I captured that shot, I sat down on the asphalt and pretended to stare up at the sky, taking my place alongside Taylor, Mama Cass, and Hershel. But really, I had the camera down in my lap, angled up at Mama Cass as she watched the heavens. There was a childlike wonder spread across her face, and I tried to capture that expression, that joyful, rapturous euphoria, with the bright sky shining behind her. I was shooting blind, though, so I couldn't be sure if the autofocus was locked on her or on the buildings in the background. I didn't bother to check on the LCD screen, and after a minute, I just shut down the camera and tucked it back into my backpack.

The street was still eerily quiet. I knew that there were people on the sidewalk behind us—I'd seen them as Taylor and I had approached—but they didn't make a single sound.

I reached out and took Taylor's hand, gently, trying not to startle her. She looked down from the sky, first glancing at our joined hands and then looking up at my face. She was perplexed and overwhelmed; I could see that in her glazed eyes. I gave her a reassuring smile, and she turned back toward the heavens.

She didn't drop my hand, at least. For that I was grateful.

The sky turned back to gray. The change from red to gray was slower than the change from gray to red. There was no earth-rending roar, no quick unnatural movement up in the atmosphere. The red just darkened gradually, and a new cloud front blew in from up north. It took a couple of minutes for the last of the red to disappear. Then it was just your typical overcast early-winter sky.

The reaction to this event, this return to normality, was surprisingly subdued. Mama Cass stood up and stretched lazily. She handed her empty beer bottle to Hershel, then folded up the lawn chair and tucked it under her arm. Back on the sidewalk, people looked down from the sky. They exchanged muted words and then walked away. I even saw one man yawn as if just getting up from a midafternoon nap.

It was over. Life—this parody of life here inside the city—could resume.

"Come back to the restaurant with me," Mama Cass said, using her free hand to gesture toward the open storefront. She was smiling, relaxed. "I'm thinking you two can help me out with something. A delivery."

"*What?*" Taylor asked. She sounded genuinely offended. How could Mama Cass confuse their relationship so thoroughly? Why would she for one second think that Taylor would do anything to help her out?

"Don't play it that way, girl," Mama Cass said. "We're in this together, right?" She smiled. It was a staged, artificial smile, and it put the lie to her words. "Besides," she continued, "if it bugs you so much, you can think of it as giving Terry a hand."

"Terry?"

"Yeah . . . Terry. Your mentor. I'm running some errands for him. I'm doing him a favor." She spit out this last word—*favor*—giving it barbs. Suddenly, her drugged euphoria was gone, and she was wielding nothing but venom. "I'm acting like an adult here, Taylor, and if you can't do the same, if you can't ditch that holier-than-thou bullshit, maybe you should just keep on running. Maybe you should get out of the way and leave the adult interactions to people who aren't complete fucking pussies."

Taylor's eyes widened with surprise, and her mouth fell open in a wordless gape. She didn't have a reply.

After a moment of silence, Mama Cass turned back toward me and smiled, once again picking up that relaxed, mellow attitude. "C'mon, Dean," she said. "I'll show you what I was thinking." Then she headed toward her restaurant.

It was as if the red sky hadn't even happened.

There was laughter in Mama Cass's dining room. People had drifted back to their tables; they'd picked up their abandoned forks and resumed their interrupted meals. The laughter, the mindless chatter—it made me think that perhaps they'd picked up the same conversations, too. Hershel went on ahead, disappearing into the kitchen, while Mama Cass paused at a couple of tables to chat with her customers. Taylor and I stayed a couple of paces back. Taylor was stewing. Her arms were crossed, and her head was turned, refusing to even look in Mama Cass's direction.

After a couple of minutes, Mama Cass waved us toward the back of the dining room. She escorted us through the kitchen and into her office.

"How's the hand?" she asked. She leaned back against the edge of her desk and gestured for me to raise my palm up into the air.

I showed it to her, and she nodded. "It's healing up all right? It isn't hurting?"

"It's getting better," I said, "but it still hurts a bit." This wasn't exactly true. In fact, it didn't hurt at all, but I was running low on Vicodin. Mama Cass nodded her head in understanding.

Taylor shot me a perplexed look. I hadn't told her about my hand or Mama Cass's help, so this was all news to her. I caught her eye, and after a second, her confusion turned to anger. I couldn't help feeling a bit guilty. Like I was conspiring with an enemy, like I was sneaking around behind her back and plotting against her.

"What do you want us to deliver?" Taylor asked brusquely, turning away from me.

"A package. Something Terry wanted me to find."

"What is it?" Taylor asked again, crossing her arms.

"I'm not going to tell you that," Mama Cass said. "It's Terry's business, not yours." She turned toward me. "Can I trust you, Dean?" she asked. "Can I trust you to be careful and discreet? Can I trust you to keep this out of her hands?"

I nodded, then glanced at Taylor. Her arms were still crossed, and she was staring angrily at the wall. "It's for Terry," I explained, trying to win her over. She just shrugged.

Perhaps Taylor would have preferred that I just let it go right there. But I was curious. I wanted to know what Mama Cass and Terry were working on, and I was pretty sure that that was what Taylor wanted, too. Despite her feelings for this mercenary businesswoman, despite her obvious loathing.

Mama Cass circled to the far side of her desk and bent low over its open drawers. There was the sound of rummaging—the crinkle of paper and change, the rattle of loose items—and when she came back up, she had a brown-wrapped parcel in her hand. It was a book; I recognized that as soon as she handed it over. A hardback book. I could feel the solid edges beneath the layer of butcher paper, the sheaf of recessed leaves.

"Be careful with it," she said. "It wasn't easy to find. My contacts had to scour all of Seattle."

I tucked the book into my backpack, and we turned to leave. Taylor stepped out of the room ahead of me.

"Dean!" Mama Cass hissed as soon as Taylor disappeared through the door. She rounded her desk and, with a huge dose of melodrama, slipped a pill bottle into my hand. I glanced at the label: Vicodin. "For the pain," she said with an ingratiating wink. The wink made me feel dirty, slimy. I slipped the bottle into my pocket and quickly followed Taylor out into the restaurant.

"I hate her," Taylor said as soon as we were alone out on the street. "I really fucking hate her. She's a game player. It gets her off. My father worked with people like that at the university. They're the ones who got all of the promotions, on the backs of their lies and their power plays."

She got quiet right then, and I knew that she was thinking about her father, remembering what had passed between them, what she thought she'd done. *Her voice, raised in anger, as he fell through the floor. His rolling eyes and searching hands.* And then her mother, doting on that floor-bound body, her hidden heart filled with blame, or love, or both, or neither.

We walked a block in silence. When we reached Monroe Street and turned to head up north, Taylor pulled to a stop. I turned to face her and found her forehead wrinkled in confusion.

"What's wrong with you, Dean?" she asked.

I shook my head, not understanding the question.

"Why are you trying so hard? With me? What attracts you?"

I stared at her for a moment, still perplexed. "You do, Taylor. You attract me."

She looked at me skeptically. "No, Dean, that's not it. That's not good enough. Not anymore." A bitter, contemptuous smile surfaced on her lips. "There's something wrong with you, Dean, something genuinely wrong. I'm sure of it now. You're not quite right in the head. You're not quite . . . sane. Not if you want to be with me." With this, she turned and resumed walking.

I let her get ahead of me. Then I dug out my new bottle of Vicodin and bolted down a couple of pills.

There was no one guarding the Homestead's entrance. No Mickey with a baseball bat. No figure hiding in the shadows. Taylor was confused.

"They should be here. They were here yesterday." There was a note of panic rising in her voice.

We stepped into the sketchy business center, and she cocked her head, listening for sounds of life inside the building. I could hear wind rattling paper out on the street, but the building itself was still and silent. After a moment, Taylor barreled forward, making her way down the dim bottom-floor corridor—past the insurance office, the office supply place, the acupuncture clinic—then up the stairs to the second floor. I followed, not wanting to fall behind.

Up on the second floor, Taylor pushed aside the plywood window cover and crawled out onto the plank bridge on the other side. I was about to follow when movement down the length of the corridor caught my eye. A door near the front of the building stood wide open. It was about twenty feet away, and in the gloom I couldn't see what the room was. Broom closet, bathroom, storage? Its purpose was lost in murky black.

But there was movement there, inside the dark. A churning motion on the floor that set my skin to crawl. Black masses in the dark gray. And it was silent, whatever it was. Absolutely silent.

The plywood cover swung back and forth from Taylor's passage, and I reached out to hold it steady, still watching the threshold down the length of the corridor. As I watched, part of the black shadow broke away, flowing smoothly out into the corridor. It was a large black spider, moving on multijointed legs. It was as big as a small dog, much bigger than the spiders that had swarmed through the crack in the wall back at the abandoned apartment building. *How long ago was that?* I wondered, not quite sure. *A week ago? Is that right?*

The room behind the spider continued to crawl with dark motion. It could have been just my eyes and my overactive imagination populating that darkness, but I thought I could see that space *full* of spiders. Moving, swarming, crawling over one another in waves of liquid motion.

My back shivered in an involuntary spasm, and the spider started to crawl my way. Before it got more than a couple of feet, I slammed the window cover aside and frantically crawled out onto the thin bridge that linked this building to the next. If I waited, if I stood there for one second longer, I was afraid I'd find myself hypnotized by the spider's smooth, almost mechanical motions—standing there frozen as it drew near, as wave after wave of its brothers and sisters broke away from the darkness, surging out into the corridor to engulf me, to swallow me whole. And the touch of those bristled legs, caressing—light, tremulous touches, gaining muscle and strength—quickly paralyzing me inside a dense spiderweb mesh.

And maybe the touch of a finger in there, too, hidden. And lips and tongue.

As I crossed the bridge, I didn't even think about the distance to the ground or the way the wood wobbled and bounced beneath my feet. I just kept going, not pausing until I jumped down into the hallway on the other side.

There were no spiders here in the back rooms of Terry's ballet studio. At least none that I could see. Just Taylor, moving quickly ahead.

I caught up with her at the end of the hallway. She didn't notice my rattled state. She was too busy looking for Terry.

She called out his name as she stepped onto the wide studio floor, but there was no one there. Terry's ratty sofa stood vacant near the window, surrounded by a scattered corona of books. She crossed the hardwood floor and circled the sofa—once, and then again—as if it were all a matter of angle, as if she'd be able to find Terry if she could just look at it from the right direction.

I paused in the center of the room and peered into every corner, checking for shadows, checking for spiders. But there were none. No shadows, no spiders.

"He's gone," Taylor said, her voice trembling. "I was here yesterday, and now he's gone. They're all gone."

"We just got here, Taylor," I said. "He could be anywhere. I'm sure he's fine." But really, with the spiders, I knew I was lying. I had no idea what had happened here, no idea what had happened to Terry, but I didn't think we'd find him again. Not really. The spiders were an omen, a harbinger of loss.

"Let's go," I said. "Let's keep looking."

Taylor nodded and hurried on ahead, retracing the path we'd taken through the building on our previous visit. I kept my eyes on the shadows as we climbed the stairs and crossed to the second bridge. The shadows in the staircase were deep, but they were motionless.

The third building was as quiet as the first and second. Taylor stopped to listen at each new hallway, but there was never even a whisper of sound. I waited as she cocked her head and slowly craned her neck, angling her ears for any hint of humanity in the air, any quarreling voices or laughter, or the tinned sound of a distant boom box. I wanted to keep moving. In those brief intervals of silence, I could feel waves of spiders cresting against the closed doors around us, on all sides, penning us in. But there were only empty rooms. Empty rooms and silence.

I was grateful when we finally reached the roof. I wanted more than anything to see the sky once again. No matter what color it might be.

We found Terry standing at the edge of the roof, near his tent and his makeshift camp. He was staring up at the gray clouds.

"Terry!" Taylor cried as soon as she saw him standing there. She broke into a run. Terry turned at the sound of her voice. His face was blank, unreadable, but he didn't seem at all surprised to see us there. He opened his arms, and Taylor fell into them.

"I thought you were gone," Taylor said, her voice choked with emotion, with relief.

"Not yet."

Terry looked older in the overcast light. The creases on his face looked deeper, and it seemed like there was more gray in his hair. "Did you see it?" he asked, his eyes turning back toward the sky. "The sky was red. Or was that just me?" There was a perplexed awe in his voice. He sounded completely and totally lost.

"We saw it," Taylor said. "Everyone saw it. It was real." She stepped back out of Terry's arms. There was concern on her face as she studied him intently. "Are you okay?"

"Yes," he said with a gentle smile. "I'm just tired. Just sick and tired."

"What happened to everyone? What happened to Mickey and the guards and everyone else? This place is deserted. We just walked right in."

"They're gone. All gone. They packed up their things and left. Last night was rough. People . . . people started to see things, in the hallways, in the shadows. They started to hear things, too, voices in the dark. They think this place is haunted." He shook his head. He didn't seem angry or sad about his abandonment. Just very, very tired. "I think Mickey took some of them and headed out on his own. But the rest . . . the rest just wandered away."

He turned and faced the city, his eyes turning from the sky to study the streets down below.

Taylor gave me a look, and I shrugged the backpack off my shoulder. "Here," I said as I unearthed Mama Cass's parcel and handed it to Terry. "Mama Cass wanted you to have this."

Terry accepted the package without looking at me. He unwrapped the brown paper and let it fall to the roof of the building. Then he glanced at the book's cover and let out a short laugh. He held it up so we could read the title: *Sustainable Small-Plot Farming*. I felt a bit cheated. This was Mama Cass's big secret?

"I'm a fool," Terry said. He hauled off and threw the book as hard as he could. It sailed out over the street, making it halfway to the intersection of Monroe and Second Avenue before finally hitting the asphalt and breaking in two, pages ripping and flying as the textbook bounced and skidded down the distant street. "What was I thinking? Sustainable farming? There's nothing sustainable here . . .

"I'm leaving," he said. "I'm getting out. It's too painful now, watching it all fall apart, trying to hold it all together while everyone else's content to just let it fade away." He paused for a moment and looked down at the street below. "We're standing at the edge of a cliff here, in the city, and the ground's crumbling away beneath our feet. I think it's time I found something new. Something solid."

Taylor took the announcement in stride. Maybe this was a good thing: Terry safe, Terry out of danger. "Where will you go?" she asked.

"I have friends in Olympia. I'll stay with them for a while, until I get things sorted out. Maybe I'll write a book. I've been thinking a lot lately about what it means to be human, about what we owe one another."

"I'd read it," Taylor said. And then: "You'll be okay, Terry. I know it."

Terry was quiet for a little while, staring out over the city.

"And you, Taylor?" he finally asked, turning back toward her. "You're strong, but I don't think strong matters much anymore. Are you going to be okay? Can I convince you to come with me to Olympia?" After a moment, he gestured toward me. "And Dean, too, of course. If that's what it takes, if that's what you want."

"You know I can't do that. I can't leave them." "Them"—her parents.

"Yeah," Terry said. "I know. You are your own woman. And when your mind is set, your mind is set."

Taylor laughed. "Yeah, that tautology . . . you're starting to sound like Mickey there. Maybe it is time for you to go."

"Yeah," Terry said, with a shrug. "Fuck, yeah."

Then he gestured toward the charcoal grill standing next to his tent and the curl of smoke stretching up into the dark sky. "While you're here, you might as well stay for dinner, though. Right?" He offered a weary smile. "It seems I've got more food in the city than I've got time, and I don't want it going to waste."

Taylor took me up into the tower while Terry cooked dinner.

When we reached the eighth floor, she gestured to an empty doorway across from the stairwell. "This was my room," she said. "After my parents . . . well, after my mom kicked me out, Weasel took me to Terry and Terry put me up here."

It was a boring room: maroon hotel carpeting, heavy drapes pulled away from a dirty window, nightstand, chest of drawers with an empty TV nook. The bed was a single stripped mattress hanging half off its frame. I inhaled deeply. Underneath a musty layer of abandonment, the room smelled faintly like Taylor.

"I wasn't in a very good state," she said. She moved about the room absently. After making a complete circuit, she approached the bed and nudged the mattress back into place atop its box spring. "Weasel found me in the park, camped out on the steps. I couldn't leave the city—I just couldn't—and I didn't know where else to go."

"It's good to have friends," I said. I crossed the room and looked out the window. The window faced the neighboring building, and four floors down, I could see Terry standing at the grill in his rooftop camp.

"Yeah, it was."

I turned and looked back at her. She was sitting on the edge of her bed now, staring blankly at the wall. "He used to hold meetings," she said. Her face lit up at the memory, a smile surfacing on her lips. "A couple of times, in the first weeks, he held them down in the hotel ballroom, just off the lobby." She pointed down at the carpeting, toward a room eight floors beneath our feet. "It's a big room, down there, and there were a lot of people back then—this was back when everybody still thought they needed a community in order to survive, in order to buck the government—and Terry refused to yell. He'd stand on stage in this huge room, in front of a sea of people, and he'd talk in his normal conversational voice. And I swear, everyone held their breath, trying desperately to hear what he had to say. He set up committees and scavenging groups, put people in charge of research—figuring out electricity, how to grow food, how to communicate and get supplies in from the outside world. He was magnificent back then. He was a complete government packed into a single body." She sighed, and her smile dimmed. "It's hard to believe that that was just a month ago."

I looked down at Terry. He was just a lonely old man down there, standing in front of his grill, flipping burgers.

"Maybe that's our attention span now," she said. "Maybe that's civilization, sped up to its natural end. Entropy. Apathy. And he's gone now. He's leaving."

I didn't know what to say. I stood at the window and watched her face move from emotion to emotion, from wry amusement to melancholy sadness. And then, whispering, she continued: "What happens, Dean, when the people you're close to don't want to be close to you anymore? What happens to me in this world?"

"You go on," I said. I moved closer, tentative at first but gaining confidence as I sat down at her side. She didn't cringe or move away. I got the feeling that she needed me right then, needed me at her side. "Besides, you've got me. And the people you're losing . . . you aren't really losing them. Your mom still loves you, and Terry—it's obvious he still cares. It's just, things come between us—that's how it happens. People move along their own trajectories. Terry's got places he needs to be, and your mother . . . she just wants to protect you." I didn't mention her father. He was gone now—I was sure of that—and there was absolutely no way I could put a gloss on that horror.

She shook her head. The violent motion dislodged tears from her cheeks, and I watched one hit the mattress next to her leg. Then she looked at me, and a gentle smile surfaced on her lips. "Like I said, Dean, there's something wrong with you. Something deeply and truly wrong." But the way she said it, it was gentle and warm.

She reached out and rested her hand on my leg. It was only a brief moment of contact, but it filled me with confidence. It felt like I was doing my job here. I was lifting some of her burden, and that made me happy.

I nodded toward the window, indicating Terry down below. "The food should be ready by now."

Taylor nodded and wiped the tears from her cheeks. Then she started a last circuit around the room, idly trailing her fingers along the hotel walls. Her expression was distant as she moved slowly through memory.

When she reached the chest of drawers under the empty TV nook, she idly pulled open the top drawer and her breath hitched in surprise. She stood still for a moment, transfixed by whatever she'd found inside.

"What is it?" I asked. And, after a moment of silence: "Taylor?"

She shook her head. I stood up and moved to her side, but her hand quickly darted into the drawer, pulling back whatever it was before I could get a good look. It looked like a piece of paper, but she quickly turned away, blocking it from view. Her hand disappeared into her pocket, and when she turned back, the piece of paper was gone. Her face was set, secretive and angry.

"What is it?" I repeated.

"It's mine," she said gruffly. "It's mine."

Then she shouldered me aside and headed toward the door.

Dinner was good. Terry served us hamburgers—fresh meat on home-baked bread, crisp lettuce, and fragrant cheese—and a selection of grilled vegetables, including squash, zucchini, carrots, and tiny potatoes. I don't know if he grew the vegetables himself or if he'd found them somewhere in the city. Despite his plans, despite his book, I hadn't seen any crops growing up here in the Homestead. Maybe he got them from Mama Cass.

Before we ate, he produced bottles of microbrew beer from an ice-filled cooler and toasted the city mockingly. "To this pile of crap at the end of the world," he said, "and to my well-deserved escape." But his tone wasn't joyous.

Taylor seemed distant throughout dinner. When she wasn't working at her food, she kept her jaw clenched, and she looked angry. It was frustrating. Up in the tower, I'd managed to help her drop one of her burdens, I think. But in that drawer she'd picked up another.

And this one seemed heavier, something she didn't want to share.

She hugged Terry for a long time before we parted. There were no tears, but I heard her voice crack as she said good-bye. Terry gave her a nod and a smile, and then we left.

When we reached the stairwell, I cast a glance back over my shoulder. Terry was standing in the middle of the roof, once again staring up at the overcast sky.

That was the last I saw of him.

Taylor didn't look back.

We found a new poem on the way home. Taylor wasn't speaking to me then. Once again, a distance had formed between us, a gulf as wide as the city. And she was standing alone on the other shore.

It was frustrating.

One step forward, twelve steps back.

The poem was on Riverside Avenue, painted on the side wall of an apartment building. There was a basketball hoop bolted next to the ten-foot-tall block of text, and a half-court boundary filled the space between the buildings. The poem was drawn in bright red paint —shiny acrylic—and it couldn't have been more than an hour old. The paint was still wet and dripping, and the smell of aerosol still hung in the air.

I glanced around, thinking I might catch the Poet somewhere nearby. But the block was deserted.

Looking up
The taste of the sky
      on my tongue
And the taste of asphalt
on the back of my head

My right eye rolled back,
in a pool of blood.

And there is a face

Above me, there is a face

Funny

   Taylor didn't even stop to read the poem. When I looked back down, she was already half a block away.

19.1

Photograph. October 24, 09:53 A.M. Green lines:

It is an abstract image. A close-up without sense or
meaning.

There is a mesh of bright green light in the middle
of the frame, stretching left to right—and right to
left—at very shallow angles. The lines are close
together, on the same horizontal plane—hundreds of
lines of light, forming a flat, tabletop surface. The
lines hit mirrors on either side of the image; re-
flections flee at oblique angles, stretching up and
out, toward the top of the frame.

The green is a bright electric green, and the lines
are as sharp as razors, cutting into the shadow-gray
background, glowing like radium in the night.

Light and line. Angle and vector. Form without context.

19.2

I slept in my own room that night.

The house around me was quiet, and as I lay there, waiting for sleep to come, I wondered what everyone else was doing. Floyd and Charlie, Sabine and Taylor—alone in their rooms (or so I assumed), silent, immersed in the dark. Were they dwelling on the past, scared and alone? Were they frustrated, like me? Were they plotting plans, getting ready to run?

Or were they just sleeping, lost to the world?

Finally, I took three more Vicodins to help me fall asleep. I was going through the pills like candy now—I recognized that—and they weren't really making me feel any better. They were helping me sleep, yeah, and during the day they helped me relax for an hour or two, preventing me from thinking all those deep and horrible thoughts. But it was only temporary. And the relief I got each time was shrinking, like a stream drying up in the midsummer sun.

And that stream was getting shallow.

But what really scared me was the thought of what I'd have to do next, when I ran out again. What would Mama Cass make me do? What errands would she have me run? It wasn't going to stay easy. I was certain of that.

As I drifted off to sleep, drugged and floating, I resolved to quit. There were other ways—better ways—to cope with stress and confusion. I just had to find them. I just had to deal.

Unfortunately, nothing's ever as easy as it seems when you're high and drifting toward sleep. I should have known that.

Charlie woke me up with a hand on my shoulder. "I know where he is. I know where he went."

I was in the middle of a dream when he woke me up, and I pulled away from his hand with a start, lost for a moment in my surroundings. I looked up from my pillow and saw Charlie smiling down at me. I was still lost.

"What's going on?" I managed, clearing phlegm from my throat. "What happened?" And why did he look so happy?

"I got an email. I think it's from my dad, or my mom, maybe— I couldn't trace its source. But it's Devon. I know where he is. I know where we need to go!"

I tried to sit up, but Charlie pushed his notebook computer forward, and I had to roll onto my side to get a good look at the screen. There was an image open on his desktop, a surprisingly high-quality image, still sharp even though it had been zoomed in to fill up the entire window. It was a street view: Devon, glancing over his shoulder, cautiously scanning the street behind him as he pulled open the thick glass door of an office building. "I know where that is. See that planter?" Charlie pointed to a knee-high bowl on the left edge of the photo. The concrete bowl was filled with dead flowers. "I recognize it. That's a research building, south of I-90, near the hospital."

I looked up to find Charlie's eyes searching my face expectantly. His smile was still there. "We can do this, Dean," he said. "We can find out what's going on. The radio . . . my parents . . ." When he started talking about his parents, his voice got hushed, imploring and desperate. "We can find them. We can find everything!"

"What's going on here?"

Surprised, Charlie and I both looked up toward the door. Floyd was standing there, resting his shoulder against the doorjamb.

His hands were busy lighting up a tightly rolled joint. "Is this when you guys hold all of the important roommate meetings? The crack of dawn? Am I missing out? Are we getting TiVo?"

"Floyd? Are you okay?" The last time I'd seen him, he'd been passed out in his bed. And before that—the last time I'd seen him awake—he'd been inconsolable.

"Yeah, I'm fine. And listen, about before, about that . . . I'm sorry." He gave Charlie a cautious look, like he might not want to talk in front of the seventeen-year-old, but he went on, anyway. "I was being stupid, but I'm better now. I'm under control." He held out his hand, palm down, and tried to hold it steady in mid-air, to demonstrate just how cool he was. When it started to shake slightly, he clenched his fist and took another drag on his joint.

I felt uncomfortable lying on the futon with both Charlie and Floyd towering over me, so I pulled back my covers and sat up in the middle of my bedding. I was still wearing my jeans and sweat-shirt. I couldn't remember when I'd last taken them off.

Floyd saw the screen of Charlie's notebook and quickly knelt down at his side, grabbing the computer and lifting it up into his lap. He handed me his joint, freeing up his hands. "Is this Devon?" he asked urgently, mousing back and forth on the image, panning it from side to side. "Do you know where he is?"

"Maybe," Charlie said. "Yes." He turned his pleading glance back my way. "I was just telling Dean about how we need to go there. My parents . . . I think Devon knows something about my parents."

"That's good enough for me," Floyd said with a nod. "That fucker's got some shit to answer for." He looked at me and tapped at his temple, his eyes going wide. "Binocular shit. Tunnel shit!"

After a moment, I nodded reluctantly. I didn't feel too confi-dent about this, following Charlie's mysterious email, looking for Devon. It felt like we were being led by the nose here, and I didn't trust that sensation; there was too much potential for traps, for disaster. But I could see that it was going to happen whether I liked it or not. With or without me.

Charlie and Floyd had already made that decision.

Floyd's joint was sitting idle between my fingertips. I took a deep drag before I handed it back.

Taylor answered her door on the second knock. She looked tired, as if she hadn't slept at all that night.

"Yeah, Dean, I'll come," she said coldly, when I told her what we were planning to do. "I'll help Charlie any way I can."

I stared at her for a while, taking in her pinched lips and wrinkled forehead, the clenched and jutting muscles of her jaw. *Who is this person?* I wondered. At times like this, I couldn't figure her out. She was wearing a mask—a cold facade that she hid behind whenever she came under assault—and I had absolutely no idea how to peel it back.

"What's wrong, Taylor?" I finally pleaded. "What did you find in that drawer back at the Homestead? What can I do to help?"

For a moment, her expression relaxed and her jaw unclenched. Then she closed her eyes and shook her head, raising a hand to cover her dark and weary eyelids.

"There's nothing for you to do, Dean," she said, speaking from behind the sanctuary of her fingers. "But don't worry about it. It's not you; it's not your fault. I just need time, okay? I need time to figure things out. Priorities, you know?"

After she finished speaking, she lowered her hand. Her eyes were red—bloodshot—but there were no tears. She tried to force a smile, but it came across as a horrible grimace, a mélange of fake, stillborn emotion.

"But you can count on me," she said. "I'll do everything I can . . . for you, for Charlie, for my friends." After the word *friends,* her voice trailed off, and I barely caught her final sentence: "I'd never let you down."

Next I went to check on Sabine. She was smiling when she opened her bedroom door, practically beaming. Her forehead was dotted with beads of sweat and smeared with graphite. I looked over her shoulder and saw large sheets of drawing paper scattered across the floor. They were dark with pencil and charcoal.

"What are you doing?" I asked, surprised at her attitude and her energy. She'd been hiding from everyone for the last couple of days; ever since she'd met with the Poet, she'd been locked away in what I had assumed was a depressive funk.

"It's a surprise," she said, flashing me a sly smile. "It's a project I'm working on. And it's absolutely brilliant. Just brilliant!"

She saw me staring over her shoulder and reached up to block my view with her palms. "No, no! It's a secret," she said. "It's not done yet, and I can't sacrifice the impact of that first viewing. It's got to hit! It's got to hit hard, like a kick to the balls." She pulled back her leg as if she were going to demonstrate the impact on *my* balls. I stepped back in surprise, and she laughed. Then she closed the door to just a crack and peeked out at me through the narrow gap.

"Are you okay, Sabine?" I asked. "You're acting strange."

Her face settled for a moment. "I'm just excited, Dean. That's all. It's my process. It's how I work. But I'm fine, really. In fact, I'm better than I've been in a long time now. I've got a plan, a purpose." She nodded toward the art on her floor. "But I've got to get back to work. The muse—she's moving, and I don't want to fall behind."

Then she closed the door in my face. I heard a playful little laugh come from inside the room as I turned and headed back toward the stairs.

The manic swings here were dizzying. At the moment, Charlie, Floyd, and Sabine were up—way up—and Taylor was down. But I got the sense that it could change at any moment. We were all fragile here, fragile and out of control.

Give the city a moment, I knew, and everything would change.

This house needs some serious *therapy,* I thought as I clambered down the stairs, cinching my camera bag tight against my back. I met Charlie, Floyd, and Taylor at the front door.

○

The research park was deserted. And it wasn't really much of a park. It was just a square of squat gray buildings with a grassy space in the middle.

Charlie knew just where he was going. He led us down a path between two of the buildings and out into the central courtyard. There was a cherry tree here in one corner, and a stagnant fountain in another. Sometime in the last couple of months, the cherry tree had toppled over, pulling up a huge knot of roots. Its bent trunk stretched across the path, ending, leafless, in a crown of broken branches. There were eight buildings in the square—two on each side—and empty windows looked down on us from every direction. One of the buildings had a broken window up on the third floor, and an office chair lay in the courtyard below, surrounded by glass and shattered computer parts. It was perfectly still inside the courtyard. There wasn't even a hint of wind inside this secluded space.

Charlie smiled widely and gestured for us to follow, breaking into an excited trot as he crossed to the far side of the square. He led us around the base of one of the buildings—the one with the broken window—and back out onto the street. The planter from Charlie's photograph was right there, at the building's entrance.

"You've been here before, haven't you?" Taylor asked. "You didn't hesitate, didn't take a wrong turn."

Charlie shook his head. "I walked by weeks ago, looking for my parents. I just remembered it, that's all. I've got a good memory for this type of thing. Places. Directions."

Taylor responded with a skeptical grunt.

"C'mon," Floyd said. "Let's see if this fucker's home." He crossed to the front door and pulled at the handle. It rattled in its frame but didn't open. "Fuck. What now? Should I knock?"

"No," Charlie said. "Look." He pointed toward the planter. On the wall, behind the concrete bowl, I saw a red light blinking steadily.

We made our way over, and Floyd leaned down into the narrow space between the planter and the wall. "It's a keypad," he said, surprise and confusion in his slow, mildly stoned voice. "It's still got power. Battery, do you think?"

The keypad was set about a foot off the ground, completely hidden in that dark crevice—even more so if the planter had been in bloom, if the flowers hadn't already wilted into mulch. *A secret keypad,* I thought. Nobody would have noticed it—not in a million years—if he or she didn't already know it was there.

"Let me try," Charlie said, and Floyd stepped back, letting Charlie take his place. The seventeen-year-old punched in a string of numbers, and the light on the keypad turned green. The lock on the front door ratcheted back audibly. "5869," he said. "It was in the email." He met our eyes one by one, then added quietly: "It's my parents' birth years: 1958, 1969."

"Did they set this up?" I asked.

"Maybe. I don't know." Charlie reached out and touched the keypad gently, as if it were something precious and fragile. "I think they're leading me here. I think they want me to find them."

I let this sink in. Then, after a moment of silence, I repeated a question that I'd already asked him once, a question that he hadn't been able—or hadn't been willing—to answer: "What does your father do, Charlie? And what does it have to do with the city?"

"He's a scientist. They're both scientists—theoretical physicists. And . . . I don't know, they might have been working here, on the phenomena. Before it got bad, before the evacuation."

"What do you mean, they *might* have been working here? You don't know where your parents were or what they were doing?"

"We lost contact. It's hard to explain." He looked genuinely confused. "Just . . . they had to be away, okay, and they couldn't tell me—they weren't allowed to tell me—where they were or what they were doing. But I knew—I suspected, at least—that they were here. It made sense timewise; this was right when the government started calling in all the experts. I had to stay with my grandparents in Portland for a while."

"And you think they were in Spokane and never made it out?" Taylor asked. "You think your parents got stuck here, inside?"

Charlie shrugged, and his brow wrinkled in pain. "I don't know. I don't know what happened." He paused for a moment, and then, suddenly, he got angry. He shot an intense, venomous look at Taylor. "But that's what I'm trying to figure out, okay? They stopped calling, and I needed to know what happened. So I came here. And now I'm getting all of these emails, and, and . . ." He trailed off, turning his eyes toward me. I knew what he was thinking; he didn't want to tell her about the radio, about his father's distant voice reaching out from the static, taking orders from Devon.

Confused, Taylor looked back and forth between the two of us. Then she nodded, and after a moment, she gestured toward the front door.

There was a blinding flash of light as soon as the door closed behind us. It was a vibrant, electric blue, brilliant and seemingly without source or direction. It dazzled my eyes, and as I stood there—blind—a loud, mechanical hum filled the lobby. The air around me grew pregnant with electricity; it felt like every molecule in the room was vibrating against my skin. Something was happening inside my body; I didn't know what, but the hair on my arms was standing up straight.

Then it stopped.

"What the fuck was that?" Floyd asked as we exchanged confused glances, our eyesight slowly returning. "Was that some type of scanner? Were we just fucking scanned?"

"Scanned?" Taylor repeated, a gruff, mocking tone to her voice. "What does that even mean, Floyd? Fucking scanned?"

"I don't know. X-rays? MRI? Something like that?"

The thought gave me a jolt, and I shrugged out of my backpack to check on my camera. I scrolled through the last couple of images on my memory card, making sure that they hadn't been erased by some strong magnetic field. They were still there. Pic-

tures of the Poet's latest work: "Above me, there is a face/Funny."
I didn't remember taking these pictures, but they were there on
the card, and they seemed completely unharmed.

When I once again raised my eyes, I found Floyd nervously
downing pills from his oxycodone stash. For a moment, I felt a
reflexive itch to follow his lead—I still had an almost full bottle
of Vicodin in my pocket—but I suppressed the urge. I was trying
to be strong here, I reminded myself. I hung my camera around
my neck and shrugged into my backpack.

"Look," Charlie said, pointing up into the corner of the room.
There was a surveillance camera up there, and as I watched, it
slowly swiveled my way. It paused for a moment, freezing with
me in the center of its glass-eyed view, and then it continued on
its circuit, turning to sweep back toward the other side of the
room. "There's still power! It's still active!" I was surprised at the
excitement in Charlie's voice. I myself felt nothing but fear.

What's going on here? What have we found?

"Is it some type of secret government installation?" Floyd
asked, voicing my very next thought.

Charlie just shrugged. He flashed us an indecipherable smile,
then turned and headed toward a door on the far side of the room.

The door opened up onto a long carpeted hallway. Charlie
paused just inside the door and ran his fingers over the nearest
wall. After a couple of seconds, the overhead fluorescents flickered on. The hallway was disconcertingly normal. It could have
been any corridor in any office building in any city around the
world—just minutes after closing time, maybe, with the workers
all gone for the day. The heater kicked on as we were standing
there, warm air blowing down from the overhead vents.

Charlie headed toward the nearest room, and the rest of us followed.

It was a small, windowless office, something for an assistant,
maybe, or an administrator. Inside, there was nothing but a desk,
a chair, a telephone, and a computer. While Charlie rummaged
through the desk drawers, I picked up the telephone handset and

listened to the sound of a dead line. The phone was getting power, but there was nothing on the wire, not even static. I replaced the handset just as Charlie lifted a thin sheaf of paper into the air.

"Office directory," he proclaimed triumphantly as he started flipping through the pages. "Biologists, physicists, psychologists, computer scientists . . . theologians. They certainly didn't narrow it down any." He paused halfway through the directory, his finger on a listing at the bottom of the page.

"Did you find them?" I asked.

He nodded, but there was no excited smile on his face, not anymore. Just a trace of confusion. He handed the pages to me and pointed to a pair of names near the bottom: Dr. Stephen Daltry and Dr. Cheryl Daltry. Instead of having a standard office number next to their names—112 or 315 or 423—they both had B13 listed as their location. A basement laboratory, I guessed. But that was not what had killed Charlie's excitement.

There was an unsteady line drawn through both of the names.

Dr. Stephen Daltry.

Dr. Cheryl Daltry.

I scanned the rest of the page and saw that most of the names had been crossed out. "It could mean anything," I said.

Both Taylor and Floyd moved into place behind me, where they could study the document over my shoulder. "Maybe those are just the people who—I don't know—people who completed security training," Taylor offered, "or signed a nondisclosure agreement, or something."

"Or RSVPed for a lunch," Floyd added, "or complained about their paltry-ass government pay."

Charlie nodded. But he didn't look reassured.

Since he had seen those names, his face had turned an ashen gray, drained of all blood and color. "Yeah, I know," he said, his voice barely more than a whisper. "But I have a bad feeling about this. Like I should know what that means." His eyes darted from Floyd to Taylor and then to me. "Like I do know already. Something bad. Something very bad."

Floyd shook his head. "Fuck no, Charlie," he said. "You don't know what that means. Those are just lines on a piece of paper. What the four of us do know—about this place, about this situation—it couldn't fill a motherfucking thimble."

Taylor nodded. "He's right." She reached out and grabbed Charlie's hand, giving it a gentle squeeze. "You can feel like shit, you can feel like the world is crashing down, but that doesn't mean you know anything. It just means that you're afraid. And you're afraid because we're getting close."

She met Charlie's frantic eyes with a calm, reassuring smile.

"So let's go, okay?" she said. "Let's go find your parents."

We took the elevator down to the basement.

The lights in the main corridor were already on, bright and institutional, about as far from natural as you can get. The first couple of doors were closed, but the third—B6, actually—was standing wide open. It was dark inside, but in the middle of the room I could make out a worktable draped under a sheet of clear protective plastic. There were microscopes and Bunsen burners hidden beneath the sheet, shielded from the dust and mold floating thick in the uncirculated air.

Charlie continued down the corridor ahead of us. He pulled to an abrupt stop in front of B13, and we all piled up behind him. The door here was open, and the lights were on.

"What is it?" Floyd asked when he finally got a look inside the laboratory. "What exactly am I seeing?"

Charlie shrugged, and we all filed into the room.

The laboratory was large—at least twenty-five feet by twenty-five feet—and most of the floor was taken up by a single piece of makeshift machinery. There was a table with several computer terminals set against the wall just inside the door, but the majority of the apparatus was in the center of the room. It consisted of two parallel mirrors standing about fifteen feet apart. There were black boxes set against the near end of each sheet of silvered glass.

The apparatus was running, and every five seconds the entire thing lit up with brilliant green light. It was very bright, and I had to narrow my eyes to get a good sense of what was happening. At first, it was all just flashes of light. Then, on about the fifth flash, I noticed a pattern in the apparatus, hundreds of lines of light—laser light—crisscrossing between the mirrors. Then, on perhaps the tenth flash, I realized what was happening. There was movement in the intricate weave—nothing I could actually see, but it was there. The line of light was shooting out of one of the black boxes and progressing down the length of the apparatus, bouncing back and forth between the two mirrors. At the far end, it ricocheted off a separate angled piece of glass and returned on a similarly sharp, crisscrossing trajectory, ending at the second black box.

It was all happening so fast, it looked like nothing but a binary switch. Off and on. Light and dark. But there was movement in there, just too fast to see. The four of us stood silent for a time, watching the flow of traffic inside this miniature city of light and glass.

Floyd was the one who finally broke the silence. "Whoa," he muttered. "This thing . . . it's better than any fucking lava lamp." When I turned, I found him lighting up a new joint.

With the silence broken, that initial period of awe left the room, and we all started moving once again. Charlie headed straight for the computer terminals, bending down to study the lit screens. Taylor moved forward and dropped into a crouch next to the apparatus. She held her eyes level with the laser and peered down the length of its path, across the field of crisscrossing lines as they blinked on and off.

I, for my part, lifted my camera and popped off the lens cap. The laser was lit for only brief periods—a quarter of a second, maybe—and it took me about twenty shots before I managed to get a picture of the bright green pattern spread between those mirrors. I would have loved to have gotten a picture halting the light in motion—with the path half lit, a visible head or tail—but there was no shutter speed that fast, no way to halt the world and capture that shot. I stayed near the "head" of the apparatus, grabbing top-down views between the two mirrors.

"Can I get a hit off that, Floyd?"

At first, I didn't notice anything strange about the voice—just words floating in the space behind me—and I kept taking pictures. Then it registered. It was Devon.

By the time I turned, Taylor, Floyd, and Charlie were already facing the doorway. Devon was standing there with his arms crossed against his chest. He had an uncomfortable grin on his lips, expectant and wary.

"It bounces over seven hundred times," he said. "Over two miles in length. That's what they said, Charlie. That's what your parents told me."

Charlie and Floyd advanced at the same time. Only a couple of steps—Floyd angry, Charlie shocked, his hands out, imploring—before they both pulled to a stop. It was synchronized almost, and they both stood there for a prolonged beat, unsure of their next choreographed step.

"Wait, wait!" Devon said, holding up his hands to ward them off. His attention mostly remained fixed on Floyd. Floyd was the angry one. Charlie was just confused and desperate.

"You were spying on us!" Floyd barked. His voice was an angry growl at first; then it trailed off into weak confusion: "Pretending to be our friend, then watching us through binoculars. Staring at us through our windows! And then . . . the tunnels?"

"I can explain. Just . . . just stay calm. All of you." His eyes flickered from Floyd to Taylor, as if he were looking to her for help, an assurance that she'd keep us all in line.

But Taylor just stared. I didn't know what she was thinking. She hadn't seen the radio, or the binoculars, or the wires beneath the house. It hadn't been her father's voice that had echoed out of Devon's radio, reporting in and taking orders. But Devon *had* been spying for Terry. It was just a minor sin in my eyes, compared with the rest of the things he'd done, but Taylor didn't give him any quarter. She remained ice cold.

"Okay," I said. "Everyone, let's just be cool."

I took a step forward and made soothing motions with my hands, trying to keep Floyd and Charlie back. I wanted to keep the situation under control. I crossed to Floyd's side and put a hand on his shoulder. "We can let him talk. Okay?"

Floyd grunted, reluctantly acquiescing.

Devon thanked me with an appreciative nod, but I just shook my head. I was not his friend. I wasn't doing this for him.

"I didn't mean to cause you any harm—none of you, really—and I don't think I did. I was just watching, making sure nothing bad happened." He took a deep breath, bracing himself, then continued. "You see, I work for a group—" He paused for a moment, then came up with a new term. "—a consortium, I guess you could call it, with national and international business interests . . . and grand political schemes. Or maybe just grand political delusions—I'm not too sure about the reality on that one. My father got me the job; he's pretty high up in the organization—sold his soul for that portfolio, right? Anyway, they placed me in the city. At first, I was an administrator in the investigative unit—" He gestured up toward the building above our heads. "—but I stayed on after it started falling apart, after the military took control. I wasn't the only one. There were other moles, but most of them fled during the transition. And of the ones who stayed, I think I might be the last one left. At least, that's the impression I get whenever they contact me. They're getting desperate, you see. They lost their bead on the situation, and they're not used to that. They're not used to losing control."

"What did they have you do?" I asked.

"Like I said, I was an administrator. It was my job to facilitate things, get the experts the gear and supplies they needed in order to do their research. I got them copy paper, I made sure their computers worked, I helped them organize their expeditions. I did anything and everything they asked me to do. That was my job. I'd get in tight, you see, and they'd tell me all of their theories, all of their hypotheses, and I'd relay it back out of the city." He nodded toward Charlie. "That's how I met your parents. That's how I learned about this." He gestured toward the laser apparatus in the middle of the room.

"What is it?" I asked.

I addressed the question to Devon, but Charlie was the one who answered. "It's measuring the speed of light," he said quietly.

Devon nodded. He looked impressed. "It's counting the length of time it takes for the laser beam to travel from one end of its path to the other."

"But why?" Taylor asked. "That's a known constant."

"Not anymore," Charlie answered. "At least, not here." There was a terrified expression on his face as he turned and gestured toward one of the computer monitors. After a moment's hesitation, Taylor, Floyd, and I approached. The screen was filled with lines of text, and each time the apparatus flashed, a new line appeared at the top of the screen. It was a time stamp, followed by a long string of digits.

As we watched, the digits changed: 299,792,457.99999908 became 299,792,457.99999907.

"Those are meters per second," Charlie explained. "It's getting slower. The speed of light . . . it's changing."

"Your parents had a hypothesis," Devon said. "They believed that the universe was slowing down. Maybe it's just stopped expanding, or maybe it's actively shrinking, but either way, physics has changed—time has changed—and it's still changing."

"We wouldn't be able to survive that," Charlie said. "Even the slightest shift. The movement of atoms, neurons in the brain—it would all fail. If something like that happened, it'd be the end of everything! No life, no substance."

"Yeah," Devon replied, smiling grimly. "That's what they tell me."

"What are they doing now? My parents—are they here, are they trying to explain this?"

"No," Devon said. "They aren't here. Not anymore."

"Then where? Where did they go?"

Devon paused for a long moment, casting careful glances at each of us in turn. "They're dead, Charlie," he finally replied. "They're dead, and you know it."

"No," Charlie said, his brow furrowing in confusion. "They aren't dead. They sent me emails. I have pictures of them, in the city. I heard you talking to my father!"

"No, Charlie. They're dead," Devon repeated. After a handful of seconds, he continued reluctantly: "Hell, you were there, at the funeral. September 15, just outside of Portland. I saw the pictures."

"No," Charlie said, shaking his head in disbelief. Then his face crinkled up in a sudden moment of doubt—*What is he thinking?* I wondered. *Right now, what does he remember?*—and he took a tentative step back. The way he was moving, I was afraid his legs were going to collapse beneath him. "It's not true. You're lying." But now there was a note of desperation in his voice.

"Your parents ran tests. They confirmed—" He gestured toward the apparatus. "—they checked interference patterns or something. And then they took a car . . . I don't think they could handle it anymore, watching the world fall apart—this was just after the mayor disappeared, when everyone in the building was starting to see things, starting to freak out. Your mother told me it was going to spread, it was going to infect the entire world. It was just a matter of time." Devon paused. His voice turned soft, sympathetic. "The official reports—the police told you it was an accident, they told you that your father lost control of the car, but I think your parents just didn't want to see what was coming. I don't think they could handle it."

"No. It's a lie. It's impossible. I don't remember . . . why wouldn't I remember?" Charlie turned abruptly and kicked out at the laser apparatus, slamming his foot into the nearest mirror. The laser tipped off its axis, and the next time it fired, it bounced high off the far mirror and shot up into the ceiling. I glanced at the tracking monitor and saw the word *ERROR* repeated a half dozen times on the topmost line. "This whole thing is bullshit. Complete and utter bullshit. The universe doesn't work that way . . . my parents, they don't work that way!"

He started toward Devon, taking hard, violent strides, and then his legs *did* collapse, sending him sprawling to the floor. At first he braced himself on the heels of his hands, then he moved his palms up to his face, hiding his emotions in a hunched-up little ball.

"But we were listening on the radio," I explained. "You were talking to somebody about plugging up leaks, about the information we were sending out. And what he said . . . whoever it was, it sounded like Charlie's father."

"I don't know what you heard, but it wasn't Charlie's father." Devon shook his head, a single shallow shake. If he was lying, he was doing a good job of it; he wasn't overselling anything, merely stating facts. "At first, we were trying to keep the more troublesome aspects of the situation contained—my bosses had no idea what would happen to their business interests if some of this stuff leaked out—but that was a while ago. Now it's just the military, with their communications freeze and their quarantine. When Charlie appeared, I was assigned to watch him, to make sure he didn't get too close to his parents' research. I still send out my reports, through the radio, but I don't get anything back, not anymore. It's just silence now. Just me—my voice—and nothing else."

"You lie." Suddenly Charlie's hands fell away from his face, and the grief written there—in gleaming eyes and on tear-streaked cheeks—was gone. There was nothing but anger now, cold, hard anger. He stood up, slowly, and the way he was holding himself—

fairly quivering with mute energy—I was afraid he was going to attack Devon. "This is all an elaborate lie," he continued, his voice level, barely restrained. "You're trying to keep me away from my parents. You're trying to shake me off their trail. That was my father on the radio, I'm sure of it, and that was my mother in that picture. They're here, in the city, and for some reason you don't want me to find them."

"Why? Why would I do that?"

Charlie stood silent for a moment, his face screwed up in thought. Then he had his answer: "Because they know what you did—you and your dirty little organization! You did this. All of this. And you're afraid . . . you're afraid because they can fix it!" He swept his hand across the room, indicating the monitors, the laser apparatus, the city itself. "They can fix it all . . . if I can just find them. If I can save them."

Devon laughed. "I wish that were true, Charlie, I really do. But we're beyond that now. There's no fixing the universe." He shook his head. "Get out of the city. Go home. Go see your grandparents before it's too late."

At that, Charlie's restraint disappeared, and he bolted forward—a scrawny seventeen-year-old computer geek, itching to stop Devon, itching to find answers . . . with his fists and blood and Devon's broken bones.

Floyd barked a loud "Stop!" and stepped between the two combatants. He grabbed Charlie's collar and pushed him back, holding on until the teen stopped squirming.

"Get the fuck out, Devon!" Floyd growled, whipping around to face the man in the doorway. "And stay away from us. Stay away from the house. You've done enough harm, you manipulative, spying piece of shit! So just go back to your tunnels and stay . . . the fuck . . . away!"

Devon nodded and made to leave; he started to turn, but then stopped suddenly. "Those aren't our tunnels, by the way," he said. "We used them, yeah, but we didn't dig them, and they most certainly aren't ours. But you know that, don't you, Floyd?

You know what types of things are down there, lurking, waiting in the dark. For you. For me. For all of us."

He paused thoughtfully, and a bitter, melancholy smile formed on his lips. "I hate to say it, boys—and girl—but our time has come. As a species, we're finished. Maybe Charlie's parents had the right idea."

Then he turned and left.

20.1

Video clip. October 24, 02:35 P.M. Sabine's graffiti:

The camera sits a couple of feet off the ground,
staring across a city street at the side of a brick
building. The view is skewed slightly, tilted a few
degrees to the left. It is day out—midmorning or
noon or early afternoon—but the street is deserted,
and the scene is not very bright; the color is all
washed away, lost beneath a ceiling of clouds. In
this light, the red brick wall has faded to a pinkish gray.

The camera jostles as the recording starts, and at
first the view is nothing but the building wall,
standing about twenty feet away. There is paint on
the wall—dark lines forming squiggly shapes—but it
is not visible for long. A young woman circles
around from the camera's rear, and the wall blurs,
the lens focusing in on this new subject. She stops
in the middle of the street and turns to face the
camera.

Really, she's not much more than a girl—small and
delicate, barely five feet tall. Her skin is white
porcelain, smeared with dirt. Her hair is charcoal
black, pulled away from her face.

THE WOMAN—SABINE: My name is Sabine Pearl-Grey, and
this is my statement.

She smiles slyly.

SABINE: There are some slights I can't tolerate, some
things that are just beggin' for my response. And
this . . . this is something I can't turn away from.
(Long beat.) I will not be ignored. If you turn your
back on me, I'll turn my fists on you. (She raises
her hands into a fighter's pose and holds it, serious, for a second. Then she lets out a tiny girlish
giggle.)

The woman turns and darts offscreen, camera right.
She is offscreen for only a handful of seconds, but
it is long enough for the camera's focus to read-
just, for the paint on the wall to come clearly into
view. It is a swarm of spray-painted spiders, surrounding a two-foot gash that starts about a foot
off the ground. It looks like they are crawling out
of that dark crevice, each one frozen in a mute
acrylic pose.

When the woman returns, she is carrying a ladder
twice her height, and there is a sagging messenger
bag slung across her back. She carries the ladder to
the wall and sets it carefully against the brick.
Then she climbs all the way up to its penultimate
rung. There is a window frame just about level with
the top of her head, a couple of inches below the
video's topmost edge.

She reaches down and back, fumbles with her messenger bag for a moment, and comes up with a can of
spray paint. She shakes the can for a couple of seconds, pops off the top, and starts to paint. It is a
long and labored process: writing words on the
wall—lines of text, starting with the left-hand
side of each line—carefully leaning out over the
sidewalk, inching down the ladder, rail by rail. She
leans out too far at one point, and the ladder
shifts beneath her weight, the right-hand foot lifting off the ground for a nerve-racking moment before
once again settling back into place. When she is
done with the left-hand side of the graffiti, she
climbs down, moves the ladder eight feet to the
right, and climbs back up to fill in the right-hand
side. The entire process takes about five minutes.

The paint is a dark green. Olive and drab. It is a
poem, drawn in bold, accusatory letters:

<u>The Poet Inside</u>

    She hides because there's no one there,

        inside.

    The heart is empty and the head is hollow.

    Her world is filled with corridors and echoes

        and shadows.

    But it is all empty space.

    And she wears a mask because she has no face.

    She hides the end of the world

        inside.

The poem ends to the right of the gash in the wall.
With just that single word: *inside*.

After she finishes writing, the woman moves the ladder a couple more feet to the right. She drops the can of green spray paint to the sidewalk and digs a new one from her bag. This one is bright red. She draws a giant arrow around the right-hand side of the poem, arcing up from the word *inside* and ending at the window above.

She's pointing up toward the Poet. Pointing into her home.

When she finishes, the woman pulls back her arm and hurls the can of spray paint far into the distance; after a moment of hang time, there's a loud clatter offscreen as the can skips across the pavement and collides with something solid—something metal and hollow that rings like a bell. The woman jumps down to the sidewalk, violently grabs hold of the ladder, and sends it crashing flat against the ground. Then she takes a couple of abrupt steps back, and—still facing the wall, still facing her poem and the Poet's window—she raises her hands and gives the building a double-fisted two-finger salute.

SABINE: Just one more thing. One more thing and my work is done. (She glances back over her shoulder at the camera. The sly smile is once again there, twisting her face, somehow wedded to her anger and not at all incongruous.)

She grabs the top of the ladder and pulls it off-screen. When she returns a couple of seconds later, she is carrying a sledgehammer. Actually, she is *dragging* a sledgehammer; its massive head trails behind her, filling the air with a loud grating/grinding sound.

Laboring under its weight, the woman lifts the hammer from the ground and squares off in front of the
gash in the wall. She swings, and the hammer crashes
into the brick with a dull thunk. The left-hand edge
of the gash caves in slightly, but the damage is
rather unimpressive—just a dent, not a melodramatic
burst of destruction. She lifts and swings again.
This time a single brick topples through the gash,
into the darkness beyond—half a spray-paint spider,
disappearing into the void. She pauses and takes a
deep breath. Already the effort seems to be taking
its toll.

But she doesn't stop. Over the next five minutes,
the woman relentlessly assaults the wall, breaking
bricks from the facade, usually one by one but occasionally triggering a miniature avalanche, sending a
half dozen or more tumbling down into the darkness,
or down to the sidewalk around her feet. By the time
the gash is about four feet high and three feet
wide, she has slowed down quite a bit. Her arms
tremble visibly each time she lifts the hammer.

She hits the wall one final time—weakly, to absolutely no effect—and the sledgehammer drops from
her hands, nearly crushing her feet. She collapses
back against the wall. Her chest is heaving. Her
arms dangle limply.

SABINE, IN A WEAK, BREATHLESS WHISPER: Fuck me, this
is harder than I thought. (She smiles at the camera
and lets out a single exhausted laugh.)

After about a half minute of rest, she pushes herself off the wall and turns to face the hole. Then
she leans forward and peers inside. Her hands are
motionless against the wall as she tilts her head

down and pauses, her face pressed into the darkness,
peering down at . . . at *something*. There must be
something down there to catch her attention, something hidden away in the dark. She stays perfectly
still for another half minute.

Then her right hand starts to move, darting
frantically—crawling like a spider—to the messenger bag at her back. Without taking her face from
the hole, she manages to dig a pen-size flashlight
from her bag. She whips it forward, into the hole
next to her face, and immediately points it down
into the gap behind the wall.

And she freezes. The scene remains still for nearly
a minute. It is a frozen tableau, a static picture
stretched across the screen: a woman—a girl—
standing, crouched, on the sidewalk, surrounded by
bricks from a damaged wall. Spray-paint spiders and
words swarming up and out while she peers down and
in, into the darkness.

Then she moves. Her left hand slides to the edge of
the hole, quivering slightly. She grabs hold, braces
herself, and lifts her leg over the litter of
bricks, through the gap, and into the wall. She
tests her weight on the other side—her foothold
isn't visible, but it looks to be about six inches
below street level—then she crouches down and
slides all the way in. Her messenger bag catches on
the right-hand edge of the gash, and she has to
reach back to pull it through. Her hands are moving
slowly now, and they are definitely quivering—maybe
from all that exertion with the sledgehammer. Or
maybe it's excitement. Maybe fear.

Once inside the hole, she pauses briefly, her back
filling up the diamond-shaped gap. Then she starts

to inch away, into the space behind the wall. She is
moving to the right but also down. Descending beneath the city streets.

Her left shoulder is the last thing we see. It is
only about a foot above street level when it disappears from view.

Then she is gone. And there is no one on-screen for
a very long time.

20.2

The sky turned red not long after we left the research facility, and it stayed red the entire way home.

Again the color changed with a roar. It was a great rending in the sky, and when I looked up, it felt like I was staring into a widening wound.

Again I got the impression of blood, and I was half expecting it to come raining down over the city. It would be a horrible thing, I thought, a horrific squall filled with gristle and teeth, and we'd have to run the last couple of blocks absolutely drenched in gore. But it didn't happen. It was the same as before: a twirling liquid red sky, suspended above our heads.

Floyd hadn't seen it the first time around, and he greeted it with stunned, wide-eyed terror.

"Oh, my God," he muttered. "Oh, my fucking God."

Taylor and I tried to calm him down. We tried to convince him that everything was fine, that the red sky would pass and the world would return to normal, but nothing seemed to work. He remained transfixed by the color above his head, his face going pale, his shoulders drooping, as if pressed down by that massive sky. And there were honest-to-God tears in his eyes.

I don't know if Charlie had seen the sky the first time around, but either way, he wasn't terrified. In fact, the sky didn't seem to affect him at all. He remained lost inside his own head. Battling demons and memory. Chasing his parents. *Are they gone? Are they really dead?* He walked like a zombie, his eyes barely flickering up toward the sky before once again fixing on his boots.

I, for my part, was surprised at how calm I remained. The sky was terrifying—objectively, it was a terrifying sight—but I couldn't find the energy to care. My reserves of horror had run bone dry. I was trying to comfort Floyd, but his confusion and fear seemed downright ridiculous to me. I'd seen all this before, and frankly, after one time, it felt old hat. Almost mundane.

I wanted to get back to the house. I wanted coffee. I wanted to wash my face and check the pantry for food.

After all, I thought with a bitter smile, *it's not like it's the end of the world.*

The four of us stayed together in the kitchen when we got home. Even terrified and confused, Floyd and Charlie wanted our company. I think they wanted the reassurance of having us nearby. This seemed like a big change to me. I was getting used to people freaking out and running away whenever something bad happened.

When we entered, Taylor immediately headed to the camp stove and started making coffee. Floyd collapsed into a chair next to the sliding glass door, where he could stare, transfixed, up at the roiling red sky. His eyes grew wide, and I watched as he bolted down another couple of pills.

"I must have missed something," Charlie said as he sat down at the kitchen table and popped open his notebook computer. "There's got to be something here, something that'll tell us what really happened to my parents. I just need to pay attention. I just need to see what's staring me in the face—in the emails, in the files they sent." His voice was loud, but I think he was just talking to himself, trying to convince himself that there was still hope. Taylor and Floyd didn't even glance up at the sound of his voice.

And then there was silence in the room.

I stood in the doorway for nearly a minute, watching my three friends. They were lost in their own little worlds, sharing the same space but completely isolated, completely alone. It made me sad. The thing that had struck me most when I had first found this house, when Taylor had first dragged me through the door, was the sense of community here, the sense of family hidden away inside these generic suburban walls. It had been such a warm place, full of laughter, full of life. But that was gone now. It had disappeared, along with Amanda and Mac and Weasel (and Devon, too, I thought).

"I'm going to go check on Sabine," I said.

There was no reply.

Upstairs, I found Sabine's door standing wide open, but she wasn't there. Out working on her project, I guessed. I peeked in through the door. Her room was still a mess, blanketed in well-used sheets of paper. I was tempted to sneak in and try to figure out what she was working on but decided against it. That would be a pretty big violation, I figured, considering her earlier reaction. Besides, whatever her project was, I guessed that it was just some manic whim of hers, a distraction, a way for her to channel her energy and pain.

I shut the door and headed back downstairs.

At the bottom of the staircase, I glanced up and saw a dark figure standing just outside the living-room window, outlined against the dark red afternoon. The figure didn't have a face.

I jumped at the sight and almost cried out, barely managing to stifle my voice as the figure backed away from the window, quickly raising its hands in the universal gesture of surrender. My fright passed as soon as I recognized who it was.

It was the Poet, her face hidden behind her dark leather hood.

She continued backing away from the window, keeping her hands raised high. As I watched, she retreated across the lawn and out onto the sidewalk. She stopped there and stood, waiting. Waiting for me?

I was confused. Why would she come here, to the house? What could she possibly want? The last I'd seen, she'd been sitting huddled in the corner of Cob Gilles's apartment, completely terrified, unable to talk. *Did she come here for Sabine?* I wondered. *Is this an apology? A meeting of the artistic minds?*

I moved into the entryway and opened the door, trying to keep it quiet. The way the Poet had retreated to the sidewalk instead of coming straight to the front door, I figured she didn't want an audience. In fact, as soon as I stepped out onto the porch, she took a nervous step back, and I was afraid she was going to flee. Then she planted her feet and stood firm.

"You're the Poet," I said awkwardly as I made my way down the front walk. "I'm sorry about before. Sabine and I . . . we didn't mean—"

As soon as I got about ten feet away, the Poet's hand darted up, frantically warding me back. I stopped, and she nodded. She wanted me at a distance; that much was clear. Her eyes were wide inside her mask's oval openings. Its mouth had been zippered shut.

"What?" I asked, holding out my hands, trying to show her that I was not a threat. "What do you want me to do?"

She held up her hand—palm flat, facing me—and urged me to stay still. Then she reached into the pocket of her paint-spattered peacoat. Her hand came out with a video camera. *My* video camera.

"How?" I asked, perplexed. I tried to think back. What had I done with the camera? How had it managed to get from my backpack to the Poet's hand?

Without thinking, I started toward her. "Where did you—?"

The Poet shook her head and took a quick step back, getting ready to flee. I stopped moving forward—in fact, I fell back a couple of steps—and after a tense moment, the masked woman started to calm back down. *She's like a nervous little bird,* I thought, *ready to fly at the slightest hint of movement.* Eventually, she nodded her head and once again resumed her pantomime. She bent at her knees and slowly lowered the camera to the sidewalk, never once taking her eyes off my face. As soon as it touched the cement, she let go. Then she turned and ran away, fleeing as fast as she could, leaving the camera sitting alone on the sidewalk.

I watched until she disappeared around a corner two blocks away. She was moving fast, running away from me as if I were a horrible threat, as if I were the Devil himself. *And what could do that to a person?* I wondered. *What could scare someone into such complete and total retreat?* Then I bent down and picked up the battered old Sony.

I'm sure it was just a coincidence, but as soon as my hand closed around the camera, the clouds started to move back in over the city, tumbling toward the center of the sky like dirty water flowing toward a drain. And once all the red was gone, the clouds opened up and it started to piss down rain.

I cast a final look down the empty street, then trotted back to the front door.

Sabine had had the video camera. That was the last thing I could recall. She'd used it to record the soldier falling out of the hospital window. Then she'd had it in the tunnel, chasing Mac into the dark. And then . . . I guess she'd never given it back.

Did she give it to the Poet? I wondered. *Why? Why would she do that?*

I ran upstairs as soon as I got back in the house. I retreated to my room and locked the door behind me. Then I sat down on my futon and turned on the camera's video screen.

The battery was almost dead, but there was enough juice to view the most recent recording, and even though the screen was only three inches wide, I could see exactly what was going on.

It was Sabine's project, her "absolutely brilliant" piece of art.

The camera didn't have a speaker, so I had to watch without sound as she took her place in front of the camera, standing there with a sly grin on her face as her lips flapped in silence. Then she started to deface the Poet's wall. I had to squint to make out the words in Sabine's "response," but the emotion of the piece still hit me pretty hard. There was so much anger there, in her words, so much venom—for the Poet, for her work. And to put it there, on the wall of her building, just outside her window—it was an act of violence, and viewing it made me feel a little sick.

Did the Poet really deserve this? Just for keeping quiet, for shutting Sabine out? Obviously, the woman had problems of her own, and her greatest sin—her huge transgression—had been merely not living up to Sabine's expectations.

I felt a jolt of fear as Sabine dragged the sledgehammer into view. It was like watching a crime in progress, an assault. Sabine was going to attack the city—I knew that, I could see it coming— and I couldn't imagine anything good happening as a result.

But when she pounded on the wall, nothing happened. The hole just got bigger. And she got tired.

I was relieved when she finally stopped. I was hoping she'd burned through all that anger. She'd let it flame brightly for that brief period, and now, I hoped, she'd be able to just walk away. Point made. Anger expressed. Bad blood gone.

But then she leaned forward and stuck her head into the gap. It was terrifying, watching that, watching her motionless body perched there at the edge of that hole, just waiting for something to happen.

What's down there? I wondered. *What'd she find? Spiders? A damaged face, a shattered body? A cache of gold, the perfect piece of art?* Or, hell, maybe there were glowing words down there, etched into the building's supports—answers to all of our questions, spelled out in bright, glowing colors (*this* is what's happening, *this* is what's going on).

Or maybe it was nothing. Maybe it was just a dark, cramped space down there beneath the street. And what Sabine was seeing, what had stopped her cold, was something that in normal circumstances would have stayed a faint whisper in the back of her head. A fear, a personal epiphany, projected into an empty, brick-ringed hole.

Whatever it was, it was a way forward. And it was a path Sabine must have felt compelled to take.

Without looking back, she moved inside and disappeared.

And that was it. That was the end of Sabine's protest, the end of her little piece of performance art.

I stared at the static scene for a long time. At first, I was waiting for her to come back out. Then, after a while, I was sure that she wouldn't. After about five minutes, I hit the fast-forward button and spun through nearly a half hour of empty street. Then there was a hint of movement screen right. I hit the "play" button once again and watched as the Poet tentatively made her way on-screen, first standing back to study Sabine's poem, then moving up to the wall to stare into the hole. She didn't look for long—she just gave the hole a cursory, uninterested glance—before she backed up and headed toward the camera.

The Poet stopped in the middle of the street, a couple of feet away. She bent down and stared into the camera lens for a long moment, her bright eyes sparkling behind her black leather mask. Then she reached out and shut it off.

The screen went a brilliant blue in my hands, and I sat there for a while, trying to figure out what to do next.

It took me about fifteen minutes to make it to Sabine's poem.

The rain was coming down hard by then, and the streets were all flooded. Spokane had been transformed into a maze of inch-deep rivers, and I cut a wake through the water as I made my way to St. James Tower, home of Cob Gilles and the Poet. By the time I got there, my clothing was soaked through. It stuck, cold, to my skin, and I couldn't stop shivering.

The poem was there. Large as life and just as angry. I noticed the can of green spray paint lying discarded in the gutter. Sabine's ladder lay flat on the sidewalk nearby.

I didn't hesitate. I went right up to the hole and peered inside. There was less than a foot of space between the outer wall and the inner wall, and that space was almost completely filled with debris. There was absolutely no way anyone could have climbed inside. It was a physical impossibility.

But that didn't really surprise me.

It was just like with Amanda and her tunnels. Where Sabine had gone, I couldn't follow. Not yet, anyway. And not on this path.

I rested my head against the wall for a long moment. I was exhausted, drained of all energy, beaten down to a pulp.

Then I turned and headed back home.

Taylor heard me open the front door and met me in the entryway.

"Dinner's ready," she said. She looked tired. Her face was long, and every muscle in her cheeks and jaw had gone perfectly slack. "You're soaking wet. Where did you go?"

"I was looking for Sabine." Taylor's eyes went wide with concern, and I paused for a moment, trying to figure out what to say. I didn't want to tell her the truth. I didn't think she could handle another loss. "I thought she might be across the street, but she's not there. She's probably with Mama Cass."

Taylor nodded and dredged up a reassuring smile. "She's a big girl, Dean. I'm sure she's fine. We'll all be fine." Her voice was faint, and I could tell that she didn't really believe what she was saying. She was just trying to be strong. For me.

I nodded. "I need to go change," I said. "But save me some food, okay? I'm absolutely famished." I forced a smile of my own. It felt wrong on my face—a weak and transparent lie.

Upstairs, I found Sabine's duffel bag tucked beneath her bed. I gathered up all of her clothing and stuffed it inside, filling it nearly to overflowing. Then I crammed her drawing papers in on top. Charcoal words jumped out at me as I worked. They smeared beneath my damp fingertips—bold but so very, very fragile. And so very, very temporary.

corridors and echoes . . .

. . . inside . . .

. . . she hides

By the time I was done, the room looked completely abandoned. The bed wasn't made, but all trace of Sabine was gone, hastily packed away. I left the door wide open and fled back to my room. I wrapped the duffel bag inside a patchwork quilt and buried it in the back of my closet, beneath a stack of neatly folded bedding.

Then I stripped out of my wet clothes and collapsed naked onto the futon.

No one has to know, I told myself. *Not Taylor, or Floyd, or Charlie. It would do them absolutely no good. It would cause them nothing but pain.*

Sabine had been talking about leaving—I could tell them that. After meeting with the Poet, she'd gotten fed up. And, frustrated, she left. Without saying a word. It would be the most natural thing in the world.

And they'd believe it. They'd want to believe it. We were all tempted to leave. We stayed—we kept staying—but we knew it was wrong. We knew we should be packing up and hiking out of here.

Hell, my car was waiting just outside the city limits. I could gather up my cameras and go. Right now. I could be in the car in a matter of hours. I could be in Seattle by midnight.

My hands started shaking in my lap. I clenched them into fists and then shook them loose. Again. And then again. Clenched and released. Clenched and released. Finally, I fished my jacket from the floor and dug through its pockets, coming up with my bottle of Vicodin. After a moment's hesitation, I popped open the lid and bolted down a couple of pills.

I wasn't going anywhere.

21.1

Photograph. October 25, 12:11 A.M. Taylor, bound:

> The shutter speed is wrong. Every edge is blurred
> slightly, giving the picture—a young woman sitting,
> bound, on the edge of a bed—a feathered, ephemeral
> quality. It is like the scene is moving, caught in
> transition.
>
> The bedroom is lit in candlelight—a warm yellow,
> burning out of frame, somewhere to the woman's left.
> Her clothing is disheveled; the shoulder of her hoodie
> has slipped down, exposing pale skin at her neck, be-
> tween strands of wild black hair. Her hands and fore-
> arms are extended out in front of her body, bound
> together with loops of gray duct tape. There is tape
> across her mouth, too, stretching from ear to ear.
>
> The woman's eyes are wide, lashes and brow raised in
> fright. She is looking right back at the camera. Her
> entire world is focused on that one point in space
> and time—laser sharp and terrified. Her right cheek
> is lost in shadow; her left is glistening with
> tears.

21.2

We had red beans and rice for dinner. It was an instant mix that Taylor had found in the pantry. I didn't have much of an appetite—my head was swimming, and the Vicodin made my arms and face feel heavy—but I ate anyway, trying to keep up appearances.

I didn't say anything about Sabine. I wanted someone else to find her emptied room.

Now that the sky was once again normal—five o'clock and already pitch black, still raining hard—Floyd seemed calmer. He was still casting nervous glances toward the windows, but he was talking now and eating. It was probably just the oxycodone, but there were bursts of bubbly delirium mixed in with his chattering nerves.

"So, now that the world is over," he asked, "what do you do?" He was addressing all of us at the table. His fork moved aimlessly through his food. "What's your final meal? Your last words?"

"The world isn't over," Charlie replied, glancing up from his computer. His voice was subdued, but there was a hint of anger there, tamped down and carefully locked away. "Devon was lying. It was complete bullshit."

"And the speed of light? The machine? The laser?"

"It was a fake. A hoax." Charlie paused, and as I watched, something inside him changed. Slowly, his eyes went wide and his back straightened in his chair. "Or maybe, maybe what's happening here affects perception. Maybe it just seems like the speed of light is changing, but really, *really,* it's just an inability to measure things. Maybe there *is* something wrong with physics, but local and not at all catastrophic." Charlie's voice gathered speed as he went along. He was getting excited. "I bet my parents figured it out. I bet they're out there right now, hunting down the source."

Taylor shot me a concerned look. Her expression was grave, and there was a question in her eyes: What do we do? What do we do about Charlie?

"We don't know anything," I said, feeling an edge of annoyance starting to slip through my numb Vicodin shield. I turned toward Floyd and continued: "And as far as planning our last words, what's the point? If it's over, it's over . . . There won't be anyone left to hear. Or care. Or remember. Just words, floating through space."

Taylor fixed me with a disapproving glare, and for a brief, surprisingly liberating moment I wanted to tell her to go fuck herself. But I stayed silent. I think I was pretty high by then.

That's when Danny showed up.

"Hello?" the soldier called as he came in through the front door. I heard him shed his rain-drenched coat onto the entryway floor. Then he stuck his head into the dining room. He was wearing a ridiculously out-of-place fishing hat, and there was water dripping from its brim.

When he saw us there, sitting at the table, he flashed a broad smile. "If you've got the food, I brought the drinks," he said, pulling a couple of bottles from a rainproof utility bag.

He glanced around the table and saw the serious expressions on our faces. His smile faltered briefly, quivering in confusion. Then it strengthened once again.

"C'mon, guys. It's time to cheer the fuck up," he said. "It's time to celebrate!" He let out a brief laugh. "We figured it out. The military—your loyal military—we finally know what's going on."

We retired to the living room, and Danny ate while the rest of us passed around his booze. One of the bottles was amber bourbon, the other a brilliant, sky-blue bottle of gin. Leftovers from the other night, remnants of his clandestine booty. I took a long draw on the gin as soon as it got within reach.

"They found spores in the air," Danny said between forkfuls of food. "It's not a very high concentration—I don't remember, something like one part in a million—but they found it. They finally found it! We've been unlucky up until now. We've been running air samples since day one, but—you see—it *moves*. In clouds, or waves, or something. It's only around at certain times, and you've got to catch it just right."

He smiled and dropped his fork into his empty bowl. "Once we knew what we were looking for, the experts were able to find the source. Earlier today, they found a giant mushroom." He let out a wild laugh, amazed at the thought, or at the sheer craziness of having to say those words. "Really, it's some type of fungus, underground, near the shore of the river, east of Riverside Park. Apparently, it's huge. It covers nearly a full square mile."

"The spores are hallucinogenic?" Charlie asked. He didn't sound willing to believe. "You're saying we've been hallucinating . . . all of this?" He gestured, weakly toward the kitchen and, I imagined, the notebook computer still sitting on the dining-room table. The emails from his parents.

"Well, yeah. It affects mood and perception. Sometimes it's subtle, and sometimes it's full-out catatonia. It blocks the receptors—neurotransmitters in the brain." He tapped idly at his temple. "Like serotonin. And norepinephrine. Just like LSD."

"But what about the sky?" Floyd asked. His eyes darted from Danny, to Taylor, and then back to Danny. "The sky was red. And crawling. There were . . . there were things up there. We all saw it. That wasn't just some fucking hallucination!"

344

Danny smiled. I got the sense that he was enjoying his role here, telling us this stuff, answering our questions. He was a fount of knowledge, a deity, if just for a minute or two, answering all our prayers. "That's part of its bloom, part of its cycle. It's been fruiting, and when enough spores reach the atmosphere, light refracts off the particles, just below cloud level . . . And I'm guessing it's not really as spectacular as you think it is. The sky was red, but everything else . . . that's just your brain spinning out of control."

Danny's expression settled into serious lines, and he surveyed each of us in turn, meeting our eyes. "In fact, everything you've seen or heard here in the city . . . I wouldn't put too much stock in it."

Danny leaned over and dug into the pockets of his khaki pants. He came up with a bottle of pills and shook it for a second, making it rattle. "This is Zoloft. It should help. It should free up your receptors." He tossed the bottle over to Floyd, catching him unaware. The bottle hit Floyd's hands and fell to the floor. Floyd quickly scooped it back up. "Take two. All of you . . . two a day for as long as you're here. The experts say it should help. They've got us all taking it."

I sat in silence as the bottle passed from Floyd, to Charlie, to Taylor, and then on to me. They all took the pills, but only Floyd seemed eager to bolt them down. He was the most desperate, I guess, and this was his life preserver. I poured two large white tablets into my palm and stared at them for a while.

This didn't make sense. Danny's explanation . . . It was all in our heads? But how could that be? "I have pictures," I said, raising my eyes. I focused on Danny at first and then turned toward Taylor. "We've seen things. All of us have seen things. *Together*."

Taylor raised her eyes to meet mine. But there was doubt there, her dark eyes quivering, refusing to stay locked on my face.

"For fuck's sake, you've seen the pictures, Danny!"

He flashed me a gentle smile. "What was your state of mind when you were editing your photos, Dean?" His voice was quiet, but there was a prodding needle buried there, inside his words. "What exactly did you do?"

No. I shook my head. I hadn't altered them. I knew that. I knew what I had seen.

"People under the influence of the spore seem prone to suggestion and confabulation. They rewrite the world around them, what they see, what they experience. And they rewrite the past. The mayor's disappearance—we think he convinced an entire room of reporters, made them believe in a shitty little piece of special effects."

No. I closed my fist around the pills, suddenly flush with violent energy. I wanted to throw the Zoloft back at Danny. I wanted to transform the drug into a pair of tiny little bullets.

"Is that the official line?" I growled. "Is that what the government's going to say? That we're all just insane? None of this is real?"

"They've already started torching the mushroom, Dean. It should be over soon. It should all be gone."

"But it's bullshit. It's a whitewash!"

My words hung in the air for a long moment. Everyone was watching me: Floyd cowed, Charlie confused, Danny looking on with those all-too-patient eyes. And Taylor . . . Taylor just looked tired.

"Take the pills," Taylor finally said. I was surprised at her voice. She sounded strong. All of her doubt and confusion had disappeared. "You don't want it to be true, do you? You don't want an answer to this place, a solution. You don't want it to make sense." She smiled sadly and met my eyes. "You want the end of the world."

I opened my mouth to protest, then quickly pulled it shut. "No," I finally managed. "No, I don't." *I'm not a monster.*

"Then take the fucking pills, Dean," she said. "And hope he's right. Okay? You don't have to believe—you don't have to believe in any of this—but you can hope. You can hope we can end this without the fucking death of the universe!"

I met her eyes for a half dozen heartbeats. Then I nodded. I downed the pills with a swallow of gin.

I had too much shit in my system. My blood was thick with it, a sludge of Vicodin and Zoloft and alcohol. *And hallucinogenic spores,* I thought. *I can't forget about those.*

This struck me as funny. As I said, I had too much shit in my system.

After he finished telling us about the army's mushroom-eradication offensive—men in full-body containment suits wielding bulldozers and blowtorches—Taylor grabbed Danny's arm and pulled him out into the entryway. They talked. Her voice started out soft, inaudible, but it grew louder as the conversation progressed.

"—following me?" she said. Her face was animated. I could see her profile—mouth pulled wide, showing off her teeth—as she confronted Danny. "And telling Dean?" She glanced my way, saw me watching, and pulled Danny out of sight. Her voice fell back into an inaudible whisper.

I crossed to the fireplace, where Floyd was arranging kindling into a neat tepee. He took time out to pass me the bottle of bourbon. I hesitated for a moment—I couldn't be too far from sloppy drunk—then took a swallow.

"This does feel a bit like an acid trip," Floyd said. His voice sounded calm, thoughtful. He struck a long match and held it to the kindling. In a matter of seconds, he had the whole thing burning. "Usually, back when I did acid, I could feel it in my balls. It was almost a pain, but not quite—like someone was giving me a bit of a squeeze. I'm not getting that now. This is mellower. I wonder if we could find this shit, bag it up, and sell it. We could probably make a killing."

"So you believe?" I asked. "You believe it's mushrooms?"

"If that's what they say." He nodded toward the entryway. Danny was still partially visible, shoulder and buttock and leg poking out from behind the entryway wall. "I don't think they'd lie about this. Not after so long."

"But they could be wrong. They're desperate for an answer. They want an answer just as much as we do."

He gave me a skeptical look. I'm sure he was remembering Taylor's words, her harsh assessment of me and my motives. Maybe I didn't want to believe. Maybe I didn't want to believe just as much as he wanted to believe. And in that case, whose judgment could we trust?

"We can wait. We can wait and see," he said.

I gave him a nod and retreated back to the sofa. Charlie was back in the dining room, sitting in front of his computer. I had no idea how he was taking Danny's news.

He probably saw it as a good thing, these mushrooms. It proved Devon a liar.

If any of that was real, I thought. *If any of it actually happened. Maybe that building down there, south of I-90, is completely empty. Maybe we built the whole thing—the laser, Devon, Charlie's parents' hypothesis—all on our own, out of whole cloth and spit and words. Some type of mass delusion, built on suggestion and re-formed, restitched memory.*

Did I actually see that man dangling from the ceiling on my first day in the city? Did I see the spiders and the face in the wall? Did I see Taylor's father and Weasel's fingers? Or is it all just hallucination, my own inner warped mind projected out into the world? Was I complicit? Was I responsible?

And those photographs. Did I do that in Photoshop?

I was scared to look. I was scared to open the images and study them pixel by pixel, looking for cut-and-paste seams, strange gradients, and out-of-place elements.

If I found it, if I found proof that those images had been altered, what would that say? About the situation? About me?

Do I really want to kill the world?

"Just stay the fuck away!" Taylor growled out in the entryway. Danny stumbled back as she pushed her way past. She darted

348

through the living room and up the stairs. She had a hand up over her face, covering her eyes and nose and cheeks, and she bumped into the sofa and bounced off without losing a single step. I heard her door slam shut as soon as she got upstairs.

"Women," Danny said as he collapsed into the sofa next to me. "Fucking hell."

"What did you see at her house?" I asked. "You followed her, right? That's what you were talking about? What did you see?"

"I didn't see shit. I followed her a couple of weeks ago, saw her mom through the window, and I left. I was just fucking curious, man. I didn't mean her any harm."

He grabbed the bottle of gin from where it sat at his feet. I let him take a drink before I continued my line of questioning. "Why'd you tell me about it, about her house? Why'd you send me there?"

"Because she likes you . . . and I thought it would help. Her. You. Whatever." He shook his head and took another swig. "I guess I was wrong." And then, exasperated: "My fucking bad!"

He offered me the bottle, and I studied it for a moment before taking a drink. The label was blurry. I was losing focus.

"I can't wait for this shit to be over," Danny said. "I can't wait for the mushroom to burn and the air to clear. I don't do well with chaos. I prefer things in their place. God in His house and man on his horse. Starbucks and movies and reliable heating. And booze on every street corner." He gestured for the bottle, and I handed it back. My aim was off, and he had to grab for it a couple of times.

"Yeah," I grunted. "Traffic and homework. Part-time jobs and cell phones on the bus."

"And Internet porn," Danny added.

"And commercials on TV."

"Fuck it," Danny said. He took another drink and lowered his head to the sofa's armrest. He handed me the bottle and shut his eyes for a handful of seconds. "If you want, if you hate modern life so much, you can start a motherfucking commune when we get out of here. I'll visit. I'll help you weed the corn and milk the cows. Or milk the corn and weed the cows . . . or milk the bulls and fuck the corn."

I was drinking when he said this, and I sputtered a laugh around the mouth of the bottle, getting the burn of gin up my nose. "Jesus Christ," I sighed in mock exasperation. "It doesn't even exist yet, and you're already ruining my commune."

"That's what you get for being a good person, Dean," he said, the words making their way out around a loud yawn. "Next time, try being a complete fucking asshole."

I woke to a loud *thunk*.

I opened my eyes and saw Mac standing over Danny's unconscious body. He had a splintered, weather-stained plank of wood in his hands. Danny's head lay still against the sofa's armrest. Blood seeped from a wound on his brow, and his eyes twitched beneath shut lids.

The room was dark. The fire had burned down to embers.

It was just the three of us here now: Mac, unconscious Danny, and me. There was no sign of Floyd or Charlie or Taylor.

In the dim light, Mac looked crazy. Absolutely insane. His hair and beard had grown wild in the days since we'd last seen him, and it looked like a dirty red corona around his face. He was absolutely caked in mud, head to foot. I couldn't tell what color his sweatshirt and pants had originally been. His eyes were wide, and his lips were pulled back away from his teeth.

He stood there for a second, staring down at me. There was a bright glimmer in the shadow of his face: reflected light in his eyes. Then a hissing sound escaped from his mouth, and he started to swing the plank.

I tried to scramble back, tried to push my way onto the floor, but I was too late. Mac, wielding that giant piece of wood, slammed a dozen pounds of darkness into the back of my head.

And, once again, I slept.

○

Danny woke me up. He patted my cheeks—gently at first and then harder—until I managed to shake my head. The shaking made my head swim. There was a searing crater of pain in the back of my skull, cutting through the remnants of Vicodin and alcohol.

"What, what, *what*?" I sputtered, cringing away from Danny. He was a macabre specter hanging above me. A wide stream of blood had congealed against his face, cutting from his hairline down to his left eyebrow, where it had pooled and dripped down to stain the shoulder of his uniform shirt. His eyes were wild. There was spit on his lips, and his chin was wet.

"It was Mac," Danny said, his voice hoarse and unsteady. Then a hint of doubt surfaced on his crinkled brow. "At least I think it was Mac. It happened so fast. He hit me pretty fucking hard."

"Yeah," I agreed. "The man can swing." I reached up and touched the back of my head, then immediately pulled my hand away. I didn't feel any blood, but the skin up there was ridiculously tender. My touch set off a siren-paced throb, and I hissed in pain.

Danny stood up straight. His eyes turned toward the ceiling. "Upstairs," he whispered, his voice hushed, cautious. "C'mon. Get up. We've got to check on the others."

He grasped my hand and pulled me to my feet. I almost toppled forward onto the floor, but Danny grabbed my shoulder, and the room settled into place around me. I gave him a nod—meeting his questioning eyes—and tried to act strong, even as I felt the blood drain from my face, even as starbursts of light obscured my vision.

Then we moved forward and climbed the stairs.

Danny took it slow, trying to keep his steps light and quiet. "He might be up there," he whispered, gesturing up toward the dark hallway.

We came to Charlie's room first. He was asleep at his desk, hunched over his closed notebook computer. He raised his head as soon as Danny opened the door.

"What?" he managed, confused and bleary. He reached up and tried to rub the sleep out of his eyes. "What's going on?"

He looked okay. It looked like he was just waking up from a sound natural sleep. Completely oblivious.

Danny raised a finger to his lips and urged Charlie to be quiet. Confused, the seventeen-year-old got up and joined us in the hallway. He fell into place at my heels, and we moved on to Taylor's door.

The door was open, but Taylor wasn't there.

There were candles burning on her nightstand, illuminating the room in a steady yellow glow. Her bed was made. She had a flowered bedspread—white and pink and blue—and the sheets were pulled tight, marred only by an indentation on the near edge, where someone had been sitting. I was surprised to see my camera in the middle of the bed, weighing down a crinkled piece of paper.

I pushed my way past Danny and retrieved the camera. It looked okay. It was smeared with dirt but still intact, still undamaged. Mac must have grabbed it from my room.

"Taylor?" Danny whispered, his voice taut and urgent. He spun and peered into the room's corners, as if maybe we'd just missed her standing there. When she didn't materialize, he stepped back into the hallway and called down toward the remaining bedrooms: "Taylor? Are you here?"

"What is it?" Charlie asked, perplexed, growing increasingly agitated. "What's going on? And why are you bleeding?"

Danny reached up and absently smeared blood across his forehead. He ignored Charlie's questions. Instead, he came into the room behind me and peered over my shoulder.

I turned on the camera and set it to display the most recent image. The screen lit, and my stomach dropped. My bruised head once again began to swim with vertigo.

"He's got her," Danny said, his voice hushed, terrified. "He took her away."

The picture showed Taylor bound at the wrists and gagged

with duct tape. There was pure terror in her eyes. I was surprised to see that look on her face. I didn't know she was capable of such stark, unambiguous emotion; it was something she had never let me see. *Would she have covered up her face,* I wondered, *if her hands had been free? Is this what she's always trying to hide? Fear? Terror?*

She looked vulnerable. She looked . . . human. Peering out at Mac, behind the camera, watching that crazed, mud-spattered lunatic. A hostage.

His hostage.

"What did he do with her?" Danny asked.

I looked up. Charlie was standing in the doorway, watching us with terrified eyes. He still didn't know what was going on, but he understood, at least, the nature of our fear: our frantic search, Taylor's absence. As I looked, Floyd appeared in the hallway behind him. The skater was mouthing a gaping yawn, still partially lost in drugged and carefree sleep.

I slung the camera around my neck and grabbed for the sheet of paper in the middle of the bed. "At least we know where they went," I said, holding up the note.

It was a familiar note. The paper was worn and crinkled, crisscrossed with at least a half dozen folds. One of the corners had been ripped away, and it looked as if the bottom third had been dipped in water and then allowed to dry. The whole thing was spattered with teardrops of mud.

But the words were still legible: "There's something I need to do, some place I need to be. I know you don't understand. I'm sorry, Amanda."

"Underground," I said. My voice was weak. As I continued, the words got caught in my throat, coming out rough, devoid of emotion. "The tunnels . . .

"He took her to the tunnels."

22.1

As soon as I told him about the tunnel in the park, Danny tore out of the bedroom like a sprinter at the sound of a starting gun. His face was set in anger, and he let out a growl as he paused briefly just outside the bedroom door. "I'll meet you there," he said, "with as many men as I can gather. And guns. Lots of guns."

Then he clumped down the stairs and out the front door.

I could imagine him hitting the street and running like a man possessed toward the courthouse and his barracked soldiers, doing absolutely everything he could to keep Taylor safe.

That's the type of person he was. Loyal. Dedicated.

My head was pounding and I felt dizzy, still drunk but getting sober now. Possibly concussed. As I turned back from the door, my vision swam and the back of my throat filled with prevomit saliva. I reached down and grabbed the corner of Taylor's bed, trying to keep myself steady. When my stomach finally settled, I bolted down two more Vicodins, hoping to push back the pain and nausea, wanting nothing more than numb, unconnected distance between me and my injured, chemically unbalanced head.

But the anger remained. And the fear.

Mac had waltzed right in and taken her. Easy as could be. Danny and me, sloppy drunk on the sofa. Floyd and Charlie, asleep and oblivious. And Taylor . . . all alone, she hadn't stood a chance.

"Get flashlights," I said. Floyd and Charlie were sitting on the edge of the bed. They had the camera balanced between them, propped up on Floyd's knee and tilted back in Charlie's hand. At the sound of my voice, they both looked up from Taylor's picture. There was fear in their eyes. They looked like children. Lost, frightened children.

"And get weapons," I said. "Anything you've got. We're going to get Taylor back, and Mac isn't going to stand in our way. At least not for long."

Danny and his soldiers weren't at the tunnel by the time we got there. I wasn't surprised. They had farther to walk, and I hadn't exactly taken my time getting us out the door and on our way—walking and running through the dark streets, but mostly running. Floyd, Charlie, and I were all panting for breath by the time we reached the dark opening.

We didn't have the breath to talk, and for that I was grateful. This situation was wrong, all sorts of fucked-up, and I didn't need Charlie or Floyd to tell me that.

It was dark, predawn. The sky overhead was clotted with clouds—the stars hidden, the moon long since crashed beneath the horizon. The rain had stopped, but the grass and trees were still dripping wet, and it was freakishly quiet. There were no animals rustling in the leaves and not a whisper of wind. If there were wolves here, stalking us through the night, they were being very quiet.

I had a baseball bat clenched in my hand, scavenged from the house's garage. Floyd had a kitchen knife. Charlie had a long-handled shovel.

I also had my camera. I hadn't even thought about it, just automatically dropping it around my neck after we finished looking at Mac's horrible photograph. It was a comfort, having it there.

The camera had always been a comfort for me, a wall to hide behind, a distance to place between myself and the subject of my eye. I was seeing that now for the first time. The camera was my way of escaping from the world.

I gave Danny a couple of minutes. The tension grew with each passing second as my imagination ran wild: *Mac, dragging Taylor through the tunnels, hurting her; wolves and spiders, stalking through the dark; buried limbs and faces; the gigantic hand of God, entombed somewhere beneath the city, dead and drained of blood.* When it got to be too much, I gathered up all my strength and headed toward the dark opening in the grassy hill.

"Wait, wait!" Floyd called, the first syllable loud before his voice dropped into a scared whisper. "Shouldn't we wait for Danny? And the soldiers?" Then, after a brief pause, "Shouldn't we wait for guns?"

"You can wait if you want," I said, trying to sound stronger, more confident than I actually felt. "But I can't do it. I can't wait . . . not while he's got her in there, not while she's in danger."

I headed toward the tunnel, making a show of not looking back. Maybe this feigned nonchalance came across as confidence, but really, I just didn't want Charlie and Floyd to see my pleading, desperate eyes. I wanted to be strong . . . but I wasn't. I was scared. And that fear—a fear of paralysis, a fear of loss—was what got me moving.

After a moment, I heard Floyd let out a string of expletives. Then he and Charlie followed me into the tunnel's gaping maw.

22.2

Photograph. Undated. Danny:

The room is small and dark. Concrete walls, underground. Dirty and wet, every surface glistening with
moisture. There's a road flare burning on the far
side of the room. A violet-red bloom—weak, but
strong enough to illuminate the enclosed space in an
eerie crimson glow.

There's a body on the floor—a male body, fairly
young—lying supine in the middle of the room. It is
illuminated in the light of a half dozen flashlight
beams.

The body is that of a soldier dressed in fatigues.
Probably dead. Lying on his back with his head
craned toward the wall behind him. He's clawed open
his shirt, but his arms are thrown to the side, one
hand inches away from a fallen flashlight.

There is pain on his face, a frozen mask of terror
and open-eyed agony.

From the taut flesh in the middle of his chest, an
arm sprouts, reaching up and bent at the elbow. The
soldier is impaled all the way up to the arm's
bicep. There are small rivulets of blood stretching
the length of the arm—from taut, pointing fingers,
past the elbow, all the way down to the soldier's
chest, where the thin streams pool and spill off
into his shirt.

The fingers are blurred slightly, the shutter speed
too slow to freeze them in motion.

I took the first left inside the tunnel. This was the way Mac had gone during our first exploration. This was the dead end into which he'd disappeared.

But there was no dead end this time. The tunnel continued on, tilting down, farther into the dark earth. I looked for wires in the tunnel walls but didn't find any. Not here.

There were paw prints on the floor, though.

And, here and there, footprints.

The ceiling dripped wet mud onto our heads as we advanced. I jumped in surprise each time a drop hit the back of my neck.

"Fuck, Dean," Floyd hissed as our flashlights stabbed into the dark, picking out nothing but tunnel and more tunnel. "I don't like this. I don't like this one fucking bit!"

I didn't like it, either, but I didn't say anything. There was no point; I wasn't about to turn around, not without Taylor. Charlie remained silent as well. I don't think the teenager had said a single word since we left the house. Whatever he was thinking, he kept it to himself.

A sound up ahead startled us to a halt. "Do you hear that?" I asked. They both nodded.

Muffled shouting. Shrill, frantic voices. And then the sharp crack of gunfire.

I jolted into a run, surging down the length of the tunnel. The mud slid beneath my feet, but I caught myself and continued on.

Gunfire in the tunnels. That couldn't be good. *Is it Mac?* I wondered. *Is Taylor already . . . ?*

After a hundred yards the tunnel deposited us into a small hub, a circular room with five new tunnels branching out into the space ahead. Floyd and Charlie slid into the room behind me. Floyd fell on his ass as he tried to avoid running into my back. "Fuck," he muttered. For a moment he just sat there, shaking mud off of his arms, then Charlie helped him to his feet.

"How could this be mushrooms?" Charlie asked, finally breaking his silence. His words were tiny, as if the dirt were trying to steal his voice, absorbing its strength and leaving behind nothing but a hushed whisper. "The tunnels—how do spores explain any of this?"

I shrugged. They didn't.

"Or are we hallucinating?" he continued. "Are we still in the house, collapsed on the floor, muttering and dreaming together? Or maybe passed out in the park while Mac and Taylor get farther and farther away?"

The thought was horrifying. I shook my head, and the room slid back and forth around me, continuing to move for a moment even after my head stopped. The light dimmed for a couple of seconds, then it returned to normal. "We can't think about that," I said. "They're in here, and so are we, and we've got to find them."

Right then, a shout sounded in the distance—indecipherable, but shrill and desperate. It didn't sound like a woman's voice. I turned my head, trying to locate the source. After a moment, both Charlie and Floyd pointed to the tunnel on the far left. I ran on ahead.

There were things in this tunnel. Objects. At first, it was just chunks of rock and wood breaking up the endless stretches of mud. Then a milk crate and an empty vodka bottle. Then there were planks beneath my feet, forming a makeshift floor. We came into another hub and found a geometric asterisk laid out in the dirt, narrow lengths of flooring that reached out into five new tunnels. There was a wooden chair set up against the wall, with an unlit lantern perched on its seat.

I swung my flashlight from tunnel to tunnel, looking for something new, something to point me in the right direction.

"Dean—" Floyd started, but I let out a hiss and he fell silent.

"Turn off your lights," I said, hitting the button on mine. "Shut them off. Maybe we can see . . ."

Charlie clicked his off. Then, after fumbling for a moment, Floyd did the same.

The tunnel dropped into darkness. It was a deep and claustrophobic black, and as soon as my eyes lost input, I got dizzy. I thought I was falling, toppling forward into the void. Without vision, without that point of reference, I lost all track of the world. *The Vicodin,* I thought. *The alcohol, the plank upside my head.* It wasn't the world doing this, I assured myself. It wasn't the spores or the speed of light. It was the things I'd done to myself, and the things I'd let happen.

I reached out to catch myself against the floor, keeping the flashlight and baseball bat clenched tightly in my hands, but the floor didn't come. I just continued spinning through the void.

"Dean . . ." It was Floyd, terrified, keening in the dark. "I hear him . . ." And I wondered at the "him." *Mac? Floyd's dead brother?*

I blinked, still toppling forward, spinning down into the pit under the city, plummeting toward the heart of the world.

"Dean!" It was still Floyd, but more frantic this time. I could hear feet clumping against wood, a terrified stutter step.

I blinked again and realized that the darkness wasn't complete. There was the dimmest of lights off to my left, sitting there, stationary, in the corner of my eye, even as I continued to spin through space.

I flicked my flashlight back on and found myself still standing in the middle of the hub. Not falling. I spun around, panning the flashlight across the room. Charlie had a confused look on his face, but there was no fear there, just a strangely distant interest, like he was buried in his own thoughts, trying to work out a complex problem. Floyd was different. He had his hand up against his chest, clutching at his heart. There were tears on his cheeks, and his mouth was moving, quivering open and shut without making a sound.

"Left," I said, pointing toward the tunnel down which I'd seen the light. "We're getting somewhere," I added, trying to sound reassuring.

I continued on, leading the way forward.

The tunnel ended at a concrete wall. There was a hole there, punched through the concrete, leading into a dark basement. I stuck my head through and panned the flashlight left and then right. It was a large multiroom basement, something you'd find beneath an office building, not a private residence.

I had no idea where we were. We should have hit the river long before we reached any type of large building. Had we somehow made it downtown?

There was the sound of scuffling up ahead in one of the adjoining rooms—feet scraping against concrete, spinning on a heel. Then the loud *crack* of rifle fire. "To the left!" someone called. There was another *crack*.

A quiet hiss: "Got it!"

And then, frantic: "Is that it? Are we done?"

I moved into the basement, and Floyd and Charlie followed, staying a couple of steps back. The room was damp, smelling of mildew and rot. Charlie shone his flashlight toward the door on the far side of the room. There was a faint red light in the gap at its foot. The sound was coming from behind the door.

I shut off my flashlight and gestured for Floyd and Charlie to do the same. Then I made my way to the door. Slowly, I turned the knob and pushed it open, afraid of what I might find on the other side.

"Shit!"

There was a blur of motion as a soldier in the middle of the room raised a rifle and pointed it at my chest. Then a collision of limbs, and a bullet snapped into the wall at my side.

"Don't!" Danny cried, after straight-arming the soldier's rifle. "Fucking stand down, man!"

My heart stuttered inside my chest. I glanced to the wall at my side; concrete dust rained down from a neat hole punched at just about heart level. The soldier with the smoking gun stood still for a long moment, his eyes wide in terror at the lethal mistake he'd almost made.

There were two other soldiers in the room, in addition to Danny and the terrified gunman. The four of them were standing back to back to back to back in its center, each covering a different corner. There was a road flare burning near a door on the far side of the room. It illuminated the concrete walls in flickering red light.

For a time, everyone was silent, stunned, not quite sure how to react.

I glanced around the room. There were dinner-plate-size gaps in each of the four walls—large, unnatural boreholes, at least a dozen of them—up near the ceiling and down at knee level. There were piles of dead spiders on the floor beneath each hole—drifts of huge twitching limbs torn apart by rifle fire. Some of them were deformed. I didn't look too closely, but I'm sure I saw human features mixed in with the battered arachnid bits. And not just fingers. A nose and an open mouth. A lolling tongue without lips. A whole fucking hand.

Danny gestured toward us frantically, and his soldiers broke formation, starting toward the door at our backs.

"We've been down here for almost an hour," Danny started. (*An hour?* I thought. That didn't seem possible.) A hint of a smile appeared on his lips as he crossed the room. "What took you so fucking—?" Then his foot caught on something. His arms cartwheeled in the air for a moment, and he toppled over backward.

He landed flat on his back. His flashlight and rifle clattered from his hands and a loud *whomp* of breath exploded from his lungs.

I started forward, ready to help him to his feet, but he began to move on his own, twitching on the floor. I froze in shock.

"Danny?" I asked. "Are you all right?"

He didn't respond. Instead, his eyes rolled back inside his head. He arched his ass off the floor, keeping his shoulder blades and upper back flat against the concrete. Then he started to make a loud gurgling sound—almost a liquid growl—and thick, foamy strings of saliva spilled from his lips. I pulled back.

"Unnnnghh!"

His quivering hands made their way up to the line of buttons on his shirt. He grasped and pulled the drab fatigues apart, revealing the pale white skin underneath. Then his eyes—until now completely rolled back inside their sockets—slowly spun forward, and he looked down in terror as his fingernails continued with their ripping motion, now working away at his flesh. It was like he was trying to pull his skin apart, trying to open up his chest and reach inside. His fingernails left behind beveled lines filled with crimson.

"Danny!" I managed, my voice choked with shock and confusion.

And then the hand broke through.

It should have torn him apart, it should have pushed him wide open, but it barely made a wound: no displaced mass, no tectonic movement inside his bones and flesh. Just a hand, reaching up from his heart, sprouting from his skin like a grotesque tree.

First fingers, then wrist. Then forearm. Then elbow. All the way up to a thin, unexercised bicep. Pale, subterranean skin, streaked with thin streams of blood.

The hand swiveled on its wrist—a graceful, artistic movement—and blood spilled from its open palm. It froze in that position, palm open and cupped—not as a statue would freeze, motionless, but rather as a human would freeze, complete with tiny muscular tremors.

Floyd, Charlie, and the soldiers all stumbled back as one, and I heard the sound of retching behind me—a violent dry heave—but I stayed perfectly still. Despite their terror, they all kept their flashlights fixed on Danny's grotesque, broken form. Some of the beams were shaking, and I heard Floyd give voice to a tiny little sob.

Danny quivered for a moment—the last vestiges of life fleeing his body—then his lower back collapsed to the ground and all of his muscles fell slack. His bladder released, and the room filled with the stench of urine. I thought I heard the sound of his last breath rattling out in a violent heave, but that might have just been my imagination, my need to put some type of punctuation at the end of this horrific statement.

It was a gruesome sight. Absolutely horrible.

Slowly, reflexively, I popped the lens cap off my camera, raised it to my eye, and started taking pictures.

22.3

The soldiers ran away as soon as they got the chance. They retreated back the way we had come, leaving behind a stream of choked obscenities. I think Floyd would have run, too, if I hadn't been there to stop him. And Charlie . . . I don't know what Charlie would have done. His face was calm despite startled, wide-open eyes.

"C'mon," I said, pointing to a door in the left-hand wall. "Taylor's still out there. We've got to find her."

"But . . . but Danny," Floyd said, his voice searching, desperate. His eyes remained fixed on the dead body. His face had gone paper-white. *"What happened to Danny?"*

"I don't know," I said, omitting all the stuff I did know, all the stuff I'd seen—Weasel's fingers, Taylor's father, merged flesh and broken form—that might shed light on the situation. "The city. The city happened." It was a statement I'd made before, and it still seemed to hold true.

Unless it's me and not the city. Unless I happened. My presence, my being here—melting Danny, punching out his heart.

Then I grabbed Floyd's forearm and pulled him across the room. I cut a wide berth around Danny's broken form and steered us clear of the piles of twitching spider parts.

Charlie followed.

We crossed through two more rooms, then back through the maw of an earthen tunnel. Once again heading down.

There were wires in the walls here, poking intermittently from the dirt. Not neat, straight lines like the ones we'd found beneath our neighbor's house, but branching and skewed, like veins in the walls of an organ, as if they'd developed here over time to push blood through the bowels of the earth.

I headed straight through an intersection, then turned left through another hub. More passages followed. I was moving at random, stopping every now and then to listen for sound in the dark, looking for something to guide me through this maze. But there was nothing, and I just kept moving. No sound. No hint. No clue.

Once I looked back and saw Charlie drawing an arrow in the wall with the blade of his shovel. Marking our path.

Then we were in another hub. There was a lantern perched atop a folding metal chair here; it was lit, supporting a tiny guttering flame. The walls danced in flickering light.

I was ready to plunge forward through the mouth of another tunnel, but Floyd grabbed my arm and pointed toward something on the floor, half buried in the dirt. He dropped to his knees and started clearing away some of the muck. It was a messenger bag— tan canvas smeared with mud, a ripped and reknotted shoulder strap.

"This is Sabine's," Floyd said, a hint of awe in his voice as he brushed aside dirt, revealing a large rectangular patch sewn into the fabric. The patch read: ART SAVES! I remembered my last glimpse of this bag—on the screen of the video camera, draped over Sabine's shoulder as she disappeared into the shattered wall. It had caught on the edge of the hole. She'd had to reach back to set it free.

Floyd's hands were shaking as he upended the bag, sending loose paper, pens, and a can of spray paint spilling to the floor.

"What happened to her?" he asked. "You said she was with Mama Cass." This was the lie I'd told Taylor back at the house. She must have passed it on. "But if this is here . . . where'd she go?"

"I don't know," I said.

But I wondered: *Could she be down here? Still alive?*

I didn't think so.

Floyd's shoulders started to shake, matching his palsied hands. I opened my mouth to tell him something reassuring—*I'm sure she's fine, she just lost her bag*—but Charlie interrupted. "Shhhhhhh," he urged. He was standing at my shoulder, and when I looked back, I found his eyes fixed on the tunnels up ahead, darting from one to another. His hands worked back and forth on the handle of his shovel. "Do you hear that? Do you hear that sound?"

I held my breath and listened. After a moment, I picked out the sound of shouting in the distance. Then there was a low, ominous growl, echoing far, far away.

The sound of wolves.

The sound of shouting and wolves.

Photograph. Undated. Amanda and the wolves:

The picture is framed in the horizontal, perfectly level. All browns and blacks, contrasting white bathed in orange.

It is underground: a dirt cave with a ten-foot ceiling, about twenty feet across. The space is illuminated from the left, where an irregular opening spills bright orange light into the earthen room. There is another tunnel in the right-hand wall, this one filled with darkness.

At least twenty wolves clog the far end of the space. Twenty muzzles face the camera, bright eyes glimmering in the half-light. And, standing in their

Floyd dropped Sabine's bag, and we once again plunged into the dark. At first, I wasn't sure if I'd picked the right tunnel, but a shout—louder this time—confirmed my choice.

A name, raw and angry: "Amanda!" It was Mac's voice up ahead. I recognized the hoarse, bass growl.

We emerged into another unlit hub and paused, once again waiting for a guiding voice. My head spun as I tried to catch my breath.

And again: "Amanda!"

Charlie darted out ahead this time, leading us into the right-most tunnel. The tunnel jibbed and bent, and then there was light up ahead. I could see it—not a steady light but flickering, strobing against the dirt walls. I could smell ozone burning in the air.

We came out into a wider corridor, still dirt but about six feet wide, much wider than the narrow boreholes through which we'd been running. Up ahead, there were two figures standing at the threshold of another, even wider space. Another hub, I guessed. The light was brighter here. We didn't really need our flashlights anymore.

It was Mac and Taylor, standing at the end of the tunnel. Mac had Taylor gripped in a sleeper hold, with Taylor's arm waving above her shoulder as he wrenched her back and forth in that incapacitating embrace. They were facing away from us, into the attached room, and as we approached, I could hear Mac growl into Taylor's ear: "Make her listen! Make her come here!"

Taylor let out a sob. The sound—so pathetic and broken coming from such a strong woman—weakened my knees and almost sent me sprawling to the floor. But I managed to stay on my feet. I continued forward, shoving the flashlight into my pocket and wrapping the baseball bat in a tighter two-handed grip. The feel of the hardwood between my fingers gave me strength, and suddenly I was filled with an intense rage.

Charlie stopped in the tunnel up ahead, pausing in indecision about fifteen feet from its end. I shoved him out of the way and continued on.

Neither Mac nor Taylor saw me coming: Mac remained focused on the room beyond the threshold, and Taylor couldn't even look back over her shoulder.

"She'll listen to you," Mac growled into Taylor's ear. "Make her—"

And I swung.

The bat slammed into the side of Mac's knee. Tendon gave way, and he crumpled to the ground, pulling Taylor down on top of him. I bent forward and slid the barrel of the bat past Taylor's head; she was still in his grasp, clenched tightly against his chest. I pushed the bat through Mac's beard and slid it right up against his Adam's apple . . . then I shoved him hard against the floor. He gagged as I applied more pressure.

369

I bent forward and rested my weight against the bat's handle.

"I owe you a fucking shot to the head," I hissed. "And if you make me do it, I'm not going to be laying down no fucking bunt. I'm going to drive your head out of the motherfucking park."

His hand loosened on Taylor's neck, and she pulled her way free, immediately recoiling in disgust against the tunnel's far wall. She let out another sob and buried her face in her hands. I kept the bat extended out toward Mac as I moved carefully to her side. Before I could put my arm around her shoulder, however, she pulled back once again, shaking her head.

"No, please," Mac said from his place on the ground. The crazed expression suddenly fell from his face, and his eyes filled with tears. "Please . . . You've got to just . . . Please! . . . Amanda . . . Amanda." And his eyes spun back toward the brightly lit room on the other side of the threshold.

I stayed where I was, but Floyd stepped over Mac's legs and looked out into the room. "Dean," he said, looking back at me after a handful of seconds, his eyes wide, his voice filled with wonder. "You've gotta see this shit."

Floyd and Charlie kept an eye on Mac while I peered into the room.

It was a disorienting sight.

I barely recognized Amanda. She was standing among a crowd of wolves on the far side of an oversized hub. They were pressed tightly around her; it looked like she was standing waist-deep in a furry, attentive pool. Since we'd last seen her, she'd lost all of her clothing, and she was now dressed in nothing but streaks of mud—intricate markings, purposefully drawn, like patterns of pigment in fur—across her cheekbones, her breasts, her belly, down the length of her arms.

I took a step into the room, and the pack of wolves tensed forward. A low groan filled the hub, a faint subvocal growl filled with warning and menace. Bright light was flooding into the room from one of the connecting corridors, and two dozen sets of fangs glittered sharply in the orange glow. I felt a twinge of pain in my hand and pulled back instinctively. *Once bitten . . .*

Amanda moved her arm, reaching forward slightly, then pulled it back toward her stomach. In response, the wolves settled onto their haunches, sitting almost in unison.

"Amanda?" I said.

She didn't respond. Her eyes were wide, curious, but completely uncomprehending. They were the eyes of an animal. An attentive animal.

"Amanda, it's me, Dean. Remember me? Remember taking me to the park, finding the tunnel. The wolves? Remember looking for your dog—" I tried to remember its name, finally managing to fish it up from the depths of my memory. "Remember Sasha?"

Her brow crinkled slightly at the name, and she reached down to touch the wolf at her side. The wolf showed me its teeth briefly—a tiny warning—then glanced up at Amanda's face. It raised a strangely jointed paw and touched her side, as if it were offering her comfort.

And there was silence. And the room was still. Her face flickered from that tiny questioning expression back to placid calm.

I raised the camera to my eye and took a quick shot. It was an amazing, improbable scene, and my hands just reacted—a nervous gesture, really, something to occupy my eye, my hands, and a detached part of my mind.

"She's gone," Taylor said in the tunnel behind me. "Mac and I have been here for the last fifteen minutes. He's been quizzing her, coaxing, trying to get her to remember who we are. Who she is." There was anger and disgust in her voice. "But she doesn't remember. They all just stand there. And they won't let us get anywhere near." She hawked up a glob of phlegm, and I heard her spit into the dirt at my back.

"Face it: Amanda's gone," Taylor repeated. "And there's just this . . . this empty shell in her place. This animal."

"No!" Mac roared. He rolled up onto his knees and pushed me

aside, nearly sending me sprawling to the floor. He moved fast. "Amanda!" he yelled.

None of us tried to stop him. None of us saw it coming.

In a matter of moments, he was up on his feet and colliding with the wolves, trying to wade through the sea of fur and muscles and teeth, trying to reach Amanda on the other side. I saw her cringe back in fear, and the wolves surged forward, putting themselves between Mac and their mistress. *That's what she is,* I realized, *that's what she's become.*

And then they were on him.

The room filled with growling and a single shrill howl. Fangs flashed as jaws clamped down on Mac's arms and legs, pulling him to the ground. Shaking muzzles. Tearing flesh. I couldn't hear him over the scrabbling claws and deep-throated growls, but I saw his mouth flash open. I don't know what he was trying to say. I don't know if he was trying to call out Amanda's name once again, or if it was just an incoherent howl of pain and anger as the wolves tore chunks of flesh from his body. I saw one angry muzzle dive in and clench shut around his face, locking tight and shredding his flesh back and forth before finally pulling back with a mouthful of cheek and lip, leaving behind blood and a glimpse of pale white bone. Then Mac was gone, lost beneath a blanket of writhing fur.

The frenzy went on for nearly a minute before Amanda stepped forward into the edge of the fray. She made a noise at the back of her throat. It wasn't a growl, more like an oscillating whine. The pack slowed its frenzy, then backed away one by one. The final wolf had a large chunk of Mac's arm dangling from its blood-drenched muzzle as it stepped back.

Amanda didn't even glance at the slab of shredded meat and jutting bone. She just turned, and the entire pack turned with her. They ran into one of the connecting corridors, soundless and graceful.

And they were gone.

I think it might have just been my imagination, but at the last moment, just before she disappeared from sight, it looked like Amanda dropped to all fours and started bounding forward on hands and feet. In that blur of activity, however, I couldn't be sure.

22.4

I stood at the threshold and watched as the last of Amanda's pack disappeared into the darkness. Then it was quiet.

I could feel Charlie, Floyd, and Taylor in the space behind me. Standing there in shock. But I didn't turn around and look. I didn't want to see their horrified faces.

They'd be turned toward me, I knew, looking to me for direction. But I didn't have the answers they were looking for. I didn't have a clue. What I did have was a splitting headache. I had a lump in my throat and a small animal turning somersaults in my stomach. But no answers. No ideas.

Mac was dead. That was about all I knew. He was dead, and he couldn't have been any deader. Nothing but a disjointed slab of meat piled in the center of the floor.

But Taylor was safe. Thank God, Taylor was safe.

I looked down at the baseball bat in my hands. Disgusted, I tossed it aside.

After nearly a minute, Charlie stepped up behind me. "See that corridor?" he whispered into my ear. His hand shot forward, pointing to one of the connecting tunnels. It was filled with flickering orange light. "That's fire down there," he said. "We must be near the mushroom. The army's burning it from the ground." He paused for a moment, letting his outstretched hand drop back down to his side. "It can't be healthy down here . . . being so near."

I inhaled deeply. I could taste the thick char of smoke in my lungs. I hadn't noticed it before. I'd been distracted—what with Amanda and the wolves, with Mac and his violent death. I coughed deeply and expelled a large clump of phlegm.

"Let's get out of here," I said, turning away from the room. "We got what we came for. We got Taylor. Let's get back to the surface."

Taylor was standing at my shoulder when I turned, and I nearly ran into her. The dirt on her face was streaked with tear tracks, and she refused to look me in the eye.

Broken, I thought. Taylor had always been broken to some extent, but it seemed worse now. Her abduction, that loss of control—she looked so fragile, so absolutely devastated. I moved to put my hand on her shoulder, but she shrugged it aside and turned away, starting into the dark tunnel. She had her arms crossed in front of her chest, clutching herself tightly, a defensive pose, like a hedgehog curled into a tiny ball.

And as she pulled away, the darkness came to life around her, reaching out and grabbing at her arms and legs.

It was like an animal, this darkness, I was sure. With thoughts and intentions, trying to engulf her, trying to suck her into its depths. Coming at her from every side. Tendrils from every shadow. Writhing blindly. Touching her and wrapping tightly around her limbs, drawing dark lines across her back. Insubstantial yet also thick, wide. Not spider joints, thankfully, but long midnight-black tentacles. Pure black. Spilled ink, etched across a paper-made Taylor.

My heartbeat quickened, and I stumbled forward a half dozen steps, trying to catch her before she could disappear, before the darkness could consume her.

I'd found her. I'd ventured into the very depths of the city and actually found her!

To lose her again, to the darkness, to the tunnel, to the city—

But my vision cleared, and she was still there, in the tunnel before me. Perfectly normal. A stark outline against the dark wall. No tendrils, no errant shadows. Nothing but her back, flickering in and out of darkness as Charlie and Floyd moved behind me, their flashlights swinging up and down.

I took a stutter step back, disoriented. What had I seen? Was it a trick of the light? Vicodin? Spores? Physical and emotional stress?

Floyd, at my side, reached out and grabbed my bicep, holding me steady. I turned and faced him. His eyes were full of questions, full of concern, but I just shook my head.

"Let's go," I said. "Let's get the fuck out of here."

At the first hub, I passed Taylor and led the way into one of the right-hand tunnels, wanting to make sure we didn't head back the way we'd come. I didn't want Taylor to see Sabine's bag or, God forbid, Danny. I just wanted to find some way up and out. Back home. Back to our little makeshift headquarters.

Then, maybe, out of the city. And far away. Far away from this fucking place, with its waking nightmares and its constant fucking wounds.

As far as I was concerned, this was it. I'd had enough. Even without Taylor—with her hidden face, always shrugging me off, always turning away—I needed to leave. No matter how painful that might be.

This wasn't a life.

This was a fugue-state dream that I needed to wake up from. I needed to move on and grow the fuck up. I needed to get real. Finally, for once in my life, fucking real. Not art and photography, not romantic chaos and confusion without a center. Not the end of the world, painted in brooding, melancholy shades of gray and red. Real.

I needed a job. I needed an apartment. I needed someplace stable and calm, something in my life that wasn't tinged with madness or melancholy or fucking adolescent dreams. I needed to grow the fuck up! And that most definitely meant leaving Spokane and Taylor behind, finding someplace and someone stable. Things I could lean on without fear of falling on my face.

I didn't need piles of shredded meat bleeding in the dark. I didn't need deformed flesh and a girlfriend who couldn't even stand my touch.

As I pressed on into the tunnel, I fumbled the bottle of Vicodin from my pocket and dry swallowed another pill. That was another thing I needed to leave behind.

But not yet. Not here.

Time passed, and I lost all sense of direction. Turning randomly. Tunnel after tunnel after tunnel. Hub after hub after hub. They all looked the same to me, and it felt like we weren't making any progress at all.

Then Floyd paused and gestured me to a stop.

"Do you hear that?" he asked, turning the flashlight back the way we'd come. Charlie and Taylor had taken the lead three hubs back, and there was only darkness behind us now.

I shook my head. I didn't hear a thing.

"It was laughter," Floyd whispered, a nervous smile on his face. He closed his eyes for a moment and took a deep breath. The smile quivered, but it didn't quite disappear. "It's my brother. It's Byron. He's down here, Dean. He's always been down here."

Charlie and Taylor paused up ahead as soon as they noticed that we'd stopped following. They were out of earshot, about twenty feet away, a semicircle of light in the darkness, their half-moon faces turned our way.

Floyd took a step forward and then stopped. I was worried that he was going to take off into the tunnel, looking for his brother. And if that happened, I knew, he'd disappear. Forever. I knew it, just as I knew that Sabine was gone. And Weasel. And Danny. And Amanda. And Mac—most definitely Mac. I grabbed Floyd's forearm and held him back. He looked down at my grip. There was no annoyance there, on his face, but no relief either.

Hell, there was no comprehension whatsoever. He might as well have been staring at the bottom of an empty bucket.

"He was looking for me that night," he whispered, "when he died, when I . . ." He raised his eyes and once again squinted into the dark. "I don't think he ever stopped looking. No matter where I run, no matter what I take, he's always there, tortured and alone, looking for his big brother."

He turned back toward me. "That makes sense, right?" he pleaded. His brow crinkled down into a narrow chevron, and his eyes collapsed into slits.

"I don't know, Floyd," I said, pulling him back a step. I urged him down the tunnel, back toward Charlie and Taylor. "I don't know what's possible in this place. But I know what's healthy, and this," I said, gesturing around the tunnel, "isn't healthy. We have to get out of here. We have to find our way back up to the surface."

He gave me a brief nod, then turned and once again started forward.

I stood there for a moment as he walked away, peering into the darkness behind us. There was nothing there. Nothing but dirt and rock.

The tunnel ended at another basement.

The basement in which we'd found Danny and his soldiers had been dark and damp, dingy concrete. This one was different. This one was brightly lit and clean, an underground hallway painted beige, with rows of flickering fluorescents in the ceiling. The floor was linoleum. There were mounds of dirt piled around the mouth of the tunnel, and a single line of footprints led the way down the corridor. Otherwise the floor was spotless, glossy clean, reflecting the overhead lights.

We paused just outside the tunnel. I held my breath and listened. Except for the buzz of the fluorescents, the building was quiet. There was the smell of cleaning supplies in the air. Disin-

fectants, wax. I wondered who was keeping the floors so sparkling clean.

Taylor cleared her throat and pointed to the wall, just outside
the tunnel's opening. There was a single word painted there, in
faded red paint—UP—and an arrow pointing toward the ceiling.
It was a small sampling, just two letters, but I was sure it was the
Poet's work. I could imagine her here, her face hidden behind
that black leather mask, spray-painting those letters. Cobb Gilles
would have been standing at her shoulder, watching, waiting,
protecting. When? When had they been here?

"They've got power," Charlie said, stating the obvious. "Just
like the research facility." There was excitement in his voice. "The
government must be keeping it running."

"Well, somebody's keeping it running," Floyd said. His voice
was slurred slightly. When I turned to face him, he was tossing an
empty pill bottle back through the mouth of the tunnel, back
into the darkness. He still had that nervous smile on his lips.
"Maybe just a generator. Somebody with their own purpose,
their own vision. There's plenty of shit in this city. It's not just
the government."

"Whatever," I said. "Let's just get the fuck out of here."

I started down the hallway, trying to avoid the footprints that
were already there, smeared like black ink across the floor. They
were abstract Rorschachs—I saw a butterfly there, a nuclear
mushroom cloud, a crying face. Taylor, Charlie, and Floyd followed.

After a moment, I heard Taylor's voice behind me, tentative
and quiet. "*Is* this the research building?" she asked. "It . . . it
seems familiar." Her voice sounded tortured and confused, as if
she were drunk and straining to make sense of something just
outside her realm of comprehension.

I pulled to a stop. The hallway swam around me for a moment.

"No," Charlie said. Then, confused: "Or . . . fuck."

I turned. Charlie was standing in the middle of the hallway, spinning, confused, on his heel. He no longer had his shovel; he must have discarded it in the tunnel. "I mean, it was different, right?" he asked. "A different color? A different sound?" He raised his hand to his forehead and crinkled his brow, thinking, but struggling at it.

I looked at the doors to my right: B24, B22. And on my left: B23, B21.

"I don't know, Charlie," I said. "This place does look familiar, but I . . . I just don't know."

I tried to remember that other place: the building, Devon, Charlie's parents' lab, the laser apparatus. It seemed so indistinct, like someone else's photograph, viewed a long time ago, or maybe a video I'd seen on the Web, seen and then forgotten. And here, all we had was . . . what? I looked up—nothing but buzzing fluorescents above our heads—then back down the way we had come, toward the tunnel's empty mouth. And still there was that single set of footprints on the floor behind us, just one, despite the passage of our muddy feet. Nothing had changed. The world remained static.

Moving through this world without leaving footprints—that's what we are, I thought. *Nothing we do makes even the slightest impression. There's nothing important we can ever really change.*

I couldn't think, and it wasn't just the drugs or my injured head. It was the world. It was this place.

Charlie dropped his hand from his forehead, and his face widened with sudden surprise—a dawning moment of clarity—then he sprinted past me, down the corridor. After a moment, I got my feet unstuck from the floor and hurried to follow.

At that point, I don't know. In that place . . .

There was a sound now at the far end of the corridor. Maybe it had been there all along and I just hadn't noticed. But that seemed unlikely.

Footsteps, echoing. A *whir* and a *hum*.

Taylor caught up to me and grabbed my arm. I looked back at her worried face, but I didn't stop running. "Don't let him go," she said as we continued to chase Charlie down the hallway. Her voice was pleading but confused. She was just as lost as I was, bogged down in this sea of incoherence, this maze of overwhelming impressions. *Bright lights overhead. Hard and shiny floor.* And the feeling that something was wrong, the feeling that we were completely, irrevocably lost.

I shook my head. I don't know why. I don't know if I was trying to shake the cobwebs from my mind or if it was a response to Taylor's request. And if so, what was I trying to say? *No, I won't let him go? No, I don't understand?* Or *no, he's gone and I can't do a goddamned thing about it?*

Charlie reached B13 and, without slowing down, twisted the doorknob and bolted inside. Taylor and I reached the door a couple of seconds later. We nearly ran into Devon's outstretched hand.

Devon. He was standing there, just inside the threshold, blocking our way. There was a smile on his face; it was a self-righteous, victorious smile, and it filled me with dread. He knew too much. Here, in this city, no one knew enough to wear that kind of smile. His palm was up, keeping us out of the room, and he shook his head: *No.*

I was about to press my way through, but Taylor let out a loud gasp, and her hand tightened on my forearm. I glanced down and saw her peering deeper into the room. I followed her eyes.

Charlie was standing fifteen feet away, next to the laser apparatus. There were two other people in the room with him. I recognized his mother from the emailed picture. In that picture, she'd been scared and confused, peering back over her shoulder; there was absolutely none of that now. The man must have been his father. Charlie's back was to us, but his parents were smiling. His father had a good grip on his son's biceps, holding him at arm's length and beaming with pride.

As we watched, Charlie's mother moved in and encompassed

him in a tight hug. A second later, his father's arms collapsed and they all pulled near. They stood like that for a time, clenched in a three-way embrace. Then Charlie's shoulders began to shake gently.

There was no sound in the room. Even the hum of the laser—still spitting out its bursts of bright green light—had gone silent.

I once again moved to push Devon aside, but Taylor held me back. I glanced back down at her face. There was a smile on her lips, warm and heartfelt. "Give him this," she whispered. "For a moment, at least."

So I grunted and rocked back on my heels. After a moment, watching this heartfelt reunion, I lifted the camera from my chest and started taking pictures. I felt like a voyeur—more so than usual—but I didn't stop.

Photograph. Undated. Charlie and his parents:

```
Through the top half of an open door: three people
huddled together in the middle of a brightly lit
room.

It is a man, a woman, and a teenager nearing the end
of his adolescence. All three are black—the man a
lighter shade than the woman and the teen. The man
and woman are dressed in light professional cloth-
ing. The teenager is decked out in a ragged ski
jacket, dirty pants, and mud-spattered boots.

The man's face is the only one we can see—the teen-
ager has his back to the camera; the woman's face is
buried against his shoulder. The man's eyes are
closed, and he is smiling warmly.

They are standing next to an elaborate piece of lab
equipment mounted atop a sawhorse. There's speckled
```

```
linoleum beneath their feet and a pair of computer
monitors on a table at their side.

A blurred figure stands in the foreground, just in-
side the door. On the left-hand side of the frame: a
single eye—barely visible—and the corner of a
smile. At the bottom of the frame: an arm, spanning
the width of the threshold.

The blurred figure is set firmly between the camera
and the huddled group. It is an obstacle, separating
the viewer from the subject.
```

Finally, after standing in his parents' embrace for nearly a minute, Charlie looked back at the door. There were tears on his face
as he gave us a smile. But the smile didn't last long. It quivered
and broke, and his eyes slowly drew wide.

Then Devon blocked our view. This infiltrator—*government
agent, demon, whatever*—once again flashed that victorious grin.
Then he stepped back into the room and slammed the door shut
in our faces.

Taylor jumped, startled at the sudden violent gesture. Her eyes
sprang wide, and her hands bolted to the doorknob. She worked
at it violently, but to no avail. It didn't even rattle. She let out a
horrified squawk, completely incoherent. I stepped up to her side
and started pounding at the door. It was like hitting the side of a
building; it didn't even shake in its frame.

"Charlie!" Taylor called. No answer. "Charlie!"

After nearly half a minute, she let out a devastated sob and
gave the knob one last upward heave. It didn't move. Her hands
slipped from the knob and flailed in the air for a moment, then
she pressed them flat against the door's surface. Dejected, burned
through all of her determination and anger, she lowered her forehead against the immovable panel and let out a pathetic sob.

"I let him go," she said, her voice choked. She pressed her face up against the door, hiding it from sight. "I . . . we could have stopped him, but I let him go."

There was silence for a moment—I didn't know what to say, I never knew what to say, not when it came to Taylor, not anymore—then a loud peal of laughter rang out at our backs. I turned. It was Floyd, standing in the middle of the corridor, braying like a moron.

"Fuck, I . . . I'm sorry," he said, trying to rein it in. He seemed confused and genuinely abashed at the inappropriate laughter. He managed to hold it in for a moment, then it burst forth once again. So shrill. So totally out of place.

The laughter echoed in the empty hallway, filling the space like blood pooling into a deep wound.

22.5

Up.

We found the stairwell and started to make our way up, toward the street.

There was no longer any light here. No overhead fluorescents, just the thin beams of our flashlights. Charlie's parents' lab had been one floor down in the research facility, but there was no door on the first landing here and no door on the second. I leaned out into the center of the stairwell and peered up toward the top of the shaft. There was a dim light up there, at least ten floors above our heads. The research facility hadn't been that tall.

As we climbed, the light from my flashlight revealed more words spray painted on the wall.

First: IN ITS PLACE. And then, on the next landing, OUT, followed by an arrow curving up toward the top of the stairs. As soon as he saw the word and the arrow, Floyd let out another shrill laugh.

"There is no out," he whispered, the laugh still in his voice. "It's just this, right? This place. And us. And the stuff that followed us in."

"That's enough, Floyd," I growled. "You're not helping any."

He laughed again, and I grabbed his forearm. He jumped at my touch and pulled away. There was fear in his eyes. And confusion.

On the next landing, we found a door. It was the first door since the basement, at least six landings down. The door was steel gray and smeared with grime—smoke grime, the exhaust of machines, layered thick and sticky against the metal. I opened it and found a hallway on the other side.

The hallway was a foreign place. Not the research facility; I was sure of that. It was no place I'd ever been. To the left, doorways stretched down both sides of the corridor, each about fifteen feet apart. About half of the doors were open, spilling muted red light onto the waxed floor. There was the smell of antiseptic in the air and, underneath it, a pungent touch of sweat and decay. It was a thick smell. I could almost feel it gathering on my skin, like pollen or lacquer.

Taylor stepped past me and let out a surprised breath. "It's the hospital," she said. "ICU." It took me a moment to parse the initials, at first hearing them as out-of-place words: "I see you."

I turned to the right, and sure enough, there was a nurses' station just down the corridor, and a line of rolling gurneys pressed up against the wall. There was a whiteboard posted behind the desk, listing room numbers, patient names, and ailments. 503, MARTIN HELDER, CIRRHOSIS—LIVER FAILURE. 504, EUNICE WEST, ANEURYSM—SHUNT. 505, PETER WILMORE, TRAUMA—FRACTURED PELVIS, RUPTURED SPLEEN, BROKEN LEG/ARM. 506, RICHARD SCALLEY . . .

It went on and on, scrawled in messy mismatched ink. Patients who were no longer in their rooms—the hospital now empty, evacuated and populated by nothing but silence.

I stepped toward the nurses' station and then stopped.

"Fifth floor," Taylor said at my back. There was absolutely no emotion in her voice, just muted, disconcerting calm. "We could find a window and jump out. Like that soldier. Remember the soldier?"

I nodded. I remembered the soldier. *Flying through the hospital window, falling through the air, hitting the concrete parking lot and bouncing. Then rising up on injured legs and lurching forward mind-lessly.*

"There's got to be an exit," I said, standing motionless in the middle of the corridor. My body felt heavy, exhausted, and I didn't want to move. "Another stairwell, maybe, with an exit on the first floor. Or we could make a rope, lower ourselves to the street."

I saw her nod out of the corner of my eye. Then she turned and peered down the corridor, first to the left, then to the right.

"Where's Floyd?" she asked. "Where'd he go?"

My stomach dropped. I turned and found the corridor empty. It was just Taylor and me, the stairwell door shut at our backs. Floyd was gone. He'd disappeared.

Frantic, I pointed her down the corridor to our right, then headed left on my own, peering into each of the rooms in turn.

It didn't take long to find Floyd. He was in the third room down.

It was a standard double-occupancy hospital room. The bed closest to the door was hidden behind a curtain, and I found Floyd seated on the second. He was perched motionless on its far edge, facing the window. The sky outside was bright red. While we'd been underground, night had become day, and the sky had lit up once again—with spores or blood, I didn't know.

"Floyd?" I prompted.

He didn't respond.

I crossed to the foot of the bed and looked at his face. He blinked and continued to stare at the window. He seemed to know I was there, but he didn't engage, didn't acknowledge my presence. I didn't press it. I didn't try to force his attention, didn't grab his shoulders and start shaking, didn't slap his face and shout bracing words.

I stepped up to the window and peered out at the city.

It was an unfamiliar landscape—still Spokane but worse, bat-tered and beaten. I-90 was visible a couple of blocks away, to the north, but it had suffered. Chunks of concrete had collapsed from its edge, diminishing its surface, and the entire Monroe overpass had fallen to the street below, leaving a wide gap in the interstate's length, filled with boulders and jagged lengths of rebar. And the destruction didn't look recent. All the buildings in sight had taken damage. Collapsed walls lay across sidewalks and streets, road surfaces had buckled and crumbled, streams of muddy water wended their way through eroded asphalt.

Time had passed somehow. The city had aged. And it had aged badly.

The sky was deep red, roiling in violent waves. *That's not spores,* I thought, *not light reflecting off of the atmosphere. That's not even sky. It's something else. Something above us, waiting to fall.*

There was smoke in the distance, up north—several columns, billowing thick and black.

"I'm right, aren't I?" Floyd asked, his voice slow and emotionless. I turned and looked at him. His face was impassive, but his eyes swam, refusing to spill but filled with tears. "He's here. This is hell and he's here, waiting for me. Just out of sight. Always here, around the next corner. And there's no escaping it . . . no way out."

Floyd slowly lowered himself onto his side, briefly curling his legs into a loose fetal position at the edge of the mattress. Then he rolled onto his back and settled his head on the pillow, fixing his eyes on the blank ceiling.

I looked up and saw Taylor standing in the doorway. There was relief on her face as she regarded Floyd. Then she saw the window.

She made her way to my side and peered out at the devastated landscape. She didn't look for long; she turned away from the window and lowered herself onto the edge of the bed, taking a seat next to Floyd's knees. She was sitting in the exact same position in which I'd first found Floyd. Her shoulders were slumped, her face expressionless.

"I can't do this, Dean," she said. "I can't be here anymore."

"We'll find our way out, get back to the house."

"I mean Spokane," she replied, her voice flat, lifeless. "I can't do this." She nodded toward the window. "I can't do *that* anymore."

I nodded. And I didn't ask any questions. I didn't ask about her father, her mother, her obligations; I didn't ask about the things that had been keeping her here. I didn't want to change her mind.

"We'll go," I said. "We'll go to California . . . or Seattle, or Olympia, if you like. We can find Terry, maybe help him with his book."

She nodded.

"You, too, Floyd," I added. "We'll get out of here. It'll get better. We'll go far, far away."

He turned his head and stared at me. There was a distance there, in his eyes. It seemed like he was already far, far away. And looking back at me through a veil.

Photograph. Undated. Spokane from above:

```
The city is in ruins beneath a bloodred sky.

The roof curves in an arc at the bottom of the
frame, the wide angle distorting the foreground.
Down below, there are no neat, rectangular blocks,
no hint of city planning, no remnant of order.
Buildings have collapsed across streets, and streets
have collapsed into rubble.

The city has lost its shape.

The view is from at least ten stories up, peering
northeast across the remains of I-90. There are ve-
hicles in the ruins, where an army checkpoint has
been—far to the left, at the edge of the city. A
```

park to the north is smoldering in the distance,
sending up plumes of dark smoke—ethereal fingers,
trying to puncture the liquid red sky. There isn't
even a hint of vegetation there, just charred black
coal.

Two blocks north of the interstate, a wide valley of
destruction has been gouged into the gray landscape,
revealing a long trough of darkened earth. At the
end of this valley, on the right-hand side of the
frame, is a downed jetliner, dented, its wings torn
free and left littered in its wake. The crash is
old. It doesn't smolder, and there are no signs of
life—no emergency vehicles, nothing but rubble. Its
nosepiece is angled up toward the heavens.

There are no signs of life anywhere in the photograph. Nothing but a shapeless city and a bloodred
sky.

Floyd led the way up to the roof. I wanted to find a different stairwell on the fifth floor, a different route to the street, but he was insistent. He had an energy that surprised me; it seemed out of keeping with his earlier mood.

"I want to see the city," he said, "from up high." Then he smiled. It was an odd smile. Delirious. It didn't touch his eyes. "You can take pictures."

Taylor looked reluctant.

"There'll probably be another stairwell up there," I offered, "on the other side of the building. Or maybe a fire escape. You saw the graffiti. Up is out."

Taylor still looked reluctant, but she nodded. And I got the sense that this was a big deal for her. She was putting herself in my hands. She was counting on me to get her out.

Back in the stairwell, we passed the doorways to the sixth, seventh, eighth, ninth, tenth, and eleventh floors. It kept getting brighter as we climbed higher and higher. Up at the top, the door to the roof was chocked open with a cinder block brick. A simple iconic eye had been spray-painted on the door's surface.

The view from the roof was amazing.

"When did that happen?" Taylor asked as we approached the northern edge of the building. There was a jetliner down in the middle of the city. A big one. The blocks immediately north of I-90 had been reduced to rubble.

"It didn't," I said. "It never happened."

Riverfront Park was smoldering on the horizon. It looked like it had been burning for quite some time. Taylor followed my eyes. "We were just there," she said, her voice hushed in reverent wonder.

I shook my head. "Not there. Someplace else." *Some*time *else*, I thought.

I raised the camera to my eye, cranked the lens as wide as it would go, and took a handful of pictures, rotating between shots to catch the full panoramic view. When I was done, I lowered the camera and we just stood there, staring out across the horrible landscape.

"Hey, guys. Check it out."

We turned and saw Floyd standing twenty feet back, next to the stairwell door. He rocked back on his heels and flashed us a brilliant smile. Then he stuck out his tongue, raised forked fingers to the sky, and started running toward the eastern edge of the building.

I didn't move. Taylor didn't move. We just watched.

Floyd took off a couple of feet from the roof's edge. He reached down, grabbed an invisible skateboard, and ollied into the void, lifting his feet to the side as he dropped out of sight.

He didn't make a sound. He just disappeared beneath the ledge. And was gone.

After a stunned moment, I managed to break my paralysis and follow him to the edge. He'd already finished falling by the time I

got there. I could barely make out his remains down in the rub-
bled street.

A rag doll, twisted and broken.

Not Floyd—not anymore. Just ravaged meat. Nothing but an
insensate piece of the landscape.

22.6

Photograph. Undated. Taylor in the boardroom:

A young woman. Her face is center frame, bright and
luminous, tinted pale red. Her eyes are dark and focused elsewhere, on some point far behind the camera. Her skin is on the dark side of Caucasian,
vaguely Indian.

She is frozen in place about ten feet away, next to
an empty chair in the middle of a deserted boardroom. The chair is magnificent—a cushioned black
leather throne, empty. There are three other chairs
in view, all empty, including one that's been
spilled onto its back. She is striding forward,
caught with her arm swinging out, toward the
camera.

There is a table on the right-hand side of the
frame. It is smooth, black, and polished to a
gleam. It stretches to the far end of the room,
where a window dominates the background. The window
is filled with red—the shape of clouds caught in

Then it was just the two of us.

Taylor didn't look over the edge. She remained where she stood, her eyes wide, staring off into space. When I looked back at her, her lips parted slightly and she shook her head. A violent denial: *No, that didn't happen. No, Floyd's fine, just fine.*

"Let's go," I said. "Let's get out of here."

I wanted to move before the horror of what we'd just seen could really sink in, before it became real. For both of us. If I paused, if I gave us time to think, I was afraid we'd never be able to move again, afraid it would send us gibbering into complete surrender. And they'd find us—who, I don't know—sitting here cross-legged in the middle of the roof. Skeletons, Taylor and me, eons dead and gone, frozen in place by the horror, the loss, the confusion.

Mourning the death of the universe. A universe broken, like Floyd, eleven floors down.

"We should have stopped him," Taylor said. "We should have seen it coming . . . just like with Charlie."

I reached for her, and she reached for me. She grasped my hand tightly, and I led her across the roof in a quick trot.

We found a second staircase on the far side of the building. The door was propped open with another cinder block brick, and there was another eye painted on its metal surface. But this eye was different from the first: this eye was closed, eyelashes hanging down from the shut lid like a line of commas.

I pulled Taylor through the door and started scrambling down the stairs. We got a single floor down before we found our way blocked. The concrete steps beneath the top-floor landing had fallen away, clogging the shaft ten feet down. I was in such a rush, I would have fallen into the gap if Taylor hadn't grabbed my shoulder and pulled me to a stop. The space was illuminated by light from the open doorway above our heads, but there was absolutely no indication of what had caused the collapse. Time, maybe. Or poor construction.

"What now?" Taylor asked in a trembling whisper.

I shook my head and pushed my way through the door at our side.

I had to find another way down.

Back to the other stairwell, maybe. A bedsheet rope through a window on the fifth floor. Anything to get us out of here, anything to get us back down to the street and back home.

I was expecting more hospital rooms up here on the top floor—gurneys and crash carts, wheelchairs and nurses' stations—but the hallway on the other side of the door was something different. Skylights illuminated its length. It was long and carpeted—speckled gray—and it no longer smelled anything like a hospital. It was in good repair. The walls were paneled wood, decorated with respectfully spaced pieces of framed art. Abstract paintings in red and gray and black, violent slashes and speckles of pigment.

There were doors on the right-hand side of the corridor. All of them were closed except for one, far down its length. Light spilled from this distant portal, tinting the carpet a pinkish gray. I tried the nearest door and found it locked.

There was nothing for us here. Nothing but the door in the distance. And the promise of a stairwell, maybe, back on the other side of the building.

Taylor caught my hand, and I met her eyes. She nodded, urging me on. We started down the corridor, breaking into a quick jog.

The walls sped past: wood paneling, shut doors, abstract art. I could feel my eyes going wide with adrenaline-fueled frustration. I just wanted this over—the corridor, the hospital, the city. Everything. There was nothing here but confusion and pain. And friends—run through with limbs, consumed by wolves, eaten by ghosts, pushed over the edge by memory and guilt. I wanted none of it. I was done.

No documenting. No shutter flash in the dark. No eye. No unblinking "truth."

I would have kept running, but Taylor pulled me to a stop. I was panting loudly. She was crying, tears streaming down her cheeks as she doubled over, trying to catch her breath in the middle of the carpeted hallway.

The open door was at our side.

We were here. We'd reached the boardroom.

It was a long room, and it ended in a wall of picture windows. There was a table stretching nearly its entire length—sturdy hard wood, black as night. In the ways of corporate excess, I'm sure the table had cost more than my entire education.

The light was pink, but the view beyond the window was red.

There were large chairs along both sides of the table, but they were all empty. Twenty chairs. I counted them. One of the chairs had been overturned, as if someone had stood up too fast, knocking it to the floor. There were pieces of paper scattered across the table, stacks in front of each skewed chair. I stepped up to the table and passed my hand over the nearest pile. There was nothing printed there. Just blank sheets of paper: white, expressionless.

Is this Cob Gilles's boardroom? I wondered. *Is this what he found when he and the Poet climbed up from the underworld?* He'd described a bright golden light and people seated at every chair . . . waiting. Waiting for something to happen.

Gone now. The room was empty, abandoned.

I glanced back at Taylor. She was standing in the doorway. She looked confused.

"I thought . . ." she said, trailing off for a long moment. "I thought I heard . . ." And then nothing. Just more confusion on her face.

She stepped into the room and started toward the window, trailing her hand along the back of the empty chairs.

I turned and noticed graffiti on the wall, just inside the door:

> I was here
> all alone.

The Poet. Her words, skewed diagonally across the wall. I couldn't tell if it was one thought or two unrelated statements. For some reason, it didn't seem right here, her words. The sentiment seemed unutterably depressing, and I wanted to erase it. I looked around for something to gouge it from the wall, but there was nothing. Just an empty boardroom.

Taylor was standing at the window now. Her hands were raised up at her sides, pressed flat against the glass. She was resting her head there, her forehead pressed against its surface. As I watched, her shoulders dropped, and her entire frame suddenly slumped down.

It was a pose of pure exhaustion. Sudden surrender, spelled out in a single moment.

Without thought, I lifted the camera to my eye and took a picture.

I was a hypocrite. And I knew it. No matter what I told myself, no matter how many times I tried to give it up, the instinct would always be there—the instinct to raise the camera and take the shot.

"There's nothing out there," Taylor said, still facing the city on the other side of the window. "I can't see a thing."

She was silent for a time. I took another picture of her back, her slumped shoulders.

"Nothing," she repeated, "and there's nothing in here. Just red destruction every way we look. And it'll be the same, eventually, outside the city. There's no running from this. No escape." She paused. "How do I know that?" she asked, sounding genuinely confused.

Then she turned and started toward me. Through the camera's viewfinder, she looked tiny, impossibly far away. I took one more picture and lowered the camera to my chest.

And she kept coming.

"Hold me, Dean," she said. She stepped right up against my body, lowering her head against my shoulder.

Surprised, I closed my arms around her back. She moved even closer, as close to me as she could get, with the camera still between us. I stepped away for a moment and spun the Canon around my neck, so that it was resting against my back and there was nothing at all separating our bodies. And I pulled her tight. I could feel her shivering against me, and she grasped me even harder, seeking comfort, seeking warmth. Seeking *me*.

She tilted her head back, offering me her lips.

And I kissed her.

This was the closest we ever got—this moment—our lips locked, our bodies pressed together—*or no, no, it wasn't*. And for a time everything was right. I forgot about the city. I forgot about Weasel and Sabine and Amanda and Mac and Danny and Charlie and Floyd. I forgot about the world crumbling down around us, the slowing speed of light, the mushrooms and the spores— everything. It was just the two of us. And nothing else existed. We formed our own universe, and here, in our universe, everything made sense.

Then she tried to pull back.

And she couldn't.

She made a sound deep in her throat, and I felt pressure pulling my lips away from my teeth. And then she was closer, getting closer. Pressure against my chin, then she was pulling back again; I could feel it in the bones of my jaw. Her hands pulled away from my back, and she gripped my shoulders, her fingers digging in, hard, scared. And this time she didn't pull away. I opened my eyes and stared deep into hers.

They were wide with terror.

I lifted my hands to the sides of our kiss. The flesh there was joined, merged together. Our lips were gone. My stubbled cheeks ended flush against her smooth flesh. And her eyes were close to mine, getting closer. I grabbed her hips and tried to push her away, but we didn't part. There was pressure against my jaw. And now my nose, next to hers, against—then inside—her cheekbone. I tried to move my hands up, but they stayed at her hips, through her clothes. And then she was closer. And I couldn't see. My eyes. Her eyes.

And then even closer.

I had an itch behind my eyes, inside my brain. And then a taste, but I couldn't move my tongue. Copper wool and blood.

And then

Taylor. Breast, chest, and I was . . . I was . . . Taylor's fear, pushing back, shivering, claustrophobic, pulling back. Taylor's fear. Mine. *God,* pulling back, please, please, God, where, my, please, *please,* my, Taylor, my head . . .

And then down to the floor.

And my head.

And the floor

And the city

And me

And Taylor

Together. And together. And together.

22.7

There was darkness.
And then we were back.

We woke up in Riverfront Park, on the side of a hill, above the mouth of the wolves' tunnel. It was a bright morning out—chilly, but the whole world was bathed in golden sunlight. The grass around us sparkled. My face was damp with dew.

I sat up and saw Taylor standing at the crest of the hill. She had her back toward me, looking out over the city. The city had once again reverted to its normal state, abandoned but not destroyed, neglected but not yet rubble.

It was just the two of us. Everyone else was gone.

"Taylor," I said. She didn't respond.

I stood up and started toward her. I rounded her side and saw her hands up against her face. She had wide, shell-shocked eyes. She glimpsed me from behind her fingers, then shook her head and once again turned away. She was remembering, I knew, the horror of our faces crushed together. The horror of that dissolution.

I stood there for a time, watching her—Taylor, in the early-morning light—watching as she tried to hide behind her hands.

Then I raised my fingers to my face and touched my lips.

23.1

Nothing.

23.2

I'm sitting at a desk in a fifth-floor apartment, just south of the river. Near the Homestead. Near the Homestead's abandoned husk.

I can see the freeway from my window. From this distance, it's just a sliver, a line etched across the buildings to the south. The army's cordon is out there somewhere, not too far west.

We moved here a couple of days after our trip into the tunnels.

Empty, the house was just too big.

And the rooms—Floyd's, Charlie's, Devon's, Sabine's, Amanda and Mac's—were filled with too many ownerless possessions.

I left a note on the front door and another on the dining-room table, beneath a half-empty bottle of gin. Saying where we were going. In case anyone came looking, in case anyone came back. That was over a month ago.

Taylor isn't doing well. She isn't talking. She won't let me come near, won't even look at me. She doesn't even want our *eyes* to make contact.

The fear is there, filling her up, where everything else had been. Taylor, her heart, her humor—it's all gone. I can see it: the belief that if we touch, if we get close, she's going to lose herself again.

And that's all she is now. That fear.

Sometimes I open the door to her room—it used to be a den, complete with sofa and leather-cushioned Eames chair, bookcases and hardwood desk—and I find her crouched there, alone in the dark. She's boarded up the room's only window, but a gap remains at its bottom-most edge, and I find her sitting there with her face pressed right up against the wood, staring out at the street. Quiet. Completely absorbed in that narrow view of the city.

I bring her food. I talk to her.

But she doesn't listen. I don't think she even hears.

And we're not going to leave.

I know that now.

It was just a dream, that thought. A fantasy. Something to keep me going down there in the tunnels. But I don't think Taylor would follow me out of the city. Not now. Not in her current state. And I can't imagine leaving her here all alone. Not anymore.

She wouldn't survive. She'd dissolve. She'd sink into the ground as soon as I turned my back.

So I stay. And she stays. And nothing ever changes.

And I'm writing now.

I don't know why. I don't know why I'm putting these words on page after page after page, crippling my hand, but I'm afraid it's the only thing holding back the darkness. And when I'm done, when I run out of history to record, I'll be all alone. And that moment's coming. Soon.

And then I'll be just like Taylor, hidden away in her little cave. Alone with the city, alone with its thoughts.

And what will that do to me? I don't know. Will there be peace, or screams echoing in a midnight-black void? Will it be painful, or will I go down nice and easy? Just close my eyes and sink.

And what does the end of the world look like, anyway? What does it sound like?

Should I keep my eyes open or hold them shut?

Should I sing along?

Danny stops by on occasion.

He showed up the morning after our trip into the tunnels. At the house. He said he never made it underground. He got to the tunnel in the park with a half dozen soldiers but found the way forward blocked. Nothing but dead ends to the left and right.

I don't believe him. I can't believe him.

I saw him down there in that basement. And I never doubted that it was him. This person, now . . . I just can't trust him.

I don't know who he is.

He says that there are other places like Spokane now, popping up all over the world. A neighborhood in Kobe, Japan. A town in Iowa. A building—a single building!—in Washington, D.C. A valley in the Ukraine.

It isn't mushrooms, obviously. It isn't hallucinogenic spores in the air. The army burned all of that from the ground, and still, nothing has changed.

People still disappear. I still see spiders on occasion. The sky still turns red.

Danny tells me that the UN has assembled a task force. Peace-keepers, to help in the affected areas. He mentioned something about a telethon airing on all the major networks. I can't even imagine what that must have been like. Celebrities and phone banks. Did it have its own song? "We Are the World"?

"We Are Spokane"?

He says my photographs have made a difference, in the effort. Raising awareness. Some shit like that.

I don't know.

I could have stopped him from posting the images, but I didn't.

I could have destroyed them when I had the chance. I could have ground the camera into dust. I could have thrown it from the top of the hospital, out into the dead red wastes. But I didn't.

He—Danny, his ghost, whatever—asked to see my camera,

and I let him have it. He popped out the memory card and put it in his pocket. I saw him do it. He wasn't trying to be sneaky or anything, wasn't trying to pull a fast one on me. In fact, I think he was waiting for me to try to stop him. But I didn't. He posted the pictures on the Web, on the message board, without text— not pretending to be me, at least, not putting words into my mouth. Just putting the pictures out there for the world to see.

I don't think I would have bothered if it had been up to me, but I certainly didn't stop him. I still had my ego. I was still *me* – aspiring photographer, artist, poor excuse for a human being— and part of me, at least, wanted people to see my work.

According to Danny, the pictures caused pandemonium on the board, and the reaction rippled out into the real world. Picked up by news weeklies and cable TV. Mainstream media. Apparently, a Republican senator printed out a poster-size copy of Danny's picture—dead, arm waving out from his chest—and paraded it around the Senate floor, demanding answers. At first, he was dismissed as pandering to the lunatic fringe, but I'm sure he's seeming more and more prescient with each passing day.

And Danny didn't say a word.

He saw that picture, obviously, he saw himself, down there underground, but he didn't ask me about the circumstances, didn't ask me about what I'd seen. Him, lying dead and mutilated on that basement floor. He didn't want to know. And that, at least, endeared him to me, whoever he is—this thing, this maybe-Danny.

There are some things we just shouldn't know. Some things we shouldn't ask about, shouldn't explore.

And I miss Danny. I really do.

Out of all of us, he was the one who had his shit together. He was the one I would have trusted with the world.

Danny brought me this bottle of Wild Turkey.

For that, at least, he's got my thanks. Even if he isn't real.

I was writing just now, and a loud roar filled the room. It was a physical sound, vibrating through my core. My desk started to shake. You can see the ink on the page—roller-ball quiver, EEG scrawl.

I stood up and looked out my window, craning my head to peer north. I didn't see much. A wing, tilting, over the line of buildings.

And then an explosion. As the plane crashed.

I don't want to be human. Not anymore.

There is smoke rising over the city. A line of military vehicles tore through the street beneath my room, and I cracked open a window. The city smells like fire.

Fuck.

I don't know about this. I don't know what to think.

And then the crowd of survivors began to pass beneath my window. They looked shell-shocked, dazed, completely out-of-their-minds fucked, but they were alive.

They shouldn't have been alive, but they were alive and marching on the street down below, the military leading the parade. They had vehicles to transport the wounded: Hummers and Jeeps. And I don't know how many died on impact in that crash. How many met their maker, here, in a crater, in the city, wrapped tight in fuselage and fire?

This is fertile land here, and things that shouldn't grow, grow. Things that land, still and static, breathe and breathe again.

And, of course, I remember the view from the hospital's roof.

It's all coming true. Plane crash and destruction. Ages come and gone.

And here I am. In my window.

I can imagine Floyd there, falling through that red sky.

Did he find peace in those final moments? His final, most successful trick. Did he kiss the sky and soar, untethered for a time, taunting gravity and God?

And when he hit, did he hit hard? Did he make a crater and fill a void?

> Or did he leave a gaping wound
> in the world,
>> a hole that nothing can fill?
>>> And we're left here all alone,
>>>> heart bruised and eye blind,
>>>>> void of breath,
>>>>>> and soul broke.
>>>>>> Watching him fall
>>>>>> still

And that room, up in the sky.

The red sky.

I'm hurt here. I can't stand it. I breathe and it hurts, a rasping grate in my lungs, like sandpaper and gravel, fingernails and coral. And . . . I don't know.

What did we find up there, in that building?

What does it mean?

Maybe the universe is collapsing. Physics has run its course, and reality has begun to contract, once again pulling back—a beat, the heartbeat of the universe—the point in the oscillating cycle of time where things stop getting bigger and start to condense. Light and time, pulling back. And the human mind is the last, most resilient part of the universe, resisting and shaping the form of reality. Before it, too, inevitably fails, collapses.

And there is a table there. And on the table, a stack of pages. And in the pages, the breath that I breathe, the Wild Turkey that I drink, the beauty that flashes in my eye.

And it resists. Like the human mind resists.

Or maybe God just left.

Maybe God got bored, pissed off, fed up, and generally stuffed. Stood up from the table and left the room. Leaving us in charge. And us in charge, with nothing—no one—to stabilize and baby-sit, we're warping and driving everything into the motherfucking ground.

Nothing left to see. Nothing left to do.

Because that's who we are. That's what we do.

And there is a room, somewhere. In a building, somewhere. In a city.

 And the world is red.

 The world is red, and the boardroom is empty.

 And I stop writing.

 And I'm here

   all alone.

LOT 1105.

Contents of black footlocker, 513 Madison St, Apt. 540
(back closet):

handwritten manuscript, 583 pages (document 511;
reference case 412); handwritten composition book
(document 512; reference case 413); loose paper,
handwritten (document 513; reference case 413);
loose paper, handwritten (document 514; reference
case 419); skateboard; notebook computer (contents
cataloged, document 515; reference case 412); Canon
Rebel digital camera; 6GB CompactFlash memory card
(contents cataloged, document 516; reference case
412); 4GB CompactFlash memory card (contents cataloged, document 517; reference case 412); newspaper
clipping (document 518; reference case 412); Sony
video camera (contents cataloged and transcribed,
document 519; reference case 412, 415)

Referencing:

Case ███ ██████, Devon. Status: ████████████. [Ex-
          punged; Executive Order #████; Executive
          Order #████; Executive Order #████; Execu-
          tive Order #████; Executive Order #████;
          Executive Order #████; Executive Order
          #██████; Password Clearance: Black Alpha and
          Higher.]

Case 012. Daltry, Dr. Stephen. Status: DECEASED. (Ref-
          erence case 013, 417)

Case 013. Daltry, Dr. Cheryl. Status: DECEASED. (Ref-
          erence case 012, 417)

Case 053. Moon, Lieutenant Daniel "Danny." Status: LO-
          CATED.

Case 117. Barnes, Sharon (AKA. "Mama Cass.") Status:
          LOCATED.

Case 222. Twill, Terence "Terry." Status: LOCATED.

Case 315. Gilles, Cob. Status: MISSING. (Reference
          case 316)

Case 316. [Name Unknown], "The Poet." Status: MISSING.
          (Reference case 315)

Case 412. Walker, Dean Andrew. Status: MISSING. (Refer-
          ence document 511, 515, 516, 517, 518, 519)

Case 413. [Last Name Unknown], Wendell (AKA. "Wea-
          sel.") Status: MISSING. (Reference document
          512, 513)

Case 414. Stray-Gupta, Taylor (AKA. "Taylor Gupta," "Taylor Stray.") Status: MISSING. (Reference case 420, 421)

Case 415. Grey, Julie (AKA. "Sabine Pearl-Grey.") Status: MISSING. (Reference document 519)

Case 416. Boyd, Floyd (AKA. "Pretty Boy Floyd.") Status: MISSING.

Case 417. Daltry, Charles "Charlie." Status: MISSING. (Reference case 012, 013)

Case 418. O'Donnell, Mackenzie "Mac." Status: MISSING.

Case 419. Siebert, Amanda. Status: MISSING. (Reference document 514)

Case 420. Gupta, Miriam (AKA. "Miriam Stray-Gupta.") Status: MISSING. (Reference case 414, 421)

Case 421. Gupta, Dr. Harold "Harry." Status: MISSING. (Reference case 414, 420)

ACKNOWLEDGMENTS

I'm the luckiest SOB in the world. I'm lucky to have editors like David Pomerico and Betsy Mitchell. I'm lucky to have an agent like Jim McCarthy. And I'm lucky to be able to call Jim Geist, Vicki Mau, Jeremy Horwitz, Margaret Danielson, Sheryl Burnham, and George Dake my readers, friends, and family. Thank you, all!

ABOUT THE AUTHOR

RICHARD E. GROPP lives on a mountain outside of Seattle with his partner of fifteen years. It is a small mountain. He studied literature and psychology at the University of California, Santa Cruz, and has worked as a bookstore clerk, a forklift driver, and an accountant. He has a hard time spelling the word *broccoli,* and in his spare time he dabbles in photography and cooking.

ABOUT THE TYPE

This book was set in Apollo, a typeface designed by Adrian Frutiger in 1962 for the founders Deberny & Peignot. Born in Interlaken, Switzerland, in 1928, Frutiger became one of the most important type designers since World War II. He attended the School of Fine Arts in Zurich from 1948 to 1951, where he studied calligraphy. He received the Gutenberg Prize in 1986 for technical and aesthetic achievement in type.